CAMP JAMESON

≈

THE CAMP JAMESON SERIES
BOOK I

WENDY LEA THOMAS
with
Chainsaw Dangerous

Copyright

ISBN-13: 978-0615935652

PRAISE for Bestselling Author
Wendy Lea Thomas
and
THE CAMP JAMESON SERIES

"Wow, I am really excited after reading this book. If I could give more than 5 stars I would! Where can I find my own Camp Jameson? I was screaming, rooting, laughing, had chill bumps at some points, and even anxiety at the end. This is a definite must read! I can't wait for the next book!"

> – Rebecca from Cover to Cover Book Blog

"Sign me up for summer camp at Camp Jameson! This book will leave you aching to join in the classes, craving more and wanting to register for camp. It truly does have it all. I not only loved the main characters, but I became attached to all the supporting characters as well. I laughed at the pranks crossed my legs with want during the games and classes, and can't wait to see what happens at the next camp! This book is absolutely worth the read and I would highly recommend it to everyone."

> – Amy Loves Reading Book Blog

"I found this book cute, funny, sexy, a hot read with a happily ever after type ending...no cliffhangers. This book made me wish there were camps like this when I was in my 20's...The intimate scenes were steamy and then there were the cute/funny scenes to balance the story...once I started reading this book I couldn't put it down."

> – KR Pink Momma Book Blog.

"This was one HOT read! I loved the book immensely and greatly enjoyed it. I found Aria very easy to relate to and the further I got in the book, the more I liked her. Avery was frustrating but still loveable. The premise of the book is unique, which makes it even more entertaining. It is a great debut by Wendy Lea Thomas. Highly…highly recommended. I can hardly wait for book 2!"

— Author Carrie Fox

"This was definitely a very different read for me. The writing was very well done. The imagination the author uses for words to describe a woman's and man's private parts were extraordinary. Some of them were quite funny. I had no idea there were that many descriptive words for those parts. The sex was very very hot and quite imaginative as well. I am looking forward to the next book in the series."

— Author Alex Grayson

"Wow! This book was quite interesting and the best kind. I was blown away by the writing style, the unique storyline, and the great characters…I would definitely recommend this book to those who love a good laugh and sexy scenes!"

— Author H.S. Strickland.

DEDICATION

To my wonderful husband, thank you for helping me on this journey. I can't thank you enough. Without you, none of this would be possible. Thank you for always believing in me, and for encouraging me when it got difficult.

You are my rock.

THANKS

To our friend Brian, whose fantastic adventures provided the inspiration for this novel. Yes, it's true; this book is inspired by true events.

Dedicated to:

My favorite rock band
Chasing Seven.

Your music has inspired me for many years.
I can only hope my readers will find their way to you
and see how truly amazing you guys are.

The following songs provide the soundtrack for
Aria's adventures:

1. Temptation
2. Comfort Zone
3. I Need You
4. Something In The Water
5. Only One
6. If I Didn't Have Eyes

Visit www.chasingseven.com
or
Download their music from iTunes or Amazon.

Camp Jameson Chapter Summary

◆Week Three

◆Week Four

◆Week Five

◆Week Six

⌘

ARRIVAL DAY
WELCOME TO CAMP JAMESON

Six weeks, I told myself. That's forty-two days of solidarity with my friends, peace, and resplendent quiet, in the backwoods of Western Pennsylvania. No more three-inch thick books to study from, weighing my messenger bag down. No more annoying classmates and no more late night study sessions.

Final exams of nursing school were officially over as I handed in my Chemistry final to my stale professor. I grabbed my Chem book and trotted out of class, then headed straight for the 'Book Buyback' line. I had half a mind to burn it. I was certain I never wanted to see it again. I never cared for Chemistry, except maybe what I felt toward the guy who sat two rows in front of me in class. His name was Colt, but he was off limits. Colt was property of my extrovert roommate, Sara. *How could one man be so gorgeous, and smart? What I wouldn't give to date somebody like him.*

I couldn't be compared to my roommate. I was everything that she wasn't – shy, awkward, quiet, with way too many introverted tendencies that people mistook as bitchiness. That is, until people got to know me, then they would learn that I would do just about anything for those I care about.

It was late June already in Northeast Ohio and Summer One classes were ending. So, when Sara suggested we go camping for the remainder of summer break, I somehow relinquished control. Honestly, I was reluctant to let her take the reigns and plan the entire trip. I tried not to over-think it. I knew either I was a fool, or in for a fantastic ride. My head told me I was a fool but my heart craved the latter. I tried to overlook the fact that I would be vacationing with the two most sexual people I knew, Sara and Colt. I made them promise that I wouldn't have to share a tent with them. Actually, I was quite relieved when I discovered that we weren't tent camping at all. We would be staying in a cabin. I hadn't gone tent camping since I was a kid and I wasn't sure if I liked it. I could only hope for a large cabin with a real bathroom and when sharing it with Sara and Colt, I knew I would need my earplugs.

∞∞∞∞

It was Sunday afternoon and we had just driven three hours east to somewhere just south of the Allegheny National Forest, in Colt's gunmetal Jeep Grand Cherokee, to a small town called Paradise Lake. We took an off-road entrance marked by a carved wooden sign, which read: 'Jameson Country'. A smaller sign below stated 'Registered Members Only'.

"So Aria, are you excited, or dreading this?" Sara twisted to look back at me from her passenger seat.

"Excited," I beamed at her. *Although, I was about to pee myself if Colt didn't stop soon!*

Sara had this incredulous energy that would pull even the most solemn person into a smile when she was around. I sighed in nervous anticipation. Colt had been a camp counselor here since it opened five years ago. He raved about this place. He explained earlier that this camp was remote and I'd be cut off from the entire world for the next six weeks. But I had nothing planned, and I loved the idea. *Now, if only I could pee because these bumpy back roads are killing me.*

The gravel crunched under the Jeep's tires as the road narrowed into one-lane. We were surrounded by forest. For about a mile, the trees seemed to darken the day, until a wide lake appeared on both sides as we went over a confined wooden bridge where another sign greeted us: *Paradise Lake.*

My face widened into a smile at its breathtaking beauty. The tires returned to gravel and we twisted and turned down the road through numerous corners until we reached a large iron gate that made the camp look more like a private upscale estate than a campground.

Colt pulled up outside the gate and waited behind a line of five cars. A young man stood by the side of the gate as the driver of each car took their turn signing what looked like a thick leather registry, and then the man punched a code into the keypad and waited for the gate to loudly slide open.

"What's with the high security?" I asked.

"Don't they have this at every camp?" Colt teased.

I felt a gentle squeeze on my knee. "Relax. This will be fun. I promise," Sara said.

An unsettling worry came over me. I nervously tugged at my long silver necklace that held my father's military tags. It was what I always did when I was trying to work through something. *Something was up. I just didn't know what.*

"Welcome to Camp Jameson. Name, please," the tanned, perfectly built, man with a deep voice said. I slyly glanced at his nametag. *Hellooo Jamie, I wished my old counselors looked like that back at Indian Princess camp when I was a kid. I would have had much more fun.*

"Colt Thompson, Sara Cox, and Aria Mason," Colt nodded at each of us as he spoke our names.

"Let me see," Jamie flipped through the one-inch thick list on his clipboard. "Is Aria short for Arabella?" He looked back at me with a bleach white smile.

"Yes," I replied, choking on my dry throat. *Whoa, he's so hot!*

His smile widened when he saw my reaction. "Here's your parking pass." He handed us our pass then he punched the code into the keypad and opened the gate for us.

"Proceed to the Main Lodge to unload your things. Cubs are housed to your left, Kittens to your right. Enjoy yourselves."

Colt nodded and pulled forward. "No turning back now, Aria," Colt winked. "Remember, what happens at camp, stays at camp," he said.

All I could think about was peeing. *Please hurry. Please hurry,* I repeated to myself.

"Stop teasing her, Colt," Sara snapped at him but her hand rubbed his thigh in another suggestive manner. I knew that it wouldn't be long before I had to take an extra long walk by myself so they could have some alone time. I rolled my eyes, reminding myself from experience that they could go all night. I felt in the front pocket of my shorts. *Thank whomever for inventing earplugs.*

Colt was twenty-five, six years older than Sara and me, and they both were the most beautiful people I had ever met. They were perfectly sculpted. Like models.

I sighed inwardly as Colt pulled the Jeep through the gate to a building called the Jameson Main Lodge. According to Colt, the Main Lodge was over 37,000 square feet.

I took in the intricate three-story design of elegant redwood and stone. The tall row of windows that lined the front enhanced the panoramic view overlooking the massive lake. The grounds were immaculately groomed and the grass was a luscious green. Vivid white and pink wild orchids were fused into the shrubs adding just the right amount of color. The pathway was lined with grey sandstone walkways and decadent lighting. This place was an extravagant estate. Not at all what I pictured a camp to look like. This place was for the elite. It was breathtaking.

Sara jumped out of the Jeep and darted inside. I followed quickly but I lost track of her as I headed for the restroom. Colt unloaded our things.

When I returned I began pulling his suitcase toward the lodge, just to help out, when his hand stopped mine. He shook his head.

"This is Kitten Territory. I'm over there." He pointed to the left.

"You're not staying with us. Why?" I wrinkled my brow.

"You'll see soon enough, newbie."

"Grab your suitcase," Sara said. In the midst of my confusion, I hadn't seen Sara return and she startled me when she spoke. "Don't forget your second one. I packed you another one just in case."

"In case what?" I eyed the dark grey extra-large suitcase and wrinkled my brow. *Sara was definitely up to something.*

"Trust me, you'll thank me later. We have to hurry to get the good cabins," she called back over her shoulder as she ran down the hill. I ran after her in hopes she'd tell me what was going on.

"Did Colt tell you where the best cabins were?" I asked, trying to get a good look around at all the cabins as we ran down a little hill away from the Jameson Main Lodge. This place was huge. There were at least ten smaller cabins surrounding me and they seemed to go on for miles.

"Yea, both Colt and Sienna told me where to go. I told you about her, right?" Sara said. I racked my brain trying to remember Sara ever mentioning Sienna.

Sara wore a tight white tank top and denim Daisy Dukes. I looked at my tan cargo shorts and navy blue Air Force t-shirt and flip-flops and suddenly I felt self-conscious. Sara and I had been best friends for two years now. We sat next to each other in our trigonometry class senior year in high school, and we hit it off instantly.

"Is Sienna the girl you had your little bi-curious adventure with?" I asked.

"I promise I will tell you all about her later." A small smile played at the edge of Sara's lips. "You'll meet her soon enough. Hurry up, pokey," she continued.

"She's here?" I tightened my hand around the leather handle and continued to wheel it behind me. She grinned but continued in a hurried fashion – more like bee lined, toward the A-frame cabin labeled 'Jasmine'.

We entered through the doorway to a rustic décor. A slate fireplace stood mid-center of the wooden living room. There was a tall picture window with a view of the lake. Even though we were about a hundred yards away from it, the view was still breathtaking. The pale accented kitchen was off to the left. Two French doors led to the back of the cabin to a small patio with several Adirondack chairs and a small fire pit made out of the same slate as the inside fireplace. *No musty smell? That's impressive, cabins always smell weird when you first walk in, until you get used to them.*

"You're here. I'm in this one," Sara said.

I walked through the living room to one of the two doorways that sat opposite each other and entered with my suitcase in tow behind me. I took a step backwards remembering my second extra-large suitcase and lifted it in my free hand. The room was very modern. It had plush bone carpet with a queen-sized bed. I lifted both suitcases to the bed and then walked into the bathroom. It was spa-like. Ivory marble floors, white garden tub, glass shower, black walnut walls. I walked back in the room to the nightstand and picked up the Jameson Camp Manual. *Why is there a manual for camp?*

"Aria, hurry. We're going to be late. Throw on your sundress and your wedge sandals and make it quick," she barked, leaving me wondering why I had to pack such fancy clothes just to go camping in the first place? *Who in the hell wears wedges camping anyway?* Sara comes from a pretty well off family so I figured when in Rome. But I mean really, *fuck the Romans. They died wearing sandals and shiny boots!*

I set the manual down and did what I was told. I changed into my navy blue sundress, black wedge strap sandals, and then met Sara in the living room.

"Ready?" she bounced with glee.

"Ready for what, exactly?" I asked adjusting my silver chain so it fell down under the front of my sundress. I could never bring myself to take it off. Not yet anyway.

Sara giggled. "It's time for the meet and greet. Now promise me you will keep an open mind. I will explain everything after we've been introduced to our instructors. Avery Jameson himself is supposed to be there. I can't wait to meet him. Now don't go all gaga on me when you see him. It's not worth it. He never gets emotionally involved with his guests," Sara sighed amorously. "He only does one-nighters with women and he never repeats. Some even say that the rich, eligible bachelor Avery Jameson is deranged. They're all fools, though. He is so…not crazy. He's just distant when it comes to women," Sara said.

What the fuck are you babbling about? I thought to myself. *Why would I care who this guy dates? He's probably some old man with a wrinkled wiener or something.*

Sara led me to a small building marked 'Infirmary'. "First, we need to have physicals. This will only take a minute." *Why do we need physicals just to camp here?*

"Wait!" I pulled Sara back by the hand, eyeing her little black dress. "What do we need physicals for and why are you so dressed up? Do I need to go change? Is this some kind of cult? Are we joining a militia? It's a militia isn't it? Even though I do look good in camo, I've never even shot a gun. Is there a supply hut or somewhere where I can buy some camo? Wait, you didn't say why you're wearing a black dress and not camo. What is going on here?"

"Shut up!" Sara snapped. "We aren't joining a militia or a cult, and we certainly aren't wearing camouflage. You look great. Stop worrying," she said. I bit my lip and hushed the thousand questions racing through my head.

At the infirmary, Sara ran off with an older nurse while I watched as a large, round woman with ebony hair quickly checked my blood pressure and drew a small vial of blood. My own thoughts drowned out her endless chatter. *Why do we need physicals? And why the hell did that woman just draw my blood?*

"Are you on any medications?" the nurse asked in a flat tone.

"Birth control pill," I answered just as flatly.

"How long have you been on it?" the round nurse asked.

"Almost a year," I replied.

"When was your last sexual experience?"

What? I blinked in surprise. I could tell she was serious. *Just as serious as you obviously take your cheeseburgers.* But I smiled calmly and half-willingly answered. "Three months ago," I stumbled over the words.

"Were there multiple partners?"

"Just one," I answered.

"Did you use protection?" *I could see this woman and I were going to tango.*

"Yes… yes of course," I mumbled. I could feel my face heat up in under her stare.

"No signs of STD's?" I shook my head. "Okay, then," she said.

I swallowed nervously. This was getting uncomfortably private and I was getting pissed.

"Many will have sex with multiple partners and this just ensures everyone stays healthy during their time at camp." She pointed at her paperwork. "Sign here and here, then you may go," she said.

"Multiple partners?" I quickly tilted my head toward her. *Why are you assuming that I will have sex with a bunch of people here? I figured they were just protecting themselves legally but did I really look like that big of a whore?*

I took the clipboard from her and signed the two pages out of spite. Sara strode over and pulled me toward the door, but I kept staring at the large nurse on my way out. If I did find someone to sleep with, I will make sure and do it in front of her cabin just so she knows about it. I turned my head back to Sara. I had never seen her so excited about camping before.

"What is going on? Did they take your blood too? Why are you being so mysterious?"

"You'll see," she said, hurriedly pulling me behind her in an almost full sprint down the path toward the Jameson Main Lodge, which was twice the distance as our cabin. *How could she run in stilettos?*

I had to fight to keep up with Sara. I almost twisted my ankle twice trying to keep up with her. I tucked my light brown hair behind my ear and tried to suppress the sick ebbing feeling that grew in the pit of my stomach as we hurried down the path. Sara spotted Colt and left me to fend for myself.

10

I walked inside and stood in a sea of abnormally good-looking men and women dressed in expensive black attire. I felt self-conscious again wearing a simple sundress. I was still wearing my ponytail from earlier. I straightened my bangs and tucked the flyaway strands of hair behind my ear again, hoping I didn't look as disheveled as I felt, while I scanned the crowd for Sara. I needed to get Sara alone for a minute, but it was obvious she was avoiding me. *Why were they so dressed up if this was simply a summer camp?* I had to find Sara. I needed answers *now*.

"Good evening Kittens and Cubs," a warm, sensuous male's voice echoed through the magnificent grand cabin as I made my way through the crowd in search of Sara.

The room was large, with a row of mirrors from floor to ceiling that surrounded the dance floor on the far side. The staircase on the other side floated in its space and was ornate with crooked carved branches resembling deer antlers. Hand carved archways rose above the doors. The artisanship was meticulous. The dance floor was made from some exotic wood I didn't recognize. We had a lot of pine at my house back home and this wasn't pine. Everywhere you looked large wooden beams braced the ceiling like giant ribs in the belly of some great wild beast.

"Welcome to the fifth annual Camp Jameson. I'm Avery Jameson. I fully expect each and every one of you to read and abide by the Camp Jameson Manual. As it notes on page one, I will not tolerate idiocy. On a lighter note, soon, I will introduce the fine men and women I have chosen for you as your instructors," he said.

Instructors…for what? Don't you mean counselors? Wait, did some guy just grab my ass? I looked quickly, but there were too many people around, I couldn't see who grabbed me and several tall guys in front of me blocked my view of the stage.

I continued looking for my traitorous friend. My eyes found Sara as I squeezed my way through the oppressive crowd. I was going to get the answers from her to what was really going on if I had to choke it out of her.

"Our attendance is high this summer," he continued. "You will enjoy the many new experiences. So many newbies, I can't wait to see what this summer holds for all of you." I grabbed hold of Sara's hand and pulled her from Colt's grasp.

"What the hell is going on here?" I said stepping in front of Sara with my back to the stage.

"Aria, can this wait until after he's done?"

"No. Why are you avoiding me?" I narrowed my eyes at her. "What are you hiding?"

Sara shifted nervously. "Please. I need you to keep an open mind," she said.

Open mind about what? Maybe it was the anxiety building inside of me. Maybe it was anger. *I'm pretty sure it was anger.*

"Spill it, Cox," I shouted.

The crowded room had just dropped to a stark quiet as Avery Jameson paused between his words, but my words continued to echo and bounce loudly across the large atrium.

Many onlookers nearby snickered. I was mortified as the room turned its attention to me. I could hear faint whispers but I couldn't make out their words. After a brief moment, he regained the crowd's attention.

"I will explain everything. Let him finish his speech first," Sara urged in a hushed whisper.

"Lover's quarrel already?" Avery Jameson's warm velvet voice gushed from the high priced speaker system. Sara froze like a deer in headlights, her face blushing.

"No," she giggled. But Sara never blushed. She was always on her toes and no one had ever intimidated her. *Why was she being so shy?*

"Do I bore you, Kitten?" Avery's warm sensuous voice trilled.

I looked at Sara. She mouthed the words 'turn around' and raised her eyebrows toward the man on the stage. I turned slowly, ignoring the gazing stares, and locked eyes on the most beautiful man I had ever seen. His brows were scrunched together, but in an instant, his eyes widened and he sucked in an audible breath. He blinked twice trying to collect his thoughts.

"What's your name, Kitten?" Avery said, as his voice echoed through the speakers.

"Aria," I choked out dryly as more and more people focused on me rather than the stage. *Take a picture, people.*

"Well, Aria, if you are quite finished, I would like to continue tonight's festivities. Take it to the mattresses, ladies, if you need to expel pent-up energy."

Take it to the mattresses? I don't need a nap. Surely, he couldn't mean it any other way. This was getting very awkward. I couldn't get my mouth to respond so I nodded politely.

"Good, now then," he said turning back to address the crowd. "Lockdown commences immediately. Your signature binds you to the contract, so does your blood," he chuckled. "Just kidding, remember as always, no means no. Never touch someone without his or her permission. Any unruliness, cameras or use of cell phones and you will be quickly assigned to aid our kitchen staff, or banned from the premises; so, once again, no one in or out from this moment on. You'll have forty-two days of magnificent bliss as you fulfill all your sexual curiosities and make all your fantasies come true. Welcome to sex camp!" he concluded.

What the fuck? Was my only dumbfounded thought.

⌘

MEET & GREET

Avery Jameson's words echoed through my head like an annoying skip of an old scratched vinyl record, forcing me to repeat the same line over and over... *make all your fantasies come true. Welcome to Sex Camp?*

The crowd milled about waiting for the second part of the program. The bar opened and lines formed as people raised their glasses of Champagne in toast.

Everywhere I looked, strangers were laughing and greeting each other, happy to start their sexual adventure while I stood gaping, pressing crescent indentations into the palms of my hands as my blood boiled. I was flabbergasted.

Sara had some audacity. My impetuous bi-curious roommate had tricked me into coming to sex camp. I had trusted her to make plans for the summer. She assured me this vacation would be everything I ever dreamed of, but sex camp? *Really, what the hell was she thinking?*

I wasn't a virgin, but I have only had sex with one man in my life and it was a one-night stand. I was inexperienced. I was living in my own Big Bang Theory like a female Dr. Sheldon Cooper.

"Don't be mad, Kitten," Colt chided.

"Fuck you, Colt," I responded.

"I'd love to. But I'm your instructor now and it's against the rules. Plus, my woman promised herself to me tonight," he said, wrapping his arm around Sara and bringing her to his side. She gave me a pathetic puppy dog look and tried to diffuse my mood.

For the second time in five minutes, I stood gaping. *I needed air.* I closed my mouth and turned to escape the chaos that was now my summer. But I hadn't noticed Avery Jameson coming up beside me. I hadn't seen anything except his button up dark blue dress shirt and black sport coat when I collided into him. I breathed in his sandalwood and citrus cologne and stepped back. I blinked, trying to reorient myself as his gorgeous face settled into view.

"Aria, I'm Avery Jameson. I wanted to personally welcome one of the most beautiful women I have ever seen to my camp."

My body seemed to come alive at the sound of his voice breathing in my name. *Why did he affect me like this?* I shook my head at him and bolted for the door. I could sense his eyes on me as I fled outside. I wanted to be alone and gather my thoughts so I headed toward the lake.

The path was inlaid with granite stepping-stones, but because I was so freaked out, I didn't take in the beauty of it for the first five minutes of the walk. I didn't stop until I made it to a clearing by the shore. I was still pushing epithets from my mouth as I plopped down on a large boulder beside the water's edge. The sun was setting and a warm orange glow glistened off the surface of the water. I inhaled, slowly breathing in the smell of fresh air, pine, and the lake for the first time. *This place was so beautiful and so peaceful…but peace can quickly give way to war,* my subconscious sneered.

16

"Your friends told me how they got you to come here," he said.

Startled, my eyes looked to the sound of the voice that made my stomach do flips. Avery had followed me from the lodge. I took in the glorious man with dark chestnut hair and emerald colored eyes. His five o'clock shadow lightly traced his square jaw and I suddenly wanted to know what he would feel like inside me. *What was wrong with me? I have never been that girl to swoon over a guy before.*

"You're still mad," he said. "I can see it in your beautiful brown eyes. Don't be too hard on them. They just wanted to surprise you. They knew you wouldn't have come if they told you where they were taking you. Soon, you won't be thinking about them." He let his eyes linger over every curve of my body. "You'll be thinking more about your body and what it feels like to be a totally free woman. And by free, I mean sexual freedom. You have a wonderful opportunity to explore your sensuality. In my camp, no one will judge you, or look down at you, or repress you. Here you can explore your every desire and your every fantasy. I promise that will outweigh any raw emotion you are feeling at this moment."

"Seriously? You don't know a thing about me. And why do you even care? I thought you were supposed to be deranged?" I asked.

He crooked an eyebrow at me in mischievous dissatisfaction. "Maybe I am or maybe I'm not, but I'll tell you what, I'll show you mine if you show me yours."

"That's juvenile," I said hoarsely.

"You're barely nineteen or twenty, who's really the juvenile here?"

He's got me there. He had to be in his mid twenties. I scoffed and rose to my feet. I crossed my arms and narrowed my eyes while locking my stare to his. *Asshole,* I thought.

He took a step toward me and I backed away. "Let me see if I've figured you out," he said, taking another step closer. I took one step back. "I can see passion in your eyes. You're confused but intrigued. Was it the moment you first saw me on stage, or just now as I step closer?" he said.

I tried to slow my breathing but the closer he stepped the more my body seemed to come alive like it was force fed by a live wire. He looked to my chest rising and falling as if I had just run a marathon.

"Careful, you wouldn't want to wear yourself out too soon. We're just getting started," he said, and he was right. I had never felt so emotional about anything. *What was this place doing to me?*

"You are so full of yourself. What makes you think this has anything to do with you?" I asked, backing away until my back pressed against a large oak tree.

He closed the gap between us. "Don't think, Aria. Just feel." His voice seared through me. All of my senses heightened. I could feel my heart pushing through every cell of my body. The tingling started in my tiniest toe and moved upward, curving through my every muscle and every tissue. The static charge widened my eyes and pouted my lips. I trembled involuntarily and my breath shortened. I didn't know my body could respond like this.

"What is your body telling you right at this very moment with me standing so close to you?" he said, as he breathed in and closed his eyes. When he opened them, his green eyes had grown darker. He brushed the back of his hand down my cheek and let his eyes drift to my lips. Unknowingly, I ran my tongue across the bottom of my lip moistening them.

"You're not sure, are you?" he said as he lowered his voice. *Oh my, he was sexy as hell when he did that. Jerk.*

"I'll tell you what I think," he whispered. "Your breathing increased three-fold the moment I stepped closer. Your pupils are dilated. Why is that, Aria? Do you like what you see?" He smirked knowingly then raised his voice a little. "They are all telltale signs of lust and desire. Use that spark to drive you. Let go of your fear and let your body guide you," he said.

I could feel his warm breath dance on my lips. I had never been so aroused by a man's words. I couldn't speak. If I did, I was sure the only thing escaping my mouth would have been a moan.

"Avery, time for Instructor introductions," a tall man called out, stepping out of the woods and interrupting our heated discussion. "Well, well, well, look what we have here. Avery, did you catch a butterfly in your web?" the dark haired, hazel-eyed man said, gawking at me.

Avery leaned closer and whispered in my ear. "A very beautiful butterfly. And she has me completely hypnotized."

I rolled my eyes in exaggeration but secretly I was barely standing on my quivering knees. He captivated me. I had just met *the* Avery Jameson and I had lost all sense of reason when he touched me. *Never say never.* My subconscious reared its ugly head reminding me that I was so sure earlier that I'd never sleep with anyone at this camp.

I returned my stare to the green-eyed Adonis, secretly begging him to touch me again. His eyes searched mine for a moment, and then he pulled away from me and squared his shoulders. I felt bereaved by this. I wanted to reach out and pull him back to me.

"Travis, let's go," Avery commanded. "Coming Aria?"

I nodded and followed behind them back to the Main Lodge. That was the second time he'd said the word come, and I smiled crookedly as my childish thoughts outweighed my anger. But there was an underlining emotion I couldn't place. Maybe I was intrigued by the idea of sex camp, or maybe I was irritated that we were interrupted, because now all I wanted was to keep Avery all to myself.

Once back inside the Main Lodge, I couldn't seem to take my eyes off Avery as he stepped back up to the microphone.

"Kits and Cubs, please allow me to introduce your instructors."

Standing on either side of Avery were thirty of the hottest men and women I had ever seen. Including Colt. Each person was of movie star quality and dressed in a white polo shirt with green trim. The logo of Camp Jameson was on the front of the shirts with *'staff'* embroidered below the logo in script text.

The crowd stared toward the stage and whispered, audibly this time, how they would like to sleep with them.

"Before we get started, I would like to go over a couple rules," Avery continued. "Do *not* frolic with the staff, and staff, vice-versa. We are professionals, not prostitutes. There will be controlled areas where we will push your body to the limits of pleasure. You will meet with your instructors tomorrow to go over your likes and dislikes. We range from petting to soft swap to full swing. You can learn pretty much whatever your little heart desires." I swear he was looking right at me as he spoke.

"Anything goes people," he continued. "Your welcome backpacks have found their way to your rooms. Use what you wish. Deposit anything you may not want in the bin beside the door. Though, I couldn't see why you'd want to waste any of it. And remember, safety first." Avery clasped his hands behind his back and looked toward me. A small smile crept on his lips. "Now, enough talk. Let's have some fun."

The meet and greet turned out to be more fun the more alcohol I drank. I watched as all the gorgeous women stood in a large circle around Avery along with a group of men.

"Brought you a treat," Colt said. "Jello shots. A whole tray of them." He was trying to kiss my ass for tricking me into coming here. I looked at Sara as she fought back a grin. They both knew Jello shots were my weakness. I plowed through five of them as I watched the women swoon over Avery. I rolled my eyes at their desperation.

"Hi Avery, I'm Caitlyn," I heard a blonde say.

The women were endless. I felt sorry for him. It was like an episode of *The Bachelor* except I was watching it from ten feet away, not through a television. Avery didn't seem phased by any of it. He spoke openly to everyone.

I ran my pinkie finger around the perimeter of another Jello shot and looked out over the massive crowd, thankful that I wasn't among them. My eyes landed on Avery as I sucked off the Jello residue from my finger, savoring the taste of whipped cream vodka. His eyes widened as I drew my finger away from my mouth. I kept my gaze on him as I tilted my head back, brought the Jello cup to my mouth, and let it fall in. Avery blinked and shifted nervously. His lips turned up into a crooked smile. The crowd faded into the background and I felt like there was no one else in the room except us.

"Avery, you have to tell me about the yacht you just bought." Caitlyn interrupted my wonderful imaginative moment by stepping between us with her back towards me. She could've been Barbie's twin and I quickly had fantasies of sneaking into her room at night and smearing Rogaine onto her knuckles and maybe the tops of her feet.

Avery's eyes never left mine until I returned the smile.

"Avery?" she cooed.

I nodded toward him and turned to share my Jello shots with Sara and Colt when a hand reached out beside me and snatched one.

"Tease," Avery's warm breath said in my ear. I swallowed nervously, forcing myself to smile at a very curious Sara and Colt.

"Avery, why did you run away? I wanted to hear about your yacht…" Caitlyn's metallic voice cut off. "Oh, hello," she said as she stepped up to our circle, eyeing Sara and me as her competition. Then her eyes fell on Colt. Colt instantly wrapped his arm around Sara and drew her to his side.

Sara smirked as she introduced everyone. She was a better person than I was. I probably would have slapped the bitch if someone were eyeing my man like that.

Avery stepped in front of her towards me and I had to fight back a snicker as Caitlyn's mouth fell open in shock. Avery blew her off for the second time in five minutes.

"Can't resist a Jello shot," he said as he ran his tongue around the rim of the cup and I almost combusted as his tongue coaxed the Jello into his mouth in one piece. I whimpered in silence as he ran his tongue over his bottom lip and looked at me. "So, Aria and Sara, what cabin are you staying in?"

"Jasmine," Sara said. I was glad she spoke for me because I was sure it was going to come out shaky.

I finally pushed away my nervousness and spoke. "How many cabins are on the grounds?"

"Just over one hundred and twenty-five. I hope to have almost two hundred by next summer. There are sixty cabins for the guests. Most are single occupancy but some are double like Jasmine. The rest are for the instructors and the wait staff. I made sure the staff had their own cabins. Except for a few like Colt here, who can only help when he doesn't have class."

"I only have two more semesters then I'm all yours." Colt looked at me. "Aria, you may not know this but Avery and the University have allowed me to study under him to complete my last year of apprenticeship for my architecture degree."

"That's great," I replied. *How did I not know this?* I had been so wrapped up in studying to even realize he landed an internship. There was a huge crash of glass behind the bar. Everyone turned to see one of the bartenders grimace at her clumsiness.

"Excuse me, I need to make sure everyone is okay," Avery hurried off to the 'Employees Only' door and came out with a broom and dustpan. Instead of letting his staff clean it up, he made everyone step back and tackled the job himself.

Later that evening, I sat on my bed in my pink pinstripe pajama shorts and a light pink camisole. After a long night of faking smiles and laughter, I was exhausted. I heard a soft knock and turned to the doorway to where Sara stood. I crossed my arms defensively and glared at her. My stubborn side wasn't ready to let her betrayal go. I trusted her and she ambushed me. *What kind of friend did that?* My subconscious sneered.

"Sara how could you?" I said with less anger than I intended. I was worn out from all the socializing. And honestly, I didn't have the heart to lay into her about all this.

"I'm sorry bestie. I really am. I didn't expect you to get so mad. I was only…"

"Don't." I took in a slow steady breath. "You could have warned me. I trusted you!"

"You wouldn't have come if I told you what kind of camp this was. You need this, Aria, whether you can see it or not. You have to stop running away from who you are and reach out and grab that sexual goddess that I know lies in there somewhere," she said.

A part of me wanted to shut her out completely but through our friendship she had always had my back and this was her not-so-subtle way of showing me I needed to spread my wings and break out of my nice tidy little box I had been living in for nineteen years. I was wavering and she could see it as she scanned my face. I was freaking out inside about having to be so open amongst a bunch of strangers. *How the hell was I going to do this?*

"You have to trust me on this one. Please, Aria. Have I steered you wrong before?"

I shut off my internal struggle after I realized her friendship meant more than me trying to overcome my insecurities and I breathed in another deep breath.

"It's fine. But you best be sure you're gonna make this up to me...for a lifetime." Sara wore Colt's oversized t-shirt. *Geez, even in that she looked like a goddess.* Sara nodded slowly.

"Did Colt leave already?" I asked trying to change the subject. Deep down, I wasn't sure how I felt about being here. I guess time would tell.

"Yes. He didn't want to leave me too sore for the first day of classes," Sara replied, glancing at my welcome backpack I was nervously fidgeting with in my hands. "Did Colt get you drunk with all those Jello shots?" she asked.

"I didn't get too drunk. I'm glad he gave them to me. It kept me from freaking out. I didn't want to make a fool out of myself on the first night. There's plenty of time for that."

Sara waited until I looked up at her then spoke. "All the men had their eye on you tonight. And the women were sizing up their competition," Sara smiled. "I'm pretty sure Caitlyn's head spun when Avery ignored her. I noticed that he couldn't take his eyes off of you."

"Were we at the same party?" I looked away as I played with the string on my backpack. She smirked at me, knowing I didn't like being the center of attention. "Did you open yours?" I asked. She shook her head and pulled hers out from behind her back.

"Together?" Sara asked.

"Together," I replied. Sara giggled nervously and jumped to the bed. I suddenly felt like a high school teenager getting away with something naughty. We unlaced the green nylon Camp Jameson backpack and spilled out the contents onto the bed. An itemized list on a thick index card fell to the top of the pile. It was broken up into two categories.

Comfort items: Dark green silk nighty with the Camp Jameson Logo over left breast. Hand sanitizer, chapstick, aloe, sunscreen, Advil, mouthwash.

Naughty items: Handcuffs & key, large box of condoms, vibrator, vibrator cleaning solution, intense warming liquid, Strawberry Lubricant, Kama Sutra guidebook, blindfold.

We jumped into a fit of giggles as we picked up each item, intrigued.

"I can't believe a place like this really exists," I said in a shaky low voice.

"I can and I've never been happier," Sara said rolling to her back.

"Are you going to be okay with Colt, you know, being with other women?" I asked rolling to my back and staring at the wooden beams of the cabin above me.

"Technically, he can't sleep with his students, but absolutely. We've always had an open relationship. That's how we met Sienna."

"Okay. Do tell, please." And just like that we were lost in the moment of this sensual surreal place and all the anger I felt slipped away.

"Sienna met Colt here when the camp opened five years ago. We had our first threesome a few months ago. It was amazing. A woman's touch is so much more sensual than a man's could ever be," Sara said.

"Seriously. I don't know about that," I answered.

"You'll see soon enough, I'm sure," Sara said.

I swallowed nervously as my heart ebbed in my chest.

"Sara, I don't know if I am ready for this." Sara studied me for a minute.

"Aria, I know your parents sheltered you. Never letting you watch an R rated movie or never talking to you about sex. They expected you to learn everything from your friends. Don't take this the wrong way, but its just sex. Don't over think it. I bet deep down you are dying to be set free. Trust me," Sara said.

I envied Sara's optimism. At 19, we were both the same age, but already she knew exactly what she wanted in life and whom she was going to spend it with. Me, I was so focused on school and nursing that I often neglected things like love…and sex.

Sara stood and gathered her pack. "I'm gonna go. I have a date with the alluring Camp Jameson Sex Manual. Maybe it will unlock some of the mystery around Avery Jameson. Colt never wants to say too much about Avery, but he did say Avery was burned very badly by a woman some years back and has never been the same since. He was devastated and decided to build this camp so he would have a playground to do as he pleased. Apparently, he made a promise to never to fall in love again. He very rarely lets his guard down. It's like he's built an invisible wall around the fortress of his heart," Sara said.

"He seemed fine when I talked to him at the meet and greet. He's very sexy but arrogant. Sometimes a guy like that only knows how to play games," I said.

"Maybe he needs someone to settle him down and turn him into the perfect man. He just needs that one special girl who can love him forever. Who's that going to be? You, the beautiful butterfly?" Sara asked.

"I never told you about that," I quipped.

"Avery may have mentioned it to Colt," Sara laughed. "Aria, not all guys are like Nate. He saw a sweet innocent freshman that got very drunk at a frat party. He was a player. But not every guy will treat you like that. I promise."

"If you say so," I muttered as I pulled my legs up to my chest and wrapped my arms around them.

"From what Colt has said, Avery has the heart of a lion but he never gets emotionally involved with his guests. He's a player that targets women from every session, seduces them and then he moves on. You don't want that to be you, but then again maybe he just needs a Kitten to soften him up," Sara chided.

I laughed aloud. I smiled at her reference and watched her leave. Her blonde curls were cut short, but just long enough she could tuck it behind her ears. I liked this new look on her.

I ran my fingers across the manual, hoping it would show me the way through this wonderful world of Oz. Because the man I had met today surely wasn't going to. But I soon realized, I wasn't looking for a wizard to get me back home, I was looking for my prince charming to show me a world that would take my breath away and make all of my fantasies come true.

I unbound the black satin ribbon tied around the outside of the loosely bound manual addressed to me: Arabella Mason.

It read:

Camp Jameson Manual

Dear Kittens,

I tried to make this short and sweet but I wanted you to have all you needed to help make your visit more pleasurable. This letter serves as your registration confirmation. Please review the following information carefully. Registration includes Camp backpack and all the items enclosed. Additional items may be purchased for a fee. I cannot stress the importance of reading the entire manual. It is provided to help ease the transition into this lifestyle, provide fundamental instructions, and advice to maximize your pleasure during the next six weeks. It is my sincere hope that you enjoy your stay with us and so with that, please read on to prepare for your first lessons.

Your Host,
Avery Jameson

I skimmed over the map, quickly noting the bars, gym, meditation chambers, salon, massage tables, tanning booths, and Turkish baths. *This camp takes its business very seriously,* I thought. *Who knew pleasure could be so much work.*

Page 1: Helpful Hints

    a. **The number one rule is no means no.** *It is a Kitten's prerogative to have sex with whom she desires and vice versa. Please respect each other.*

    b. **No cell phones, cameras, or recording equipment of any kind.** *If you are found using any of these devices, you will be ejected from the camp and your equipment and phone will be confiscated. Cell phone jammers have been installed. Any calls needed made can be done so in the main office but must be authorized during the allotted times, except for emergencies.*

    c. **Relax:** *Nerves are the hardest part of this camp to overcome - no pun intended. Meditation and hot baths are highly recommended. Massage is a must. And the drinks are complimentary. So, loosen up…but not too much.*

    d. **Don't play too much, too soon.** *You don't want to be sore for what we have in store for you — trust me; you will learn to push your* *body to its limits and beyond. It's not just about reaching the common orgasm, it's about the experience that leads to the mind blowing – holy fuck – breathtaking – I see stars orgasm, see the difference?*

e. **Drunkenness: 1ˢᵗ *offense* -** *I will* NOT *tolerate drunks. You will spend the hangover confined to quarters and then suffer kitchen duty: washing dishes, emptying dirty ashtrays, peeling potatoes, and listening to loud music. PAYBACKS are a bitch. You fuck with my business – I fuck with you. Don't waste my time. I won't waste yours.*

f. **Drunkenness: 2ⁿᵈ *offense* –** *We have a zero second offense tolerance policy. No redo's. No excuses. No refunds. You will be expelled from the camp. It is what it is. Be an adult and be responsible. Control your intake.*

g. **Topless Sunbathing ONLY.** *No Nude sunbathing. Clothing is not optional. Leave something for the imagination. Think sexy, not vulgar. Nude sunbathing leads to unmonitored sex.*

h. **Sex is to be restricted to designate areas only.** *Instructors must be present at all times. You are here to learn and that means we will correct you when you're doing it wrong. <u>Please respect each other. Always remember:</u>* <u>**No means No.**</u>

i. **Be responsible** and put on sunblock. *SUN = SUNBLOCK. It's that simple. You*

31

don't want to be the one that missed out on an experience because you baked into a lobster. Umbrellas are at every chair side. USE THEM.

j.   **Performance Anxiety:** *(Viagra) Nerves will be taken into consideration if unable to perform- but you only get 3(10mg) complimentary Viagra tablets. Additional tablets may be purchased for a fee. So I recommend eating right, getting the proper sleep, and exercising regularly. Whenever possible it is preferred you perform naturally.*

k.   **Wooded Recreation:** *Sex in the wooded areas is for the more adventurous guests. An Instructor must be present at all times.*

l.   **Orgasm:** *I am here to make your sexual experiences more desirable. Sex will not be more desirable if your body can't function at its optimal level. Let's face it Cubs - Cuming prematurely makes you look soft, boring, and flat. Kittens – taking too long to orgasm makes you cold and distant, so do as I say and I will help you reach your peak sexual fitness. Defy my instructions and kitchen duty will be your new station until you take me seriously. Hotheads need not apply. Know-it-alls, there is no such thing when the human body is different with each individual. So check your attitude/ego at the main entrance and say hello to the best orgasm you've ever experienced and*

*to a world of sensuality and tantalizing
sexuality.*

m. **Safe Sex**: *Safe sex is sexual activity engaged
in by people who have taken precautions to
protect themselves against sexually transmitted
disease (STDs). Safe sex is effective avoiding
STDs only if both parties involved in sexual
intercourse agreed on doing so and stick to it.
During sexual intercourse using condoms, for
example, the male might intentionally pull off
the condom and continue penetrating without
the female's consent and notice. This high-risk
behavior betrays trust as well as spreading the
disease.*

n. **Sex toys:** *Putting a condom on a sex toy
provides better sexual hygiene and can help to
prevent transmission of STDs if the sex toy is
shared, provided the condom is replaced when
used by a different partner. Some sex toys are
made of porous materials, and pores retain
viruses and bacteria, which makes it necessary
to clean sex toys thoroughly, preferably with use
of cleaners specifically for sex toys. Glass sex
toys are non-porous and more easily sterilized
between uses. All sex toys have to be properly
cleaned after use.*

Page 2: Some Sexual Helpful Hints:

1. **Try talking dirty**. *If you're too embarrassed, make
sure you have the lights off, then try it. You may find you
love it!*

33

2. **Get her or his motor running.** *Whisper or write sexy messages to your partner throughout the day.*
3. **Stop by the camp boutique and buy new undies:** *Bring your guy or girl with you and let them pick some out for you.*
4. **Break out the Sex toys.** *Let your partner share a little of the vibrating action and both will enjoy.*
5. **Kittens strap on your high heels** *and give a sexy lap dance.*
6. **Mix it up during Sex.** *Take a bath together as foreplay, change positions often during sex, use lubrication.*
7. **Share your fantasies with each other.** *You may be surprised by what your partner finds hot and sexy.*
8. **Role-playing:** *Role-playing may seem a bit awkward at first, but that's just because you haven't tried it. It's the perfect addition to everyone's sex life.*
9. **Bring on the kink:** *with some furry handcuffs. If you don't like being cuffed (or tied) to the bed, have your partner strap them on and take control of the situation.*
10. **Sweet treats:** *We all know how delicious chocolate and whipped cream is; why not take them to bed? But get ready to get sticky. Remember you can shower off together, afterwards.*

I skimmed through the six-week itinerary and endless pages of detailed descriptions of what each class entailed. I wasn't ready to dive in yet. I turned to the last page and found a portrait of Avery grinning mischievously back at me. Below his half page photo was an excerpt.

About Me - Avery Mathew Jameson:

> *First things first: I believe in keeping a professional distance with my guests. I don't believe in rumors or gossip. If you have a question about me just ask. Gossip will not be tolerated. I am 26 years old. A Capricorn. Born January 3rd. I am 6'2". I was born and raised in Pennsylvania. I am the second of three children. I have two husky-wolf mixed breed dogs named Bo and Luke. I love long walks off cliffs. No, not suicide, bungee jumping. I live each day in the moment, and I want to teach that to everyone I meet. Making the billionaire of the month club pleases me. But what makes me happy is...well, even I don't know because I am never satisfied.*

I turned off the bedside lamp with only one thought in my mind. *What have I gotten myself into?*

◆<u>**Week One:**</u>

⌘

DAY ONE:
MONDAY MORNING
MEET SIENNA

"Damn you, Sara!" I seethed, in consternation at all the items I had sprawled out on my bed. It was the next morning and I had just opened my second suitcase, the one Sara had packed for me.

"You called?" Sara asked.

I didn't have to look up to know Sara was standing there grinning at me. I reached down for the shiny red platform shoes and held them up to her. My face wore an expression of pure distress.

"That goes with your sexy nurse costume," Sara said, as she reached into the suitcase and shuffled around the clothing until she retrieved a very short red and white naughty costume. Then she continued to rearrange the piles of dangerously revealing and sexual clothing. "I bought all of these for you to help with your little adventure."

I looked down to see fourteen pairs of matching lacy bra and panty sets from Victoria's Secret, one of every color.

"This is the standard uniform. You can wear whatever you want over them to class but when you are in class you wear one of these, or nothing at all," Sara giggled.

Besides my matching lacy bra-and-panty-sets there were a pair of thigh high leather boots, Black Mary Jane's, 5 inch stilettos, a sexy Cinderella costume, a school girl costume, a sexy Santa costume, corsets that were red, white, and black with red accents, lace teddies, garter belts and an assortment of thigh high and knee high stockings, some with the line up the back of the stocking.

"Am I really supposed to wear all those?" I asked modestly.

"Didn't you read the manual?" Sara asked. I shook my head as she continued. "There are theme parties twice a week. Everyone goes. I bought you this lacy shirt and latex boy shorts to wear to the first party. But by night's end, I'll bet you'll be wearing just your panties," she said.

I thanked her for bringing me a more modest outfit for the first party but honestly, I didn't see the difference. All of it was too revealing. I wasn't used to showing off so much of my body. My face was as red as the platform shoes Sara gave me. The only thing I was comfortable with was the boy shorts. I just wasn't sure if I had the ass for hotpants. I couldn't look at the rest.

I moved the bra-and-panty-sets to the top drawer of my dresser and thigh-high stockings to the second drawer. Shirts and shorts in the remaining two drawers. Sara hung up the remaining items and put the boots and heels in the bottom of my armoire. I hung my head over the dresser and closed my eyes. *How the hell was I going to do this? I wanted to leave but damn it, I couldn't. The camp was in lockdown. Maybe I could skip all of my classes and avoid all parties. Possibly, stay in my room the whole time. I could volunteer in the kitchen. I grimaced as I thought of kitchen duty. Working in the kitchen in a place this size would be awful. I could just imagine cleaning cum off a dinner plate and mistaking it for tapioca. I had to laugh at that. Why would somebody cum on a plate? But who knows what kind of kinkiness they get into here? The thing that really scared me was that soon I was going to find out…firsthand.*

"Hey Aria, don't stress too much about it," Sara said. "Colt and I will help you through the hard stuff."

"The hard stuff? Like what?" My voice cracked as I sat down hard on the edge of the bed unsure of myself.

Sara chuckled. "It's hard to pick the classes at first, when you've never really experienced anything like this before. So, I will help you find something that will fit your preferences, and your inexperience."

"I don't think I can do this." I shook my head at her.

"Don't be afraid of the unknown," Sara said. "Colt will be a good instructor. He's patient and very knowledgeable. He's taught me everything I know. Besides, Sienna can't wait to get to know you and she knows her way around a woman's body and will help you tap into sensations you never knew existed." I fought to keep the blush from my face as I thought of the endless sexual experiences that Sara and Colt shared since they started dating. There was no other way to say it…Colt was a sexual machine.

My eyes met hers as I studied her sincerity and my face reddened a bit as I thought about how cute she looked right now. "I'm not like you, Sara. It's hard for me to open up to people, let alone strangers. Now you expect me to have sex in front of them!" My voice was more questioning than assured.

"Aria, don't over-think this. You know Colt well enough to know he won't let anything bad happen to you, and you'll love Sienna, too. They can help you relieve your anxiety and show you the pleasures of your body, pleasures that will blow your mind. Just give it a chance. After we register for classes, you'll have some time to sit and talk with them. Nobody will force anything on you. They are very good at dealing with people's fear. You can go at your own speed. I'm betting by the end of the first day, that you will see that you're more than a little curious and will probably want to know more. Just remember, we're all here for the same reason, so there's no need to be shy. It's everybody's first day. No one is here to judge you."

"Colt isn't going to be your instructor?" I asked.

"No, because we're dating, he's not allowed. I asked him to choose you as a student to help ease you into this," she said.

"Thanks. I think." I was wondering just what the instructors would say or do. Colt has almost seen me naked a few times back at home. But now, Sara had practically set him up to see me naked and who knows what else? I was embarrassed at the thought of someone I know teaching me about sex and yet, it did kind of excite me to think about Colt seeing me in those sexy outfits and teaching me about sex. I forced myself to clear away my thoughts. They kept saying instructors weren't allowed to have sex with the guests but how can they really enforce that?

"You're welcome," Sara said. "Now come, Kitten. We've put this off long enough. We need to get breakfast then Colt's taking us on a tour of camp and then it's time to register for classes." I couldn't suppress my giggle at Sara's willfulness. As I walked with her, I tried to convince myself that I would be fine, no matter what.

CAMP JAMESON

Breakfast took longer than usual on this first morning. The lines were long as we waded through the crowd staring at a very nice layout of breakfast food aptly named with bad sexually suggestive puns. I opted for syrup soaked flapjack-offs while Sara chose the French-kiss-toast. The thought of six weeks of bad sexual puns made me giggle, but really, what else would you expect at sex camp. The staff kept muttering the importance of carb-loading as they loaded our trays. Usually, I only ate fruit and maybe a protein bar for breakfast, but these people take their sex seriously saying we needed the calories. *I mean how much energy does it take for a girl to just lie there? I know, it was a bad joke. Good thing nobody could hear me think that.*

As I looked around at my future classmates, I could sense that I wasn't the only one nervous about what today would bring. I overheard one married couple that sat to our left. The husband kept telling his wife to relax. She seemed much more nervous than me. She wore a loose sweater that made her look very frumpy and jeans that clearly screamed, "I'm the mother of a sixteen year old." Her hair was gray halfway down to her shoulders where it suddenly turned blonde. *Why wouldn't you get it colored before coming to camp?* I thought. *Have some pride, girl.* She wore librarian glasses with a little nose that resembled a mockingbird. It was clear this woman only liked to have sex one Sunday a month. She was so timid, like a little squirrel trying to eat a nut from your hand. I actually started feeling sorry for her husband until I heard him speak. Her husband kept scolding her as others around them took turns staring. He was such an asshole. I heard him say "Tara, we paid good money so you could learn how to fuck, so you're going through with it." I wanted to smash his face into my flapjack-offs but I held back, mostly because I didn't want to end up peeling potatoes while serving kitchen duty.

"You need to stop by the salon and get a spray tan," Sara said.

"Why?" I asked through a mouthful of pancakes...I mean, flapjack-offs.

"Aria, you're pale. The first theme party is Wednesday. It's the sexy lingerie party, and Saturday is the leather and lace party. This is your first time in lingerie. We have to make sure you look good for any potential suitors. So, you need to go tanning, get your hair cut and get a mani-pedi."

"I'm not a poodle you're entering in a dog show, ya know," I giggled.

"We have a lot to do to get you ready. The first two parties are important. People will be judging you. Seeing if they want to have sex with you or not. Most of these people here could be models, so you don't want to be the only girl at camp who doesn't get laid," Sara said.

"That's not a bad thing," I said.

"Yes it is. Believe me. These parties are going to blow you away," Sara said.

"How do you know so much?" I asked.

"I read the fucking manual!" she said. We both started giggling at ourselves.

After breakfast, Colt gave the Kittens a tour of camp. "This is Prentice cabin," Colt said, passing the light two-story redwood cabin. It was long in length with a large wooden door and lengthy darkened windows. "This building houses twenty-five pole dancing suites and a large bar. Cocktails are free, Kittens, so drink to get loose," he said, and then he continued. "Oh, before I forget, each room has a one-way mirror so that anyone can watch from the hallway. We don't want you being shy," he said. I sighed inwardly.

"On your left is the co-ed gym. There's a variety of exercise equipment like treadmills, ellipticals, rowing machines, and weight benches. There is also a lap pool, boxing, and an array of different exercise classes. See your manual for the specifics. Next to it is the full service salon and spa. It also houses the camp store where you can purchase your club wear and dancewear as well as extra accessories. Please take advantage of it ladies, it's important to make yourself beautiful for your men." I stole a glance over at the bird woman, Tara, just in time to see her asshole husband nodding in approval at Colt's misogynistic words. Sara caught me staring and leaned into my ear to whisper. "I bet he likes to give her Strawberry Shortcakes."

"Strawberry Shortcakes?" I asked.

"Yea, it's where the man cums on his wife's face, and then he punches her in the face. The cum and blood mix like red and white icing in the filling of a strawberry shortcake," Sara said.

"Oh my god. You're so rotten!" I said, giggling, as Sara just laughed.

"Ladies, if you please," Colt admonished. My face turned red as I sunk into my shoulders. I felt like I was back in grade school.

Next, Colt showed us Kit Kat cabin. "The Kit Kat cabin houses a variety of classrooms, twenty rooms total including the mechanical pancake swiveler and the feature hit of Kit Kat cabin, the Sybian." Colt wriggled his eyebrows and grinned widely at me. I had no idea what a Sybian was, but Sara rode one once saying it was the best orgasm she ever had, which was saying a lot because I heard quite a few of her orgasms over the years, and if this Sybian was the best then that was really saying something. The Kit Kat cabin was largely beautiful, also made of redwood, but the darkened windows were normal size.

"Okay, moving on," Colt continued. "Up ahead is the Jameson Main Lodge. All of you were there last night so I won't spend too much time covering the main room. Except to say, that this is where all the theme parties will take place, the closing ceremonies are there also.

Before I knew it, I quickly blurted out "Where does Avery stay?"

Colt glared at me mischievously, "He's not far, but I can't disclose that information. It stops star-struck guests from flocking to his doorstep," he smirked as I narrowed my eyes at him. He then held open the door to the Main Lodge for everyone. "Now, in you go." We all stepped into the entranceway lined with black walnut floors. He escorted us to the long rectangular bar. "Alcoholic drinks are here to help everyone get relaxed and open up. Do not get drunk and stupid. The bartenders and servers will monitor your alcohol. Avery recommends no more than four. You want to loosen up but don't get sloppy. Shots, mixed drinks, beer, whatever you like, it's a full bar stocked with only top shelf liquor but they do keep some cheap stuff under the bar if that's your preference."

"Okay, moving on. As you can see, it has floor-length mirrors and three dance poles. So, feel free to let yourself go." *Why does he keep looking at me when he says stuff like that?*

He continued, "The DJ booth is on the far side of the dance floor up the steps to your left. He has all the current music so make lots of requests."

He pointed to the hallways. "On either side of the bar you will have two main hallways. They are identical. Bathrooms on the left and hot tubs are on your right. No lotion or drinks in the hot tubs. Please, we can't stress that enough. Lotion junks up the filters so keep it clean people. This is a high-class place. A connecting hallway ties each one together. On event night, it's like a swingers club," he said, then turned and walked down the hall. *Swingers? I saw that movie. I love swing music, it's so 90's and so Favreau.*

"During the day, we sometimes use these rooms as extra classrooms. 12 rooms downstairs, 12 upstairs. During the parties, remember that there are 80 guests to accommodate so rooms do fill up fast. Here, let me show you a room. Follow me. If you need service at any time dial 7 on the phone beside the bed," he said. The rooms were very nice with lavender walls and hardwood floors. The beds were king size with extra sheets and towels stacked high on the dresser.

"I don't understand. What are the rooms for?" I whispered to Sara.

"To have sex in…duh," Sara said.

Okay, mental note, quit asking stupid questions, I thought.

"There are showers in every room. Towels and sheets are re-stocked as needed. Condoms can be found in every drawer. Any scares, please see the camp nurse." He cleared his throat. "Please remember safe sex is best. Okay, back to the fun stuff. You have been given toys in your camp bags and whatnot, so make use of your time here. For most of you, this will be the only time in your life you can experience this lifestyle, so enjoy it. Swings are available in rooms 10-14. Those usually fill up first. Middle rooms are the exhibition rooms, you can leave the door open, or you can leave the blinds up and people can watch through the windows in the hall. We are all one big happy family."

What? People watch other people have sex? Sara must have felt me stiffen because she squeezed my hand.

"At the end of this hall is the round room. You can enter from either side and as you can see, it could house a small crowd. This room was designed for group orgies."

My mouth fell open at the size of the mattress that was centered in the middle of the room. It could easily hold ten people. The perimeter of the room was lined with long narrow red couches ensconced in velvet.

"Up the stairs we have our smaller, more private rooms. They decrease in size the farther back you go. Some of you who are newer to this lifestyle may want to start there. Ease your self into it before you're ready to let it all hang out in the public room."

I looked around at all these astoundingly beautiful women. *Who was I kidding? I felt like the ugly duckling amongst a flock of beautiful swans except for Tara, who could be beautiful if she would just get to the salon.* Some of these women were tall and some were short. I was in the middle at 5'5", but several were curvy in all the right places, and their breasts were so goddamn perky. I'm amazed that some of these women didn't have bruised chins from their tits hitting them while they jogged. I had a slim hourglass figure with an athletic build. I had been a gymnast up until this past spring. My greatest feature was my muscular calves and arms. Okay, I couldn't complain, my bra size was a 34C but I didn't look at myself as sexy. I had always been an athlete and wore a sports bra to hold my tits in place. I wasn't used to wearing sexy bras that lifted and accentuated them. It was going to take some getting used to.

"So, this brings us back to the main bar. The exits are at the end of every hallway in case of emergencies. Otherwise, please use the main double doors." We headed out the main entrance and proceeded down the main path.

"This way, Kittens. Up the hill here we have a classroom being built now."

I could hear the pounding of the hammers and electric saws echoing off the area ahead of us as we walked closer. There was talk of building measurements between two men going over floor plans at a bench nearby. My eyes rested on a tanned, muscular body atop the roof. *God, it was Avery. How was he built like that? Damn, I caught myself drooling.* This place was amazing. He was golden tan and shirtless as he slid his hammer in his tool belt, then descended the ladder in front of us in one long sliding move. *He made that look sexy.*

When he arrived at the bottom, he wiped his forehead and brushed his hand against his holey ripped jeans, then strode toward the men at the workbench. He muttered something about a peak then looked up to the onlookers. He smirked at the many mouths that hung gaping. *Oh, he definitely noticed all of us gawking at him.* Even the guys, but it didn't seem to make him uncomfortable. He was confident in everything he did.

"Kittens, where are you off to?" Avery asked.

"Tour of the grounds," Colt replied. "Come along everybody."

I stood a moment longer taking in his well-defined back muscles before me. *Jesus, he was glorious.* The sight of his muscular physique made my heart thump loudly in my chest. Sara didn't seem phased by Avery but rather kept her eyes on me as she smirked. Even the bird women Tara seemed caught up in Avery's spell, much to the chagrin of her asshole husband. I watched Avery take a swig of his water bottle then recap it. He turned and noticed me. Our eyes locked for a moment but he seemed lost in thought as he stared at me. I looked to his tight abs and the obvious bulge in his crotch as my face reddened. I recomposed myself and moved to catch up to Colt's tour, but as soon as I turned, I tripped on an errant rock jutting out from the hard clay ground. I landed face first against the hard earth and dust lifted all around me.

I lifted my top half up slightly as I looked back to see Avery still staring. I quickly stood as his eyes raked over me. I was in my ripped jean shorts, a white sleeveless button up shirt, and my dark grey running shoes, hardly a thing of beauty, now dust covered, but he stared anyway. A small smile played on his lips and he winked at me.

I turned away from Avery, feeling dumbfounded, and almost stumbled into Colt who had come back to help me.

"Lose something?" Colt asked.

I giggled nervously. "Just my dignity." My heart was beating wildly in my chest. I had no idea anyone could affect me like this. I took in a shaky breath trying to find the ground that just leapt out from under me.

"Good. Because it's time for your first class." It didn't register. My thoughts were too scrambled from Avery's beautiful body…I…uh…mean his eyes, but he had such beautiful glistening skin. *Pull yourself together girl.*

I walked with Colt to Peak cabin while the rest of our group went to meet their instructors. We walked into room 2B where we met up with Sienna. She was beautiful and mesmerizing. Her skin glowed like cherry blossoms in the hope of spring. I wished Sara was here to help with the awkwardness, but she was off with her group. The room reminded me of a small massage suite. The folding wall opened up on one side, leaving room for three soft chairs for Sienna, Colt, and myself. There was something very intimate and relaxing about it while at the same time every nerve in my body screamed to run for the door. I sat in the soft plush chair fidgeting nervously and trying very hard not to have a meltdown. I had no idea what was going to happen next. *How was I going to get through this?* My heart raced and my stomach churned.

Sienna handed me a frosty glass filled with a crimson and orange liquid. "It's never too early for a cocktail. It's Sex on the Beach," she winked at Colt and I. *Of course it is.*

I smiled gratefully and looked to Colt as he stared at both of us with a dangerous hunger in his eyes. But soon he shook it off and continued the orientation.

"Theme parties are Wednesdays and Saturdays. Sunday is recovery day. A day to swim, hike, bike, and go horseback riding," Colt said breaking the tension in the room. "Remember you only participate when you are ready. There's no rush."

"If I may, Aria, for class structure purposes, when is your period?" Sienna asked.

My face reddened immediately. I looked around the classroom. The massage room was dimly lit. Cotton sheets draped over it, making the room warm and cozy. I looked hesitantly back to Sienna. "Today is my last day."

"Good timing. At least you won't have it twice at camp. You don't want to be sitting on the sidelines while the rest of your group parties. It will show up during week five but that shouldn't be a problem. We'll do other things that week. Now, here's your schedule, Aria. Monday through Saturday, we will meet here at Peak cabin in the morning – nine o'clock – for exploration/masturbation/massage class. After lunch, meet us at Prentice cabin for pole dancing, lap dancing, and strip tease lessons. After dinner, excluding Wednesdays and Saturdays meet us at Kit Kat for and all other classes," Sienna said. "Some of your classes will revolve around Kama Sutra, or how to use the sex swing. You will also have workshops on threesomes, hand jobs, and fellatio. Some nights, we will have you do activities on your own so that you can help to build up your confidence. Tonight you won't have class but you will be assigned some homework. Is all of this okay for you so far?" she asked.

I looked at both of them. My head was spinning. They seemed so relaxed about the whole thing, like this was normal everyday conversation for them. They both sat staring at me, waiting for my reply.

"Sure," was all that I could mutter then I brought my straw up to my mouth and took two big sips of my sex on the beach. *Yummy.*

50

"Okay, let's talk about your likes and dislikes. How many sexual encounters have you had?" Sienna asked.

"One."

"Oh, yea. The one night stand," Colt said to Sienna. My eyes widened at his revelation. I hadn't realized Sara told him. But then again I couldn't see that they kept any secrets between them. Not even about Sienna. I studied the two. Colt had blonde shaggy hair, blue eyes, and an excellent football physique. Sienna had auburn wavy hair with a light dusting of freckles on her nose, lean, with perfect breasts.

"We're here to help you open up to new experiences. So tell us, what was it like the first time you had sex?" Sienna asked.

"Short," I said.

"Was it missionary position or doggie style?" Colt asked.

"Missionary," I said feeling exposed. I shifted nervously in my seat waiting for the awkwardness to pass.

"You are going to learn so many things in the next six weeks about different sexual positions, techniques, role playing, and fantasies. Everything you need to be an empowered lover. We will help make you comfortable in exploring each one," Colt said.

Comfortable exploring? I'm not even comfortable talking about it! I took another sip of my cocktail and couldn't wait for the inquisition to be over.

"Have you ever reached orgasm by sexual penetration or masturbation?" Sienna asked.

"Yes." I could see they were waiting for me to clarify. "From masturbating." My face reddened even more.

Seeing my hesitance, Sienna continued on, "I need you to be bold here, Aria." She handed me a sexual questionnaire. *So the inquisition wasn't enough, now I have to put it down in writing.*

"As you read through this, think about what you might like and what you might enjoy, try to be honest and open. I want you to do the same for your dislikes. The check off sheet keeps you from having to put it into words. Sometimes it helps our shyer guests confront taboo topics and behavior. It's designed to help you open up and answer honestly."

I scanned the sheet and checked my likes. *Ok, I was guessing at some of it.* Then I went through my dislikes. I shivered inwardly at the thought of anal fisting. *No way!* Sienna and Colt waited patiently for me to finish. I looked up at them feeling surprised by some of my own acknowledgements. Sienna took the list and scanned down the page.

"Aria, I am going to check the Sybian under the likes column for you, Sara signed you up for that class and quite frankly, I don't know any girl who hasn't liked it," Sienna smiled to me and I found myself smiling back. "I reserved your day and time for that class already. Because there is so many that want to get into that class it fills up quickly. On Friday morning of week two, you will have your first class at Kit Kat cabin instead of your usual meeting cabin." I nodded.

"I think we're good here," Colt said. "Sienna will give you a massage to help relax you then you have a couple of homework assignments. First, I want you to practice walking in your platform shoes around your cabin for the rest of today. The second thing is tonight I want you to pleasure yourself. It will help get you warmed up for the weeks to follow. The more you do it, the more control you will have and the more intense it becomes." *Boy, Sara really knew how to set me up. What a way to spend the summer.*

As I walked back toward the Jasmine cabin, I was so relaxed by my hour and a half deep tissue massage that Sienna gave me. She had worked out a few kinks in my neck and back from being hunched over the last week cramming for finals. I felt like a new person. However, my anxiety soon resurfaced as I pulled open the doors of the armoire and stared at the two pairs of shiny platform shoes. One red pair, one white. I picked up the white ones, maybe because that made me feel less brazen, and sighed. I tugged off my running shoes and low cut socks and slipped on the right platform heel. I wrestled with the strap. Then, once it was secured, I did the same with the left. I stood unsteadily and braced myself with my right hand on the bed. I stood up slow and tall trying to find my center. That was one of the first things my gymnastics coach taught me in tumbling. *Easy enough.*

I took a small step and fell over like a great oak tree. My rumble lodged a bowl of potpourri that was barely resting on the edge of the dresser and it found it's way onto my head covering me in small fragrant flowers. Sighing loudly, I raised myself up on my hands, then grasped the edge of the bed, and lifted myself for another try. I felt my ankle wanting to buckle right away. I took another step, forcing myself to walk opposite of what I had been taught since I was a year old. Toe then heel. Not heel to toe. I held on to the armoire then the dresser and moved toward the doorframe of my room. *I felt like Bambi learning to walk on ice.*

I held on the outside wall and furniture and walked the perimeter of the room a few times then I let go at the doorframe of the bedroom, stepped out into the hall, and hit the floor again, where oddly enough, housekeeping left another bowl of potpourri on an end table, that I now wore. *Aww, come on!*

I dusted myself off and rose again with the aid of that same end table. I walked across the hardwood floor to the kitchen and decided I would go to the refrigerator and get a bottle of water. The steps I took were unsteady at first and I kept my knees bent, ready to catch myself if I fell again.

"Try standing up straight and tall then lean back a little in your heels," Sara said. She was standing in her bedroom doorway barely curtailing a giggle. "You smell very nice. Is that lavender?" As I glared at her, I could see her lips trembling, threatening to break with laughter.

"I will pay you back for this, Sara!" I'm pretty sure I looked like the most awkward duckling that still couldn't fly. I stood up feeling uncomfortably taller.

"Good, now relax your shoulders and lean back just a little. You're not going skiing," Sara chuckled.

"Maybe I am," I said sticking my tongue out at her. I sighed heavily and let my shoulders fall, then straightened my legs. *Ugh.* I was so frustrated that I couldn't think straight.

"Think of yoga," Sara said.

"Huh?" I mumbled trying to reign in my nervous thoughts. "What does Star Wars have to do with platform shoes?"

"I said yoga, not Yoda," Sara replied.

I snickered. "Oh."

"Find your center and imagine there is an invisible line running through you. The taller you stretch, the easier it is to find your center, and better balance will follow," Sara said.

"You are wise, Jedi Master." I closed my eyes and tried to center myself. After a few moments, I opened them and stepped toward her. With the first step, I was still unsteady, but then after a few more my feet felt almost weightless. I wasn't concentrating on the tall shoes anymore. I was concentrating on centering myself.

"It actually works. You were right," I said. I walked across the room to the back patio and sat in one of the wooden Adirondack chairs looking out at the woods around me.

Sara strolled out with a bottle of wine and two glasses as she joined me. She sat the bottle on a small table at the far side of the patio. Sara lit the fire in the stone fire pit and we sat sipping on our red wine and reminiscing about our freshman year. In between our conversation, Sara forced me to get up and walk across the patio to get the bottle of wine to refill our glasses. As I listened to her talk about the fashion industry and her dreams of owning her own clothing line, I was glad to be with my best friend.

It was almost midnight when I took off my platform shoes and climbed into bed in my snug fitted t-shirt and panties. I turned off the light and let myself get accustomed to the darkness. No light, no sound, just my breathing in the surrounding darkness. The darkness, with the help of some wine, helped me to relax, and the image of Colt came to mind. I had gotten to know his shirtless, muscular figure since he moved in with Sara and me at our place back home, but I quickly forced the thoughts away. He was my best friend's boyfriend. I couldn't.

I tried to calm myself and clear the thoughts from my head. If this was going to happen, then I had to force myself not to think, but feel. The image of Avery was there as his words came back to me... *just feel.*

The image of yesterday played out in my head. I could remember exactly what he was wearing – black dress pants and a dark blue button up shirt open at the collar. I could remember the smell of his cologne invading my senses. I stepped away from him and my back pressed against the oak tree. Then my imagination took hold...he closed the gap between us and his hand traced my cheek then draped down to my breasts through my sundress. His hand slid further down. He lifted the hem of my dress and let his hands slip under and trail over my bare skin.

I closed my eyes and let the fantasy play out in my head as I slipped my fingers beneath my lace panties, mimicking his gesture in my fantasy. I felt his warm hand find refuge as he slipped his fingers inside me. My pelvis pushed closer to him feeling his engorged self beneath his dress pants. I was growing hotter and wetter as I unbuttoned his shirt. My hand ran over his exposed muscular chest. He rushed to kiss me and drew his fingers deeper inside me. He pulled them out, and then moved them deeper within me. He moved them back out then moved to my clit.

My fingers in my dark room mimicked his and encircled my clit. The more I stroked, the more I desired him. I let the thoughts of his forbidden body flood into my head.

"Just feel, don't think." And *that* was just what I was doing. I felt him unzip his pants. I felt him lift me up over him and pull my panties to the side. I felt his engorged penis enter into me. I looked into his emerald green eyes and felt his smile on my lips as he kissed me and then ground deeper into me. I closed my eyes and let him thrust and grind into me. *God, it was heaven.* He swiveled his hips drawing out, then in, out, then in. Soon my legs were burning and I was about to fall over the edge.

"That's it, Aria. Let go, baby," he breathed in my ear and that was my undoing. My body convulsed around him sending white stars to my periphery as he let go inside of me. Then he disappeared from my fantasy and I was left alone, breathing heavily in my dark bedroom, wishing I could have more of Avery Jameson.

⌘

DAY TWO:
TUESDAY MORNING
EXPLORATION CLASS

At 8:55am the next morning, I walked into Peak cabin. I had rushed Sara through breakfast so I could arrive early and ease some of my anxiety. Sara was annoyed that I was rushing her but she could see my nervousness.

After breakfast, Sara gave me a hug and hurried off to her first group and I headed here. When I walked in, Sienna handed me two glasses. The first was a shot glass full of whiskey. The second was a tall reddish-orange Alabama Slammer. I looked at her with appeasement in my eyes and downed the shot. *It burned all the way down into my belly!* Then I sucked down half my cocktail and felt my body relax for the first time since I arrived. *Alcohol before noon is yummy. There's an old Naval axiom that says you don't drink before the sun passes over the main yard arm, which, is about noon. I shrugged. I'm not sure why they said that, but I was glad no one here believed in Naval axioms.*

"This exploration class is to help you learn your body's magic spots. Everybody is different. I know it sounds intimate but what you learn here should pique your curiosity of what is to come," Sienna said. She wore a tight cheerleader costume emblazoned with the Camp Jameson

58

logo. It was short and green with her shirt tied near her cleavage so her breasts almost spilled out of it. She had white skintight lycra shorts and black strap high-heeled platform shoes. Her hair fell down her shoulders to the middle of her back. She was drop-dead gorgeous. She guided me over to the massage table on the far side of the room as Colt came in holding a bottle of massage oil.

"Good morning, Aria. Why don't you go ahead and strip down to your undies then lay back and make yourself comfortable on the table. Try to let your mind relax," Colt said, lifting off his tight Camp Jameson polo and exposing his six-pack. He was only wearing cargo shorts and sandals.

"I'm a little warm," he said. "You don't mind if I take my shirt off do you?"

I quickly shook my head 'no' as my eyes shifted nervously. *God, he's hot.* I downed the rest of my drink and unbuttoned my sleeveless shirt. I shimmied off my shorts and placed them on the chair beside the bed. I lay down on my back and stared at the rustic wood of the cabin ceiling around me.

"To heighten your senses, I'm going to put this blindfold on you. Sienna is going to sit this one out until you are comfortable with me touching you. Then we'll help you get comfortable with another woman touching you," he said slipping the mask over my eyes. *Oh*, was all I could think.

I heard Sienna move over to the wall then slow, sexy jazz music filled my ears from the speakers over head. It was very soothing. Colt's hands began to rub light strokes over my shoulders to my bare arms. I shivered slightly. I couldn't believe I was lying in my burgundy bra and panties in a very dimly lit cabin with Colt and letting him give me a massage. *I hope Sara doesn't get jealous but I always wondered what his hands would feel like touching me and it feels reeeaaallly good.*

Colt's warm, dexterous hands slipped off my hair tie and my loose bun unraveled so that my hair cascaded around me. It was the first time I noticed my long hair touch my skin sensually. His hands rubbed lotion over my clavicle then down my arms and back up again. His forefingers dragged my bra straps down and let them fall past my shoulders. He continued to rub circles from my neck to my shoulders, back, and arms. I was finally starting to relax when his last stroke skimmed over my breasts. I inhaled slightly. He moved back up to my shoulders continuing his repetitive motion like before, and each time, his last stroke pressed a little harder over my nipples through my bra. After the fifth time my body bowed upward off the table begging for him not to stop there. I had no idea my body would respond to his touch like this. *Better yet; what did he put in my drink? Colt wouldn't do that. But would Sienna?*

"You're doing good, Aria." He then slipped his fingers underneath my bra and exposed my nipples. The air wasn't cold by any means, it was late June and the temperature was in the low eighties now, but the air mixed with his touch left my nipples hard and sensitive. Colt restarted his tantalizing touch as before, this time letting his hands tweak my nipples just long enough to make my breathing go faster and my heart race. I felt sexy for the first time. I moaned softly and wiggled my hips, craving more. He moved to the bottom of the table and began stroking my abdomen, my legs, and my calves. Repeatedly he stroked his hands over the same areas then at the last minute, he gently slid his hand over the apex of my thigh. *Oh my.* Before my body could commit, he would move on to another area. Each stroke teased me, bringing me to the edge where my body begged for some unknown mercy. He traced over my crest once more then moved to my feet. His hand stroked the instep of my right foot. My insides almost convulsed at his touch. *How in the hell was I feeling that all the way up my groin?*

"Is this too much?" Colt asked.

"No," I wriggled. I craved more.

"You're doing fine, just relax. You're in total darkness now. Let go, Aria," Colt said, rubbing his thumb up my instep. My body quivered, but something was stopping me from letting go. I tried to drown myself in the music. I wanted to let go. I wanted to feel that burning desire but the sensations were becoming too much.

"It's too much," I gushed.

"Okay," he said. He covered me with a sheet and walked to the head of the table. "Great job for your first day, Aria," his voice was hoarse when he pulled off my blindfold. *How could he not be affected by this?* But then I noticed the tell tale sign of a bulge barely visible in his loose-fitting cargo pants.

"Get up slowly and get dressed when you are ready," he said stepping over to where Sienna had been sitting and watching.

After I finished dressing, I couldn't bring myself to look at him. Sienna smiled and motioned for me to take a seat in the chair next to them while Colt scribbled notes in his notebook.

"Did you put something in my drink?" I asked Sienna.

"No. That was all you, honey." She smiled wider. "Feels great, doesn't it?" My lips curved upward in a small smile when I realized she was right. "I just observed today, Aria and I could see you trying to overcome your fear. Just relax. It's very normal. You're strong, but you let your mind control you. Let your body and feelings lead once in awhile. I could see you started to think too much near the end of your massage. What were you thinking about?"

My eyes flashed to Colt. "Colt, being Sara's boyfriend. It started to feel kind of wrong," I said.

Colt leaned in toward me and rested his arms on the table in front of him. "Sex, is just sex. It doesn't mean anything unless you want it to." I nervously wrung my hands in my lap as he tried to find another way to state what he meant. "Look. Sara 100% agrees with this. Remember this was her idea. She wants you to have the full experience. You are allowed to have sexual feelings, and she wants you to embrace those," Colt said. He cleared his throat. "It doesn't matter who is touching you, it's all about how you feel while you're being touched. If I make it easy for you to cum, then don't be ashamed of that. That is why you're here. Avery set up this camp to help people like you explore the endless possibilities that sex has to offer. But you have to clear your mind and let your body rule in order to do that. Don't think about me as Sara's boyfriend when I am giving you pleasure. No one is judging you here."

"How do you do this?" I asked. "You're obviously turned on right now. How do you give me pleasure without being able to do anything about it?"

"Sara's meeting me here after this. I can guarantee we won't make it to the massage bed," he said.

"I thought the guests weren't supposed to have sex with the instructors?" I chuckled. "I think I get it. It's part of that whole sexual freedom thing."

"Yes," Sienna said.

I sighed inwardly. I had only been intimate with one man before in my life. And that was a disaster. I had promised myself that my first time was going to be glorious, romantic, maybe even seductive, and it was the complete opposite of that. I never thought my first guy had to be madly in love with me, but he would make love to me like he was. It would be something that I would want to remember forever. But it wasn't any of those things. It was some upper classman at a frat party just looking for a one-night stand. We attended the same high school but he was older than me and graduated early. We never hung out before. He got me drunk for the first time. It was a big mistake because he didn't care about me at all. He wasn't passionate. He was cold. I felt used and betrayed afterwards. He wasn't any of the things that I wanted in a man. There wasn't a mind-blowing kiss or a big jolt of electricity when he touched me. There weren't any fireworks or earth-shattering earthquakes. *Whom was I kidding? A man like that could only ever exist in my fantasies.*

⌘

DAY TWO:
TUESDAY AFTERNOON
POLE DANCING CLASS

It was just after lunch but my nervousness had made eating almost impossible. I was only able to force down a few slivers of wet lettuce and there's nothing more nasty than wet wilting lettuce leaves. It makes it hard for the dressing to stick to them and it just runs off and pools in the bottom of your bowl. *It's so gross.*

After giving up on eating, I made my way to class a few minutes early so I could get dressed for pole dancing. Every activity in this place has an outfit or lack of one, that's why Sara packed my second suitcase. The classroom was similar to a strip club. There were six poles lining the dance floor with another single pole out in front of the others and I could hear the low dance music pulsing in the background. The room was dimly lit and I could see a small collection of people standing in the hallway looking in through the large windows wanting to get a peek at the hot mess of newbies learning to dance inside. I was silently cursing myself for taking this class.

I only wobbled once. Okay, twice. Nope. Now it was three times, as I walked in my new red platform shoes toward Colt, Sienna, and the five others in my group class who were waiting for me beside the dance pole in Prentice Cabin. *Ugh. Focus.* I was wearing only my black bra and panties. Up until last year, I was a gymnast and I proudly wore my leotards. But for some reason I felt so weird being barely dressed in front of these strangers and Colt. *I had to find a way to get used to this. Not just the shoes, but also the sexually charged atmosphere.*

"Here, down this," Sienna said handing me another shot. I didn't care what was in it. I needed liquid courage. I grabbed the shot glass with a double and tossed it back. *Christ, that burned!*

"That's my girl," Colt teased. It was my first day. I had just consumed my fourth shot plus a fruity drink since breakfast this morning and one at lunch. I took a minute to think about that. I could feel the alcohol heat my body and calm my nerves instantly. *Works every time.*

I took in my surroundings once more as I moved to the stage where Sienna now stood next to one of the center poles illuminated in alternating colored lights. Colt stepped over to the side of the room and sat on an old wooden oak bench.

Sienna began, "This is one of the main events in the Camp Olympics, for those of you hearing about this for the first time, read your manuals. Each class you take here at camp corresponds to an event. There are a variety of points given for each event won. This is one of the big three. The winner with the most points is crowned the Kitten Queen and wins an all-expense paid trip to Hawaii on Avery Jameson's private jet and will stay at Avery's private estate in Maui for the week. So for all of you who are interested, this is one event you will want to win. Pole dancing is one of the hardest things you will do while you're here at camp and therefore it awards the most points. It takes proper training and endurance. We'll start slow then build on your strengths. You can't rush this or you could get hurt. Everyone step up to your pole. We're going to approach the pole with confidence. Let your shoulders fall back, then let your fingers slide around the bar as you revolve around it."

I walked several circles around the pole squeezing my hand tight around the cold brass.

"Keep your grip loose. Don't over-think it. It's about touch and feel."

Ugh, there were those words again. I loosened my grip and strode uncomfortably around the bar, keeping my eyes to the ground. I wobbled again in my heels and almost twisted my ankle. *Damn it, platform heels suck.*

Sienna giggled and I looked up to see her smiling at me. "Aria, try not to look at your feet. You're a runner aren't you? Do you look at your feet when you run?"

"No," I replied.

"Exactly," she smiled. "Now class, chin up. Let your eyes fall on something in the distance. Let that be your center focus. If you spin too much around the bar not fixating on something you'll make yourself dizzy. Always focus on something in the distance," she announced to the class. "For those of you that have never seen a pole dance up close, I will show you a short routine just so you can get the feel of what I hope you'll all learn while you're here."

I watched as Sienna danced in her short shorts and tight tank top with the white and green Camp Jameson logo just over the center of her chest. She didn't falter once in her black platform shoes. Her routine was glorious. Her movements were smooth and seductive. *I could be that seductive,* but I knew it was just the whiskey talking.

"Okay," Sienna said regrouping everyone back up to the poles. "First we're going to start off with a pirouette pose." She stood with her back to the pole and raised her hands in the air and grabbed the pole behind her then bent her left knee. Okay, simple enough. Sienna turned and faced the pole. She stretched her left arm up the pole and stepped seductively around the pole. Her right hand traced the curve of her hip and leg then back up again as she strutted around the pole once and stepped back to the same spot she left. *She made that look easy.*

"This is called a leg hook," Sienna said, lifting her left leg and wrapping it around the pole. She gripped the pole with her right hand and leaned back, letting her left arm trail behind her. "I'm going to do the steps again but I'm going to do it without stopping in between so you can see the end result." She repeated the first three moves again, this time it was all in one fluid movement. Pirouette pose, seductive walk, leg hook, and then she planted her feet back to the ground. "Okay, Tara, you try first," Sienna instructed, motioning Tara toward her pole.

Tara was average height with sandy blonde hair and slim narrow hips. She wobbled terribly in her high platform shoes and I wanted to ask Sienna why we couldn't go without the shoes until we got more comfortable but I knew this was part of the torment, I mean, lesson.

Tara stepped in half steps to the pole and her nervousness radiated through her tight grip on the pole.

"Loosen your grip," Sienna said stepping up next to her. Sienna pulled her shoulders back and let her hand fall to the middle of Tara's back. Tara was a nervous wreck. Her chest was moving hard and fast and her eyes were wide with fear. Sienna urged her forward. Stiffly, Tara teetered around the pole and came back to her original spot. On her last step her ankle buckled and she tumbled into Sienna. Sienna just caught her in time before she face planted to the ground.

"I can't do this," Tara said with tears in her eyes. We all knew her dumb husband was glaring at her from the hallway through the thick glass windows.

"Take a break, we'll try again in a bit. Start by practice walking around the room in your shoes. That's half the battle."

"Now Aria, you try," Sienna said.

"I think I need another shot," I muttered. Colt chuckled and moved to the mini sized bar and poured me another double. He quickly hurried back to me and I tilted the glass back. I felt it burn all the way down my throat.

"Geez. What is that stuff?"

Colt smirked. "It's Jameson whiskey. Good stuff isn't it?"

I nodded as I felt my shoulders relax. I closed my eyes and just escaped into the moment. I let the music fill my head and flow over my body. I stepped up to the pole and turned my back towards it. I reached both arms up behind me and grabbed the pole and bent my leg.

"Good. Now arch your back a bit more. Show us your goods," Sienna commanded. "Good. Now turn and grip the pole with your left hand and walk around it. Stop when you get to the same spot you started." I did as she asked, feeling more confident by the second. "Sway your hips some… good," Sienna continued. "Now hold the bar with your right hand. Lift your left leg and curl it around the pole. Let your left arm fall back behind you. Great, that's it. Let your head fall back a little and look at me. Pretend I'm the man you want to seduce. How do you feel?"

"Ridiculous," I said angling my neck at a weird angle to look at her.

"Well you look hot," Sienna said. "Okay, do it again. This time try to build up some speed." Then it happened. My eyes saw movement by the door and I felt my grip falter when I saw Avery Jameson leaning against the doorframe with his arms crossed and staring right at me. My sweaty palms slipped from the pole and I flew backwards as my feet slipped and pointed up at the ceiling while the rest of my body landed hard on my back. *Bwhump!*

Giggles filled the room. I groaned and stood up trying to gather what self-respect I had left and tried to ignore the rather large crowd that had gathered to watch me through the windows.

"Don't think about the pole or the people. Just feel the music. You're the entertainer; the pole is an extension of your body. Whether you're straddling it or spinning around it, whatever movement you choose will bring life to it, not the other way around," Sienna said.

I watched as Caitlyn spiraled around the pole like she had done it for a living. She was desperately trying to hold Avery's attention but his eyes kept wandering to me. Caitlyn noticed where his eyes rested but she was confident on her heels and showed no fear. My eyes shifted toward Amber

69

to see that she was struggling a little with her grip on the pole. On her other side Tara held her wide-eyed gaze as Caitlyn straddled the pole and hung upside down. Okay, maybe I wasn't doing as well as I thought. I sucked compared to these girls, then Sienna announced to the onlookers, including Avery, that it was time for them to move along. Avery looked like a little puppy dog that had just been kicked, and it really seemed like his eyes lingered on mine as he retreated to the shadows of the hallway.

I took in a deep breath trying to calm my nerves. My hands shook but I squashed my nerves down as I reached out for the metal pole once again. I repeated the same steps with the help of Sienna calling out what to do. As I made my way around the pole, I genuinely smiled for the first time since I arrived. *Maybe I could do this.* I looked around at my surroundings and groaned inwardly. *I was almost naked dancing on a stripper pole. Didn't I have morals? Isn't this what society says not to do? Then why did I feel so free? I'm here for six weeks. This was only my first day of classes and I was feeling overwhelmed.*

Colt and Sienna stepped away to help Amber and Lucy in the group, I could see Amber's dark eyes showed confidence in herself as she approached her pole. Her straight ebony hair was pulled back into a ponytail like mine. Lucy had golden brown shoulder length hair. She had a larger frame with curves. I was studying Lucy when Sienna instructed us to practice a bit on our own while she and Colt worked individually with Lucy and Amber.

I spent most of my time trying to mimic Sienna's more difficult moves, learning how to place my hands and how to hold myself up on the pole in different positions. I learned how to spin around and lift myself up on the pole with just my leg and hands as an anchor. It was hard trying to land back in the same spot I took off from but I found that I actually liked it.

Somewhere in between it all she threw out terms like 'climbs' and 'inverts' and continued to show off different poses like 'Cleopatra' and 'Daphne'. I laughed at myself when I screwed up. I laughed harder when my hands slipped from the pole and I fell on my ass over and over again. After a half hour, I closed my eyes and just danced. I lost myself in the music. I swayed my hips and straddled the pole. Dipped down, and shimmied around. It was just me and the music. Nothing else. *God, how I loved to dance.*

"You're a natural, Aria." Sienna's voice broke my trance. Her heated look said more than I was willing to admit. I recomposed myself and glanced around the room. Everyone was starring. Several men I didn't know had their mouths agape. *Shit, the guys never left.*

Caitlyn huffed beside me. "Do you always have to be center of attention?" she hissed.

"That was awesome, Aria. I think you're ready to learn your routine." My high was short-lived when Sienna started taking me through the steps and the group of others stood behind me and observed.

"Kick your legs up over your head like this," Sienna's voice called out over the bass of the dance music.

I shook my head at her. "No fucking way." I was wearing my 'you must be crazy' look.

"Colt said you were a gymnast in high school. You have excellent upper body strength. You can do this. Grab here and swing your legs upward in a scissor kick to heighten

71

your jump." Sienna demonstrated. These moves were way more than the other girls were asked to do. That is, except Caitlyn.

"Tighten your hands as soon as your legs make contact with the pole. When you feel secure, squeeze your legs around the pole and hold yourself there. Release, then dismount." I crossed my arms, not budging.

"I have to hang upside down from that? Are you crazy?" I ignored the others watching me as Sienna stepped up to my pole to wipe it down as I tried to hide my scowl.

"You're over-thinking it, Aria," she whispered calmly. "Think of it like you're hanging upside down from the parallel bars. Watch again," Sienna said continuing. Sienna demonstrated it again.

Oh, I see. Why didn't she just say that in the first place? I didn't know why I couldn't cross the one thought into the other, but as soon as she put it that way, I could instantly see what she meant. I stood watching this beautiful swan swing her legs around the pole and hang upside down. She was graceful and seductive. I could be graceful, this much I knew. But seductive, I wasn't sure.

Sienna continued, "My hands are here, my legs are here. My butt is here touching the pole. I squeeze them around the pole, then I let go." She dismounted and urged me to try. I sighed, and then swung my legs around. With a small amount of grace, I swiveled my legs around the bar and squeezed them tight.

"Angle your head back," Sienna added. I followed her instructions.

"Good, now squeeze your thighs together and let your hands fall down by your head." I followed her instructions.

72

"Re-grip the pole and kick off." I re-gripped the pole and descended to the floor. "Excellent." She squeezed my biceps. Man, you are one tough little cookie. Maybe in few weeks we can try a back flip. You might want to consider making this your event at the Olympics. With a little effort you could do really well."

I laughed aloud. "Now you're talking."

"Well, look who's finally getting her wings," Caitlyn sneered as she continued her routine.

I smiled at her. "Will you teach me, Caitlyn?" My eyes fell on my classmates. Amber, Tara, Lucy, and Kennedy they all seemed genuinely friendly while Caitlyn stood there with a scowl on her face and rolled her eyes.

"Okay, class. Before you leave, I just wanted everyone to know all this hard work does have a payoff," Sienna announced. "It will excite your lovers and those of you who can't get enough of Avery can sign up for this event at the Camp Olympics. If you win this event and the Sybian Rodeo you'll give yourself a great shot at Maui and who knows…maybe you'll get to spend the whole week with Avery Jameson," Sienna said. "Okay, class dismissed. See you all tomorrow," she said.

As we stepped outside, Caitlyn followed closely and spoke so only she and I would hear. "Don't bother signing up for this event, Aria."

"I wasn't planning on it," I said as my eyes narrowed at her.

"Good, because even if you did win the Camp Olympics, a pathetic little thing like you would only disappoint a man like Avery," Caitlyn said.

My eyes widened as she strutted away like a little princess and as I watched her bony ass walk up the path, I thought to myself, *you know what? Game on, bitch!*

⌘

DAY THREE:
WEDNESDAY MORNING
EXHIBITIONISM IN THE FOREST

There was a light mist over the forest in the morning. The lake had steam rising up from its still waters that came from the air being cooler than the water itself. The sun rose up slowly from behind the trees. I didn't sleep much last night so I decided to go for a run to relax a bit and explore the camp before everyone else arose. There were only a few gardeners out this early, tending to the walkways, and applying mulch around trees that lined the path. I jogged past one of them named Rodriguez, his name clearly displayed on the patch of his uniform. He barely looked up at me as I passed him. I decided to explore the camp a little further down some pathways that I hadn't seen yet. I could feel the wind stir the forest around me through my tight, low-cut, pink tank top and black lycra shorts, courtesy of Sara's shopping spree before camp. It was going to be hot today and the breeze felt good against my skin.

I followed the narrow path, past the horse barns that housed Avery Jameson's prize Arabian pure breeds lost in thought about my changing feelings about camp. It was only the third day and I was already feeling more confident since my breakthrough at pole dancing class. It made me wonder what else I might be a natural at.

I passed some outdoor classroom areas with picnic tables and small shelters. A little farther down the path there was a small meadow beside a rocky stream. There was a small group of people standing in a circle barely lit from small beams of sunlight that poked through the thick tree canopy.

When I got a bit closer, I was shocked to see Tara kneeling on the ground with her obnoxious husband standing over her in a circle of five guys who were completely naked. I hadn't seen her since class yesterday, and since yesterday, I could see that she had lightened her hair. Her eyebrows were groomed, her glasses were gone and she wore a touch of makeup. My guess would be that she got a makeover at the salon last evening. She looked uncomfortable kneeling in the dewy grass as her husband held her by the hair and barked orders at her on how he wanted her to get him off. She stroked his cock as she pointed it towards her pursed lips. The remaining men stroked their own shafts long and steadily around her, moving in slowly. Their chests heaved as they watched her with hooded eyes as she licked her lips while stroking him and one other guy in anticipation of their climax. As her husband started groaning in orgasm, she opened her mouth. Each guy took turns stepping forward as they tossed their heads back spilling their loads onto her face one at a time. Each one aiming for either her open mouth, lips, or cheeks. Her hands were reaching out in all directions grabbing and stroking their manhood's.

I stared with widened eyes as I took in the explicit scene. She let them smack her face with their penises as they dribbled their spider webs across her lips and button nose. One very hot guy shot a massive load coating her eyes in thick glaze. *That's going to ruin her nice makeup.* I think some of it may have bounced off her eyes and onto her husband's fat belly as she held his penis near her lips. *Oh man, that's not good for anybody.*

Discreetly, I closed my hanging mouth and backed away so I wouldn't disturb their bombastic scene until I could silently continue my run deeper into the woods. From what Sara had told me, that must have been a Bukake session. *I'm not sure whether I'd like a bunch of strangers blowing their climax in my face like that, it really mats up in your hair and burns your eyes…at least that's what Sara used to say.*

I couldn't tell whether Tara enjoyed it or not but she certainly was having an interesting first couple of days at camp. If her husband brought her here to loosen her up and experience some new things, I'd say it's working. I hope he appreciated it.

A few minutes more down the wooded path, I could hear another woman's moans of pleasure before I saw her. *I was surrounded by sexuality this morning.* I don't know what I was more uncomfortable with, the fact that people were up so early in the morning out in the middle of the woods, or that they were all exhibitionists. I was going to turn away to give them a private moment, but what I saw made me stop and stare. I never knew there was anything like this. The woman was blindfolded standing up with her arms over her head and tied to a tall wooden X with brown leather straps. I couldn't turn away. Her chest heaved upwards heavily as she feigned struggling against her capturer. An instructor named Travis was standing in a dominant stance in front of her. His shoulders were wide and his large build made the girl look small. He snapped something against her skin. I recognized it as Sara's newfound toy, a riding crop made of black leather. She flinched at the temporary pain as she let her head fall back and moaned loudly again. My muscles clenched deep in my belly and I was surprised by how turned on this made me watching her bound and writhing in rapture. She was in her early twenties, fully naked with a Brazilian wax. I wasn't one for BDSM, but watching this woman in ecstasy really made me wonder. *Would I like it?*

Travis smacked the woman's clitoris with the riding crop and I could see her body quiver with anticipation. I'm not sure how long she had been tied up there, but her skin was pink and she was getting close to orgasm.

A small crowd had gathered around her, enjoying her splendor. Travis was shirtless and I couldn't help but notice his well-defined abs. My eyes scrolled up to his chest where the name 'MAYA' was tattooed in black across the left side of his chest. Even with all the people gathered around, his hazel eyes were focused solely on bringing the woman pleasure through pain. He rubbed the crop across her chest, winding down to her sex. She lifted her hips in anticipation toward him, craving him and his touch more and more. He reached and smacked her bare breasts. She gave a sharp gasp. Then he stepped back and pressed the crop into her vagina, stroking it in and out, teasing her, and pushing her farther over the edge.

My wide eyes scanned the crowd. I couldn't get a grasp on these fantasies that these women were living out. I guess the real problem was I didn't know what my true fantasy was in order to act on it.

I shifted nervously as my doe-like eyes locked with Avery's green gems. I hesitantly looked back to the woman in restraints as Travis teased her again. She wriggled in her restraints and begged him for more. He smirked and paced around her letting the crop brush against her deep pink skin. He whispered something in her ear. I swallowed nervously and shifted my eyes swiftly back to Avery. He wasn't watching the scene in front of us. He was watching me, and for the life of me, I couldn't figure out why. There was a tall, lengthy blonde-haired woman in front of me, and a model-like brunette beside me. I was in a sea of beautiful women and he was looking at me.

"That's it, Kaley. Now you may cum," Travis said in a deep low voice. My eyes shifted to see Travis tuck a strand of her blonde and black streaked hair behind her ear and I could hear Kaley whimper. Travis unleashed his final slap with the riding crop to her clit and Kaley cried out as her body spasmed out of control. "Good girl," Travis purred.

My face heated up. My pulse escalated and my breathing quickened. I turned to look back at Avery. He was gone. I scanned the crowd for him when I felt warm hands go around my waist.

"You're glowing," a warm voice whispered just below my ear. I was frozen by his touch around my waist and the heat from his breath on my neck. His breath became small kisses that sent little electrical quivers racing up my neck. *Holy hell.*

I clenched my thighs together and tilted my head back toward him and a soft moan escaped me. I stiffened, embarrassed that I had just moaned aloud to a stranger.

His hands slipped over me touching me in places that sent ripples across my skin like a stone skipping across a pond. His right hand drifted onto my lycra shorts caressing between my legs as his middle finger traced upwards over my clit, pressing firmly through my shorts. His left hand cupped my breast, then squeezed tight over my nipple. I exploded in orgasm immediately as dampness soaked through my panties.

After my tremors subsided, I pushed out of his grasp and looked up to see Avery smirking knowingly at me. I stepped back and my foot caught on a tree root and once again I fell backwards. He laughed and took a step with an outreached hand. I shook it off, straightened and took another step to right myself and stubbed my toe on a large rock. He stepped forward to help me and I shook my head at him again. I turned away and limped down the path that headed back to my cabin. I was embarrassed and excited both at the same time.

One of my little fantasies of Avery had just played out and the feel of his warm hands through my shirt had made me sizzle with desire. It was very real, not in my head. He must have been working on a cabin again or just decided to see what activity was happening in the woods. *That must be what Avery meant when he said the woods are for the adventurous.* I pushed the thoughts of Avery from my head and quickly trotted down the path toward my cabin.

I clenched my fists to my side as I neared my cabin. I slammed the door of the cabin hoping it would diffuse some of my frustration. Then abruptly, I strode to my bedroom, not sure what to do with myself. I collapsed on the bed and tears ran down my face. I just lay there, not sure if I had just been violated or if I loved it. I was mindlessly playing with my father's military tags around my neck and staring up at the ceiling when Sara spoke.

"You're freaking, aren't you?" Sara's kind voice interrupted my pessimistic thoughts. My eyes widened then drifted upward toward the ceiling again. I hadn't counted on Sara being here. I thought she would have gone to breakfast by now. I rubbed my forehead, and let my hand fall to my side. I just shook my head at her, trying not to burst into tears.

"You're doing great. Colt and Sienna say you've really taken to pole dancing," Sara said.

I glared at her. "This is all too much. Do you hear yourself right now? I've taken to pole dancing! My father did not raise me to be a pole dancer. He raised me to be a strong, independent, successful woman!" I said raising my voice.

Sara narrowed her lips. "Let me have it. Go on. Scream at me. Do whatever you have to do to get all this frustration out of your system. Better yet. Go for another run. What are you up to now? Five miles? Why don't you make it ten?"

I looked over to Sara. "How can I not, when everything I was taught tells me that society frowns on all of this."

Sara took a step closer. "I have news for you. All of society does not frown upon this lifestyle. In fact, business is booming for Avery. He can't build those damn cabins fast enough." I scowled at her but not for the reasons she thought. I just didn't want to hear his name right now.

"Look, there is no reason to feel ashamed of yourself. These classes turn you on. You are not alone. There are 79 others that have made the journey to get into this place and paid a lot of money to do it. You're in the greatest place in the world. It's safe. It's secure and you can let go and just be yourself. And it's a hell of a lot of fun if you'd just let yourself relax and enjoy it. Turn off that incessant mind of yours and just fucking let go!" I looked at Sara with uncertainty. She took another step toward me and reached for my hand.

"I know you're scared," she said lowering her voice. "This is all new for you. It's unusual. You feel out of place. I know it freaks you out but instead of running from what you fear, try embracing it. You might be surprised to discover a wild side in you."

Sara brushed away my bangs from my forehead. "You have no idea how beautiful you really are. Your innocence is sweet and what makes you so beautiful. I bet you will have all the guys and most of the women here lining up for you before the six weeks is over."

My eyes flickered away from her. I shook my head. "I don't know what to do," I cleared my throat trying to fight back the tears.

"Just enjoy the journey. You'll find out what you like and what you don't. It really is that simple," she added.

One thing kept leaping to the front of my mind. *Avery.* And all the desire in me kept chanting, *I want Avery. Only Avery.*

"How can all these people take off work for six weeks at a time?" I asked, trying to change the subject.

"Most of these people are doctors, lawyers, trust fund kids, CEOs, VPs, and their spouses. They can afford to do whatever the hell they want," Sara stated plainly. Sara came from a high-class family. Her parents just bought a house in the Hamptons just after her high school graduation. They had money to burn. Their graduation gift to Sara was our apartment. Sara fell in love with it, so they bought it. It was as simple as that. *Jesus. I was so out of my league here.*

"I know what you need. Come on, get up," she smiled. I studied her eyes trying to see where she was going with this. A smile spread over my face.

"Ice cream for breakfast," we both gushed.

Sara and I made our way to the Main Lodge. As I buried my worries in a heaping spoonful of mint chocolate chip ice cream, I pushed away my thoughts of all the sex, away from all the people, but one thought kept plaguing me. It was no secret. Avery didn't get emotionally involved with his guests. But the way that he was making me feel when he was around, I had to stay the hell away from him. *He was toxic.*

⌘

DAY THREE:
WEDNESDAY NIGHT
SEXY LINGERIE THEME PARTY

It was just after ice cream breakfast and after hurrying to class, I kept fidgeting as Sienna kneaded my lower back.

"Aria, you have to relax. Stop thinking and enjoy the massage," Sienna insisted. I sat up taking the sheet with me to cover my half naked body.

"I'm sorry. I'm nervous about tonight. What if something happens and I'm not ready for it? What if I embarrass myself?"

Sienna stepped around me and let her hands fall to my shoulders. My eyes lifted to hers. "Look, I know you're overwhelmed but I promise you, you will have a good time tonight. You're in the sexiest place on earth with the sexiest men and women I've ever had the pleasure of meeting and Avery throws one hell of a party. So, don't worry. Sara, Colt, and I have your back. You'll hang with us and we'll break you in slowly," Sienna smiled.

"Break me in to what?" I stuttered. Horrible images of me chained to the wooden X with a shirtless, dew-glistened Travis pacing around me like a lion, and me bound, gagged, and tortured. That's what came to the forefront of my mind. The more my mind raced, the more my eyes widened.

Sienna noticed my mental freak out and sighed. "Okay, poor choice of words. We will ease you into this slowly. You set the pace, Aria. If a guy approaches you, just smile and tell him you're not ready. They're just as nervous as you are. Trust me." I nodded reluctantly at her words.

"Speaking of guys. What kind of classes do they have? What are their experiences here?" I asked.

"The Cubs go through something similar to a mini boot camp where they exercise six days a week to help build their stamina and make their bodies stronger. There's cardio, weight training, canoeing, kayaking and rock climbing. The more fit they are the better lovers they will make in order to please their women."

"So, no sex classes? They workout the entire time they're here?"

Sienna snickered. "Of course they have their own sex classes. Their work out regimen takes up most of the morning. But in the afternoon they get to indulge in the fun stuff. Their classes focus on things like tantric breathing and how to properly give cunnilingus. Most of them have come here to become better lovers and it's our job to help them with that." I smiled crookedly up at her.

"Shall I go on?" Sienna asked. I nodded. "There is a class that teaches proper technique on how to pleasure a woman in every way imaginable. From touching, kissing, oral skills, sexual positions, g-spot techniques, penetration of vaginal and anal, and care of her afterwards. Some of the Cubs here are into BDSM and are in training to become a sub or dom. Men are also very visual so Avery made it possible for the Cubs to watch the Kittens in some classes like pole dancing." I felt my body tense when I remembered how the guys watched all of us during pole dancing class. "Okay, enough talk. Time to relax," Sienna urged.

Knowing I was still too wound up to enjoy my class, Sienna gave me a half-hour massage and sent me on my way.

For my afternoon class, Sienna helped me get more confident in walking in my platform shoes. At least my worries of rolling my ankle were leaving me. It's a real trick to stop walking heel to toe and lead with the balls of my feet. I only wished they made chunkier heels in these things, it would help me to balance. She gave up on showing me more moves on the pole. My hands were too sweaty and I couldn't concentrate on a single move she tried to teach me.

The first Theme Party at the Jameson Main Lodge was tonight. It was a sexy lingerie theme. The idea of walking around half-naked in front of over 110 strangers was freaking me out. Every time Sara had me convinced that I could handle it, I would look in the mirror at what I had to wear and changed my mind. Sara layered me just to try and make me feel more comfortable. I wore a sexy black sheer and silver sequin dress that was ultra short. Underneath the mini dress, I wore a sexy satin-and-chains padded underwire bra top and matching black satin bikini panties with chain accents. It came with removable garters that held my black fishnet hose followed by black shiny platform heels, which I still wished had a chunkier heel. When it was time to go, Sara and Colt had me by each arm, dragging me toward the Lodge.

When I walked into the massive room and stood amongst the throng of people, I felt small. It was otherworldly. The energy of the room was lively and filled with sexual suggestiveness. I was a bundle of nerves. Colt was quick to deliver a cold beer to my trembling hands. I fidgeted with the beer, trying to expel my anxiety as I picked at its dew-ridden label. I was so overwhelmed. I didn't know how to act except to down the frosty drink and beg for another. *What was expected of me?* I understood gymnastics – the pressure to perform, to nail each tumble and each step with precision and grace. I understood running – the feel of my feet hitting the ground at a steady pace on the asphalt or navigating through wooded trails on the hot summer days that Ohio drops on us every year. I often took long runs in the summer just to clear my burdened thoughts that Nursing school can leave burned in your psyche. But none of this I understood. Not the vapid sexuality or the rapid feelings I was starting to develop for Colt or the fact that I couldn't explore any of those feelings until camp was over. *If I could even go through with it.* Nor the heated looks I was getting from Sara because of either what I was doing with Colt or if she was into me. Sara was bi, saying she liked the touch and feel of a woman every so often. But she's never tried it with me. I guess that's a good thing because I'm not sure how I would act in that situation. *Why was the music so loud in here?*

My face reddened slightly as I kept stealing peeks at the huge TV monitors that played porn scenes constantly. The guy on screen was doing it with two women at once. My face broadened seeing how well endowed that actor was. It was impressive how the woman took his manhood so far inside her. I could sympathetically feel the pain she must have felt in her cervix. I averted my eyes and smiled politely to those I passed by as I made my way to the round table that accommodated ten people.

Colt quickly introduced Sienna's boyfriend Sean and Travis's girlfriend Maya. I sighed inwardly then took a gulp of my beer as I wondered if Travis ever whipped Maya the way he did Kaley this morning. Sara grabbed my hand, stirring me out of my ponderence.

"Don't worry. This will be fun. You'll see," Sara said.

I was trying hard to hide my nervousness, but it was useless. Sara could read me so easily. It was a gift, and a curse. I smiled crookedly and glanced at all the tables that were filling up with beauty queens and male models with hard bodies. So many were smiling, beaming with excitement and here I sat trying to get the knot out of my throat. *More beer, please.* I downed the bottle and felt my shoulders relax. *Nice.* Colt had arrived with three more beers and set them in front of us.

"I thought our intake was monitored," I questioned.

He winked to me. "Not tonight, ladies, not ever. Just let me know and I'll hook you up."

I had never been so glad he had all the hook ups. I was afraid that until I got used to all of this, I was going to need a lot of liquid encouragement. I took a sip of my new bottle of beer and promised to pace myself. 'Temptation' by Chasing Seven pulsed in the background and I could feel my body relax.

I loved to dance. I loved music. No one could judge me when I enveloped myself in the music. In the past, I constantly forced myself to be the best that I could. It was ingrained in me all my life by my strict parents. I reached for my necklace and realized I hadn't put my father's military tags on this morning. My father always strived for better. My gymnastics coach, too. Unfortunately, I learned that from them, and often I was too hard on myself even if I didn't want to admit it. My work ethic took the fun out of life. I hadn't found a balance yet. I was working on it. That's probably why I was drawn to Sara. She was so carefree and outgoing. She was my balance. I respected her and I listened when she told me to relax, to loosen up. I had to admit this camp was above and beyond the extreme. I was totally swinging the pendulum in the opposite direction now. *Could I ever get used to this lifestyle?*

Avery took the stage and the voices hushed around me.

"Welcome, everyone. Tonight, being the first Theme Party, I have set beads on the tables in front of you. I usually wait for Mardi Gras, but I thought it would help loosen everyone up. We have a couple surprise prizes for the Kitten with the most beads at the end of tonight, a complimentary body piercing or tattoo at the salon. So enjoy yourselves and each other," he grinned widely. "As a reminder, cell phones are banned when naked bodies are present. Just so you can resist temptation, leave them in your cabins from now on. For those of you that brought them, turn them off now, and don't let me hear that you've disregarded my instructions. I'd hate for anyone to have to be forced to leave the camp during the first week." Avery scanned the crowd, watching as a handful of people turned off their phones and tucked them away.

"Good. Use this time to get to know one another. That's what the parties are for," he winked then turned on his heel and walked off the stage. He carried himself with a confidence that made it hard to take my eyes off him.

The dark-haired server, named Molly, dressed in a black corset with a garter belt and black stockings came to take our dinner order. As she walked away to place our order, I couldn't help but notice how graceful she was in her platform shoes. I listened to Sara, Colt, Sienna, and her boyfriend, Sean, as they chatted to Maya and Travis about how sexy the women were dressed as they passed by on their way to the bar. Even in their half-dressed state, these women were upscale. I felt self-conscious in my sheer mini dress and hoped no one could see this beer was kinda bloating my tummy. *Was everyone as nervous as I was?* Sean passed around some Jello shots and we downed those quickly.

"Did you see that Kennedy is wearing Bordelle? She looks hot in the new collection," Sienna said to Sara. *Who was Bordelle? Was that a man or woman?*

"Your line will be better. It's going to kick some serious ass. Don't worry," Sara replied. Sienna smiled her heart-stopping smile and relaxed. Both Sienna and Sara were getting their degrees in fashion and their shoptalk was way over my head.

After dinner, people were stopping by to introduce themselves. Many people, actually. I lost track of how many after my fourth or fifth beer and the Jello shots. I had lost count of them, too. *So much for pacing myself.* This was turning into a good night. I didn't care about anything now. My mind was numb. So were my lips. I smacked them together and smiled to myself. *If I could feel like this every day, it was going to be a great summer.*

Sara looked over at me and yelled… "DONKEY!"

I burst out laughing as the others around the table joined in. Whenever Sara got me drunk, she would make me do my Donkey impersonation from Shrek, which I supplied at her command by clicking my tongue obnoxiously on the roof of my mouth. Everyone laughed. It made me feel better.

I rose to my feet and steadied myself. *Yep. I was drunk.* I set off to the restroom. Afterwards, I didn't feel like going back to the table so I made my way through the back halls and went to explore the lodge.

In the main hallway, there were several women with men in various states of undress. The men sat on one of the long red velvet benches and the women were straddled across their laps and grinding in the throes of passion. I looked away to give them a private moment then I realized they were the ones out in the open and didn't seem to mind if I stared.

A dark-skinned man and his friend, both in their forties, wearing a charcoal grey suit that probably cost more than my tuition for a semester, both propositioned me. I did what Sienna said to do. I smiled and politely declined. The taller man was named Griffin. The other was Neil. They seemed nice enough. *Hey, I'm actually walking in these heels…umm… anyway,* I tried not to stare at the porn playing on the LCD televisions that played behind them. I moved down the hall and kept my eyes down as three couples were going at it as I passed the group sex room.

I carried on my way through the hallway and Tara and her husband, who she introduced as Jim, invited me to accompany them in a room. Without waiting for my answer

Jim grabbed my hand, and followed by Tara, we entered the room. I was having trouble forming some of my words and before I knew it, we were standing at the foot of the bed. Jim pushed Tara and me together, ordering us to kiss. I inhaled sharply and stood in shock as Tara nervously moved her mouth toward mine, then pressed her lips timidly into mine.

For a second, I accepted her lips into mine then quickly snapped back to reality and stepped back. By this time, Jim had mostly undressed. Shocked and taken aback by how quickly this happened, I graciously declined then turned towards the door and made a hasty exit. I could see Jim was disappointed and hoped he wouldn't take it out on her. Tara was so nice. She didn't need a man like that, but if anything, he needed a dentist. He reminded me of Mr. Cunningham from Happy Days, only with greasier hair and a fatter belly. He looked like he swallowed a small volleyball. Everyone in camp was so much more physically sculpted than Jim and Tara. I think they got in because of his wealth, because earlier Tara said he was a doctor.

As I ventured farther down the hallway, I could hear the moans of ecstasy coming from behind closed doors. It was early and people were already in their bliss. I stepped into the main room and a server fluttered by with a tray of shots. I wondered if it would be okay to take one. A place like this wouldn't put up with someone drugging someone else's drink. Just as I was lost in thought, a man in his mid thirties introduced himself as Braden and asked me to join him in a room. I declined him as well even though he was cute. What had happened with Jim and Tara sobered me up and I really needed to fix that.

Everyone seemed to be chatting amongst themselves and I almost felt like an outsider until I approached the table and Maya smiled warmly up at me. I settled back into my chair and breathed a sigh of relief. I had just walked around the whole place in my high heels, drunk, and didn't stumble. *Maybe I was getting the hang of this.*

I had spent most of the night watching women undress without shyness of any kind in order to get the most beads. *Is this what Mardi Gras was going to be like?* Women wanted to take their clothes off for a few beads. I'm sure I looked like a deer in headlights most of the night.

"Playtime," Sean announced. My eyes widened as Sean brought out a pair of red oversized dice and rolled them on the table in front of us. Each side of the dice had a sexual favor printed on it. He smiled happily at Sienna. Sean had wavy dirty blonde hair, hazel eyes, broad shoulders, and a swimmer's physique. He looked amazing in his white button up dress shirt, vest, and black dress pants. I was sharply pulled from my people watching when he spoke to Sienna.

"Lap dance, gorgeous." Sean stood and turned his chair so that it was facing away from the table. A techno song rang out in the background and Sienna was more than happy to seduce him. I watched as Sienna stepped out in front of him and moved her body to the beat of the music. His eyes never left her body as she strutted her stuff. She turned her back to him and lowered her head so that her behind was forced in the air. She skimmed her hand over the crack of her buttocks and slid it up over her sex. Then she turned and faced him, letting her leg fall over him, but never touching him. Her breasts hovered close to him, just

93

inches away from his face. She cupped her breasts and teased him with her eyes, never breaking eye contact.

I sat mesmerized by her grace and beauty. Those nearby stopped to take in the view. Colt draped his arm around Sara and she stroked his leg suggestively while they watched Sienna. The beat of the music only seemed to amplify her movements. She narrowed her hips over Sean's lap then continued to pulse and tease him. Just as she was about to touch him, she'd move away. His breathing had changed now. His chest heaved up and down and I could see his hand itching to touch her. One second later his hands wrapped firmly around her hips and he pulled her down on his lap and forced her mouth open with his tongue. He growled as she deepened the kiss. He stood abruptly, lifting her with him, and they soon disappeared down the hall to a private room. I swallowed nervously and looked around the room. *All of it was turning me on.*

By midnight, Sienna joined Sara and I on the dance floor. Sara and Sienna were both topless and each had a neck full of beads. I watched as many of the Cubs that passed by sucked on their nipples. They were half-naked and very relaxed about it. This wasn't their first time doing this. I had no idea this kind of world even existed. I was in a room filled with men and women getting naked like it was an everyday occurrence. Maybe for them it was. *I didn't know.*

As we danced, Both Sienna and Sara took turns grinding on me, often with me in the middle of both of them as Sean and Colt watched from their seats. The girls took turns teasing them by caressing me. I could feel their hands caressing over my butt cheeks and up around my waist. Sara turned me towards her and Sienna pressed light kisses on my neck. Then she and Sienna lifted the sides of my mini dress and raised it upwards as Colt and Sean cheered along with several other men. I simply raised my arms upward and allowed them, against my better judgment, to slip it over my head. I danced in my black satin bra and panties and black-chained garter belt and I still felt overdressed. *Christ, I was overdressed.*

Both girls took turns dirty dancing with me. They planted light kisses all over my body and we danced all night amongst half-naked men and women grinding and gyrating to the loud music. Sara and Sienna would break away for a moment to kiss and fondle each other. I was in a state of disbelief as their tongues wove into each other's mouths. *That was pretty hot.* I could tell I was right by the continued cheers from the guys at our table. Still, I was doing my best to maintain composure.

Sara grabbed my hand, and Sienna my waist, and both girls escorted me off the dance floor and into the hallway. Colt kept feeding me beers all night and I was past slurring my words by this time, as I tried to form a complete thought and ask them where we were headed. They took me into room number ten. Sara walked me in and lowered me onto the king size bed. It was so comfortable I just wanted to close my eyes and go to sleep. Sienna closed the door most of the way but left it cracked slightly, probably figuring Colt and Sean would join us soon.

My head fogged over with alcohol as I lie there looking up at the ceiling in a daze. Sara and Sienna started massaging me, rubbing their hands over my tummy and down my smooth legs and then back up. All I could do was moan from their caresses as my head turned from side to side. Sara's hand rubbed over my breasts and pinched my nipples lightly. I moaned slightly louder. Sienna must have noticed my approval and started kissing up my arms as I reached out and touched her thigh. Sara lowered her head and kissed lightly by my ear. I moaned even louder but refused to open my now closed eyes.

Their hands were all over me when Sara reached my mouth with hers. I accepted her tongue into my mouth and lavished it. Sienna moved upward as she kissed my arm and neck and then when Sara moved off my lips, Sienna placed her mouth over mine and then deepened the kiss with her tongue. I reached up with my hand, grasped onto the back of Sienna's head, and pulled her head tighter with mine. I lifted up as Sara released my bra and moved her mouth over my right breast. I moaned into Sienna's mouth then both girls switched places and Sara was the one kissing me again while Sienna moved lower to kiss my left breast. My hips started gyrating back and forth, as Sara slipped her hand down into my panties and let her fingers slip inside me. I moaned deeper into Sara's mouth. I couldn't believe how easily I was letting this happen. But I think I wanted it, at least with the room spinning I was able to determine that. I wanted so badly just to give in and let go. The alcohol made it so much easier to quiet my thoughts and accept the pleasure they were giving me.

Sienna continued caressing me and sucking my nipples, Sara's fingers were magical. They worked in and out of me, coaxing me nearer to the orgasm I so desperately needed. Until now, I didn't know how much I needed it, but I wanted it badly, so very badly. The room was spinning as pleasure rolled over me. Sienna and Sara both grabbed the sides of my panties and coaxed them down my legs, sliding them slowly over my thighs teasing me, then down my calves. It was agony and pleasure at the same time. I lifted my legs together and they slipped them off me. Both girls spread my legs as Sienna's fingers now entered me. Sara started moving her mouth lower from my lips, to my chin, and around my neck, then over my breasts. She started going lower and lower over my belly. My hips were responding to Sienna's fingers intently as the anticipation of where Sara was going intensified. She kissed lower and still lower. I had never been kissed down there by any man or woman. *Oh God.* Sienna's fingers were equally as magical as Sara's was.

Sara removed Sienna's fingers from me as her kisses neared my pelvic bone. I rolled my eyes back in my head, waiting for release and ecstasy when the door suddenly opened and in walked Jim dragging Tara by the hand. His tiny cock was hard and thrusting upwards against that soccer ball of a belly. He started telling Tara to get on the bed to join us. Then he said he was going to fuck each one of us until we screamed. *Well he got his screams all right.* Both Sara and Sienna angrily yelled for them to get out. Tara looked mortified.

"Why did you leave the door open then? Come on. Let's have a party. I want to fuck you dumb broads!" Jim said.

I snapped back to reality and grabbed my bra, panties, and minders that lay next to us on the bed and ran out of the room into the adjoining bathroom. Although the room was spinning, I knew I wasn't ready for any of this. I closed the door behind me and could hear yelling from the other side as Sienna ordered them out and threatened to report him if he barged into anyone else's room like that. I heard the outer door slam, as I got dressed.

Sara knocked on the door and asked, "Aria, are you okay?"

I leaned against the door on the opposite side and gathered my thoughts. After I composed myself, I opened the door and stepped into the room.

"I don't think I'm ready for this yet." She hugged me, followed by Sienna, saying they both understood. I was so confused by my feelings and the alcohol made it harder to figure this out. But I knew I was embarrassed at my reaction.

"Honey, when you're ready you'll know," Sara said. She and Sienna just held me and smiled.

"You guys aren't mad at me are you?" I asked somewhat sheepishly. Sara simply hugged me again and both girls grabbed me by the hand and escorted me out into the main ballroom.

"Let's get a drink, honey. We'll continue when you're ready. Just know that we both love you," Sara said referring to her and Sienna. She was right. I knew they'd take care of me, *apparently, in more ways than one,* I thought.

This time we headed over towards the bar. The room had stopped spinning by this time. I was happy to have Sara in my life. My breathing had only very recently returned back to normal. My eyes scanned the room and found Avery. We were heading right towards him. He was leaning against the bar, engrossed in a conversation with Travis. A group of gorgeous women surrounded him. Many were topless with handfuls of beads around their necks. Others were hanging on every word he said. He didn't seem to be paying any attention to the array of naked bodies that was within reach. Maybe Sara was right, he had no intentions of really getting to know the women. We were just an accessory.

I studied him from a distance. He had his sport coat and tie off, his shirt was unbuttoned halfway, and his sleeves were rolled up. He held a beer in his left hand and threw his head back in laughter at something Travis said. "Oh," was all I could say. A slow grin spread across my lips. *God, he was beautiful when he smiled.* I wished that I could hear his laugh but we were too far away and the music was pulsing loudly. My head was definitely starting to spin.

"Shots!" Sienna called out. *Oh, no more shots,* I thought. I followed in tow behind them as we made our way to the bar. We were fast approaching Travis and Avery. *Just Perfect,* I thought. I stood at Sara's flank as Sienna ordered us a round of shots.

"You're wearing too many clothes, Kitten," Travis smirked at me. *If you only knew what just happened.* I shrugged and stepped to the far side of Sienna. We all downed our shots and I was glad to have my buzz back.

"She's just getting warmed up, aren't ya Aria?" Sienna winked. I smiled and nodded but deep down I felt like a prude. I was trying to wrap my head around all of this.

"Sweet Jesus," a voice rippled toward me. I glanced up to see him eyeing me from head to toe…twice. "You are exquisite, Kitten. What's your name?" he asked.

I introduced myself and studied him. He was a younger version of Avery but he had blue eyes. Colt snuck up behind Sara and planted a soft kiss behind her ear. I watched as her eyes filled with love and I was instantly jealous.

"Down boy," Colt said. "Sara, Aria, I'd like you to meet Pierce, Avery's brother." His eyes devoured me and I unconsciously took a step back. He wasn't as reserved as Avery.

Maya approached Travis and wrapped her arms around his chest and slipped her hands into his half unbuttoned shirt. She was topless too, with a neck full of beads. She'd been busy.

Sean came up behind Sienna and lifted her onto the bar. She let out a squeal of delight and laid back. The bartender poured her a shot and Sienna held it in her breast. Sean moaned and rolled his eyes back in his head as Sienna poured salt over her nipples.

"God, woman, you're beautiful, and all mine," Sean growled in delight, licking the salt off of her breasts. He let his mouth fall around the shot glass and tipped his head back, letting the liquid fall back in his throat. He pulled the glass from his mouth while Sienna held the lime in between her teeth. Sean ran his tongue between her breasts then her neck then let his mouth fall over hers. I fidgeted nervously and watched as all the couples, half-naked women, and Avery huddled near the bar, grinning at the seductive scene in front of them.

Sean helped Sienna off the bar and my new crowd of friends fell into small talk about their classes. I had done my second shot in the last fifteen minutes and set it down when my eyes flashed to Avery as he laughed at Colt's joke. My mouth curved up into a smile. I had gotten my wish.

Avery's eyes flashed to mine. "A beaded necklace for your thoughts," Avery said leaning in towards me, dangling an emerald green beaded necklace over his fingertip.

"I'm just taking it all in," I said, trying hard not to squirm under his stare.

He lowered the necklace over my head and let his hands brush over my shoulders. I shuddered under his touch. His eyes danced as they took me in. He lowered his head to my ear. I could feel the heat of his body next to mine.

"I apologize if I offended you this morning," he breathed. I just stared up at him.

"You didn't," I answered.

⌘

DAY FOUR:
THURSDAY EARLY MORNING
THE BEAUTIFUL BUTTERFLY

It was 5am when I tied up my running shoes, stretched, and followed a wide trail into the woods behind the Kitten cabins. The trees brushed by me quickly as I pushed myself to sprint the first mile. Then I backed off some and fell into my usual pace, trying to unwind from the stress that this new place had brought me. It was day four and I still hadn't been able to relax enough to cum in front of Colt and Sienna. At this point, I didn't know if I ever would.

I distanced myself from my thoughts and continued running another mile and a half to a clearing with a large circle of neatly groomed orchids and woven ivy when I heard footsteps coming toward me. My stomach knotted up as Avery approached from the other direction. I waved politely as he passed by and circled back in the direction that he originally came. He was surprised to see me at first then his delicious lips curved up in that smile that made me weak in the knees. I almost stumbled on another tree root as my thoughts filled with nothing but his chiseled body. *I was usually a well-coordinated woman. Why was I going weak-kneed every time I saw him?*

I pushed myself harder and looped around the trail that brought me back around heading in Avery's direction, trying hard not to think of his hungry eyes and the way he looked at me last night at the Theme Party. I pushed on toward his direction but his stride was too great, the thick forest already swallowed him up. I finished another mile, which left me spent. I moved into a clearing and stopped for a moment. I let my hands fall to my knees to catch my breath. Gracious hands handed me a bottle of ice-cold water. I should have been startled but instead I composed myself and stood upright. I took a swig as Avery studied me. I ran my arm across my brow to wipe the sweat away and tried to slow my breathing so I could speak.

"Hi," was all I could manage to say. He chuckled as I regained my breathing. "Thanks for the water."

"You're welcome, Aria." His voice was like a red velvet cake dipped in delicious chocolate. I stared up at him, speechless. "You better walk with me before you cramp up. That was a pretty hard run. Working out some issues? I always find running helps me clear my head. How about you?"

I realized I was holding my breath and let out a huge sigh. "Always."

"You never turn your mind off for a second, do you?" he teased, walking toward the direction of a large cabin laid with tall windows and ornately carved doors. I followed behind him and frowned knowing that was true.

He glanced at me sideways. "Sorry, I didn't mean to pry."

"No, you're right. I'm working some things out. Running helps me think. I can just shut out the world, only concentrating on my feet hitting the ground."

I studied him. He was wearing black running shorts that rested just above his knees and no shirt. I looked at his chest and suddenly I couldn't form a thought. I walked beside him in silence as we approached a cabin. He looked over at me.

"You are sworn to secrecy from this moment on. What I am about to show you could potentially wreck havoc if you mutter a single word of it to anyone at camp. I mean it. Don't get drunk and blab my secrets to everyone. Okay?" he said.

"You don't trust too many people do you? Why is that?" I asked.

"I've been burned before, that's all I'm going to say." He stopped to wait for my response.

How cliché. "I will not tell a soul. I promise." I wanted to tell him he could trust me. But for some reason I didn't think it would matter. Avery had been hurt. That much was true. But seeing the vulnerability in his eyes, I realized it had to be brutal. *Maybe it was just women, in general, that he didn't trust.* My heart ached to help heal him.

Avery escorted me into his very large two-story timber frame cabin that left me at a loss for words. It had floor to ceiling windows. It had a wide-open floor plan with a touch of rustic mixed with contemporary. It was decorated exactly like I would do it. The first thing I noticed was the large fireplace in the living room inlaid with stone from floor to ceiling. There was a large black leather L-shaped couch and matching oversized chairs. We walked down the hall and he showed me two spare bedrooms fully furnished, his office, a game room with a pool table, dartboard, foosball, large monitors for gaming, card table, and a fully stocked bar. My eyes landed back to the pool table – *oh do I have thoughts about that pool table – me naked on it, for starters.* My mind took me away to the image of him kissing me everywhere and my face heated instantly. He cleared his throat and headed toward the kitchen. The layout was very modern in here also, the appliances were stainless steel but with a 1940's retro style. So, even though they looked and functioned in a very modern way they looked liked they belonged in a very high-end hunting cabin. It was awesome.

"You like to cook?" I inquired.

Avery smiled softly. "When I have time. Yes. It's a passion of mine."

To the right of that was the dining room – all of it was an open floor plan decorated in dark walnut. We stepped to the large spiral staircase that matched the exposed beams of the cabin and moved onto the balcony. We passed the laundry room on the way down the hall. He opened two black double doors and I followed him into a large bedroom. I swallowed nervously and waited near the doorway. I glanced around his enormous room and took in his king-sized, elevated platform bed in the center. A large flat screen was on a nearby wall. *A true bachelor's dream.* What enamored me more was the breathtaking panoramic view of the surrounding mountains.

"My room," he breathed. I looked to see his chest rise and fall quickly and all I wanted to do was wrap my arms around him and calm his anxiety. He looked lost for a moment then turned toward his long walk-in closet. I stepped into the adjoining bathroom with French doors and I melted on the spot. Lavish garden tub, dual sinks, open shower with dual showerheads. Control panel on the wall for temperature control. I peered upward to see skylights above me. He had this designed so nature was all around us. It really brought the outdoors inside.

Avery stepped into the doorway and pulled on a plain grey t-shirt and I stepped back into the bedroom, thinking he needed a moment. A warm hand embraced mine and pulled me backwards. He stepped in front of me. I looked up at him. Suddenly, I couldn't imagine being anywhere else in the world. He lowered his face to mine. He brushed his hand over my reddened cheek and studied my face. His eyes lingered on my lips and I was begging for him to kiss me. His breathing was fast like mine. I was certain he could hear my heart pounding in my chest. *God, I wanted him. I had never wanted anything more in my life.* But he stepped away and whispered, "I'm sorry. I keep touching you without your permission. I apologize for that." My hope crashed down around me.

"Anytime you want," I blurted out the words before I could stop myself. "I mean you have my permission anytime you want it…I mean…uh…never mind…I mean you don't have to ask…umm…apology accepted," I said, nodding my head his way. *Ugh, I'm such a dumbass. Get it together girl. I'm so lame…so lame.* Then I smiled a very fake wide smile toward him and cocked my head slightly to the side. Apparently, my super cuteness worked because Avery didn't answer but just flashed his megawatt smile and took my hand.

"Have breakfast with me," he asked.

"I'd love to."

I tried to hide the frown that had replaced my shit-eating grin as he let go of my hand and stepped to the intercom. He pushed the button and spoke into it. "Daniel, there will two for breakfast and I'll take it lagoon side."

A deep voice acknowledged Avery's request and we walked through the tall glass windows to his back deck and down the large staircase. The sun was just rising over the horizon and bathing everything in its golden glory.

We passed the in-ground pool but we didn't stop at the pool's edge. He continued through the yard down a narrow path that led to a small lagoon at the base of a mountain. I heard the roar of gushing water as we approached.

"Look there," he leaned into me and I breathed in the smell of Avery's cologne mixed with sweat. My heart skipped a beat as I stepped through the wooded forest and stood before a most beautiful sight. I was surrounded by nothing except nature, trees, sunlight, and a breathtaking narrow waterfall. Time stood still as I felt encased in all of nature's beauty. I looked up at the sky past the thick maple trees that hid us from the rest of the world.

Avery pulled out a chair at the small rustic iron table and I sat down on a plush cushion. "What do you see?" he asked, scanning the forest landscaping.

I wanted to say, *the sexiest man I had ever known,* but I didn't. I took a moment to look around at the vivid, magnificent scenery that only the Allegheny Mountains had to offer. I noted the vast wall of wild orchids next to us at the breakfast nook. Next to it was a queen sized outdoor mattress encompassed in wild orchids. A calming peace fell upon me and suddenly I knew there was no other place I'd rather be. My heart ached with wanting. I wanted to spend every minute here with him. I wanted to be the one that made him happy, to make him smile, to make him laugh. I wanted to be the one that touched not just his heart, but also his soul. I barely knew him, yet I never felt more at home before.

"Home," I said, wishing I hadn't. My eyes flashed to Avery's as he sucked in a breath. His eyes lit up then a soft smile spread over his lips. *What the hell was wrong with me?* The man hadn't even kissed me yet. He seemed like he wanted to when we were standing in his bedroom but I could tell he was scared. That much I could see in his eyes. I wondered then – *did he always hide this side of himself from the world. Why was he showing me?* This was the most romantic place I'd ever been and I was here with Avery. *What more could a girl want?*

I was thankful when a short bald man stepped up to the table with a heaping tray. He set down two ice waters, two orange juices and two covered platters.

"Thank you, Daniel. This looks great," Avery said taking off his lid to his breakfast. Daniel lifted the lid of my platter and set it to the edge of the table.

"Enjoy, Miss…?"

"Aria," I said.

"Of course…Miss Aria…Sir." Daniel flashed a look toward Avery and nodded then turned away. I'm sure he didn't approve of me. I blinked and tried to take in the lavish breakfast that he served to me as Avery sat across from me just out of reach. The stack of French toast was drizzled in strawberries and syrup, and on the side was crisp bacon. I tried to hide my squeal of delight but it was written all over my face. I glanced up to see Avery grinning at me as I dug in. I took a bite. *Jesus, the syrup was warm.* I moaned in delight.

Avery stopped mid chew and locked his eyes on mine. His gaze was interrupted as his eyes drifted to the right and I followed his gaze to a radiant blue and black monarch butterfly. A warm feeling fell over me thinking of his words bedside the lake the first time I met him — *a beautiful butterfly, and she has me hypnotized.*

We watched it hover directly over us then it landed on the dome plate cover. Its wings pulsed for a moment.

His eyes softened as he looked at me. "Beautiful butterfly," he breathed. I smiled nervously. We drew our attention back to the butterfly now stilled. It waved its wings then rose up and fluttered away. Our eyes never left it until it faded into the blue sky.

"Is any of this real?" I chuckled nervously. I could feel Avery's eyes on me as I ran my hand over the soft petals of white and fuscia that rested in the vase at the center of the table. "Wild Orchids. Don't tell me you love gardening also?" I said.

"Some secrets even I will never tell," he teased.

"So, tell me a secret Avery," I said looking into his green eyes.

He blinked and I could see him trying to hide his surprise. "I already gave you one. Well, two actually," his eyes sparkled. His look would haunt me for a long time. I wrinkled my eyebrow at him in confusion. He looked around at his paradise. "Where I live inside my camp is one and the camp itself is number two. You should come horseback riding sometime. It's wonderful riding through the mountain trails." He was trying to change the subject.

"Fair enough. Tell me something else I don't know," I said chewing another bite of French toast.

"I was an architecture major. Still working on it, actually," he said taking another bite. "Your turn," he said looking at me with hope in his eyes.

"You don't like to talk about yourself, do you?" I asked.

"Look who's talking," Avery said with a wolfish grin.

I narrowed my eyes at him as I took a few more bites then set my fork down. I couldn't eat anymore. I was too nervous. *Okay, Avery. Have it your way.*

"My favorite meal is steak. My favorite sport to play is gymnastics although volleyball is a close second. My favorite sport to watch is football. I think basketball is boring. I love running, hiking, and riding four-wheelers. I love to dance. I drink beer really fast when I'm nervous, I like wine when I want to be social, and I have found that whiskey is becoming my new spinach. Sorry, I know, I just used a Popeye reference. I can't help it; my dad loved the classics, Popeye, Road Runner, Bugs Bunny and The Three Stooges. My first pet was a kitten named Knuckles." Avery's eyes lit up in humor. I shrugged. "I was five. Anyways, I love the sound of an acoustic guitar. My favorite band is Chasing Seven," I rambled nervously, trying to keep to a general topic. He was right. I didn't like to talk in depth about myself. It was easier when I didn't. People couldn't judge me. "My favorite actors in order from oldest to youngest are Morgan Freeman, Liam Neeson, Vin Diesel, Anne Hathaway, & Mila Kunis. I have both read and seen Pride & Prejudice more times than I can count, and I'm secretly in love with Mr. Darcy, and I'm a nursing student. I love medicine. But my true passion is to someday write a novel. Your turn," I said all breathy.

Avery raised both eyebrows. "You're a hopeless romantic through and through aren't you?" Avery reached down to pick a long branch of pink and white blossoms from beside us. He leaned closer to me, our eyes locked in a stare. "Close your eyes, Aria," his sultry voice said.

I hesitantly closed my eyes. I felt the gentle caress of soft silk brush across my forehead. Then he trailed downward over my nose and I inhaled, smelling the sensual scent of the wild orchids. I tilted my head back and he traced the petals gently over my lips and down the length of my neck. And then it was gone.

"Aria. Or as Mr. Darcy would say, Miss Aria," he said in a seductive voice. My eyes fluttered open to his heated stare. *Oh my.* That sent quivers down my spine. Suddenly, I could imagine him saying my name as he cried out in an orgasm and it left me breathless.

"Tease," I said giving his words from the first night of camp back to him. He held out the stem of wild orchids to me and I took it as he rose from his chair and looked lost in thought. *Oh no, I was losing him.* "Have you heard Chasing Seven's newest song, 'I Need You'?" I said walking up beside him and quickly trying to downplay what he'd just done.

He smiled genuinely. "It's great isn't it? They're coming to Pittsburgh in January," he said stepping to the edge of the mattress beside the waterfall. "Should be a great show," he added, twirling another long branch of those seductive flowers in his hand.

111

"So tell me about architecture," I said steering the conversation back to something he might openly talk about. Avery walked over and stretched out on the mattress and I sat down facing him with my legs crossed in front of me.

It seemed like we were there for hours and I relished in his talk and love for architecture. We talked of nature. How the bold, vivid colors of the Pennsylvania forest were the perfect scene and canvas for anything he wanted to build. Nothing seemed to matter except being with Avery. We exchanged little looks and small smiles as we tossed pebbles into the water. He brushed dirt from my face when I rubbed my cheek after I picked up a muddy rock. I listened to his warm, husky voice talk of the new phase of cabins he was planning to build and that he had owned almost a thousand acres now. I listened to his breathing, the waterfall, and nature all around us. The sun was bearing down on us and I had never been happier in that moment.

Out of habit, I reached for my necklace only to find my neck bare. I lowered my hand then studied Avery and all his beautiful features, his square jaw, his perfect nose, his soft sensual lips, even the thickness of his eyebrows that perfectly matched the color of his brown hair. He was watching a bird drinking from the water's edge while his back was propped up against the boulder behind him and his leg was stretched out brushing against mine. He closed his eyes and let the last rays of the sun hit his face. I wasn't disappointed that he didn't make a move to seduce me. I understood he was taking this slow.

"Why am I here, Avery? Why all this?"

Avery rubbed the back of his neck while he pondered my question. "I don't know, Aria. I seem to be breaking all my rules when it comes to you," he said bending his knees, crossing his legs, and leaning closer toward me. He cupped my face with his hands and let his eyes roam over my face. "Sweet Aria," Avery purred. I could feel his breath on my lips and I never wanted to taste someone's kiss so badly. He let his head rest against mine. His chest was rising and falling rapidly and I could see his torment playing out in his eyes. He closed his eyes and pulled away, dropping his hands and leaving me feeling like a part of me was taken away with him.

"I can't let this go any further. I don't get involved with my guests." Avery's phone rang and he reached in his pocket and pulled out his phone. "Damn it," he cursed when he noted the time. "I'm running late, Pierce. I'll be there in ten." All of Avery's tenderness was gone when he looked at me. He was all business again. "Let's get you back to class."

I stood and looked up at him, afraid that this would be my last moment with him. He could see my panic and he gently lifted my hand and pressed his lips to the back of it. *Oh, Avery, why don't you kiss me?*

"I have a meeting and I'm most certain that you are late for your group oral class."

"You know my schedule?" I flushed.

"Yes, of course," Avery mumbled, looking away. He led us to the back door of his house.

"Wait here. I'll only be a moment." He was back to his professional montage. I nodded as I watched him disappear into the house. *One step forward, two steps back.* I wondered how late I was. Avery pulled the door behind him and ended his call on his cellphone. "I just spoke to Colt. He knows you'll be late." I followed him to the side garage and I entered, blinking into the darkness. It was short-lived when the door rose up and light flooded the room. I moved to the BMW SUV. He shook his head and pointed to the quad. I smiled at his sentiment and climbed on. "Aria, I can't let anyone see us together. It will start rumors and appearances are important. Everyone must follow the rules here...even me," he said. *I'm not so sure that's true,* I thought.

"We will have to go the back way into camp." I shrugged. He eyed me warily. "I will drop you at the clearing next to the Peak cabin." I smiled politely. He started up the quad. We raced through the doorway and the door closed behind us. "Hang on. It's going to get bumpy." He smiled his breathtaking smile and I was more than happy to hang on tightly. *Avery was a kid at heart.*

We moved over hills and through the trees at record speed. The trees brushed my arms. He leaped over mounds of dirt and we splashed down into a medium sized stream. I giggled as the water soaked my feet and legs. He chuckled then revved up the engine, pulled back around, and spun us in a circle. I squealed as he spun two more donuts in the stream. Water splashed high up my legs. He steered straight out of the ravine and slowed the quad to a coast. I don't know if he was caught up in the moment but he turned to me and let his hands cradle my face. He was breathing hard and I could feel his heart pounding in his chest. We were so close. Our lips were almost touching but I could see the internal struggle in his eyes. He was fighting to keep his guard up. His phone rang out and he cursed under his breath.

"Pierce, I'm coming," he barked into the phone. He listened for a moment then growled. "I won't be ready." He paused a minute. "No. They can't come sooner. I don't care. I have the Hawaii trip to contend with in August. They're not scheduled to come until October, he urged and hung up the phone. Avery looked torn as he turned back to the accelerator.

He caressed my hand then threaded his fingers through mine and guided my hand around his waist. It was such a simple gesture but it felt so intimate. He placed his other hand on the handle bar and pressed the accelerator. The tires spun. Water flew up behind us again and I could feel it spray the back of me. I laid my head against his back. I breathed in Avery, again. Inside, I was purring with happiness. This feeling had made me lose all my rationale. All I knew was I wanted him any way I could get him.

When we got to the clearing, I could see Peak cabin. It was a short jog from where we were. Avery let the quad idle and I climbed off. I stepped forward intending to kiss him.

"Don't, Aria." My face fell and I couldn't hide my confusion. "I'm sorry. I just can't," Avery said looking away.

My heart fell to my stomach and I was left winded. Avery grimaced. I nodded my head to him stiffly, turned away and walked out into the clearing. I forced myself to put one foot in front of the other. I was shocked by his words. *Why would he spend hours with me next to a romantic waterfall and not make a move? Why would he hold my hand like that? Why would he almost kiss me? Then not.* Then it occurred to me. *It was just another man with another game that I didn't understand. Sara Cox, you were wrong. He was exactly like every other guy.*

By the time I heard him pull away, I was seething. I took off in a full sprint and ran as far away from Avery Jameson as I could.

⌘

DAY FOUR:
THURSDAY MORNING
ORAL SEX CLASS

I hurried through the heavy wooden door of Peak cabin and I tried to bury my mixed emotions as I ducked into classroom B. Sienna was passing out bananas to the other five women in my group. I hurried to join them and Sienna handed me a large banana.

"There will be a quiz at the end of the lesson." I couldn't help but wonder what kind of quiz it could be. "Today's class we're going to be practicing oral and the best way to do that is with a banana. Now watch what I do then in turn each one of you will do the same. I want you to let yourself go and really get into it. Don't be afraid to experiment just don't bite down or your banana will break and that's bad. The purpose of using bananas is so you can have real world practice not using your teeth."

I watched as the rest of the class unpeeled their bananas and as Sienna stepped next to them they each let their lips fall over the top. Caitlyn could fit the entire thing in her mouth. Tara went all the way down and started twisting it in her mouth with her tongue. *Jesus. How the hell did she do that?* Sienna smirked.

"Good, Tara, I want to see more of that during the quiz." Tara flushed three shades of red and looked away with a slight nod.

"Okay class. Hold the base with one hand and then use your tongue to slowly lick it from the base to the tip." She paused and watched as everyone complied. "Good. Now mix it up a little by moving your tongue side to side as you go from the base to the tip. Even swivel your hand in the process and trail it behind your tongue." I held the base of the banana in my hand and trailed my tongue from the base to the tip and then straight back down. On the second pass, I twirled my tongue around and let my other hand trail behind my tongue. My eyes landed on the now silent class as Sienna gleamed at me.

"Excellent technique, Aria." She turned to the rest of the class. "You all seem to have the basics. Let's see how you do with the real thing," Sienna announced.

Colt stepped up beside me in a dark green robe with the Camp Jameson logo emblazoned on the left chest and untied it then he stood there proudly exposed in all his glory. That was the first time I ever saw his manhood. It was huge and thick. I could tell why Sara talked about it like it was its own person. Sienna was saying something about the quiz and telling us to line up. She coached us on how providing gentle but firm strokes was essential, but all I could focus on was that Colt was very well endowed. *Oh my!*

Caitlyn sidestepped me and pushed to the front of the line and knocked me over in the process. As I landed on the ground Sienna called aloud.

"Relax, ladies. There's enough to go around. I know it's big but don't kill each other," she chuckled. "Caitlyn, go ahead. I'll let you get him hard the rest of the way then you can tease him. But remember class, you must stop before he climaxes. This is just an exercise in technique and the fine art of foreplay. If he comes, you fail. We need to get through the entire class so, although I want you to be viscous and make him suffer, there will be no orgasm. Remember that Colt. No cuming," Sienna chuckled.

The class giggled in nervous energy and I watched as Caitlyn's rough hands gripped Colt's penis like she was milking a cow. Colt flinched a little at her rough dexterity. Her technique was sloppy and brambly. Her mouth sounded like the tongue of a basset hound deprived of water for a day. Squeech, Squeech, Squeech filled the room. She was fast and very loud as Colt grimaced.

"Easy, Caitlyn," Colt finally spoke up. "It's a marathon, not a sprint," Colt said through clenched teeth. I saw Caitlyn go down his shaft with unsheathed teeth and Colt backed away quickly, grabbing his manhood.

"Oww, you're done. Return to the practice bananas with Sienna." He looked down at his manhood. "Jesus! There are little indentations on little Colt." He glared at Caitlyn. "Do it until there aren't any teeth marks on that banana."

Caitlyn huffed and crossed her arms. Colt scowled and pointed to the bananas showing her that he was serious. Caitlyn stuck her nose up in the air and walked heavy-footed toward the bananas. I could hear Sienna tell her not to be so rough when I realized I was next.

"I'm all yours, Aria." I studied Colt for a second then stepped up to him. He was now leaning against the massage table with his feet on the floor. I sank to my feet and ran my hands up both his thighs. *I could do this. Christ, I've imagined this moment for so long that I was almost giddy.*

I felt Colt's body relax under my touch and I leaned in to take him in my mouth. Colt stiffened and I looked up at him. He was smiling looking down at me.

"No biting, please," he begged. I nodded then took his glorious cock in my hand.

I started with a gentle hand job to help build the tension. I felt him relax more. I leaned over and softly kissed the head of his penis then trailed soft kisses all over his shaft. I blocked out the rest of the class and began licking the underside of him. I took it in about an inch into my mouth and used my tongue in a circular motion to massage the head. While massaging it with my tongue, I wrapped my hand around the base with firm pressure and swirled my tongue around his tip, then let my hand stroke his shaft up and down. The mixture of wetness and firmness caused his head to fall back and a low moan to erupt from his throat. I continued to stroke him up and down in my mouth then I thought, *what the hell, I'll try the tongue squeeze technique Sienna was going on about during her lecture.*

I took him deep in my mouth until I felt the head of his penis press against the roof of my mouth. Then, I trailed my tongue down the underside of him while the tip was still pressing on the roof of my mouth. Each stroke I pulsed my tongue so that it squeezed the head up against the roof of my mouth and trapped his shaft completely with my tongue. Then I took my other hand and gently palmed his balls and massaged gently.

I heard Colt hiss under his breath. He reached down and put both hands on the sides of my head to anchor himself further. I felt him swivel his hips and draw himself deeper into me. The only sound in the room was the moisture I was spreading around with my tongue all over his cock. I felt him harden further. *Geez, he was big in my mouth.*

I teased him further letting his shaft glide in and out then I trapped him against the roof of my mouth and pressed with my tongue again. I heard Colt moan louder and suddenly, I wanted more than anything to bring him to climax. I sped up my motions and pulled him further into my mouth and tightened my grip a little more on his length. He was hard as steel but his skin was soft as velvet. And he tasted delicious.

"Jesus!" Colt muttered. I heard his breath catch in his throat and before I could react, I felt his warm fluid hit the back of my throat. I stiffened a moment and then relaxed swallowing all that was Colt Thompson.

"Fuck, yeah, that's it baby. Suck it," Colt gushed. I heard the class gasp around me but it wasn't until Sienna called out in an authoritative voice that I regained my senses.

"Colt, can I see you in our office for a moment?" I was on my knees in front of Colt and he just came gloriously in my mouth. *Fuck.* Sienna told us not to make him come.

Colt was smiling down at me like an eight year old on Christmas morning that got his first Gnip Gnop. I could see that Sienna's words finally registered because when he blinked, his euphoric state was replaced with a nervous *I fucked up* kind of look. He quickly recomposed himself and wrapped the robe back around him. He winked at me then strode toward the office.

121

"Let's call it a day, class," Sienna said, dismissing us and ushering Colt into their office. I sat back on my knees and watched Sienna close the door behind her. I was torn. My body was quickly recovering from an intense high from bringing Colt to climax but another part of me didn't want to disappoint Sienna. I was afraid it was too late for that. Then there was Sara. *How was I going to tell her Colt just came in my mouth?* My guilt had just tripled.

⌘

DAY FOUR:
THURSDAY NIGHT
KITTEN'S NIGHT

I paused briefly from pacing the hardwood floors of the cabin kitchen to down my beer. I was torn. It had only been a half hour since my class, I could still taste Colt in my mouth, and I still didn't know how I was going to tell Sara. I heard the turn of the doorknob to the cabin door and Sara stepped through the doorway with her hands full of grocery bags from the camp store.

"I went shopping," Sara said in her usual bubbly manner. A part of me wanted to say something just to piss her off. It would make things so much easier if she were mad at me. I swallowed down my anxiety and it helped free up some of the psychological weight on my shoulders.

"Did you walk from the store with all of these bags?"

"No. I took the golf cart," Sara replied, handing me a bundle of bananas. *God, I wanted to die. Bananas...damn you Colt. How do I tell her?*

"We can use the golf carts?"

Sara chuckled. "You'd know that if you'd read the manual," Sara narrowed her eyes at me. I hated when she did that. I knew what question was going to follow. "What's wrong? You look stressed." My eyes widened. I opened my mouth to tell her and then shut it immediately. I tried again but nothing came out. *How do I tell my best friend that I just sucked off her boyfriend who is the love of her life? No matter how much I enjoyed it, in that moment, I now felt terrible.*

"Are you feeling okay? Honey, you look pale. You weren't at lunch today. I bought some protein bars. You should go into A's Market sometime. That place would put our grocery store back home to shame." I mind-numbingly took the protein bar that she held out for me but I didn't open it.

"Maybe you'd rather have a banana?" Sara offered. *Lightning, strike me now.* I shook my head. "Do you want to go to Kitten Night with me? We can drink lots of beer and forget about the guys for a night?" Sara asked. I answered with the only word I could spit out.

"Sure." I helped Sara put the rest of the groceries away as I wrestled internally to tell her. *Okay, calm down girl...I don't have to tell her right at this moment. It's been a hard day...oh boy...even in my head I knew that sounded bad...But I would tell her tonight...yea for sure...I would tell her tonight when the time was right...after I got a few beers in her to soften the blow. After all, what's the worst that could happen? Yea, that's a good plan...tell her tonight. Kitten night meant that she wouldn't be seeing Colt. That's good. At least I had a few hours until I absolutely had to tell her. I could do this. I had to...probably have a couple beers myself first.*

The time really seemed to fly by fast now that Sara and I arrived at one of the four campfires burning high behind the Main Lodge. I glanced up at the balcony to the large gathering of Cubs and Instructors. By the looks of it and the noise level, Thursday night Cub cocktail hour with Avery started early and was going well. I could hear their laughter echoing off the back courtyard as Sara and I made our way through the torch lit path to the Kitten campfire where Sienna and Maya greeted us.

It was a dark night and the Main Lodge was coated in shadows except for the golden glow of torches and dim landscape lighting. I had tried to tell Sara about what I did with Colt several times on the way over here, but each time Sara seemed to endlessly ramble on about every gorgeous guy she met today. But then I welcomed her ramblings so I didn't have to tell her the sad truth yet, even though deep down, I knew it was only prolonging my agony.

I smiled at the group that had gathered around our sundry orange fire and hoped that tonight I could forget about everything, especially Colt and Avery.

After my rendezvous with Avery, I had to lie to Sienna and Colt and say I got lost in the woods while I was running and Avery found me while riding through. He brought me back to safety. I made him out to be the hero. I could literally just have choked on those words. He was no hero. He was heartless and an emotional tease. Sienna and Colt seemed to buy it anyways.

The fire crackled intently, filled with bright greens and blues as Sienna put another log on. So here we were, just us Kittens and our female instructors, sitting around a campfire behind the Main Lodge, telling stories about what else?...*Men.*

I reached into the cooler and pulled out a beer. I popped the cap off and chugged half of it. This was my fifth beer since Sara came home and I was finally starting to relax as we all took seats on horizontal logs that were graciously placed in geometric order around each fire pit.

"Look everyone, I think Aria's getting bored," Sara said. "Let's play a game," Sara urged. *Man, that sounded sarcastic.* I tried not to roll my eyes at the implications and just stared at the fire instead.

"The game is called 'Spill It'." *Great, more games.* Then she continued. "It's kinda a mixture of Truth or Dare and Bullshit. For every round there is always a 'Truth' and for the first round everyone has to tell a story about how they got revenge on someone from their past who cheated on them. We've all had that happen to us at some point in our lives, or tell us how you got back at the girl your boyfriend did it with." *What?* Then Sara went on. "If someone is suspected of embellishing or holding back someone calls out 'Spill It' and as punishment, that person caught telling the lie has to shotgun two beers and then afterwards spill their guts. *Oh fuck! She knows. Could this possibly be a coincidence? She's gonna kick my ass for sure.*

I kept looking around to see where I could go…where I could hide. It must be a coincidence. *Yea, that's right. Just a coincidence.* She didn't see Colt today. *It was Caitlyn.* I bet she told her. She's been after me since the beginning just because Avery talks to me and not her. *Goddamn her! If she told Sara, I will kick the ever-living shit out of her! Okay, calm down, she doesn't know. I'm just freaking myself out. I swear to God, Caitlyn, I will rip your fake fucking fingernails out, you fake blonde slut bitch! Take a deep breath, Aria. Nobody knows. Nobody knows…except Sienna and everyone else at class. Ugh…I'm dead. It's my own damn fault. I give one blowjob at camp and now I'm dead and buried…oh wait…I'm about to be buried.*

"Sienna, you go first," Sara said, making sure that everyone agreed.

"My revenge on a guy that cheated on me was with a guy I dated for five months. I had stopped by to pick up takeout at our usual place in a small café in New York City when I saw him lip locked with my best friend," Sienna said. I gulped.

"We had plans to see each other that night so I played it cool and went along with the date. We ordered in Chinese that night and I made him drink until he was obliterated and passed out. Then, while he was sleeping I had a friend – I'm never saying who, so don't ask, give him a Prince Albert."

The women all gasped in unison. Sienna smiled deceptively as she stared into the fire. Her auburn hair glowed even more with the flames dancing off them.

"Let's just say when he woke up, the pain lasted a lot longer than if I kicked him in the balls," Sienna smiled to us.

Tara covered her mouth with her hand. "Jesus, that's brutal," she grimaced.

"What was even better, he couldn't have sex with my ex best friend for months," Sienna added. *What the fuck is a Prince Albert? Strike that, I don't even want to know.* I didn't really want to ask so I sat still.

"I'll go next," Sara blurted. I eyed her suspiciously. *Ugh.* I was getting more paranoid by the minute. I shifted nervously but stared straight at the fire. I kept telling myself Sara would have said something, wouldn't she? I took another swig of my beer. Damn, it was empty. I reached into the cooler and brought out another one.

Sara started. "Aria knows this story. So she can call it if I don't tell the truth." I flinched as soon as she said my name. I rolled backwards right off my log. I did my best not to spill my beer but it was useless as my feet pointed at the sky my beer spilled out all over my shirt.

"Aria. That's not how you play spill it," Caitlyn chided condescendingly as everyone burst out laughing.

"Eat a full bag of shit, Caitlyn," I said very sweetly through my fake smile as my feet still pointed upward towards the dark night. I slowly dug my hands in the soft earth and pushed myself back onto my log.

"Be nice, ladies," Sienna added. Then Sara continued on.

"So there was this guy Jake that I dated in my senior year of high school. We'd been dating about six months when he started canceling our dates out of the blue. At first, I really believed he was sick, like he said he was. Why wouldn't I believe him? But then, a guy friend of mine took a picture of him all over another girl at the same party that we were supposed to go to together. He of course denied it was him. The picture was kinda blurry but he swore up and down it wasn't him. He kept saying he loved me and blah, blah, blah. I was naïve back then and I forgave him. Then he started blowing me off again and going to parties by himself. That didn't sit well with me. The night that I finally caught him, I had borrowed Aria's car so that he wouldn't know I was there. I hid outside in the tall grass across the street from his house and watched him arrive with this other girl from our class. My plan was to wait until he went inside but they never made it." Sara looked at me and smirked. "They started going at it before they made it to the porch and he pulled her right into the bushes," Sara said leaning forward. *This wasn't the story I knew.* "She sunk to her knees and unzipped him. She pulled out his cock and started to suck him off." My eyes widened as Sara went on. "I watched as she got him off. He didn't even pull out. He shot it right in her mouth and she swallowed his entire load. She was a natural." I gulped, then coughed a bit and spit up some of my beer as I quickly caught it in my hand. Everyone stared over at me until I finished hacking.

"You okay there, Aria?" Sienna asked.

"Yea, I'm fine." I said.

"I waited until he went inside then I grabbed my baseball bat. I went back to his truck and put dents in every surface of it. I smashed out his headlights, his mirrors. But I was still pissed off, so I jacked up the truck on cement blocks and took all his tires. They were heavy as hell and I couldn't carry them, so I rolled them down the hill into some poor guy's yard and then put a 'Free' sign on them."

"Is she lying, Aria?" Sienna asked.

My head was spinning from all of the beer. "Spill it," I bleated very softly. "Everything was true except for the blowjob part," I said as a feeling of anxiety swept over me like high tide.

"Speaking of blowjobs," Amber said. "That was hot as hell today in class, Aria," she added, looking at me.

I gulped and cringed at the same time. I rose quickly and stepped in a circle unsure if I was leaving or heading toward Sara. Then I gave in, stepped toward Sara, and looked down at the ground. I couldn't look her in the eye.

"Sara, I gave Colt a blowjob today in class…and…" I stuttered. Then giggles started to break from the girls sitting around us.

"Wait," I said, pausing to look at Sara. I studied her face for a minute. She didn't look angry; she was fighting back a grin. Sienna nudged her with her arm and winked at me. Then everyone burst out laughing. "Holy shit. All this time you knew and you didn't say anything? You little bitch!"

Sara giggled and confirmed my suspicion. Everyone was laughing so hard that we garnered stares from the other campfires along the back lawn.

"Yes. And it was a blast torturing you," Sara said.

"Serves you right for not telling her right away," Caitlyn quipped.

"Thanks from the peanut gallery," I said to Caitlyn as she scrunched her face back at me.

"What does peanuts have to do with this?" she sneered.

Everyone snickered then I turned my attention back to Sara as she continued on, "We've spent two hours together and you still didn't have the guts to tell me. I gave you every opportunity when we were unloading the groceries. I kept handing you the bananas and you never said a word."

"Oh man, I was wondering if that's what you were doing," I stood gaping at my best friend. Laughter spilled out of me joining in the chorus with the others.

"I stopped by Colt's before I went to the Market. He didn't let me get in the door before he took me," Sara said. "The whole time he bragged about how you gave him the hottest blowjob he's ever had. And he wants *you* to show me how *you* do that thing with your tongue and the roof of your mouth and coming from Colt, that's saying something. I'm a little jealous. Colt can last a long time and you made him cum in two minutes. Not to mention he doesn't cum in anyone's mouth, except mine. So, sexy little Kitten, want to tell me where you learned that little technique from?" I smiled sardonically and shook my head. "Suit yourself. I'm sure he's up on that balcony describing in full detail what sweet little Aria did in class today and I can assure you the more people you teach that to, the better."

"You're such a bitch," I playfully bantered.

"Whore," Sara grinned wickedly.

"Yea, whore!" Caitlyn blurted out.

"Caitlyn! How bout we take it easy there, sister," Sienna countered.

"Oh, sorry. I just thought that was the thing to do," Caitlyn responded as she rolled her eyes in sarcastic apology.

Sara and I both laughed as everyone joined in and just like that, my slutty escapade that I was trying so hard to hide became center stage. *Damn.*

"It's all in the tongue," I said sitting back down on my log beside the fire.

"Okay, ladies. Sara made up that last game just to see Aria squirm. How about some real Truth or Dare," Sienna said. "Sara, since you're sitting to my right, you first. Other than here, where is the kinkiest place you've ever had sex?"

Sara took a second and contemplated the question and then she blurted out so matter-of-factly, "In Aria's bedroom, on her bed."

"What?" I said as everyone started laughing uncontrollably.

"Well, since we're all telling the truth here tonight," Sara said as she shrugged her shoulders at me causing everyone to laugh even harder, "Remember a couple weeks ago when you thought your bed was a little sticky? Yea, that was us," she joked. Everyone laughed harder. Our group was definitely the rowdiest and most animated among the campfires.

"Oh, that is so gross!" I said.

"What's the difference if the cum was in your mouth or on your sheets?" Sara asked. The laughter roared on. I knew she was kidding but my face still reddened in the glow of the fire.

"Aria, it's your turn. Truth…who did you think of the first time you masturbated to orgasm? Give us his name," Sienna said grinning.

I laughed aloud for the first time today. "Colt." I just smiled at Sara. "Like Amber said, he's hot."

"I know," Sara leaned in and giggled with the others and me.

"That was when you had your first orgasm? Oh, you poor thing," Caitlyn snickered.

"What-evs," I said, batting my eyes toward Caitlyn. *I never would admit this to anyone but there were times I would hear Colt and Sara going at it for hours in our apartment that we shared and I would get so turned on. I would imagine Colt was making love to me instead. He was a machine and they would go for hours on end. I would hear them cry out with orgasm after orgasm. I could even tell when they were getting close to climax. Then I would slip my hand down into my panties and build up with them. Sadly, I had to pleasure myself while Colt rocked Sara's world but the fantasy in my head made me feel less pathetic.* After all our laughter died down we continued the game.

"Okay, here's a question for everyone. Did anyone else here masturbate to Colt?" Sienna asked.

"Yes," everyone chimed in. Sara beamed at all of us. We laughed until it was getting hard to breathe. At least I wasn't alone in my desire.

"Another truth, has anyone masturbated to the steamy Avery Jameson?" Sienna said, raising an eyebrow to everyone. Everyone erupted into laughter and giggles. "I'll take that as a yes," she chuckled.

"Oh, one more Truth question for you, Aria. How embarrassed were you when you yelled 'Spill it Cox' during the meet and greet?" Sienna asked.

"Mortified, " I said having just finished my sixth beer. This only seemed to make Caitlyn laugh.

"I heard that Avery is wild in bed. A regular ol' steam engine," Caitlyn said. "They say he designed the Sybian himself and that the cock on the machine is an exact latex replica of his," Caitlyn added. She had a raw timbre about her voice like when someone scrapes their fork across a plate.

"He can seduce me anytime," Amber said. Amber had silky ebony hair, with big dark eyes, pouty lips, and olive skin. *And there it was. Everybody wanted Avery.* He was such a player. He built this camp for his own personal playground.

"I think I would die and go to heaven," Caitlyn's voice purred. But to me it sounded like a cat crying out in a bathtub.

I stared at the crackling flame, watching it devour every piece of wood. Its coals were red hot. Embers were trailing into the night sky. I lifted my head in the direction of Avery's cocktail hour and in that moment I couldn't help myself, I was wondering if he thought about earlier today. *Probably not,* my subconscious sneered.

"Could you imagine having sex with that man? He's a god. Ugh, I'm wet just thinking about him," Caitlyn pressed on. *Okay Caitlyn, you made your point. You're a whore.*

"I know, right," Maya trilled. Maya was tall and had a dark pixie haircut and dark brown eyes. Her ears were pierced three times and a she wore a hoop in her upper right part of her ear. I could see a tattoo on her right shoulder but it was too dark to make it out. I thought back to the tattoo on Travis' chest. *He must really love Maya*, I thought.

"I would love to have the chance to rock his world," the bartender named Kim said. Kim was petite and pencil thin. Her natural color was dishwater blonde but she wore it with highlights.

I looked to Sienna to see a small smile move to her lips. I wondered if she had ever succumbed to the ways of Avery Jameson. The thought of Avery's closeness on the four-wheeler and how I wanted him to devour me seemed to suffocate me. My wicked thoughts were doused in ice water as I remembered how quickly he rejected me. I couldn't take anymore at that point. Before I knew it, I was on my feet and frowning.

"Aria, what's wrong?" Sara and Sienna both asked.

"I gotta pee," I lied. Well, it really wasn't a lie. I really did have to pee. I started to head in toward the restroom when I ran directly into Caitlyn. In my drunken state, I lost balance again and hit the ground.

"Oh sorry," she exclaimed. "Here let me help you up." I could tell her pleasantry was fake but I reached out a hand and she yanked me up. "I'm heading into the restroom. You'll have to wait your turn," she said.

"I can't," I exclaimed. "I really have to go!"

"Just go out there on the lawn," she said. "It's pitch black out. No one will see you. Just step out there twenty yards or so." Then she turned and ran toward the Main House.

"Why don't you?" I hollered after her.

"I had really spicy Mexican earlier," she exclaimed as she hurried away. *Great, I don't wanna go in there after that anyway.*

"Just go over there and hurry back," Sara said.

I shrugged. Sara knew there have been many drunken nights, more so in high school than in college, that we were too drunk to make it to the bathroom so we squatted in the middle of the woods. I snagged a napkin beside the bag of hotdogs and buns that Sara brought and headed toward the dark middle of the courtyard.

The back lawn was very large, at least the length of several football fields and about as wide. I stumbled away from the campfires and still farther away from the lodge where it became extremely dark.

My head buzzed from the alcohol and I took in the sound of the frogs and crickets singing to the hot humid June night. The party up on the second floor terrace was really humming. *God, I loved this place.* I hadn't lied when I told Avery that it felt like home.

I came upon a spot that I thought was far enough away. The moonless night helped me feel more at ease. The lodge glowed beautifully but the darkness shielded me perfectly. I couldn't wait any longer so I unzipped my shorts and pulled them down to my knees and squatted in the grass.

I really loved the outdoors. The seclusion of darkness and nature, it made it liberating in so many ways. That was what I was thinking when someone hit the lights and the courtyard lit up bright white like a playoff game at Cleveland Indians Stadium.

Have you ever been driving down the road when a poor little defenseless animal just sits in the middle of the road looking surprised as hell that someone is there, when in fact, it was perfectly happy to be going about its own business in the dark all by itself. Well, that was me; the deer in headlights, the poor raccoon, or maybe even the possum. There I was with my pants around my ankles in mid-stream flashing the whole camp. The bright lights running along the entire length of the lawn illuminated everything including me. I'm sure the whites of my eyes were clearly visible for miles as I squatted in the middle of it.

It was then I realized I really hadn't wandered that far at all. Here I was on full display to everyone looking out the back to the courtyard, including Avery. Everything stopped. The music stopped. The crickets stopped, and even the frogs. The DJ on the second floor balcony even pulled the record. At first, it was still, so very quiet. It was sadly beautiful, but then it came. It started out so distant but it quickly grew like a small wave breaking against a rocky shore but this one grew into a tidal wave. The laughter rose like a thunderous tsunami until it reached my ears. The entire camp roared. All the Cubs stood overlooking the balcony laughing at me joining the chorus of Kittens crowded along the fire pits. I'm pretty sure someone even whistled. I was right smack in the middle of the courtyard for the entire camp to see.

At that very moment, I was praying to God, like that poor defenseless animal that someone would knock me out and put me out of my misery. But then my subconscious reared up and reminded me, *you'd just be a knocked out drunk with her pants pulled down around her ankles.* So, I did what any sensible drunk would do; I hurried to pull my pants up, I lowered my head, and ran like hell.

⌘

DAY FOUR:
THURSDAY LATE NIGHT
HERE BUNNY, BUNNY

The laughter echoed throughout the camp as I pushed quickly through the bushes that lay off to the side of the great back lawn. *Why was I too lazy to walk to the bushes? Other people were sneaking into them to piss when the restroom was busy. I should have, too. God, I was such an idiot. That's what I get for being stupid and not going inside the Main Lodge to pee, I could always count on my fucking head to tell me what I did wrong. Well guess what? Everyone just caught you peeing in the middle of the lawn,* my subconscious sneered.

I clenched my fists and ran toward my cabin. I didn't want to be alone. But I couldn't go back to the fire, certainly not now after the most embarrassing moment of my life. I slammed the door of our cabin hoping it would diffuse some of my frustration. Then abruptly, I strode to my bedroom determined to pack my things and find someway out of this hell. I was sure that if I started hiking west through the woods I'd come out on a road eventually. I didn't care if I had to walk all the way back to Ohio. I was out of here.

The door opened behind me and Sara stepped toward me. I just turned my head into her shoulder and cried. I could feel her try to sooth me, but I could feel her tension even more. I pulled away and looked up at her. Sara was beyond pissed. There were only two times since I knew Sara that she had been this angry. The one was when she caught Jake cheating. The second was when Nate Gregor took my virginity and tossed me away like a piece of trash. This was number three and she was furious.

"What is it?" I looked back at Sara.

"After the lights mysteriously lit up the lawn like a football stadium guess who came back laughing her ass off and gloating that she felt like giving you the spotlight tonight," Sara said through clenched teeth.

"That bitch!" I seethed. "I'm going to find her and kick her fucking pretty girl ass," I said, heading towards the door.

"Wait! We have to deal with this by more sinister means," Sara said. "But not in a way that will get us kicked out. I want to see her suffer publicly. We need to humiliate her in a more dignified manner and knock her out of that ivory tower and it's going to take some thinking. We have to study her and find out what makes her tick then use that to embarrass her. But first I have an idea to get things started in the right direction. Think of it as an appetizer. Wait here a moment." Sara turned on her heel and headed toward her bedroom.

"Where are you going?" I asked.

"I'll be right back," Sara replied. She disappeared into her bedroom and in few minutes she returned clutching a brown paper bag. I looked at her quizzically. "Come with me," Sara said.

I followed her out the rear sliding door and down the steps of our back deck. Sara scanned the area looking around to make sure no one saw us. Then we headed across the back lawns and decks at the rear of the cabins, paying attention to remain covered in the shadows hidden from any pathway lights.

The new moon made it extremely dark and we moved easily undetected toward Caitlyn's cabin. Once on the back deck, Sara dug in her pocket and pulled out two slim metal pins. Actually, they were bigger than pins but much thinner than pencils. Sara handed me the bag as she knelt down and started working the two rods into the keyhole, picking the lock. My eyes widened.

"I didn't know you knew how to do that," I said. The door popped open and Sara smiled proudly at me and stood.

"Who do you think broke in and stole that Chem final our senior year."

I gaped at her. "That was you?"

"Later. I need you to focus, Aria." She stepped into the cabin and checked to make sure we were alone. I was sweating bullets. I had never done anything like this. My stomach was doing somersaults. An owl screeched outside and I nearly jumped out of my skin. I sucked in a deep breath trying to calm myself down. I didn't know what Sara was up to. *What the hell was in that bag?*

I followed Sara into one of the rooms as she opened up the closet. She shook her head. That must have been Kennedy's, her roommate's, room. We ducked out of the room and moved across the living room to the other bedroom. The layout was exactly like ours except the color scheme was beige and burgundy.

Sara moved to the closet, bent down, and pulled out a black pair of Jimmy Choo's. She squinted at the shoe size and smiled valiantly. *What the hell was she going to do with an overpriced pair of designer shoes?*

Sara set the bag down in front of her and pulled out an identical pair. She quickly swapped them out and closed the closet door.

"This will be a good opening salvo. Now come on, let's get out of here," she whispered.

We were halfway to the front door when we heard the voices outside the door coming down the walkway. It was Caitlyn and she had someone with her. Sara gripped my hand and pulled me toward the back sliding door, but before we could get there the front door started opening. We quickly reached for the hall closet. We both dove inside and miraculously Sara was able to get the door closed as I fumbled to catch the sweeper from falling over and crashing into the wall. I righted the sweeper back to its standing position and breathed a sigh of relief. *That was close.*

I turned slowly, rubbing against Sara but making sure I didn't bump anything else in the process. Sara cracked the door and peeked through. The space was not more than an inch but surprisingly we had a decent view of the living room. The lamp burst on and I could see Caitlyn guiding an older man to the couch. She leaned forward, grabbed his chin and kissed him roughly on the mouth. The Spanish man smiled widely up at her.

"Wait here, Rodriguez. I have something very special for you," Caitlyn's snarly voice said. Rodriguez was one of the gardeners at camp. He was somewhat short with balding peppered black and gray hair with a belly that looked like it encased a bowling ball. It hung bubbling over his belt like it was its own country. I passed by him often when I was out for a run or heading to class.

Rodriguez shifted in his seat in anticipation and when Caitlyn turned away he quickly adjusted himself. *Yuck. How could he be turned on by this woman?*

Sara let the door creak open and took a step forward but then quickly snapped back. Rodriguez was too close to us. We couldn't sneak out without being seen. *Damn it. I was going to kill Sara for this.* I took a step forward to follow but when Sara jumped backwards I slammed into Sara's back. My feet tumbled over the sweeper and I stubbed my toe. I threw my hand over my mouth to try to silence my outburst.

"Shhh," Sara whispered. *Damn that hurt.*

Caitlyn returned to the living room wearing a black see-through teddy and carrying a large beige nylon bag and handed it to Rodriguez. "Go put this on and meet me back here. Hurry, I'll get us some shots of Patron." He nodded and stood. He disappeared into her room and Caitlyn turned toward the kitchen. *Shit.* We still didn't have a chance to bolt free. The kitchen and living room were wide-open layouts and both Sara and I could easily see her and she could see us if we tried to move. I was afraid we'd be here for awhile.

"What are we going to do?" I whispered to Sara.

"We'll wait them out. They can't go all night, can they?"

I scowled at her. *God, I hope not. Why couldn't they go back to her bedroom? Why did she have to make such a show of all this?*

Then I realized whom I was talking about. Caitlyn made a show of everything. She probably wanted her roommate to come home and join them. We both peered through the crack of the door as we heard bobbling from the other room. Whatever he was doing in there sounded like a lot of effort. I'm not sure what was happening in there but it sounded like he fell over.

Finally, the doorknob jiggled and turned and out walked Rodriguez in a large white furry bunny costume. Caitlyn stepped back into the living room carrying two shots with her and not looking like anything out of the ordinary was happening. Meanwhile, in the tiny flyspeck closet both Sara's and my eyes were so wide we could have passed for owls.

"Sit," she commanded to her bunny fellow, setting down the shots on the end table beside the couch. Rodriguez, in his full bunny suit, sat in the middle of the couch. Caitlyn downed her shot then straddled the gardener and started grinding on him.

"Oh my god, I know what this is. She's a furry!" Sara whispered. A *furry what…rabbit?*

I didn't know what she meant. So, I peered around Sara to see Caitlyn reaching into his crotch and pulling out Rodriguez's penis or rather it looked like a penis but much smaller. I fought back my snicker at Caitlyn's grimace as she continued to use her thumb and index finger to stroke him. She was having a hard time pulling on his little wee willie and trying not to bump into his belly with her hand as she stroked him. Then she started getting angry as her little fingers started pumping really fast like the piston of an old Chevy.

Rodriguez winced in pain from her rough hands…er…

fingers but then he wrapped his hands around her waist and drew her near. He moved Caitlyn on his lap as she groped his tiny tent pole trying to get it inside of her. They fumbled and bounced as she tried everything to get him inside her. It was so bizarre. His petite penis, soccer sized bulbous belly, and furry rabbit costume were all working efficiently to keep his winky from entering her cold cut combo.

Several more tries and a moan later and Rodriguez was cuming all over Caitlyn's very expensive manicured hands.

Sara smothered her giggle and I could feel her tense up in front of me. I was so close to losing it that I thrust my hand in my mouth and bit down. It really hurt but it was worth it for this show. Suddenly, I felt so much better.

"Get out," Caitlyn barked at Rodriguez as he pulled off the head to the bunny costume.

"I'm sorry, Senorita," he apologized.

"I said. Get. Out."

Rodriguez quickly jumped up and changed back into his clothes and in record time he was flying out the door.

Caitlyn flipped the light off, stormed back to her bedroom and slammed her door so loud that the walls shook slightly.

I could hear the sound of the shower stirring. Sara grabbed my hand and pulled me to the back sliding glass door. We stumbled onto the patio barely containing our laughter. Sara and I took off toward our cabin. As soon as we were a hundred yards or so from Caitlyn's we fell into a fit of giggles and both fell to the ground rolling over and over covering ourselves in dirt and leaves as we laughed hysterically.

"What's a furry?" I said as I tried to catch my breath enough to form the words.

"You just saw it first hand. He was going to fuck her with the bunny suit on."

We laughed even harder then as I paused catching my breath. "Why did you switch out her shoes?"

"You'll see tomorrow night at the theme party. Come on," Sara said as she rose to her feet. "First things first, you need wine and a hot bubble bath." I smiled as we headed back to our cabin.

⌘

DAY SIX:

SATURDAY
LEATHER & LACE THEME PARTY

Saturday night came quickly. I kept mostly to myself
yesterday preferring to blow off the day's activities. But Sara
would not let me skip tonight's theme party. Sara and I
entered the Jameson Main Lodge. I wore my black hot
pants, a black rhinestone leather corset with a sweetheart
neckline, and little black lace panties with leather platform
knee boots. I really wasn't ready to face such a massive
room full of people, but Sara forced me here.

Tonight's party theme was Leather and Lace. As we got
comfortable, I left Sara to go to the bar for a shot. I
ordered my usual, a double. I scanned the crowd and
realized everyone was here. Forty Kittens and forty Cubs
with thirty instructors and the handsome Avery Jameson all
crammed into the same room. *What could be worse?*

"Isn't that the girl that was peeing in the courtyard?" A
woman in an uptight bun said to her friend. *Scratch that. My
night just got worse.*

I almost let the comment get to me but I finally found
my bearings, calmed down and headed to the ladies' room.
I quickly closed the door behind me and leaned my back
against the wall. I rubbed my eyes, trying to block out my
inner thoughts. I stopped mid-rub, remembering the inch

of make-up that Sara had applied. I looked at my hands and I was thankful nothing rubbed off. I stepped to the mirror to check my makeup.

Caitlyn wobbled in wearing an irritated expression. She quickly replaced her scrunched up brow with a fake smile. I tweaked my eyeliner, running my finger under my eye to remove a light smudge, as Caitlyn took narrowed unstable steps toward the sink.

We exchanged brief acknowledgements. I kept expecting her to gloat for being clever enough to expose my peeing habits to the whole camp but she was definitely preoccupied. So, after finishing, I decided to head to the bar. I found a different bartender, in case the other one was counting my drinks. We're not suppose to get too drunk... 'Inability to perform if in a drunken state, blah, blah, blah,' Avery said. I ordered whiskey because I needed something with a little more edge and a little more pain, plus it numbed my mind. I liked it. *Yummy.* They weren't counting. Maybe Colt said something to them.

In a short time, I've had three shots on an empty stomach. I was pretty sure that I was swaying in my boots.

Avery's voice resonated through the room, welcoming everyone, and I quickly asked the bartender for another shot, trying to block out his voice and the constant whispering around me.

"Tonight we'll be having the first qualifying rounds of the pole dancing competition. Second round will not be held next Wednesday as it's the Fourth of July Masquerade Ball but qualifying will resume next Saturday. The other judges and I will choose three Kittens each night to advance to the semifinals. Top six advance to the finals that will be held during the Camp Olympics. Remember, the winner of the Olympics gets an all expense paid trip to Hawaii. So good luck, Kittens," Avery said.

"There you are. I wondered where you disappeared to." Sara studied my face. "What's wrong?"

"Nothing. I'm just getting drunk is all." *Liar.* I quickly snuffed out my relentless subconscious.

She narrowed her eyes at me and frowned. "You need food."

I didn't have the strength to argue so I shrugged my shoulders and said, "Okay." I downed another shot then followed Sara to our table. We joined Travis, Maya, Sienna, Sean, Colt and Pierce. Colt quickly introduced Sara and me to another instructor named Kara.

Everyone settled into idle chat and dinner was served. I munched on my roll and enjoyed my buzz.

"You better sober up some," Sara said handing me the roster for the pole-dancing contest. "You're on the list to dance tonight. I'm counting on you to win this." *What a fucking buzz kill.* I took the paper from her and glanced down at it. I was last.

"Are you serious?" I asked. *So much for getting drunk tonight.*

"Once you're up there dancing no one's going to remember you're the girl who peed. Well, they might remember, but they won't care because they'll be so turned on. That is if you do a good job," Sara said.

"Fine." I scanned the crowd and took in the sea of black leather and lace. The women were magnificent. Each outfit was different. There were so many variations of each one pressed firmly against their skin. I noticed that it was mainly the women who dressed up for the Theme Parties. The men as usual, wore dress pants and button up shirts.

By the time dinner arrived, my mouth was watering for the chicken and veggies I ordered, or Sara ordered, I wasn't quite sure. I giggled to myself because this was the first time I could honestly say I didn't have the answer to such a simple question, and I didn't care.

After dinner, the chatter of the room escalated. I sipped on my beer when the DJ's voice rang out into the microphone. "Judges, please report to the judging table."

Colt, Sienna, Travis, and Maya stood and went to the judge's table to join Avery.

"Kennedy Myers, please report to the DJ booth," the DJ's voice added, then a Chasing Seven song 'Comfort Zone' broke the silence of the room.

Kennedy sashayed up to the booth in her killer black leather knee boots and emerald green lacy panties. More than one set of eyes were on her as she smiled and leaned over to give her song request to the DJ. She had poker straight medium length blonde hair. Her platform boots made her 5'4" frame appear taller. Her sun-kissed skin glowed as she stepped up onto the stage into the dancing lights. The song changed to a dance beat as she braced the pole. Now all eyes in the room were on her. The room had never been more full. *Was everyone going to watch?*

Kennedy sauntered around the pole, dipped down and shook her ass. She lit up the stage with her megawatt smile and her seductive moves. Her rhythm was flawless. She was confident in her technique and as she finished the 'Cleopatra' and 'Daphne' moves the crowd applauded loudly. Then it was Caitlyn's turn.

Sara leaned over into my ear and whispered, "Did you know that I am a whole shoe size smaller than Caitlyn." I looked at her curiously. "Bet she can't for the life of her figure out why suddenly her shoes don't fit."

My mouth fell open and I couldn't stop the laughter that burst out of me. Caitlyn very clumsily took the stage like a new baby calf learning to walk just after its birth. Caitlyn glared in our direction as I quickly tried to muffle my laughter. Now it all made sense. Sara's plan was brilliant.

Caitlyn was awkward and very unsteady. Her legs were knocking as she wobbled, trying to steady herself by gripping the pole as the music began to play.

Caitlyn was shaky as she slipped and stumbled, trying to keep her balance and kick off the ground with momentum. She tried to kick her legs upward but had no strength as she barely got her legs over her head to meet the pole but then she drifted downward until she knocked her head on the floor. The couple at the table next to us nearly spit out their drinks as Caitlyn slid downward. She was floundering on moves that she had done so well before in class.

Giggles started near the back of the room and crept forward, spreading like a sage brush fire in a dry forest. Her flopping was beyond any amount of description. Sweat clung to her skin and nervousness ground into her eyes as I could tell she had no idea why her shoes didn't fit anymore. The harder she tried, the more frustrated and confused she got. She had little control over her steps.

She bounced higher on the pole and slid downward but when her feet hit the floor they wobbled and gave out and she crumpled downward like a poorly built house of cards.

Booing replaced the laughter as it began to echo through the crowd as someone yelled 'get off the stage'.

Finally, to end her agony, the DJ cut the song and Caitlyn was forced off the stage.

A small part of me felt bad for her, but then there was the larger part that truly felt that she deserved everything she got.

Lucy went next and her moves were seductive and strong, as she teased the pole between her legs.

The night continued on as the next contestant, Amber, was called to the stage. I took off my hotpants and then readjusted my leather corset and smoothed my panties as I waited for my name to be called. I could see Sean watching me out of the corner of his eye. So was Sara. *Ahh hell, the whole room had just watched me undress.*

They all smiled to each other like they shared in a secret that I did not. *Why were they all staring at me?*

I quickly pulled my hair into a loose ponytail and refocused on the stage. I shifted nervously in my seat, waiting for my name to be called. *Of course I was last.*

I could feel my conviction falter after I stopped at the DJ booth to request my song. I made my way to the pole center stage in my five-inch high knee boots with front laces and centered myself in front of the pole. *The pole is not the main attraction, I am,* I told myself.

I spread my legs wide and raised my arms above my head, grasping the pole behind me, and waited to begin. The lights were blinding. I squinted to see all in attendance. I could see movement out of the corner of my eye and Colt talking to the guy at the sound booth. The lights in the audience went out and the only table I could see was the judges table bathed in a soft white light. I gave Colt a grateful smile as he sat down at the judge's table. Sara stood behind him, beaming with a proud smile.

The judges, who were Colt, Sienna, Travis, and Maya sat with Avery who was dressed in a black button-up pinstripe dress shirt, black pants, and a black two-button vest. I wanted to breathe him in. I thought of his sweet cologne mixed with sweat and my mouth was watering. I didn't know why, but I wanted to do this for him.

I closed my eyes and let my thoughts take me back to this first week of camp at how shy and timid I had been. I knew, because of the alcohol, I was more relaxed but my thoughts were fuzzy and at the same time it had also given me courage. I could let go and embrace some of my sexuality. I could do this.

The music began and loud guitars ripped through the loud speaker as 'Something In The Water' played from Chasing Seven. It was one of my favorite dance songs. I remembered what Sienna told me, 'find your focus in the crowd.' My eyes locked on Avery and I knew what I had to do. *Don't think, just feel the music.*

I saw him lean back in his seat and drape his arm over the back of his chair and spread his legs wider under the table. He ran his fingers over his bottom lip and a slow seductive grin followed. My smile widened in return and now I was ready to do this for him, only him.

A few beats into the music and my hips started swaying. I pressed my buttocks back against the pole and rubbed it back and forth to the music. I lowered myself to the floor with my legs together and my hands trailed down the pole. I let go of the pole and slid my hands down my legs to my knees and pushed my legs apart. I stroked my thighs, my sex, and moved up my flat stomach and over my breasts. I reached for the elastic band in my hair and let my hair cascade down my shoulders. I rotated my hips into a bucking motion and rose to my feet. All the while, my eyes were locked on Avery's and his were locked on mine. Suddenly, I was only dancing for him.

I rounded the pole and circled to build up momentum. I spun around with my leg curled around it like Sienna had showed me. I planted my feet on the floor then dipped down and back up.

I paced around the pole and turned my ass toward the audience. I bent over and rubbed my hands across my buttocks slowly, holding it there for Avery to see.

I stood and sucked in a deep breath and built up momentum again. With my upper body strength, I lifted myself up mid-spin and wrapped my legs tightly around the pole, then climbed to the top of the pole. I kicked my legs up to the space above me and squeezed my thighs. I gripped the pole between my legs and held myself out horizontal, holding my arms outright like a beautiful swan. Then, I bent at my waist, gripping the pole in my hands, and arched my back, swinging my legs around gaining force to ascend once more to the top of the pole. I kicked my legs upward then spun my feet around into the pole, pushing my body outward as I flipped and dismounted.

I kicked into a helicopter and twisted until my back landed flat against the pole and reached my arms back to find the pole above my head. I let my hands skim the pole as I bent my knees and sank to the floor. I arched my back, showing off my breasts, and held the pose as the song ended while I bit my lip seductively.

Everyone cheered as the lights of the Jameson Main Lodge turned back on. I looked at Avery one last time and smirked. The heated look in his eyes only fueled my desire. I saw Colt and Sienna flash a look to each other, then Avery. Their eyebrows were raised in surprise. I took in a shaky breath and stepped to the stairs. Familiar arms swooped around me, picked me up, and spun me around.

"That was fucking hot as sin," Sara gushed. I beamed at her, completely blown away that I could even do that. I just went with the moment and that is where it took me. "You're no longer that girl who peed in the courtyard, you just blossomed into a sexy-ass Kitten and made every guy in this room want to get in your panties."

"Thanks for reminding me," I grimaced.

"Let's hear it for the contestants," Avery's voice echoed out into the Main Lodge. When the applause died down he continued.

"I will take the top three highest scores from tonight and next Saturday and those six will proceed to the semifinals. Here are the results. Third place goes to Amber Bensen." The crowd cheered and whistled.

"Second place goes to Kennedy Myers." The crowd grew louder.

"And first place goes to... Arabella Mason."

They went nuts and cheered wonderfully as their applause rang so loud it hurt my ears. I just grinned and waved at everyone as hands appeared from all sides congratulating me and hugging me. Avery smiled widely.

"Great job, Kittens. Enjoy the rest of your night, folks,"

he announced, and then stepped off the stage and swung his arms around a tall blonde and then a brunette and brought them into his sides.

I frowned as they disappeared down the hall toward a room. Sara elbowed me in the ribs and I tried to hide my disappointment as she nodded toward Caitlyn. She had kicked her shoes off and was rubbing her feet with sullen anger on her face. *Revenge was sweet. Especially, when it came in the form of giant blisters.*

◆Week Two:

⌘

DAY EIGHT:
MONDAY MORNING
MASTURBATION CLASS

Monday morning breakfast was quick today as I actually looked forward to class. I still felt proud about my win Saturday night and hoped that today's lesson would allow me to relax. I secretly hoped it would be sensual massage. They never told us in advance what each morning's lesson would be. They said it would heighten our senses and excitement. It usually worked.

As I entered the cabin I greeted the five other girls in my class as I took a seat on the floor. The carpet was thick and plush in this room with pillows strewn all over and padded posts spaced evenly around the room. This room was definitely made to be comfortable. We were gathered in a semicircle as Colt stepped in front of us.

"Today class will be a mixture of masturbation and toys," Colt said. *Bummer, I wanted a massage.*

"Sienna and I are going to mix a few techniques to bring you the most pleasure. I'll have you start with some deep breathing exercises to help you relax." Sienna lowered the lights and lit a few candles. "Take off your panties and lay back and make yourself comfortable. There is no one here but us. No distractions."

I must be getting used to all this because I simply obeyed and shimmied out of my panties. I laid back on the thick plush floor covered with pillows, and closed my eyes. I let the vanilla mixed with lavender scent fill my senses as I concentrated on my breathing. Soft classical music filtered from the speakers around me. Colt knelt close to me as Sienna instructed the others.

"In the past classes you've found it hard to relax enough to climax. And I understand that it's difficult to do so when someone is watching and not sexually involved. So today, I want to aid you in the final delivery by using a vibrator. I can assure you that if you lay back and enjoy its pulsating rhythm that you will reach orgasm. Most women can't resist their charms," Colt said to me. I smiled softly up at him as he clicked on the wand.

"I want you to tease yourself with it until you're squirming in need then I'm going to take it from you and push your body to its limits and ensure that you reach your climax." I nodded, obeying his every word. He could have asked me to punch an old man in the head and I would have done it for him. I was nervous with anticipation. I felt my insides clench in desire as I opened my legs for him. Colt had a way of dousing me with his words and I was instantly squirming in need.

"Start by letting it massage your clit softly and relentlessly," Colt said. I closed my eyes then skimmed the vibrator over my Helmut hide-a-way and let it work its magic. I gyrated my pelvis into it and before I knew it, Colt took it from my hands and switched it off. *WTF?* I opened by eyes to see why he stopped.

"Aria, I'm going to have you lift your arms above your head. And then I'm going to put a pair of handcuffs around each wrist and then restrain your hands to that post." *What?*

I glanced over at the post that lay a few feet from me and then quickly at him and saw Colt's calm smiling face looking back at me. I wasn't sure about being restrained. Giving up control to someone else can be overwhelming. Even if I did trust Colt more than anyone else, except Sara, I wasn't sure I could let go enough for restraints.

"I know you've never tried anything like this, but I promise you, I won't be doing anything other than using the vibrating wand. Sienna's soft touch will aid you in your relaxation."

Sienna joined me on the floor after giving the other girls their instructions. I gathered that I must be the slow kid in this class judging from all the extra attention I was getting.

Colt continued, "These cuffs are leather so they won't be tight on your wrist. I want you to push your own limits. Our goal is to bring you extreme pleasure at the same time we are expanding your boundaries. So trust me when I say, we'd never hurt you."

"I know," I said nervously. I held my arms out to the post as Colt clicked the handcuffs in place and I watched with interest as his dexterous hands restrained my small wrists. I shivered as he ran his fingers down the length of my arms. A small smile splayed on his face as he took in the scene of me cuffed and at his mercy with no panties on and my legs parted. His face darkened as his eyes roamed over my body a second time. *It's a good thing I shaved this morning.*

"It's not too tight, is it?" I shook my head at Colt as he checked the leather handcuffs to make sure they weren't hurting me. "Good. Here's your mask."

"You never said anything about being blindfolded?" I said, but the words fell on deaf ears as neither Colt nor Sienna responded as I lifted my head and let him pull it over my eyes. His hands were warm and I couldn't wait for him to touch me. Something changed in me this week. Maybe it was because I wanted to erase all the thoughts of wanting Avery or maybe it was because over the last week Colt had been the one constantly turning me on, but I was starting to crave it.

I could hear Colt switch on the vibrating wand as I closed my eyes. After a moment, I felt it touch my shoulders. It had a warming setting and my body relaxed into it. He ran it between my breasts and down my belly. He stroked it around my navel and down my hips. He traced the line of my legs to my feet then ran it up my inner thighs.

As I lay there blindfolded, with the music playing, I could feel my breathing pick up and I could hear Sienna's getting heavier. I wondered if this was getting to her like it was getting to me.

Colt teased me with the same sensual strokes until my hips squirmed with desire for what he brought next. I heard the wand click and he sped up the intensity and let it rest against my silk funnel. I moaned in pleasure as the oscillations coursed through me. My sweet briar grew moist instantly and I tilted my pelvis deeper into it.

"That's right, Aria, feel it," Colt said in a low voice. I heard Sienna move forward then her tender touch kneaded my arms in sensual strokes. I had spent the last eight days with her and I was becoming very comfortable.

The sledgehammer combination of Colt stroking my clit with the vibrator and Sienna's soft touch, forced my body to burn with intense desire. I loved their touch and I really loved how quickly my body responded. I loved feeling seduced. I was really starting to enjoy the dynamics of each class as I could hear the other girls moaning from their own fingers as they watched my show before them. I was in darkness behind my mask. This helped to amplify the sensations that my body was experiencing. I loved the touch and the feel of hands all over me. Then I felt other hands on me, more than just Sienna's, At least two more sets of soft female hands followed by another then another. They glided and caressed all over me. *God, it was intense...so amazing....ahhh....it felt so good.*

Colt trailed wet soft kisses on my hips and across my navel. My body bowed off the floor and tugged on my cuffs that anchored me to the post as it craved more. I moaned softly and felt my legs tighten. The hands were all over me now. No place was sacred as they explored every inch of my being.

Colt continued to rotate the vibrator over my clit and someone slipped two fingers inside me.

"Aaah..." I moaned as the intensity of so many touching and stroking my arms and chest, the vibrator quaking over my kitty cage, and the fingers inside me, pushed me higher and higher. Fingers dipped in and out of me slowly. I let my head fall back and pulsed my hips in rhythm to them.

I knew by Sienna's warm hands that she pulled my bra down to expose my nipples and rolled them between her fingers. *God that felt amazing.* I had never had so much stimulation all at once like this and my body was humming loudly.

With Sienna rubbing my nipples, Colt pressing the vibrator over my clitoris, and the luscious rhythm of fingers going in and out, tipped me over the edge. My body convulsed around their fingers and just when I thought it was over; they didn't stop. Colt replaced the feminine fingers with his rougher masculine ones and rubbed his two fingers against the front wall of my mystical fold and the orgasm intensified. My breath took and the burning within my legs and sex got stronger, building me higher and higher. My legs went numb and I could feel nothing except Sienna's fingers pulling at my nipples, the vibrator, and Colt's fingers pushing me more and more. My heart was pounding in my chest. My face felt heated, my ears thumped to the beat of my heart then it hit me quickly like a giant wave. I cried out in ecstasy as my mind spiraled out of control emblazoned by white stars, my entire body burned with fire and convulsed beyond any orgasm I had ever experienced, making all the others look like the tiny waves created by a skipping pebble on a shallow pond.

My chest heaved as Colt let his fingers slip in and out of me while the walls of my crimson palace shuddered hard and I pushed the fire through my veins. I was tied to a post, and I loved it. My best friend's boyfriend coaxed me into the best orgasm of my life, so far, because that is what she wanted, and I loved it. I was letting other women touch me, and I loved it. I was breathless and speechless.

Sara was right; I could see what drew her to this camp. This moment had surpassed everything I had ever known and my body soared like I was flying.

⌘

DAY EIGHT:
MONDAY AFTERNOON
NATE GREGOR

As I sat down at the lunch table, I thought about how it was the eighth day of camp and how this lifestyle was starting to take hold of me. I was wondering if everyone else was feeling the same kind of high that this place brought to me. After my class with Colt and Sienna I could honestly say that my curiosity was piqued. Sara gave me a warm smile and set her tray on the table and stood beside me.

"Why are you not sitting?" I asked, peering up at Sara.

Sara nibbled at her bite-sized cut up cantaloupe. "My V…A…G. is S...O...R...E. I rode the Sybian this morning in class. God, that thing was exquisite."

"Ugh. Spare me the details," I rolled my eyes and took a bite of my grilled chicken sandwich.

Sara giggled. "I plan to win the Sybian Rodeo. It's one of the main events in the Camp Olympics."

Colt kissed Sara softly on the lips and lowered himself to the chair beside me. Before I could stop myself, I wondered what it would be like to have Colt's lips on me. Then I started to really study them. The top lip was thinner than the bottom. He had just run his tongue over them and they were still moist. I squeezed my legs together under the

164

table, fighting the craving that was blossoming between my legs and the memory of what he did to my body this morning.

Colt raised an eyebrow at me and said calmly, "Aria, what are you staring at?"

I lowered my head as I flushed seven shades of scarlet and pushed a large bite of my sandwich into my mouth, trying to find an excuse for drooling over him the way that I was. I finally settled for an over-exaggerated shrug of my shoulders.

"Oh, no you don't. You can't look at me like that and not tell me what you're really thinking," Colt urged.

"Fess up, Aria," Sara said, leaning over in my direction and resting her hands on the table. She kind of stuck her butt out like she was trying to get her vagina some air.

I swallowed the large bite in my mouth. "What am I, an open book?" I said, looking back to Colt.

"Not your mind, Aria. But your body sure is," he wiggled his eyebrows knowingly.

"You suck, you know that. Both of you," I replied. They both laughed.

"As you so eloquently shouted the first night here at camp, spill it," Colt pressed.

I looked to see Sara take a sip of her iced tea and then she sat gingerly on the chair beside Colt. *She must have gotten her V..A..G enough A..I..R.* I looked at Colt and before I knew it, the words were tumbling out of my mouth.

"Okay, if you must know, I was thinking dirty thoughts about your delicious lips."

Sara spurted tea all over the table in front of her and choked on the small part that went down her throat. Colt patted her back and let his eyes melt into me.

"That has to be the sexiest thing I've ever heard come out of your mouth," Colt said, leaning closer. "It's amazing what a week here has done for you."

I shrugged nonchalantly back at them and then went back to my sandwich while they stared wide-eyed at me like I was a two-headed alien.

After noticing their stilled gaze not leaving my presence I decided to continue, "So, I can't help it if I like what I see. What's wrong with that?"

Colt let his head fall back in laughter. Sara's blue eyes lit up behind her long lashes.

"I think we've created a monster, how about you Colt?" as they both laughed.

"Hmmh. Yum," Colt replied. They both looked at me with a hunger in their eyes and I squirmed nervously in my seat.

"Stop it. You two are starting to really freak me out." Colt and Sara beamed and their laughter trailed off. Sara's face fell as her eyes fell on someone in the distance behind me.

"Don't look now but crazy bitch is glaring at you," Sara said. I froze in my seat and forced myself to only move my eyes to Sara.

"Who's crazy bitch?" Travis asked sitting down next to Colt with his lunch tray.

"Caitlyn," Sara said, answering Travis's question. Travis shuddered then dug in to his pulled pork sandwich. Sara's eyes moved back to me. "She has been on a rampage since you won the pole dancing contest. You are not her favorite person right now," Sara said to me.

"It's not like I had any control over the judging," I said, trying to keep my voice down as Maya, Sienna, and Sean all joined us.

"True," Sara agreed. Maya and Travis were Sara's instructors. *With all the couples sitting next to me, I always felt like the odd man out.*

I was pushing around a bite-sized piece of watermelon when I heard the sound of Avery's voice. Everyone looked up at him. Avery had a way of commanding the entire room.

"Travis, are you able to sub a Sybian class for Pierce? He's not going to make it in today."

"What time?" Travis asked.

"Two o'clock," Avery replied.

"Sure," Travis nodded.

"Great." Avery scanned the table and let his eyes land on me for a moment before he turned to leave. My heart sank and fluttered at the same time. I watched him walk away and disappear into the kitchen.

I frowned at the memory of a few days ago, and the image of him and the two women he was with. Then the memory of the waterfall flashed in my mind. That will be as intimate as I will probably ever get with Avery. *Who am I kidding? Why did I think he'd be into me? I knew the rule. He never falls in love with his guests. Why did I think that there could be something more?*

"Does that man ever have any fun?" Sara said.

I didn't answer Sara. I knew first hand that Avery was all business. My shoulders sagged. I didn't feel much like

167

eating now. I stuffed down a few bites, trying to pass the time, and pushed away my thoughts of Avery.

"What's up with you? You seem far away," Sara said. I could tell she wanted to delve further, but she didn't.

I shrugged, afraid of what may come out of my mouth. It might have been tears or words of anger. I was teeter-tottering on the edge of the abyss. *What better way to drown your sorrows than in a class designed to free you from all your inhibitions? A class that teaches you to let go with a metal pole between your legs. If I fall, who will be there to catch me?*

My thoughts continued to spiral out of control but I pulled myself back toward my ambitious side, forcing myself to go through the motions and get ready to head to my next class. Sara really knew how to read me like an open book. It was a good day at first, but now I wanted to hide behind my shame. Hide behind my feelings for the one man I could never have.

I stood when the group stood. I followed behind them to the trash and deposited my leftovers when I was rudely brought out of my self-wallowing by a hard elbow that dug into my upper arm.

"Watch it!" Caitlyn bellowed tossing her tray in front of mine. *Are you fucking kidding me? It's like we're back in high school.*

I grimaced and rubbed my arm hoping that *Barbie* didn't leave a bruise. *What was her problem?* As I was contemplating backhanding her, I didn't see the man stand up from the table behind me and turn toward me. I felt his cold salad dressing seep through my shirt. I felt his hot coffee burn my wrist and trail down my legs. The silverware and heavy glass plate made a huge racket as it clanked to the ground making a huge scene. *This day couldn't get any worse.*

He hurried to help wipe off my shirt with a bunch of napkins and handed me some. I dabbed my wrist and heard his voice before I made eye contact with his brown puppy dog eyes that always lured me in.

"Aria?"

I dropped the napkins and pushed his hands away. "Nate?" I said, all breathy as my eyes turned upwards. I sounded like a moron. *I stand corrected; my day just got a hell of a lot worse.*

"I'm sorry, are you okay?"

"Yea! I was just peachy when you forgot to call me ten months ago." *Damn. I really needed to say things in my head first.*

"I meant, did I burn you when I spilled my coffee on you?"

"Just stop, Nate," I said through clenched teeth. I hated this man. He crushed me. He made me weep like a little girl because he treated me like dirt after he took my virginity. He fucked me – then left me.

"Look Aria, I can explain. I was in a bad place back then, but I've changed. Maybe you can let me make it up to you. Let's get together tonight and have dinner or maybe a couple drinks," he said.

"Nate Gregor. I have only one thing to say to you. Fuck off!" Sara said, stepping up beside me and helping to wipe the ranch dressing off my shorts.

He smirked at her. "It's good to see you too, Sara. Listen Aria, if you change your mind I'm in Tigger Cabin. Come see me, please. I'll buy you a new pair of shorts from the camp store," he said as he walked in the opposite direction.

"Aria, you okay?" Colt and Avery said together as they walked up to us. Colt glowered at Nate but I could see Avery was trying to figure out the connection I had with Nate. I felt my cheeks turn fifty shades of gre...I mean red, as I shook the salad dressing from my shirt and shook out my hands.

I drew my lips into a straight line. "I'm fine. I just... I need to go change," I said and stepped toward the door.

"Good to see you again, Aria," Nate said, as I passed him on my way out of the lunch hall. I stopped and glared back over my shoulder.

"No, it really isn't, dickwad," Sara interceded as the group followed me out a few seconds later. I took that opportunity to leave. If there was one thing I loved and hated about Sara, I could always count on her to give it to ya straight whether you wanted to hear it or not.

After I changed my clothes, I slowly walked towards class, wishing I could expunge some of the memories from my head. It was hard gathering my thoughts after seeing Nate. *What was he doing here anyway and how did he find out about this place? Could he finally have come to his senses and decided I'm the girl for him?* I admit I did slightly stalk him for about a month or so after our night together. I just couldn't figure out why he didn't want me.

I sat in a daze for a few minutes, waiting for the rest of class to arrive, just looking out the window at the properly manicured garden stones and pathways trimmed with accent lighting that always left me at peace.

"Aria, do you want a massage before the others get here? You seem tense," Colt said.

I shrugged my shoulders at him and resumed staring out the window. I saw him look at Sienna out of the corner of my eye. Colt knew my history with Nate but it wasn't just that, I was feeling a little off this afternoon.

"Is there anything you want to talk about?" I shook my head and wrapped my arms around myself. Sienna nodded at him, and then he turned back to me. "Aria, you've had a great breakthrough this morning. Why don't you take the afternoon off? Go for a hike and enjoy the sunshine. You've earned it. We can pick up again tomorrow."

"What?" I said bringing my focus back to my instructors.

"Now that you've opened yourself up to the possibilities of new sexual encounters, there will be a point where you feel torn about things. You might feel guilty because you are reprogramming your values."

I blinked at him in confusion. Colt stood and walked near the massage table. "Okay, look at it this way. It's like your body has just been pumped full of sugar for the last week and you're crashing."

Sienna interceded. "To put it simply, you need a day to recharge."

I stood up and thanked both of them with my eyes. "Can I go?"

"Yea, see you tomorrow morning," Colt said.

I hurried for the door. I stepped outside the door and made a mental note not to run in Avery's direction. I didn't want to be near his house or any section of the woods behind his house. I just needed some space. I needed an ass-kicking run that would deplete me and recharge me at the same time. I turned right and ran towards the Cub section of camp. I hadn't been down many of those pathways yet so it seemed liked the right thing to do. I ran past A's Market, a work shed and a water station. A canoe station was set up beside the water's edge and I could make out the lake glimmering like a mirror as the sun hit its surface. I squinted and veered toward it. I wanted to stop and take in its beauty but I hadn't gone that far yet.

As I crossed into the cub section, I ran through several rows of cabins. I passed Tigger Cabin on my right, hoping that Nate wouldn't see me and think I was stalking him. I was just about to run past the cub communal area when I heard several Cubs hooting and hollering at me.

"Aria, come here for a second," Sean called out, bouncing the basketball in front of him on a small clay basketball court. I smiled nervously and forced myself toward him and his friends. I slowed my pace and trotted up beside Sean.

"I wanted to introduce you to my friends. This is Ethan and Wren Cartwright."

"Hi guys," I replied standing with my hands on my hips trying not to sound winded.

"Hi to you too, gorgeous," Ethan smiled widely. His eyes were dark like his hair. He was sexy as hell.

"Where have you been hiding all this time?" Wren smirked.

My eyes drifted to his well-cut chest as I glanced over both of them. They were twins with similar builds and hairstyles that if the light were dim enough they both could pass for Avery Jameson's brothers. That fact alone made them very appealing to me.

They looked me over for the second time. I just smiled. Sean chuckled as I shifted nervously on my feet under the heat of their gaze. I felt like a pork chop on a fat man's plate and my sweat from running provided the glaze.

This was that awkwardly pristine moment during a lull in conversation where I wasn't sure if I should continue my run or just close my eyes and let them rip my clothes off. The thought of being seduced by twins was thrilling to me. But then Sean broke that moment and handed me my exit. *Damn.*

"We'll let you get back to your run. I just wanted to take a second and introduce you. See you later."

I smiled appreciatively to Sean and gave them a little wave. They got back to their game and I continued my run.

I picked up the pace until I was in a full sprint and ran toward a lightly wooded area. I could see picnic tables at random intervals in the woods. I was excited to be somewhere new. I took some curves at a brisk pace, careful not to step on any roots or misplaced stones that lay near my footfalls.

In just a few minutes, I was heading down one of the more secluded pathways. The air felt warm and the sun broke through the tree canopy, illuminating the forest. I crossed over a small brook, careful not to slip off the large flat stones as I used them to cross the water then headed around another curve and up a steep hill.

I was about a mile into the deepening forest. I could feel the burn in my calves as I made it to the top and was just about to turn around when I saw Pierce and two girls sunbathing nude on a wide rock embedded in the earth at a small clearing near the edge of a ravine overlooking the lake.

I looked closer to see Pierce resting on a soft blanket on his side. His hips were angled to the side and a blonde woman was leaning over him. He moaned in delight as the woman stroked his shaft up and down. I stared as he wrapped his hands around a redheaded woman's pelvis and drew her closer. She quickly lay on her back and spread her legs wide for him. He pushed two fingers into her and I watched her writhe under him while his tongue found her clitoris.

I stepped behind a tree and looked around to see if anyone was nearby. I was panting from the strenuous run and my heart was beating against my chest, but my mouth fell open at the sight before me. *God, it was hot.*

I watched as the blonde submerged Pierce's cock with her mouth and his hips gyrated in anticipation. He reached up and pinched the redheaded woman's nipple in one hand. She rose off the blanket and cried out. He watched as she quivered underneath his vigorous tongue and continued to pulse his fingers in and out of her until she fell quiet.

Pierce lay back as the blonde moved to straddle him. She sunk down onto his engorged shaft and groaned with pleasure. Pierce hissed between his teeth and grabbed hold of her hips and swiveled his hips deep into her. He lifted her rapidly and I could hear the sound of skin against skin smacking.

The redheaded woman got to her knees and let her hands stroke gently over the blonde's body. She pinched the blonde's nipples between her fingers and the blonde threw her head back in pleasure. I was breathless as I watched the scene unfold. It was the most erotic thing I had witnessed so far.

Pierce sat up mid-thrust and the blonde was now sitting in his lap. He gyrated slowly as he cupped the redheaded woman's breasts then dipped down and sucked her nipples. He kissed her roughly and included her in his pleasure. The blonde was on his lap with his manhood buried deep within her. The redhead was lip-locked with his seductive tongue while she rubbed her clit with one hand and twisted the blonde's nipples with her other. Pierce kissed the redhead harder and thrust into the blonde deeper.

"Yea, baby, that's it. Cum for me. That's right," Pierce said. His voice was heavy and deep. The blonde bucked hard against him and shook as her body unleashed. The redhead rubbed her clit twice more and cried out with pleasure again. Pierce pumped once more, fell forward, and unloaded inside of her. All three were panting and left satiated.

I turned my back against the tree and hid behind it while I caught my breath. I was shaking, turned on, and for the first time I wanted to do those things. I wanted to feel that kind of pleasure. I could see the pleasure pool before me and I wanted to dive in. I stepped back out onto the path and ran back to camp, toward my fantasies.

⌘

DAY NINE:
TUESDAY MORNING
SENSUAL TOUCH CLASS

"I heard you met Wren and Ethan Cartwright yesterday. Did you like either of them? They're both pretty hot aren't they?" Sienna said.

"Sure, I mean yes, they are both quite attractive," I said, distracted. I was thinking about the masquerade ball tomorrow night. I didn't have anything to wear. Sara didn't pack me anything for such a fancy ball. All I had were costumes, corsets and sundresses and from what I've heard this is the second biggest ball of the camp.

"Sean said they were both really into you. And that if you want to hang out with them sometime, that he could arrange it." I shrugged not really hearing her.

"You seem tense again, Aria. You have to relax," Sienna said. She turned toward me and began to rub my shoulders as I sat on the edge of the massage table. I let my head fall back enjoying the feel of her hands. The continual strokes really helped relax me.

"Lay down," she commanded.

I laid on my back on the soft blanket of the massage table and let Sienna stroke my shoulders. I found myself wondering what it would be like to be with Sienna. She was gorgeous and I was flattered that she was here giving me a massage. I closed my eyes.

It was only Sienna and myself today, at least for the moment, so I let her rub my shoulders, working away knots in each one. She then moved down my arms, giving gentle squeezes. A few more strokes and my body was even more at ease. I thought of Avery and how badly I wanted it to be his hands caressing me. Then I started thinking of Ethan and Wren when Sienna let her hands trail down my breasts and rolled my nipples between her fingers. I could see myself with either one of them. My body arched upward in response. My thoughts then drifted to Colt and how I yearned for him inside me as I felt a gentle fur glove cascade down my shoulders, breasts, nipples, and belly, over the apex of my sex, then down my thighs to my feet. But when Sienna opened my legs wide then repeatedly caressed my inner thighs moving up again to my breasts and down again to my inside thigh, I forgot about men altogether.

My breathing increased and Sienna climbed over me, letting soft kisses reign down on my neck. *That's it. I was hers.* I wanted her lips on me as Sienna encouraged me to let my stress go. Sienna's lips were soft and warm on my skin.

I heard footsteps and looked to see Colt enter the room and sit in the far corner. Sienna ran her hand over my face and closed my eyes. Sienna gently kneaded my breasts and nipples then kissed my navel. My mind went numb and I wanted so badly to cum.

"Relax your mind and your body will follow. Block everything out except my voice and feel the heat of your skin rise as I touch you."

I could feel Sienna's gentle hands now gliding over my skin in the same pattern as the fur gloves. *Just feel,* I told myself.

"That's it," Sienna encouraged. Tenderly she touched me from head to toe and a gentle wave of warmth began to spread throughout my body. My nipples rolled between her steady fingers. My body arched again. Soft tender hands led down over my kitty and concentrated there with swift quick strokes, then my inner thighs one at a time. I moaned softly.

My legs stiffened as the touch went from my nipples to my apex and back again. My breasts burned and my sex was wet with anticipation. I ground my hips against her merciless hands as they reached my clit again. Steady fingers pressed small circles against me. I tilted my pelvis forward.

Her tempting hands continued on. The other hand gently glided down my inner thigh to my foot and in one swift motion pressed the nail of her thumb up the instep of my foot from heel to toe. That sent a quiver up my groin. With the circular motion on my clit and the spasm to my groin, I cried out. My vision fluttered and a mind-blowing orgasm erupted from within me.

I opened my eyes to Sienna and Colt smiling. I smiled nervously back at them. "Holy shit! Damn you're good," I said.

Sienna chuckled. "I know. I made you forget your worries didn't I?" I nodded my head appreciatively, and then I got dressed slowly, allowing my head to clear, and headed back to my cabin.

When I stepped through the doorway, Sara was grinning wide at me, which, usually meant she had been up to something.

"I have something for you. Well, two things really." I looked at her sideways.

"What did you do? The last time you were acting like this I got swept away to sex camp."

"Don't ruin my fun. It's an early birthday present." She reached behind the door and held up a garment bag.

I nervously undid the zipper and peeled back the bag to reveal the most stunning blue corset dress. My face broke into a smile. "Wow! This is beautiful." My eyes met Sara's and she was bouncing with joy.

"I knew you'd love it," she said.

"When did you get this?" I asked.

Her face fell a little. "Don't be mad, but I didn't like what you were planning to wear so I bought it today at Avery's boutique."

"He has a Boutique?"

"Yes. It's in the spa cabin. It features Sienna's new lingerie line. I'll have to take you there sometime," Sara said. I looked back at the dress. It would just cover up my behind. I could feel Sara eyeing me. I turned back to her and smiled.

"You did good," I said.

She squealed in delight. "You sure?" I nodded. "Okay, I got you some black thigh highs and you can borrow my stilettos. I brought two pair," she said, excitedly.

"This is going to be so much fun. I can't wait until tomorrow night. Maybe you will have hot sex with a masked stranger?"

I looked to the ground nervously. Sara grabbed my hand and stepped closer.

"Aria, it's been a week and a half, it's okay to hook up with someone," she said, studying me. "I know what you are thinking. There's the side of you that is a romantic at heart and secretly, you want to be swept off your feet. Then there's the part of you that is telling you that men will only hurt you. Don't let how Nate treated you in the past keep you from exploring who you really are. The guys are great here. It's all consensual sex. There are no misunderstandings this way. Just promise me you will think about it. One way or another, I'm getting you laid. Even if it's just you and me," Sara winked.

I laughed aloud. "I promise I will try to be more open about having sex," I said. "Geez, the things you make me do," I teased.

Sara let go of my hand and reached over the side of the bed and brought out a medium sized white paper shopping bag with handles.

"This is for you, also." Her eyes sparkled with excitement. I reached into the shopping bag and brought out a black satin pouch. I unraveled the strings that bound it and pulled out an elegant, laser-cut metallic blue butterfly-shaped eye mask with satin ribbon ties. It had silver sequined crystal-rimmed eyes. I gasped.

"Isn't it perfect?" Sara squealed. "This is a masquerade ball after all. We have to wear our masks until midnight. That's the rule. No matter what happens, keep it on until midnight, but you're allowed to take everything else off," she winked.

I loved this mask. It was so elegant. I could only think how it matched the colors of the blue sundress I wore when Avery and I met the first day of camp down by the lake, and his reference to me being a beautiful butterfly that had him hypnotized. I swallowed hard, trying to bury how it made me think of the morning we spent at the waterfall. The butterfly we saw was a blue monarch. It was too much. My heart thudded against my chest wanting to escape the pressure it was feeling as I tried to force a barrier up around it. *I would never have Avery.*

I ran my hand over the sequined lined eyes. It really was beautiful. And no matter what happened tomorrow night, I couldn't disappoint her.

"I love it," I whispered.

"Awesome." Then Sara rambled on about how she and Colt swapped with Sienna and Sean after the pole dancing qualifying rounds Saturday night and how fucking hot it was. But all I could think of was how this costume *was* perfect. If only the rest of the fairy tale could come true.

⌘

DAY TEN:
WEDNESDAY NIGHT
MARDI GRAS MASQUERADE BALL

Sara made a point that we should start getting ready for the party early. She even had jello shots ready for us while we got dressed. I admit Sara knew what she was doing when it came to dressing me. She had a knack of putting me in the right clothes to accentuate my curves. I did look pretty good as I checked myself out in the mirror. If Nate was there tonight, he was going to eat his heart out for dumping me.

Sara kept teasing me about Ethan and Wren, telling me that I'm only allowed to pick one and I teased her back saying I couldn't pick one without sampling both, even though I'd probably never be able to go through with it. I assured her I would do my best to feel sexy and we'd see what happened after that.

As we walked into the ballroom, there were signs everywhere that read: "Welcome to the Camp Jameson Fourth of July Masquerade Ball."

Everyone looked so elegant and beautiful in their masks and costumes. The decorations of an almost life-like New Orleans were breathtaking. The walls were lined with the very ornate French Quarters of Bourbon Street and the motif was steeped with history and folklore. Avery even

182

had a live jazz band playing beside the DJ booth. The beauty of it seemed to capture everyone as they were milling about seeing if they could recognize anyone. I followed Sara and Colt up to the bar. With all these masked people, I felt like I could have been swept away to Louisiana.

In the dim party lighting, I watched as the barmaid poured the Jameson whiskey into the round shot glass and recapped the bottle. I tilted the glass back. I felt the whiskey burn as it went down my throat. Sara and Colt were beside me and they followed suit. We all three clinked our glasses back down on the bar and smiled at each other.

"Reload!" Colt said, and we quickly downed another.

"It's gonna be a good night. I think I'll have another," I said.

Meg, the woman with big breasts behind the bar poured me another. "Four's the limit tonight, honey," she said with a deep cigarette voice.

I frowned and threw back my third one. Damn, they were counting tonight. Colt winked at me and I realized I didn't need to worry. I followed Sara and Colt to our table.

"Fair warning, Aria, Ethan's on the hunt for you tonight. He practically begged me to tell him what you were wearing. So did Wren. They've got it bad for you, girl," Sara said, taking a sip of her red cocktail.

I picked up the large red index sized card from my dinner plate and read it as we sat down.

> *Tonight, Roses are a bloom,*
> *And Violets are as bright as a moon swept night.*
> *To keep the Mystery in the darkened room,*

Don't take your mask off until MIDNIGHT.
Only then, can you reveal your true self,
And allow your fairy tale to come true.

"Don't take your mask off until midnight, Aria. Those are the rules under which we all play tonight."

I smiled to myself as I looked at Sara. She was radiant in her very short Mardi Gras spaghetti strap dress. The bodice of the drop waist dress was a deep purple with gold braided straps. A short tulle petticoat underneath was gold and green. Sara was all-legs in her black high stilettos. She accented the outfit with purple feather eyelashes. Her blonde curly hair was pinned back on both sides of her head. She wore a violet Venetian lace mask with rhinestones. If I hadn't come to the ball with Sara and Colt I would have never been able to find them.

The lights dimmed around us and I could see that they kept it dark in the ballroom tonight just to make it harder. I guess tonight's all about the mystery.

The men were dressed in button up shirts with bright colorful masks that hid their faces perfectly. I scanned the room trying to find someone I knew, but part of the fun this evening was that you were supposed to sit with people that you didn't know. Avery just loved to mix things up to get people talking to one another.

Several couples sat down at our table and try as I might, I couldn't tell who they were, not even by their voices. I didn't see how I was going to be able to find Ethan or Wren at this party but I was at least sure that Nate wouldn't recognize me.

Full-length mirrors lined the Main Lodge and I garnered several looks at my new sexy costume. It was a dark blue corset mini dress with a low cut sweetheart neckline that unzipped in the front. The skirt was pleated and very short. A harlequin diamond print mesh panel ran down the center. I had borrowed Sara's extra black high heels. I wasn't wearing a bra, just sexy black underwear and black thigh highs. The costume barely covered my behind. And I smiled to myself. *I felt sexy.*

Light jazz music started and the staff began to serve dinner. I let the music fill my ears and tried to block out my thoughts except one. *Tonight — all I wanted was to get drunk and maybe find Ethan or Wren to have sex with and make Sara proud. Was that so wrong?*

My heart plummeted into my stomach when I realized I wasn't sure I could even go through with it. But I told her I'd try to relax and go with the flow. I realized wearing a mask had its advantages. I smiled at my next thought. *In the dim light, no one would know it was me.* Tonight was about letting go with total anonymity. *What could go wrong?*

After dinner and a few more shots thanks to Colt, I was feeling good and drunk when Sara pulled me to the darkened dance floor. The jazz band had disassembled and the DJ took the reigns. The only thing illuminating the dance floor were several strings of lights fanned out from the middle to the corners.

Beads were dangling around most of the guys' necks. Their faces were unrecognizable. A woman with ebony hair beside us was letting a man tease her nipple with his mouth. She threw her head back in pleasure. He slipped some beads over her head and she winked through her mask and moved on to the next man.

Song after song played as I cleared my mind and let the music move me. Several guys danced with me but they didn't hold my attention long. I wasn't satisfied. They had asked me if I wanted to join them in a room but I declined every time. I kept dancing even when Sara and Colt wanted to escape to a room. For a moment, I thought they might take me with them, but in Sara's guilt she latched onto the next guy that walked by the dance floor and shoved him toward me.

"You. Come here. Dance with her." She pulled the strangers' hands and mine together, gave me a small wave, and took Colt in tow behind her to a private room.

"Go get 'em, tiger," a familiar voice across the table said. I tried to recall whose voice it was but my brain was too fuzzy at this point to care. The man beside me slammed the rest of his drink and set the glass on the nearby table and pulled me back to him on the dance floor.

He paced a circle around to the back of me. I was contemplating leaving until strong hands wrapped around my waist and pulled me back against his chest. He didn't speak as he moved to my ear and planted a soft kiss behind it. My knees went weak. I kept wondering if this was either Ethan or Wren. I was sure it was one of them. Sara knew them well enough to grab one of them for me because in my current state it was all I could do to keep standing. I was clearly drunk.

He twirled me around and brought us nose to nose. He was still several inches taller than me and I was in four-inch stilettos. *Or was it five?*

I studied him, trying to find out who had me so enthralled. I couldn't wait to unmask him and see which one was my prize. They were twins so I figured my odds were good either way. It was hard to see the color of his eyes with the scantily lights. His delicious looking lips and square jaw were the only features I could make out behind his full-face black satin Venetian mask with gold trimmed eyes. It was exquisite with diamond crest, which sprouted a number of black feathers mixed with black and gold ribbons draping from the temple and tried to place him.

The lights and the music pulsed through me as I let him press against me. He was dressed all in black. He had wide shoulders. I could feel his muscles through his button-up shirt. *That didn't narrow it down any. Everyone here had tight abs.*

His hands moved like magic under my long curled hair that Sara took an hour to do, to reveal my bare skin underneath. His lips trailed across my neck and shoulder as his fingers teased my bare arms and I lost all sense of logic and the idea to find out which twin this masked man was. I had never craved anyone's touch more than I did in that moment. When his fingers met my hands, he intertwined them together and brought them between us. He softly kissed each one and smirked valiantly. My foggy thoughts lifted for a moment and I was intrigued. I wanted more.

"Who are you, Ethan or Wren?" I asked.

He startled for a moment then a slow seductive grin spread across his face. He completely distracted me as he trailed kisses across my jawline then down my neck. He unzipped my dress down past my breasts and slipped his hands inside then cupped my breasts. *Fuck.* His touch was electric. I stepped closer. *Why did I want to know?* The only thing I could concentrate on was that I wanted more.

My lips parted and I ran my tongue across my bottom lip and left it wet. His eyes dropped instantly to my lips and his mouth fell open slightly. Within seconds, his mouth found mine, and a low moan escaped his throat. I moved my hands to rest on his arms while he pressed his lips harder to mine. His lips were all consuming. *Jesus, this man could kiss.*

We were in the middle of the dance floor but it was only him I could see and only him that I wanted. He still had his hands cupping my breasts beneath my costume as our tongues explored one another and our hips ground against each other to the beat of Britney Spears 'Slave for You'. He tasted of tequila and sweet lime. I couldn't get enough of his warm velvet body, his tart cologne, and his lips. He leaned away, grasped my hand, and pulled me behind him. I followed him down a dim narrow hallway with closed doors on each side. I had never wanted someone to touch me like this. I never wanted him to let go of my hand. I couldn't wait to be alone with him.

He brought me into the round room with ten or so people on a large platform bed. People were all interwoven together and with the shadowy light, I couldn't tell who was who. I looked up at him when he gripped my hand tighter in a possessive manner and pulled me through the endless sea of naked and grinding bodies. The nearby speaker in the corner still playing Britney drowned out their moans. He led me up a rope-lighted staircase past a smaller crowd of people – six or so, and pulled me to the other side of the hall toward a more private room. We almost made it to the room when we were finally alone. He spun towards me and pressed me against the wall. His lips found mine again and he buried his pelvis into mine. I could feel his excitement through our clothing. His tongue invaded my mouth and I did what I always wanted to do. I let go.

Our breathing was erratic now as our desire built beyond anything I had ever known before. My hands urgently moved to unbutton his pants. I slid the zipper down his black dress pants and let my hand dip down beneath his boxer briefs. I was holding my breath when I wrapped my hand around his quickly hardening cock. He gasped when my hands made contact with his warm skin. I could feel my heart pounding like a jackrabbit in my chest as I stroked his shaft up and down. His chest rose and fell rapidly. His tongue pushed further into my mouth. When that was no longer enough, he lifted my legs around his waist and pressed my back harder against the wall. I wrapped my legs around him as he pulled my lacy underwear to the side and tilted his pelvis towards mine. I felt his shaft sink into me and I tilted my head back in sheer pleasure as his hands firmly moved to my hips. He thrust deeper into me. I felt him lift me then I fell back upon him. His mouth urgently found mine again.

Thrust for thrust he ground deeper inside me. I was quickly building toward my orgasm. His hands dug into my hips and he lifted me like I was light as a feather. Up and down he moved me over him. Our breathing was hard and fast. Our movements were urgent and I was building higher in the darkened hallway. His touch shook something inside me. I couldn't get enough of him and I let the moment move me. My legs stiffened and I couldn't stop my body from convulsing around him in an instant. He thrust twice more and poured himself into me. He pulled away and I could see the question in his eyes.

"I'm covered." I switched off my always-interfering thoughts and relaxed against him. Before I had time to really study him he smiled in relief and lowered his head down and kissed my neck. He breathed in a slow deep breath and reached behind me. He tightened his grip as he twisted the doorknob to the closest bedroom and kicked it open with his foot.

He carried me across the room with my legs still wrapped around his waist toward the bathroom and set me on the cold countertop. The entire bathroom was glowing in a soft flicker of light. I reached for his mask. He shook his head no. His gentle hands wound my hair up and I felt a hair clip pinned to the back of my head. I looked at him curiously. He kissed the top of my head and reached for the shower stall. He turned on the two-headed shower and adjusted the controls. The top shower turned off and I realized what he was doing. He only left the body showerhead on. We weren't supposed to remove our masks until midnight. Avery's rule. I rolled my eyes. I was not going to think of Avery at a moment like this. Ethan or Wren, whichever one this was, distracted me from my thoughts as he pulled his shirt from his body and let his pants and underwear fall to the floor.

All my thoughts escaped me as he sauntered toward me. He was perfectly fit. I was buzzed and I couldn't quite place which twin I had. *Ugh. What a time to be impaired, to not be able to think clearly. Damn it, I really wanted to know which one he was.*

He spread my legs with his hands and he devoured me with his mouth. My body was a flame under his touch. *I guess this means round two.*

He finished unzipping my costume and pushed it over my shoulders. It fell to my waist as he rushed to kiss my bare skin. I tilted my head back and my body bowed, craving his touch. His lips alternated from warm and soft, then wet and firm. My body hummed underneath his command. His dexterous fingers trailed down my legs and he swiftly removed my high-heeled shoes. They clumped to the ground, then my stockings followed. He wrapped his arms around my waist and set me on my feet. My costume fell to the floor just leaving my black lacy panties. He lowered those to the floor with his teeth and then pulled me into the shower. It was no time at all before I was pressed to the darkened steamy shower walls and he was having his way with me again.

We never spoke a word. We simply moaned, both of us. We just lost ourselves in each other, over and over again. It was only when we had rinsed the soap away and my body shook from exertion that he reached over to switch off the shower.

I toweled off, careful not to dislodge my mask and then I reached for my panties. I was strangely comfortable in his presence. He smiled greedily and before I knew it, I was straddling him on the bathroom counter again. His penis was growing hard against me again. He pulled away a moment studying me. He intertwined his fingers with mine and pulled me to a standing position. His head motioned for me to follow him. *I guess we're not done.*

We both grabbed our clothes and I followed him out to the queen sized bed against the far wall in the attached semi-private room. *Round three.* Yes, I was counting. This man was hot, sensual, strong, and *oh my, did he have stamina* – it was everything I ever wanted in a lover. I was not letting him out of my sight – or my grasp, for that matter.

The fast music that was pulsing through the walls quickly changed to a slow seductive song and the masked man seemed to be moved by the music of Joe Cocker's sexy voice. His kisses were soft as he undid my hair clamp and let my hair fall around my naked shoulders. He looked at me like I was the most beautiful thing he'd ever seen then laid me down on the satin sheets. His body, heated by the shower, covered mine. He traced my body with his hands and threaded his fingers under the sides of my black lace panties.

A slow grin crept over his face and before I knew what he was doing, he twisted them in his grasp and shredded through them with his fingers. He pulled away to take in my naked body and purred in delight at not having enough of me. I smiled crookedly, letting him take me in.

I ran my hands through his silky hair. He ran the palm of his hand down my chest between my breasts and traced the line of my stomach, navel, and let his hand cup my sex. He placed soft kisses on the heated skin of my thighs then moved to his knees. He spread my legs wide and let his kisses trail across my hip to my clit. He pressed two more kisses over my kitten and then slowly let his tongue rotate around it.

My body instinctively rose off the bed and I groaned. It was so sensitive. He had made me cum four times already and my body wasn't slowing down, it wanted more. I didn't find it weird that besides the contraceptive topic, we still hadn't spoken a word to one another except our groans of pleasure. Who needed words when all I wanted to do was feel him. All of him.

He slipped two fingers inside of me and let his tongue work his magic on my sensitive clit. The burning from the orgasm in the shower had barely subsided. When he stroked me, my body picked up right where it left off and I was climbing higher than I ever had before. Maybe it was the fact that I never had four orgasms in a row before. Maybe it was the fact that they were so close together. No, it was all him.

My attraction for this silent stranger helped me to open up to a place I never knew I could reach. My thoughts turned to Avery and how grateful I was to him that he created this place, whatever the reason was for doing it. I pushed the thoughts of Avery away as my legs burned for release, my body was still building and climbing, then I convulsed around the stranger's fingers. He let my body quiver under his heated look and my legs fell limp from pleasure. He smirked, leaned over, and kissed my silky pop-tart, causing me to gasp.

My eyes met his and he grabbed my hips and brought me on top of him. I sunk down on him and cried out in pleasure as his hard powerhouse buried deep within me. I tried to catch my breath but then he moved to missionary position and then he began to move slowly over me. His hardness filled me resplendently and he stopped when he could enter me no more.

My eyes burned with curiosity as his eyes opened to look at me. His hard muscles trembled over me. I didn't know if it was from fatigue, or fear. He pulled out slowly then pushed back in even more deliciously slower. He hovered over me with his hands on the sides of my face and stopped to really take me in. Passion and caring filled his eyes. I could feel my body tremble as well. His mouth curved up into a smile and all I wanted to say was; *I feel the same way.* He was making love to me. I beamed back at him and he took a slow steady breath and moved out and in slowly, feeling every inch of me. His eyes never left mine. My smile never went away.

He delivered a slow, delicious thrust in and out of me. My hands memorized every detail of his body as I traced his wide shoulders, his back, and his abs. He was perfect. I heard the words of Joe Cocker's 'Feels Like Forever' for the first time. Word for word it matched how I felt in this exact moment. How this man was turning my world around and I never would forget him. How one moment in my life when everything felt right and how my heart was exploding in my chest for a stranger that could melt me with just his touch.

My hands ran over every inch of his skin now beaded with sweat. The song embraced us. In that moment, his soft lips covered mine. I closed my eyes and felt him inside me, all around me, embracing me like he was holding on for dear life.

A deep groan filled the back of his throat and he picked up the pace just slightly. I opened my eyes to see his passionate glowing eyes. He threaded his hands through mine and moved them above my head. When I stretched them above me something about it made it feel more intimate.

Palm to palm, lips to lips, body to body, and soul to soul. In one night, we had connected deeper, more than anyone I had ever met. He pressed harder and faster. We reached the brink and both our bodies climaxed together without warning. I pulsed and quivered beneath him. Our eyes still locked on each other, closing only briefly while we orgasmed. He moved his head to the side of my chest and we both tried desperately to catch our breaths as the song finished.

Midnight was fast approaching and I couldn't wait. He lifted his head and leaned up to kiss me gently. Then he moved directly over me and cradled my face in his hands. I knew that shortly, I was about to learn who he was. He kissed me more passionately than he ever had before then leaned his forehead against mine. Our breathing was uneven but slowing.

The chime of the clock rang throughout the speakers. Fireworks exploded outside over the camp. Their glow illuminated us in crimson through the windows. It was finally midnight and that was the signal that all would be revealed.

⌘

DAY TEN:
WEDNESDAY LATE NIGHT
FOURTH OF JULY FIREWORKS

As the fireworks intensified outside down by the lake, his eyes flashed to mine. My heart was pounding in my chest as I waited in silence for him to say something. He still didn't speak. I could see the gears starting to turn in his head. The fireworks seemed to be sobering. I was holding my breath waiting to see what he was going to do next.

He stiffened, as the fireworks bathed the room in gold and blue. They seemed to call his attention to something. He sat up quickly and let the sheet fall to his waist. I followed, sensing his nervousness. He ran his hands through his hair in frustration as the lights of the entire Lodge increased in intensity– I was sure it was that he was more frustrated with himself than with me, but I couldn't be sure. I knelt in front of him.

"It's okay," I said moving closer to him. "This was right. For me, this was everything I ever wanted." My voice was drowned out by another salvo of deepening booms outside our window. Then another pushed through the quickly building awkward silence. He shook his head and rubbed his forehead as the rockets whistled into explosions. His hands trembled. He seemed to be trying to figure something out. He was growing more distant by the minute.

The bell chimed again and he sighed heavily. He seemed to be weighing his options. Then something dark passed over his face, and like a switch, I saw his guard go up.

He stared at me like I was a snake that was about to bite. I untied the satin ribbon and removed the mask from my face and I tugged lightly on his arm for him to turn toward me. When his eyes met mine, he wasn't surprised. It was fear I saw instead.

I moved to undo his mask. I wanted to see all of him before I lost him for good. I couldn't understand his behavior. The passion, the closeness felt like it was getting pushed further and further away with each moment the clocked ticked from midnight. I reached for his hand first and kissed the back of it, trying to diffuse the situation.

Another explosion rang out again and he stood frozen, watching me with curiosity and uncertainty. The finale started roaring in the air above the lake as my fingers slid under his mask. As I brought the mask away from his face, the finale outside intensified, his shoulders stiffened and by the look in his eyes, the man I just spent hours with, was gone.

"Avery!" I said breathless.

"Aria!" Avery cursed under his breath and grabbed his mask forcibly from my trembling hands. He rushed to put it back in place then glanced around the room. Relief flooded his eyes when he could see we were still alone.

My shoulders sank. They looked so much alike. They could have been brothers. Avery, Ethan and Wren were so similar in hairstyles and builds. My magnificent bubble had just burst. I knew he had been hurt before and he never got emotionally involved with the guests. He was a player. He was spiteful of women and never allowed himself to fall in love. He built this camp to serve as his own personal amusement park and now I was his latest ride. I felt ashamed.

His naked body stood and in a hurried pace he rushed to get dressed. He was glorious but at that moment, I hated myself for succumbing to his charm. I watched as he quickly threw on his shirt.

I sat seething. He didn't acknowledge me any further. He didn't look at me. He didn't address me. He was now cold and distant and he was too busy getting dressed to see the tears running down my face. *Didn't he hear me sniffle?* My heart was broken. My first love rose and fell all within a span of one evening. *How pathetic was I? You don't come to sex camp to find love.*

He was stomping on my heart like it meant nothing but I know we felt something together. I quickly lost my empathy for him. I purposely held my gaze away from him. But I knew he never once looked to me. It was like I didn't exist.

A man burst through the door in a drunken stupor, laughing and devouring the two women in front of him. I didn't care about the details as I pulled the sheet up around me and felt my heart close down. I was numb. My body wouldn't move from that spot. I was weak but not from any orgasm or from the night of pleasure, but from the betrayal of a man that when he took his mask off, revealed his true self.

Avery stopped short and turned with regret in his eyes. I didn't look in his eyes. I avoided his soft lips. I could only look at his forehead. His mouth fell open like he was trying to find the words to appease his guilt. I held my hand up in warning and shook my head. I don't know how I found the strength, maybe it was my anger, but I rose to my feet, leaving my shredded panties lying on the floor, and reached for my dress.

He watched me nervously. I turned my back to him and quickly dressed. I forced myself to turn to him. I reached down and lifted my panties – they looked more like webs. A small smile played on my lips and I stuffed them into his hand. I frowned knowing this was it.

"To remember you once had a beautiful butterfly," I said stiffly. I was fighting back the tears that were threatening to spill at any moment. I was more frustrated with myself that I was in this position, that I could let myself believe that I would find love in a place like this.

I didn't want to touch him anymore so I pulled my hand away and let it fall to my side. I turned my back to him, grabbed my stockings and shoes, and pushed through the door.

I didn't notice any of the naked bodies that filled the multiple rooms on my way out. My sights were only on the exit. And I never looked back. It was after midnight. Today was officially my birthday. *Happy fucking birthday to me!*

⌘

DAY ELEVEN:
THURSDAY AFTERNOON
BEACH BIRTHDAY BLAST

"Uhhh," I grumbled. To say I was hungover was a gross understatement. I crawled out of bed slowly and only because the noonday sun was shining through the window right on my head. I made it into the shower then as I went into the kitchen, I found Sara's note on the table telling me to meet her at the beach. It also instructed me to down a quick beer to beat the hair-of-the- dog back and that's exactly what I did, but it actually took two beers.

"Happy Birthday, Aria!" Sara and Sienna squealed and pulled me into a group hug as I arrived on the beach. I smiled, trying to make the best of it. *My life couldn't get much worse could it?*

It was midday Thursday and Avery decided to throw a barbeque with shrimp and steak. Avery knew I loved steak. Maybe he was feeling guilty for last night but everyone was excited for the change up, everyone except me.

The beach filled up with every Kitten, Cub, and Instructor at Camp Jameson. Everyone partied in swimsuits and either sat baking in the hot sun or swam in the crystal clear lake while my favorite band Chasing Seven played in the background through the giant Bose sound system.

I glanced to see Nate talking with Avery. I couldn't help but see the similarities. They both were one-night stands and they both fucked me over afterward, like either I had the plague or my vagina smelled like swamp juice. I'm pretty sure it wasn't the latter.

Sara had her eagle eye on me as I watched the two men converse. I quickly diverted my attention to the beer in my hand, trying to hide my true feelings and numb the sick feeling in my tummy from drinking last night.

"Aria, can you go get me a Long Island Iced Tea?" Sara asked. I saw her narrow her eyes at Nate as I nodded and headed in the direction of the outside bar. When I came back I could hear Sara's voice over the music.

"I don't care if you were engaged and made a mistake. You fucked her over asshole. Stay away from her," Sara scolded Nate. "No one screws over my best friend and gets away with it."

I saw Avery's eyes widen at Sara's words. I could see how much those words stung him. I stepped beside Sara and handed her the Long Island. I was met with two pairs of merciful stares. Sara could be harsh when she wanted to and I could tell both men secretly wanted to flee.

"Sara, let it go," my voice cracked and held more emotion than I was willing to show. Nate looked at me apologetically and turned toward the bar and Avery stood looking at me with a mixture of guilt and regret. *Geez, I knew how to pick 'em.*

"Fine," Sara huffed and dragged me to the sand volleyball court, mumbling under her breath.

I quickly drowned myself in the music and found the strength to play beach volleyball with my friends. And drank beer. Lots of beer, and after a bit, I did start to feel better.

I was on the team with Sara, Colt, Travis, Sienna, and Sean. The sun beat down on us but we were unstoppable.

After the third game, I fell to the ground in exhaustion beside Sean's feet after I scored the winning point. Sean collapsed next to me and braced his arms on either side of me then hovered over me. His eyes were burning with desire.

"Birthday girl, I can't take it anymore. Kiss me, you beautiful athlete."

I kissed him reluctantly at first. His lips were soft and seeking. Then with the mix of alcohol and his tight body laying over me I decided, *what do I have to lose?* So I wrapped my arms around him and deepened the kiss. That's when Avery cleared his throat and announced the steaks were ready.

"Damn girl, you can kiss!" Sean called out. Everyone chuckled. But I could feel Avery staring at me. I didn't make eye contact. I closed my eyes and laid my head back in the sand. I didn't want to think of Avery.

Before I knew it, Sean had cradled me in his arms and lifted me from the sand. He spun me around and I squealed in delight as he spun me faster.

"Let's go, hottie! We need to feed that little body of yours," he said, carrying me into the grass and setting me down next to the pavilion. He growled in delight then smacked my ass. I jumped and smiled back at him. My skin prickled on the back of my neck and I knew Avery was watching, but I never turned around. I couldn't. I was afraid that the tears would come when I looked into those green eyes that now haunted me. I wasn't feeling strong enough to find out. I was still too wounded from last night.

"Looks like Sean has a new pet," Sienna smirked at me. My eyes arched upward and I smiled nervously to her. I had no idea what that meant.

After we ate, I stood amongst the usual crowd with Sara, sipping on my beer and listening to Sean, Travis, and Colt banter about who could bench press more.

"Dance with me, beautiful," a deep husky voice purred. I turned and my eyes landed on Ethan. I smiled softly and nodded. *I needed a distraction.*

He lightly gripped my small hand in his and led me to the makeshift dance floor occupied by several dozen couples enjoying a beautiful summer evening. Chasing Seven 'Only One' began to play. And I let myself get lost in the music as he pulled me near. *Why couldn't I have found him last night?*

"Where you from?" Ethan asked.

"Northeast Ohio."

"Are you a student?" he asked.

"Yes. At Kent State."

"What's your major?"

"Nursing."

He smiled wickedly at me. "A hot nurse. You're the spitting image of every man's wet dream. How did I get so lucky?" he teased. My face flushed red. I tried to hide my face and turn into him but he was studying me so closely. "You're adorable when you blush." I giggled.

"Thanks," I said softly. "Where are you from?" I asked trying to change the subject quickly.

"San Francisco."

"California. Nice," I replied.

"Ever been?"

"No. But I always wondered what it would be like to live in California."

Ethan ran his hand down my back and let it rest on my hip. "I won't bite you know. We're just dancing. Getting to know each other. Aria, I gotta tell you, ever since I saw you in your little running outfit the other day I've been hoping to get a moment alone with you. You're quite popular these days."

"Why do you say that?"

"You're with Avery's friends. You're popular. And very hot, I might add."

I stiffened at his comment. "Oh," was all that I could say. I wasn't with Avery, though. *I never would be.* I studied his soft brown eyes. He was being gentle with me and I smiled, glad that I made a friend.

"I have only one regret," he said.

"What's that?"

"I'm sorry it took me three days to get up the nerve to finally come talk to you. I'll be honest, I was afraid I'd get turned down."

"Really," I raised my eyebrow at him. "Do I come off that hardcore?"

"No, I just meant I thought you were particular about your men. You had only been hanging out with a select few here at camp. I didn't think I'd fall into that category."

"It takes me awhile to get warmed up to people," I said.

He shrugged. "I knew you loved to dance so I thought at least I could get a dance with you."

"You know what, Ethan." I moved closer to him. "I think you're hitting on me," I flirted.

He laughed louder. "Whatever gave you that idea?" he said mockingly. I felt myself relax against him. He was nice. And I liked his honesty and he did resemble Avery.

"Is it my turn yet, Romeo?" Wren cut in.

"Fine," Ethan huffed. "We'll finish our chat later, Aria."

"Sure I'd like that," I replied.

Wren scooped me up and twirled me around away from Ethan. He growled in my ear flirtatiously. *It must be a twin thing.*

"God, you're beautiful. I could spend every day devouring you," Wren lowered his head and drew in a slow sensual breath. I giggled. "I couldn't keep my distance anymore. I want to get to know you," he said.

"I'm flattered," I answered.

Wren stepped closer as a faster song began to play. He swiveled his hips into me and led my arms around his neck.

"Go Aria," Sean called out as he pulled Sienna to the dance floor beside us. *Why did he have to do that?*

I was glad that Wren couldn't see my face as I buried my head further against his shoulder. He was a good dancer and I felt at ease beside him.

We didn't talk like Ethan and I did. It was purely physical. I got lost in the dance music with Wren. I looked to Sara across the dance floor talking with Colt and Avery. She looked over to me and winked. My eyes met Avery's. He was listening to Colt with his arms crossed, but his eyes were fixed on me. *Why? He made it clear he didn't want me. So why were his eyes filled with jealousy?*

I turned my head away from Avery and let myself get drowned in Eth...I mean Wren and the music. *Damn, they look so much alike.*

I danced the day away taking turns with Ethan and Wren. The twins were sweet, smart, and strong in their own way and incredibly funny. My cheeks hurt from laughing so much. It was exactly what I needed. I kept my back to Avery, knowing that he was watching me. But I forced myself not to go there.

I excused myself to go to the bathroom and when I came back, I was a little relieved when I saw Wren and Ethan starting a game of volleyball. I walked to the edge of the lake and waded my feet in the water, letting my mind drift away from everything. The water was warm from the summer sun. It was very calming.

As the sun set, Pierce, Travis, and Colt lit the many fires along the beach and crowds of people gathered around to each one. I moved to the seat nearest me and took in the laughter that could be heard all around us as Pierce lit the one closest to our group. Avery and I kept at opposite ends of the group. We were back to being strangers.

Sean, Colt, and Sienna were good friends with him. There was no avoiding that. Sara and Sienna were chatting non-stop about a new clothing line that had just hit New York.

Travis and Colt were talking about the homerun that someone hit on some baseball team today. I wasn't really listening. I was lost in thought staring out at the lake, sitting in my chair and sipping my beer. *God, this place was beautiful.*

Maya and Amber were giggling about something but my thoughts were too distant to care. I looked to see movement beside me and my mouth fell open. I quickly composed myself and tried to reign in my emotions as Avery and Pierce brought out six acoustic guitars and set the cases on the nearby pavilion. Avery handed Travis, Colt, Maya, and Sienna each one. Pierce grabbed his, then Avery held one and they both sat in their chairs.

I had no idea Avery played. I had no idea any of them played. Each one dexterously strummed and tuned the chords to their liking. I hadn't realized I was staring at Avery when his eyes met mine. The campfire seemed to brighten his eyes. My insides sank and Sara broke my internal disorientation by placing her hand on mine. My eyes shifted to her.

"You okay?" she inquired.

I looked back to see Avery still looking at me and tuning his guitar. He mouthed the words 'Happy Birthday' and my eyes quickly fell away. I nodded to Sara and gave her a small smile. It was the only thing I had the strength to do.

"Here's a new one I've been working on," Avery's velvet voice purred. My eyes met his in surprise. His eyes were locked on mine. "It's called 'Falling'. Hope you like it," his voice sounded strained, like he was holding back some heavy emotion.

My heart broke out into a fast patter and I wanted to run. *I couldn't do this.* So I did the only thing I could think of. I reached for my beer and downed it. Then I leaned over to the cooler and dug out another one while Avery taught the group with guitars the chords. They ran their hands down the neck of their guitar with ease. Avery hummed the melody.

After a few minutes Avery spoke. "Ready?" Everyone nodded and let him lead.

I tried to keep my breath even as Avery began singing about a special woman. He sang about how he liked the feel of her name on his lips. How she took his breath away with just one look. How her eyes dance when she laughed. How he tried to steal every moment he could to be with her.

My heart pained as he sang of a sweet girl that turned his whole world upside down. How he couldn't trust his heart anymore. He sang about blue wings of a butterfly and the stillness of the world as he took in its innocent beauty. I pushed the lump down in my throat as he described the waterfall and compared the moment to paradise.

In the next verse, he sang that he hated how he didn't make the most of the situation when he had the chance that day. He sang of how he wanted to make love on a bed of wild orchids.

I don't think I took a breath as he sang about riding the aftershocks of the most intimate night he's ever known. How her scent lingers when she's not there. How one touch from her shattered his guard he worked so hard to keep in place. How he wonders if she'll ever forgive him for hurting her.

The next verse he sang about his crumbling walls falling down all around him. How when he sobered he looked up and saw the most beautiful woman he's ever known. He sang of his fear. Even though his words tormented me, I was mesmerized. I loved watching him play. I didn't realize how much one man could surprise me and make me fall for him all over again, but he did. I hated him for it.

I gripped my beer tighter and listened to the words of his new song. His voice was sexy, strong, and desirable. He was in his element and so at ease with the six-string guitar beneath him. The strings danced under his beautiful fingers. Those same relentless fingers that touched every part of my body and brought me pleasure, just last night, in ways I'd never known before.

The others followed along and that only added to my despair. The more he sang the more my guard fell, crumbling like the walls of Jericho. I tried to distance myself but his lyrics kept pulling me back.

When he got to the end, he sang of his regret of watching her walk away. How he tried so many times to apologize but the words got stuck in his throat. The song came full circle when he sang about putting the words in a song.

I secretly wiped the tears away. I knew it was for me. But it only made me angry. I should have loved that a man would write a song just for me but he had ripped open a wound that hadn't healed yet. He was making me relive these precious moments with him and I didn't want to relive that. I had forced myself to suppress those feelings because he pushed me away two seconds after fucking me. Now here he was confessing his feelings to me in a song. I hated his games. I pounded another beer and felt my body relax. *Yes, getting drunk was exactly what I needed.*

I didn't look to Avery when the song finished. Every one clapped and praised him. I wrapped my arms around myself and bit the inside of my lip nervously. In that moment, I knew that I had to push Avery Jameson out of my heart, out of my life, or he was going to break me.

Sara moved around to the side of the pavilion and I sat in a trance and stared at the fire. I didn't want to look across from me. I didn't want to see those beautiful sad eyes staring back at me. I was too angry. I was too hurt.

The chords of 'Happy Birthday' broke through my self-wallowing and I looked up to see Sara with a large cake with candles blazing. I smiled widely at her.

"Twenty?" I crooked my eyebrow at her.

"Of course," she beamed up and down while everyone sang Happy Birthday to the six acoustic guitars around a campfire. I smiled for the first time, feeling lucky that I had made so many friends over the last few weeks.

"Make a wish," Sara urged.

I tried with all my might not to look at Avery. But I wore my heart on my sleeve. I would have to wait one more night until I placed the shield back around my heart. Until I could be strong enough to lock him out of my life forever. *Tomorrow.* My traitorous eyes found Avery and I watched as his fingers finished the last chords of the song. His eyes locked on mine.

"I already got my wish." I watched as Avery's soft smile fell and he swallowed hard. My eyes moved back to Sara.

"I have all of you here with me. What more could I ask for?"

As I drew in a deep breath I knew that I would never have another chance with Avery. As the flames of the candles fell dormant, so did my heart. Looks like everyone had a good time tonight. *Everyone, except me.*

⌘

DAY TWELVE:
FRIDAY MORNING
MEET THE SYBIAN

So, here I was, Friday morning, and my head pounded to the rhythm of my heavy heart combined with a second hangover in as many days. I sat there pondering the hours that led up to this moment. I realized then I had to treat my problem with guys just like a hangover. Pretend it never existed. Push past it and never look back.

As I lay there staring at the wooden rafters of the cabin, I was surrounded by everything that Avery's own hands had built. *God, it sucked!*

He created this world that until two weeks ago I didn't even know existed. I knew one thing for sure. I liked these new sexual experiences. I didn't come here by choice – not this type of camp anyway. I came because Sara said it was a getaway from the pressures of life especially from school. I had to admit, this place was exhilarating. There was no better way to blow off steam than to feel the rush of an orgasm taking over your body – leaving you satiated and your mind a little fuzzy.

A smile grew on my face and I knew in that moment what I needed to do. I was definitely going to dive in. First stop – Sybian class. I'll be honest – I was intimidated by the thought of it at first but now I felt it was calling to me.

211

I stood and stretched my arms as my eyes landed on the fresh wild orchids on my dresser. I sucked in a breath, trying to remember where they came from. I wanted to throw them across the room. I didn't want to be reminded of him. I saw the card sticking out of the top. I shook my head and ignored it. *How many times could I break until I shattered?*

After my shower, I pulled on my lace bra and panty set, tight low cut shirt, and short workout shorts then hearing a noise, I left my room. I moved closer and I could hear Sara heaving in the bathroom as I approached. I tapped lightly on the door and peeked my head in. She was green.

"Sara, are you okay?"

"Uhhh. No," she mumbled as she hung her head lower.

"Can I get you anything? Hair of the dog?"

"Funny," she said spitting into the toilet. "I called off from my classes already. Sienna is hungover too."

"How's Colt?" I asked.

"I can't get a hold of him." She heaved into the toilet again. I turned my head.

"Feel better," I said as I grabbed my backpack and left, wishing I could help make her feel better.

The camp wasn't bustling with people like it usually was. *Was everybody hungover this morning?*

I made my way to my first Sybian class. When I entered the cabin, I waited to shed my shirt and workout shorts. I had planned on going for a run after class. I waited hoping class wasn't cancelled. The room was empty except for the masterful piece of equipment. I couldn't help but to get nervous and excited at the same time. I paced around it, staring it down, and turned my back to the door while I studied it.

"Bad news. Colt and Sienna are both hungover." I stiffened at the sound of his velvet voice. I closed my eyes briefly, opened them, and turned around with a wry smile.

"Avery." *Damn it!* He didn't look as nearly as uncomfortable as I was. He was his well-composed, hot and steamy self and I was just another notch on his cigar case.

"I guess that was my fault. I didn't restrict the alcohol consumption yesterday, but then it was a special day," he huffed. "So, I am forced to oversee a few of the classes that are actually occurring today. Pierce is helping me along with five other instructors," he rambled on. "I cancelled all other classes for today. You don't seem worse for wear," he said that like maybe he was more nervous than he let on.

"No. I'm good," I lied coldly. *Crying has a way of sobering a drunken girl up.*

"Okay, good." He pushed his hands into his pockets and rocked back on his heels. "So, the Sybian. Have you ever seen or had any experience with this kind of heavy duty machinery?" I shook my head.

He stepped up to it. "The Sybian is one of the main events at the Camp Olympics. We hold it just like it was a real rodeo. The Kittens will ride a rocking horse that has been converted into a full Sybian. Only no one's allowed to see it yet. It's a surprise. Every year we find a new design for the Sybian. Last year, it was a dime store racecar. This is a normal Sybian for training new riders."

I blinked up at him as he pointed to the intense looking machine and rambled on.

"The Sybian rodeo works just like a real one where the Kitten rides the bull and see how many seconds she can stay on while the attendant slowly cranks up the power. No Kitten has ever made it to ten without jumping off or yelling stop. The highest mark ever achieved was an eight."

He ran his hand through his hair nervously. "Anyway, Colt and Sienna feel you're ready to try this. I'm just not so sure from what I've seen but I'll switch it on so you get used to its mechanical lore and we'll see how you do."

I didn't like what he was implying by that comment, but then he went on.

"This is my own design."

I purposely stared at his forehead. I was not going to look into those beautiful eyes that made me melt two nights ago. I wasn't going to stare at his perfect round lips, the ones that had devoured me and seduced me. I switched gears and remembered the story about the Sybian during girls' night around the campfire.

"The saddle-like feature makes it easier for the Kittens to reach climax," he swallowed nervously.

I listened to his instructions but I wasn't really listening. My thoughts took me away to two nights ago. His gentle touch. His loving eyes. I pushed the memory away, gritted my teeth, and stormed to the credenza that held my only escape. I covered the name up on the Jameson whiskey bottle and poured a small amount into a glass and slammed it back. *Yes, at that moment, I was that petty.*

I didn't want anything to remind me of him. I still hurt too badly. I could feel Avery's eyes on me. I made myself not look into those gorgeous emerald eyes and let the alcohol work its magic. *Gotta love Irish whiskey.*

214

"You really are my little whiskey girl," Avery said. The corner of his mouth rose up slightly then he cleared his throat. "Get on your knees on the table and pull your mask on." I looked to him curiously. "Colt's notes say you like being blindfolded," he smirked.

I quickly downed a little more of the liquid courage and blocked out Avery's chuckle as I slammed my glass back down on the counter. I went to my backpack and dug through it. My shaky hands found my mask and I sighed inwardly. I guess there's no point in fighting any of this. This was his camp. I was bound to run into him at some point. *Why not every damn day!*

I shimmied off my shorts and t-shirt with my back turned toward him. I left my light pink bra and panties on. I wasn't going to give him the satisfaction of seeing me naked yet again. I breathed in a shaky sigh and tried to look unaffected by him being inches away from me. My insides were quivering, though. *God, how was I going to do this?*

I knelt on the soft plush blanket beside the machine and pulled the mask over my eyes. *Damn him. Why does it have to be today of all days that he has to cover classes. I'm not going to let him ruin this for me.* I kept telling myself that. I let the blackness fill my world. The machine still purred beside me. The constant noise drowning out Avery's steady breaths helped. I could feel him nearby. This couldn't be more awkward.

"I would recommend pleasuring yourself first. You really need to be turned on for this," he said softly.

I stand corrected. It *couldn't* get more awkward than this very moment.

"Fine," I huffed. Colt never mentioned that you had to be turned on prior to using this machine, besides he could just let me have some lube if it mattered that much. But if that's the way he wanted to play, then he'd better prepare himself because it was about to be one hell of a show. I reached down into my panties and began to play. The alcohol was helping to relax me and was giving me the courage to show him what he was missing out on. Still, I wasn't giving him the satisfaction of seeing me naked just yet and judging from the outline in his pants before I put my mask on, I was having an affect on him, whether he wanted to admit it or not. I was going to ride this out until the very last minute.

I rubbed my magic spot, blocking everything out. I was just beginning to get wet when Avery gasped quietly. I tore off my mask.

"No, Avery. You don't get to enjoy this." I tried to sound angry but my voice shook unsteadily instead.

He swallowed hard and nodded then took a step back. My anger calmed and I slid the mask back on.

"I need music, please," I said, weakly. "Something hard and fast. No more love crap for me," I muttered.

The music blared to a guitar solo and I pushed all my anxiety down between my thighs. I reached down and continued my ministrations. *This wasn't for anyone, just me. I had to show Avery what he would miss out on by rejecting me. Worse yet, I had to prove it to myself.*

The burning took hold of me shortly afterwards and my legs began to stiffen.

"That's enough. If you're going to cum, you will want to do it on the Sybian – trust me," his voice was surprisingly steady. *Trust you!* I was glaring at him through my mask as I slid off my panties. I lifted my blindfold and waited for Avery to guide me.

He never spoke as he stepped beside me and reached for my hand. With every fiber of my wounded heart, I wanted to pull away but I knew he was doing this for me. I was to move forward up over the machine. He had already cleaned the vibrating phallus and I was glad that there wasn't a long interruption.

I lowered myself down onto it and repositioned my mask. The machine began vibrating and grinding slowly and the Sybian began to move inside me.

It was slow and steady, not as overwhelming as I had imagined. As my body relaxed around it, I could hear Avery click the remote in his hand and the gentle, smooth grinding increased. I anchored my knees on either side of the beast.

"Squeeze your thighs together, Aria, as you start building again. Move up and down now, like you're cantering on a horse. Good." *God, this was so deep.* I threw my head back and let my fingers find my clit.

"Nice," he purred. "Feel the vibrations move through every part of you."

The humming of the machine was extraordinary. My fingers circled faster while I cantered up and down. I found my clit burning and seeking release faster than I had ever thought was possible. The relentless machine moved inside me. I fell deeper into it against its gyration. I rose up and fell back down on it, repeating the maneuver over and over.

It only took a few moments more of gentle rubbing to reach my release. My body quivered and soared. A moan erupted from deep inside me. My vision blurred and stars crept into my periphery. I was panting hard. The machine clicked and slowed but kept going.

"One more, Aria. Let go."

"I'm too sensitive." *From you, two nights ago,* my subconscious sneered.

"Use it. Push past the initial response and I promise you, you will build faster and harder to an even more intense orgasm."

I nodded, not sure if I could do it. My insides still quivered. I reached down and rubbed my fingers over my wet clit. I spread the moisture and rubbed in circles. He was right. Within moments, I was building harder and faster. The mixture of vibrations of the machine that was slow and steady, my numb legs, and the burning inside me pushed past my usual orgasm and I was climbing higher than I ever thought I could.

I circled my clit a few minutes more. Without warning, his fingers clamped around my nipple over my bra and my body convulsed hard and fast. I cried out uncontrollably. The machine sped up and I cantered up and down as the thrusts of the machine prolonged my orgasm. I was trembling when the machine slowed to a stop.

"That was amazing," I breathed drowning in my new euphoria. I felt warm hands touch me and lift my mask. I opened my brown eyes to see his emerald green ones staring back at me. I saw so much in his heated stare. Lust, desire, and something else he was trying to hide, need. His breathing matched mine and he took a step forward between my legs.

"That was wonderful. You made it up to number two," he said. *Oh my god, that was only on two?* I thought, but then he ruined my amazement. "Aria, I'm sorr.."

"Don't," I said hopping down from the table to the side away from him. My legs were wobbly as I took a step toward my clothes. My hands shook as I pulled my underwear back on.

"I don't want to hear your excuses, Avery." *I gave you my heart and you smashed it.* He reached out toward me. His eyes pained. His despair was overwhelming. "I can never forgive you for how you treated me. It was like I didn't matter to you," I whispered fighting back the tears that pooled in my eyes. *Just like Nate.*

I pulled on my shorts and my t-shirt, then my socks and shoes. I grabbed my backpack and pushed it over my shoulder.

"Don't go," he pleaded.

I glanced to him for a moment then looked away. "That's what you should have said two nights ago." I shook my head. "It's too late."

I took a step toward the door then stopped. I let my shoulders sag. I tightened my grip around the strap of my backpack and pushed through the door. I let the door slam behind me, never looking back. I wished that he would chase after me. But I knew deep down…he never would.

⌘

DAY TWELVE:
FRIDAY AFTERNOON
POWDER-PUFF FOOTBALL

"**W**hat's the deal?" I asked Colt as Sara and I arrived at the back lawn of the Jameson Main Lodge. It had been painted with white lines running down the field. I was wondering why we'd been summoned with only the instructions to wear athletic gear and running shoes. It had only been two hours since I left Avery standing in my Sybian class and I wasn't looking forward to seeing him again. This was getting painful.

The sky threatened rain, and the humidity pressed down on me like a suffocating wet blanket. I was lucky to be feeling as good as I was considering I had a hangover this morning and from the looks of most, everyone was still hungover.

The Masquerade Ball was only two days ago and my birthday was yesterday and yet it seemed like a lifetime ago. I was glad for any distraction at this point.

Colt reached Sara's side and threaded his fingers through hers briefly then nudged me playfully with his shoulders.

"I want to welcome you ladies to Challenge Friday," Colt said, quickly turning and catching a football then tossing it back to Travis as he wiped his brow. "You two up for it?"

"Always," Sara and I said in unison.

"Great. One more practice play then we'll get started."

I looked toward Avery. *Why was it that no matter where he was in the room full of people, or football field, I could find him instantly?*

He glanced my way then turned back to the team of shirtless men. Colt ran back to the field and stood in the huddle next to Avery. Avery called out the next play and the shirtless men lined up against the men in shirts. His muscles rippled as his teammate snapped the ball to him and he hoisted it up in anticipation to throw it to Travis who ran down the field.

Travis weaved through everyone as Avery threw the ball down the field. Travis caught it and ran it into the end zone. Sara and I cheered as Colt's team scored.

I tried my hardest not to look at Avery's perfect body. How it glistened with sweat. How my tongue had run down his happy trail that night... I stopped myself. *What was I doing? Better yet, why was he still affecting me like this?* I scolded myself. He had stomped on my heart. I was pathetic.

The men moved to the sidelines toward the two groups of women. Most of the women were gawking at Avery.

"Colt. What did you call us here for?" I asked a little more irritated than I wanted to admit.

"On Challenge Friday we pick one sporting event for everyone to play as a team building exercise. Today is the Powder Puff football challenge but too many women opted out because they're still hungover from last night so we're improvising. We're going to play no-tackle coed football.

You're both athletic and we need you. Can you throw a football, Aria?"

I grabbed the football from Colt and spiraled it to Travis as he stepped towards us.

I nodded and watched Avery out of the corner of my eye as he handed out flags to his team. He began instructing the women in front of him and motioned them to follow behind him. I turned my back to him.

"The Powder Puff challenge. It doesn't get any better than Kittens duking it out on the gridiron," Colt sighed playfully.

We followed him to the sidelines and I smiled to Sienna and Maya. These were strong women and I was glad that I was on their team, even if they were still hurting from their hangovers.

"Aria, you're the quarterback for our team," Colt said.

Gray heavy clouds rolled in but no one seemed phased by the threatening downpour. It looked like we wouldn't have much time before it opened up on us.

I beamed at him. "Let's do this," I said, putting my hair up in a ponytail. I had so much pent up anger that this was just the non-sexual release I needed.

I recalled all the Sundays that I watched football with my dad before he got deployed to Iraq. He had taught me everything I knew about football. I was pretty good at the powder-puff game in my senior year of high school. It had a lot to do with our family reunions every year. We'd play for hours. My cousins weren't the kind to take it easy on their little female cousin either. They bloodied my nose several times over the years.

I listened as Colt ran through the first play. He rattled off a play, hoping the women would understand. The few men that played shook their head in understanding then he walked several women to their positions behind the forty-yard line. Some giggled endlessly. They all stood staring at Colt with a deer-in-headlights look. I would say by now I knew these women fairly well. I knew who was strong and athletic and who didn't want to break a nail. It was just common sense. After a few minutes, Colt seemed to be a bit overwhelmed and before I knew it, I stepped forward and seized control.

"Maya, you run the wide out down the right side and I will get the ball to you. Sienna, you try to push in front of her and block anyone who gets in her path. Maya, stay in the center and don't let anyone get past. Colt's going to block Avery. Sara, you're on my left flank so don't let anyone get a hold of me."

My eyes landed on Avery as he approached Colt standing beside me. He stared wide-eyed at me. I glanced to Colt who wore a shocked expression on his face.

Colt rubbed the back of his head and chuckled. "Errh, okay. Everybody got it?"

I could see everyone nodding. Colt passed out the green jerseys, white flags, and belts and I quickly pulled on my jersey and wrapped the belt around my waist, careful to not meet Avery's eyes. I could feel him watching me. His teammates stepped to the cooler and cracked open a few beers.

"What's our team name?" I asked, as Sara, Colt, and I approached the cooler. Colt offered me a beer. I shrugged. *Why not?*

Colt smirked. "The Colts of course," he replied, tipping back his beer.

"Hair of the dog?" I asked.

"No better way to cure a hangover," Colt replied.

"Let's go guys!" I clapped my hands together.

Sara took a gulp of her beer then smirked and took her place on the field next to me. She was feeling better already. *Maybe hair of the dog really did work.*

Colt hurried by helping with some last minute coaching. I heard him point out a few details and lined up his team in white jerseys in front of us, then stepped to the defensive line.

"No tackling. Leave that for the mattresses ladies. Just grab onto the flags and the play is complete," Avery instructed, stepping to his position across from Colt.

I was already sizing up the opposing team. *God, I loved football.* Then there was Caitlyn who was crouched down opposite of me on the scrimmage line with a look of disgust. *Great.* I studied her determined expression. *Who would have thought Caitlyn was athletic. I bet she's so happy to be on her little Avery's team.*

The ball was snapped toward me, and I let the pigskin fall into my hands. I raised my chin looking for Maya. Sara blocked a girl coming toward me and Sienna helped out Maya. As smoothly as if I had done it my entire life, I cradled the ball next to my head and waited until Maya was open. Colt blocked Avery. Pierce blocked Sean. I threw the ball and watched it spiral across the fifty, then forty, then thirty-yard line. Maya gripped the ball and ran down the field leaving everyone else eating her dust. *Yes!*

"Touchdown!" Travis yelled out into the microphone.

Sara picked me up in a bear hug and spun me around. "That was awesome!"

I laughed as my feet touched the ground. Sienna and Maya followed suit. The whistle blew and I quickly shouted out the defensive play.

I lined up in front of Caitlyn on the forty-yard line. She was all legs, and all boobs. After I had won the first round of the pole dancing contest, she had her mind made up she was going to get with Avery. I thought of how Sara and I had switched out her shoes for a smaller size. I smirked sardonically to her and she narrowed her eyes at me. *Bring it on, Barbie.*

Her team snapped the ball and I set my eyes on tackling her before the ball ever left her possession. I dove out of several women's grasps and lunged for her. I watched her hips turn to the right and I turned with her. She barely had the ball back to throw it when I rushed her and snatched her flag. The whistle blew and I held out the flag to return it.

"Ohh. Caitlyn sacked by Aria. Five yard loss," Travis's voice rang out.

"You're going down, Aria. You won't win this one. Avery's mine this time," she said snidely.

"You can have him!" I answered.

"What is she talking about?" I asked Sara as we lined up against the thirty-five yard line.

"Winners get a cocktail party with Avery tonight."

The clouds broke and rain started coming down lightly at first, but quickly escalated to pouring sheets of stinging droplets. I blinked away the water from my eyes. I didn't know if I really wanted a night with Avery again anyway,

225

but I was pissed at this woman's animosity towards me so I wanted to take her down. No matter how hard it poured.

"Let's take this bitch down," I said to Sara. She chuckled, tucking her wet short hair behind her ear.

"You're on," she answered.

The rain was soaking all of us from head to toe but no one seemed to care. Maybe it was the alcohol from last night burning all our brain cells but we were already dripping from the humidity, so why not. It just showed me how much these women really wanted Avery. Deep down, even me.

I glanced over at Avery to see him eyeing me while he called another play to his team. He winked at me arrogantly and I suddenly wanted to tackle him to the ground and show him how angry I was with him. He'd hurt me. And because of him and Nate, I didn't trust any guy with my heart anymore.

I drew my lips into a straight line in determination and turned back toward my team. We lined up at the forty-yard line and I waited for them to snap the ball to Caitlyn, who really seemed put out by this downpour. She kept trying to fix her hair before giving up entirely. I ground my teeth together in anticipation as they snapped the ball. I watched the movement of her hips and I was just about to rip her flag from her belt when Avery tackled me. I threw him a cold glare as Caitlyn passed the ball clumsily off to Kennedy. Kennedy ran it into the end zone.

"Homerun!" Caitlyn cheered. Everyone erupted in laughter. She scowled. "What?" she asked.

Avery chuckled and got to his feet. I held my stomach and laughed harder. Avery held his hand out to help me up and I begrudgingly took it. As I stood, Caitlyn threw me her 'fuck you' look over her shoulder, then I quickly forced my team into a huddle, not waiting for Colt. I wanted to crush this team.

"We have to switch it up. Maya, you start a crossing pattern behind me then buttonhook down the left side. Sara, watch out for Caitlyn. She has it out for me now. Sienna, help block anyone who goes after Maya."

I called hike and threw the ball as Avery, playing safety, stepped up to cut off Maya's route and intercepted the ball. Caitlyn couldn't wait to jump into Avery's arms. She was so happy when he spun her around. *That's it. This means war.*

"Colt!" I shouted. "You take Caitlyn, I'm going after Avery," I said it with severity in my voice. His mouth dropped open. He quickly recovered and nodded. I wasn't taking no for an answer.

I gave a few more instructions to Kennedy and Nora and walked to the forty-yard line. We lined up and I let my guard down for an instant. I ignored the growl I heard from Caitlyn and looked to Avery. His eyes were glued on me as his hands rested on his knees, waiting to run their last play. The side of his mouth drew up in a smile and his eyes sparkled with that cocky look that up until two days ago would have melted the panties right off me. That arrogant look of his sparked something in me.

When Caitlyn's hand gripped the ball, I didn't even look at Caitlyn. I knew Colt had her. I lunged for Avery. He had the same idea. My world tilted and before I knew it, Avery blocked me and had me pressed into the mud. His wide smile gleamed at me. That only fueled my anger more. I pushed at his chest for him to get off me.

"I love it when you're feisty," Avery said. I scowled at him. He chuckled. "And you're cute as hell when you're mad," he said touching the tip of his finger to my nose like I was a toddler and rose to his feet. He held out his hand and I reluctantly took it. I grinned sarcastically at him. It was my turn.

We gathered onto the soggy forty-yard line and I waited for Caitlyn to get the ball then I lunged toward her. *Screw the play.* She faked the ball and for a moment, I was distracted by it. She launched the ball in the air, lost her step, and face-planted into the mud. I leaped into the air and my hand closed around the ball. My feet hit the ground and I slipped and slid in the mud. I quickly found my balance then took off into a full-on sprint.

"Interception by Aria," Travis shouted into the microphone. I pushed through the cluster of girls and ran for the end zone. I ran the length of the field and into the end zone. Just as I made it into the end zone warm, arms tackled me to the ground. We stumbled together, rolling in the mud.

When my world stopped spinning, I blinked Avery into focus. He pressed his wet, heavy body against mine and pinned my arms to the side. The heated look in his eyes was the most scrumptious thing I'd ever seen. Then reality seeped into my senses and I stiffened.

"Touchdown by Aria!" Travis called out into the microphone.

"Get off me," I barked.

"Make me," he said wiping mud away from my brow. I squirmed under him and he pressed me to the ground harder. I could feel the cold mud soaking through my shirt but my body burned from the feel of his body. Avery felt my shiver but I wasn't going to give him the satisfaction of knowing he turned me on. I slid my leg out and rolled Avery to the side. He looked surprised as I rolled him to his back but as I tried to straddle him my knees slid out from under me and I fell into him. I tried to stand up again but my shoes kept slipping in the mud.

The rain was coming down stronger and the field was a giant mess. Avery tried to get up but his feet failed quickly. We rolled around the mud pit until finally, I rolled to my back next to him and we both lay there trying to catch our breath. His eyes danced over me.

"You're so beautiful, Aria," he said softly pulling a wet strand of my hair away from my eyes. I blinked in disbelief. *I was a muddy mess.* I felt his warm hand on my face and leaned into it. *God, his touch was electric. It always sucked me back in.* His eyes bored into me and I squirmed under his stare.

"What?" I asked.

"You playing quarterback is the sexiest thing I've ever seen. You made me fall in love with football all over again."

I cringed at his choice of words. *Avery had hurt me.* My guard immediately went back up.

"Is that right?" My eyes fell away and I tilted my head away. "Look who's finally feeling with his heart."

Colt and Sean ran up next to us.

"Need help?" Colt asked.

I turned away from Avery, instantly feeling bad for what I'd said.

Avery and I both tried to get up again but quickly slipped and we both fell face first this time. I could hear the teams laughing at us. We rolled onto our backs and broke out into laughter. The tense conversation was now gone as our pathetic attempt to get to our feet only made things worse.

Colt planted his feet next to Avery's and instead of helping Avery up, Colt's feet lost traction and he fell into Avery. Avery cried out as Colt's knee slammed into Avery's groin. Avery jerked back and smacked my chin. I grabbed my chin and cursed.

"Fuck!" Sean's eyes lit up when my leg tripped him and his feet went out from under him. We held our sides in laughter as Pierce made his way over to us.

"Don't!" We all shouted at him at the same time.

"Idiots," Pierce chuckled, and reached out for my hands. He dragged me a few feet out of the shallow mud pit and pulled me to my feet. He did the same thing to the others. That only made us laugh harder. *Why didn't we think of that?*

"Colts win!" he announced. And just like that the competitive side to the game was gone. The game was over and I made my way to the sidelines for some water.

Sara and Colt both slapped my hand and cheered at our victory. I was so happy to have my friends. Avery congratulated all of us on our win. My knees shook with weakness. I forced myself not to look back over my shoulder. I didn't want to see the hurt in Avery's eyes. I was mean to him and I felt like hell about it now. *Damn, I have no filter.*

I let Ethan and Wren take turns spinning me around. Each one saying what a great job I did. Ethan had his arm around me when Avery spoke.

"Be at the cocktail lounge at ten o'clock." His eyes landed on mine. "All of you."

I gulped nervously. He was a jerk to me that night of the Ball. But god, he was beautiful, sexy, and desirable. I tried hard to find the silver lining in all of this. At least this time we weren't going to be alone.

⌘

DAY TWELVE:
FRIDAY NIGHT
COCKTAIL PARTY

It was just before ten that evening when Sara and I walked up the back deck stairs toward the second floor cocktail lounge. The blanket of radiant stars flickered like diamonds glimmering in the moonlight above.

I stepped up to the deck in Sara's stilettos to see that it was decorated in very expensive lighting with delicate curves in the carved wood. All the women were in heels and little black dresses. I ran through several scenarios in my head as I was putting on my new gorgeous black dress that Sara had also bought me, thinking of ways to get out of this tonight. But I couldn't muster the energy to come up with a good excuse. And I definitely didn't have the strength to tell her the truth about what was going on between Avery and me.

I let my hands fall over my hips and readjusted my dress in hoping that I looked as good as Sara. *I liked this dress.* It was cinched tight at the waist and just covered my bottom by an inch. The shoulders of the dress set just off my shoulders and hugged my breasts tightly so I opted not to wear a bra. I didn't bother with stockings, preferring to show off my tanned legs.

I let my lungs fill and let out a deep breath slowly hoping tonight I could avoid Avery at all costs. I stepped to the doorway and let Sara go first. As I stepped in, I was met with applause and cheering.

"There's our star quarterback," Colt announced.

I cringed knowing Avery had everything to do with the beauty of this night. I plastered on my fake smile and glanced around the room. Twinkling white lights draped from the ceiling and the lights were dim for a more intimate setting. Sienna scooped me up and spun me around.

"You were so awesome. Thank you for not letting Caitlyn win this one. She is seething. You've burned her twice now." *Great, just what I needed. I'll be sure not to stumble out on the lawn to pee tonight. Just in case she's lurking in the shadows waiting to get me back.*

Our small team of sexy ladies, with Colt and Sean, moved to the bar beside the back windows. I tried to keep my eyes to the floor as I searched for Avery. I didn't want him to think I was looking for him. *Because I wasn't.* I just wanted to make sure I kept my distance.

Sara handed me a glass of champagne and I sipped on it slowly, trying hard not to have a repeat of my birthday or the masquerade party. Sara and Colt were reenacting the powder puff game with Sean, Sienna, Tyler, and Maya and I let myself step back against the bar, letting my gaze drift out to the forest that lay behind the great lodge. Fireflies flitted around the back lawn like tiny little explosions of canary-colored light. It was soothing as a gentle breeze wafted through my hair with the remnants of the storm system that had moved through earlier today.

The night was humid and I could feel my skin beginning to swelter when the breeze died down. I let my thoughts reflect on the past couple of weeks of camp. Never in my best fantasies could I have come up with this lifestyle.

I let my shoulders relax realizing how comfortable I was growing in all my endeavors. I liked my new friends. I liked the closeness that camp brought us. My sexuality was peaking. I had learned so much about myself in such a short time and I had only one person to thank. My eyes registered movement next to me. I glanced up to see Avery stepping toward me. *Damn, he was gorgeous.*

"To you, beautiful Aria," he said clinking his glass with mine. I smiled softly in awe of him. I knew then that I could never truly hate this man. I was still under his spell.

"Thank you." I tried to ignore the sparkle in his eyes. I sipped my champagne, keeping my eyes locked onto his. "Avery, I'm sorry about the mean things I said earlier," I rushed to say.

"I deserved that. It's forgotten, Aria," he said, holding my gaze. "Will you walk with me?"

I looked to my team to see their backs were to us. I nodded shyly and stepped in front of him. We walked the length of the room in silence and up a couple of steps to his private deck. I could feel the chilled glass in the palm of my hand. Crickets sang out in harmony throughout the night. I wobbled in my heels and Avery reached out to steady me.

"Thanks." He guided me to the railing and I took in the beauty of this night. His hand that still rested on me brushed up my arm and I turned to look up at him. "Please don't. I'm trying my hardest not to run from you, all of this, how you make me feel. When you touch me, my guard that I've worked so hard to put in place, shatters."

His eyes broadened. "Your honesty is overwhelming at times. But I like it. Don't ever lose that," he said softly lowering his hand. My eyes drifted to his half-unbuttoned soft grey dress shirt and I found myself tracing the curves of his muscular chest below.

"I won't." I swallowed dryly then took another sip of my champagne. "What do you want from me, Avery?"

"I wanted to apologize. I'm sorry for the night of the masquerade ball. I never wanted you to get hurt. I don't get emotionally involved with my guests. I crossed a line with you that I never intended to cross."

"I get it. Really I do. Are we done here? I want to get back to the party."

Avery let his head fall back, closed his eyes and breathed deeply, taking in the sounds of the night. He exhaled then opened his eyes and looked to me again. I could see something he was trying to shield me from.

"Was the song you sang at my birthday party about me?" I asked.

"Yes…it was."

"Why?" I said more forcefully than I intended. His eyes shifted back and forth searching mine for something. I could tell he was struggling with opening up to me.

"Avery, Aria, appetizers are being served," Pierce said, breaking through our private moment. Avery stepped away looking defeated.

"Be right there, Pierce. Give us a minute," he said not taking his eyes off me. I could see Peirce studying us for a moment then he turned and walked away. I tried to fight the tears that were pooling up in my eyes but this was all too much.

"Just tell me why you're fighting this. Us," I whispered as a tear fell down my cheek to my lips. He reached up and wiped it away. All I could do was stare up into his eyes waiting for his answer. I could see the fear in his eyes like a child afraid of the darkness that surrounded him knowing that at any moment the monster in the closest was going to step out.

He ran his hand through his hair in frustration. Laughter rang out as the noise of the party on the deck below seemed to break our private moment.

"I can't be that guy for you, Aria. I'm sorry, I really am."

I watched the man I was falling in love with run away from me, again. It proved once and for all to my heart that he didn't love me. *There was never any room for you in his world,* my wicked subconscious reminded me.

Anger boiled inside of me. *Fuck this!* I hated how Avery made me weak. I was not a weak person. I was a strong, independent woman for Christ's sake. *But if I was so independent, then why did I care so much?*

I pushed away the snide mental comment that I could always count on from my subconscious, straightened my shoulders, and made my way back toward the bar. I needed a drink. And you can be damned sure it won't have Avery's last name on the bottle. *I think I'll switch over to Jack Daniels tonight. He seemed friendly enough.*

⌘

DAY THIRTEEN:
SATURDAY NIGHT
NAUGHTY FAIRY TALES THEME PARTY

The next afternoon, after nursing yet another hangover, we were in our cabin getting ready for the Naughty Fairy Tales theme party. I didn't want to think of Avery anymore. I promised myself I would concentrate on a man that wanted me instead of one that ran away. I was done with Avery Jameson. There were forty Cubs in this camp and I could be with any of them. *If I really wanted to.*

Sara met my eyes in the mirror and I quickly diverted them away and smoothed out my dress and petticoat. At tonight's party, I would be naughty Cinderella. I had on a brocade corset dress with a crown brooch and embroidered accents, a venise lace trimmed underskirt with a white tulle petticoat and a satin bustle bow. The black choker was a contrast to the white elbow length gloves and a satin light blue headband with white trim accents. Lastly, I wore white thigh highs with bows. The length of it hardly constituted it as a dress.

"Jello wrestling and the final qualifying rounds of the pole dancing are tonight. Can't wait for Jello wrestling," Sara squealed.

"Jello wrestling?" I quirked my eyebrow questionably at her. Sara threw her head back and laughed.

"Read the fucking camp manual already," Sara urged.

"No. I refuse to read or study. I'm on break until the end of August." We both laughed.

"Anyways," she said, unplugging the curling iron and setting it down on the dresser. "I softened the look of your bangs by curling them a bit so they tucked under." I looked to see that Sara pulled my hair up onto the top of my head and curled the ends. I smiled widely at her. "You're ready Cinderella. Now scoot, so I can get ready."

"What are you going as?" I asked standing up from my chair.

"Princess Jasmine. I thought it would be fitting," she grinned.

"Cute," I said. I looked to my best friend and I could see how much she glowed. This place really made her happy. She was in her natural element. I went to put on my black platform shoes and couldn't help but wonder why I still felt like a fish out of water.

As Sara and I entered the Main Lodge, I noticed seven Cinderella's and three other Princess Jasmine's but for the most part everyone kept a nice mix of fairy tale characters.

The music helped to take away some of my stress. Everything was doused in silver and gold decor. Avery even had a large chandelier installed in the center of the room. The only thing missing was my Prince Charming.

"Tonight is the second night of the qualifying rounds for the pole dancing contest and for a little more fun, tonight's the first qualifying round of Kitten Jello wrestling," Avery announced.

238

I looked at the green-eyed heartless man and his eyes found mine through the sea of fantasy characters.

"The Winner of tonight's Jello wrestling event gets a once in a lifetime bungee jumping trip with me as your host," Avery hummed.

I saw Tara's husband elbow her like he wanted her to win the prize. But she quickly shook him off. *That a girl.*

Avery smiled that slow seductive smile at me and gave me that heated look that almost melted my panties right off. *Seriously?*

It took everything in me to move my feet. I had to keep my distance from him. He was like an emotional vampire calling out to me but I wasn't going to enter a Jello contest with the prize being an evening spent with him. *No fucking way am I putting myself through that.*

I finally turned my back to him and found Kim, the bartender. She smiled politely to me and nodded, knowing that I always ordered the same thing.

As I waited for my shot, Caitlyn arrived with Lucy and Becca flanking her. *The wonder triplets,* I thought to myself.

Caitlyn wore a Belle of the Ball costume. It was a satin yellow corset dress with off-the-shoulder sleeves and a small red rose applique. Her red chunky high heels accented the red petticoat.

Lucy wore a divine little red riding hood costume. Her mini dress was trimmed in black ribbon and lace-up bodice and a black petticoat. It had see through puff sleeves and an attached hood and she accented it with black gloves and black fishnet stockings.

Becca wore a pink Sleeping Beauty costume with off-the-shoulder sleeves, lace-up front, pale pink under skirt with silver trim detail and white petticoat. A long pink over skirt draped down behind her. She even wore the matching crown headpiece. Amber ran up to them squealing in delight.

"You guys look awesome," Amber said. Amber wore a purple fairy costume with a shimmer baby-doll dress with luminescent fiber optic lights. At her waist was a silver rope belt. She had her hair curled and accented with a headband. She even had the white glittery wings and a light-up wand.

"I know. Right," Caitlyn said in her scratchy voice. I could tell she was throwing looks of steely contempt my way.

Nate appeared out of nowhere wrapping his arms around Caitlyn's waist and pulled her against him. She smiled like they shared a secret and I suddenly felt more determined to get drunk.

I downed my double then nodded for her to pour me another. She winked at me and handed me another shot and a beer. I downed my second double and smiled widely to her. *Thank you, Kim.*

I carried the beer with me to our table. The alcohol hit me hard. I needed to eat. My eyes fell to Avery sitting at our table. He was talking to Travis about the Jello wrestling match and I did everything I could to avoid his gaze. I nervously sipped my beer.

Sara and Sienna were talking fashion. Sienna wore an evil queen costume. It was a black and purple mini dress and it had a black chocker. She even wore the crown.

Maya was Snow White. She wore a dark blue stretch velvet knit dress with red satin ribbon and a lace up front. Maya was laughing at something Sean whispered in her ear.

Colt sat next to me and handed me another beer. I thanked him. I took the last gulp of my first beer as Colt joined in the conversation with Avery and Travis.

Pierce was letting an instructor, Meredith, lick a dollop of whipped cream from his finger.

As we ate dinner, I couldn't help but let my foggy thoughts drift to Avery as he sat across from me. I hadn't thanked him for sending me the bouquet of wild orchids. I couldn't. *Why did he send them anyway?* He got what he wanted from me already. Frankly, the man confused the hell out of me.

I found myself staring at Avery's lips as Colt brushed his elbow against my arm. Avery was looking right at me with a knowing smirk like he knew what I was thinking. *Damn it.*

"Aria, your opponent is Lucy?" Colt asked.

I blinked over at him. "For what?" *I slurred that a bit.*

"You haven't heard a word I just said have you? No more shots for you tonight," he grumbled. "You're in tonight's first tier. You're taking on Lucy in the first round. If you win, you proceed to tonight's second round and wrestle the winner of Kennedy and Tara. Sara, you're in next week's tier, wrestling Amber. The winners of these tiers advance to wrestle in the final rounds at the camp Olympics. You did say you wanted to win that trip to Hawaii didn't you?"

I totally spaced out again. Avery had licked his lips and that was all I could concentrate on. *Wait, so I have to wrestle in Jello?*

Colt cleared his throat. I nervously glanced around the table. I was grateful that everyone was looking at Colt and not at me drooling over Avery. I scolded myself. I needed to move on from Avery. He made it plain and simple when he said that he didn't want me.

"Don't make me do this. Oh, please. No, I'm too fucked up," I begged.

"Hey, if you win you may get a shot to kick Caitlyn's ass, she was raised wrestling in Jello," Sara jumped in.

"How many rounds are there tonight?" I asked.

Colt rolled his eyes at me and set a glass of water in front of me.

"Here, drink this. I need you to sober up. The match starts just after the pole dancing qualifying rounds."

I mentally shook myself. It wasn't the alcohol. I just didn't want another evening with Avery but I couldn't tell him that. Nobody knew that I let Avery have his way with me and I wasn't going to start trouble between Colt and his friend. I knew Sara and Colt would protect me. They always did. Sara and Colt both warned me not to get involved with Avery. But here I was involved and regretting that decision.

"Two rounds, Aria. We have three pools set up. It should go fairly quickly. Got it?"

"Yep," I chirped. "Wait. When does it start?"

Colt sighed and looked to Sara. "I got this." Sara stood and pulled me up to the bar. She ordered me an energy drink and an ice water. Sara quickly made me down them both, then we made our way back to the table.

The DJ called the judges to the center table and I was relieved when Avery left our table. I was better already since I didn't have Avery's eyes distracting my every thought.

The second round pole-dancing contest quickly got underway and I was still buzzed, even after dinner. I kept myself busy with conversation with Sara, and Sienna's boyfriend Sean.

In my haze, I looked at Sean. He was wearing a black button up dress shirt that was unbuttoned twice at the collar, revealing his chest, and black dress pants. I could see his eyes shift to me and his lips curved into a crooked smile. These theme parties were definitely about the women. The men simply dressed up either in suits or collared shirts and dress pants that usually favored black.

"You like what you see, Aria?" Sean's sultry voice said.

"Yes," I stated confidently.

"Me too, baby," he winked and deep down in my groin I felt a burning desire.

"I think we have Jameson to thank for bringing Aria out of her shell," Sara winked to me.

"What?" I barked. My eyes lit up. *Did they know about Avery and me?*

"The whiskey, Aria," Sara replied. *Oh.* I felt my face heat up. Sara wore a light blue Princess Jasmine costume with a blue short-sleeved mesh top accented with a gold pattern and blue waist see through harem trousers to reveal blue lace panties. The hat with a veil complimented it.

I looked around the room at all the sexy fairy tale costumes. A sexy wolf costume caught my eye and I grinned when I realized it was Tara as she waved to me and strutted to the DJ booth to request her song.

Tara was the last to finish up the pole dancing contest and the crowd cheered and whistled. She had some sexy moves. She really had blossomed here at camp. Avery announced the three winners and I smiled when he announced Tara as one of the winners.

Avery called the participants for Jello wrestling over to the side. Three large pools were set up on the side of the ballroom. They were circular but a square boxing ring type enclosure encased each pool with the main ring for the last bout featured in the center. The earlier qualifying rounds would be in the smaller pools on either side of it. Small bleachers were set up on the far side of the pools nearest the wall and tables lined the other side where I was sitting. The lights all danced to the beat of the music with lasers banding about rhythms on the floors and walls. It was sensory overload.

Begrudgingly, I stepped out of my high heels and stockings and waited for Colt and Lucy to make their way to ringside. Lucy unzipped her revealing little red riding hood costume and took off her black fishnet stockings. Her body was gorgeous.

The spectators moved closer to us and idle chatter filled the crowd. My anxiety spiked high as most of the camp had spilled into the ballroom of the Lodge for these events. Music poured out from the overhead sound system.

"Strip," Colt said, coming up beside me. I glared at him. He chuckled. "Take off your costume. You can leave your bra and underwear on. But you can't do this fully clothed."

I nodded and shimmied out of my very short dress.

"Good girl," Colt said, not trying to hide his smile as he stepped to the side of the wrestling pools to announce the rules of the competition.

I kept my eyes to the ground. I didn't want to know if anyone was looking at me.

"Hello, ladies. The rules for this event are as follows:
Remember to be nice or be disqualified. No head butting,
hair pulling, biting, kneeing, kicking, gouging, or choking. If
you slide out it's an automatic point for the other person.
Referees, as always, have the final say. Pin your opponent
and you win the round. The winner moves on to the
second round. Be safe, be silly, and have fun. Got it?" Colt
asked, looking at all four of us.

"Ready, Kittens?" Colt said. *Damn, this was really
happening.* I really didn't want to win this contest. I didn't
want to be in the contest in the first place. But Colt didn't
leave me much choice. I would do anything for him, all he
had to do was ask. We all nodded.

"On my count, three, two, one, go," Colt shouted.

Colt urged Lucy and me forward. We slipped our feet
into the cold lime-green Jello and I only had a second to get
used to it. It was so squishy.

Lucy didn't hesitate. She nailed me with a good
clothesline to the chest. I slipped and landed on my back in
the Jello. I rose up at my waist and ran my hand over my
face trying to clear my vision and then rolled onto my knees
just as Lucy fell toward me. Instinctively, I rolled onto my
side away from her and I heard the crowd hiss as Lucy
glided hard into the side of the kiddie pool with her body
halfway out.

"Point for Aria." *This stuff was getting into every crevice on my
body.* "Go again," Colt added.

I clenched my hands to my sides, staggered to my feet,
and swung around to face her. My adrenaline was finally
clearing the alcohol-induced fog from my head. I took a
step back from her but she lashed out and dragged me

down with her. I choked on the Jello and brutally struggled to breathe. My heart was drowning out the music and the cheering around me.

I climbed on top of her so she would stop splashing Jello in my face and finally took a deep breath in. She grunted and wiggled out from under me like an eel.

We both stood facing each other. Lucy looked more determined than ever. As she leaped forward, Lucy slipped and fell on her face. She slid forward into me and I fell over on top of her, sprawled out like I was a baby calf learning to walk. Lucy tried hard to get her hands under me to push me off her but they kept slipping. I was about to roll off her to let her get up when Colt blew the whistle.

"Pin. Aria wins!" Colt shouts. People nearby cheered and I frowned up at Colt. *What? The match was over?*

I helped a scowling Lucy up and stepped out from the pool. Colt handed me a towel. I wiped off my face and looked to see Sara smiling. Kennedy stepped into the pool in front of me with her eyes set on Avery. These women were vicious. They wanted to win this so bad. I was nervous that I might.

Colt called the match to a start and I tried for the same moves as last time but Kennedy was ready for me. I dodged the clothesline move that she stole from Lucy. She turned quickly and I could see the surprise on her face as her feet went out from under her. Her body was submerged in Jello. She tried to stand but she couldn't get her footing. Before I knew it, my feet were knocked out from under me and I lay stunned, looking up at the rafters. Kennedy lay beside me. I crawled to my knees but Kennedy was already to her feet with her arms out in front trying to balance herself. She took a step forward and fell again. I tried to get out of the way of her misstep but I landed face first on top of her and I ended up half straddling her. The move pinned her beneath me and I couldn't get any grip to move myself off her. My hands kept sliding out from under me.

After three seconds, Colt called out, "Pin. Point for Aria."

Kennedy stood, looking nervous and frustrated. Losing a Jello-wrestling match was harder than I thought. I tried not to make any sudden moves. I waited for Kennedy to make the first move but she had the same idea I did.

"You have to wrestle, Kittens," Colt urged. Kennedy and I were comparable in build but she was a few inches taller than me. I saw her hesitate then she tackled my waist. She raked her nails down my arm as we fell into the Jello. *Kennedy wasn't fighting fair and she just pissed me off.*

I leaned all my weight onto her using her nails in my skin to fuel my rage. Her legs kicked under me as she rolled me over. I squirmed underneath her and we both could hear Colt counting.

"Pin. Point for Kennedy," Colt said.

She rose to her feet and paced around as I scrambled to my feet. We were too close of a match in strength. I had to think of another way.

Colt resumed the match, urging us on. I could hear the mixture of cheering for her and me throughout the crowd.

"Tackle her, Kennedy," Nate's voice called out and that was all she needed. Her lip curled in determination and she dove after me in a blind rage. I quickly stepped out of her way. She skidded across the pool and up over the side onto the dance floor. *Fuck you, bitch!*

247

"Point. Aria, wins," Colt said.

Kennedy pounded her hand on the ground below her and stormed away. Colt handed me my towel and I quickly scraped the Jello away from my face. I groaned inwardly. I had just won again.

Sara walked over with a long hose and sprayed me down as most of the guys stood nearby watching. I rolled my eyes inwardly as she toweled me off. I followed Sara toward the bar. We downed our shots and I looked to the stage to see Avery bringing the room to his attention.

"Aria, please come to the stage, Kitten," his decadent voice said.

Sara quickly swiped a napkin under my eyes, wiping away the excess mascara and sent me on my way. I stepped to the stage in my soggy Jello infested underwear and bare feet.

Avery took hold of my hand and I couldn't hide the shiver that ran through me. His eyes locked on mine and his lips spread into an arrogant smile.

"Kittens and Cubs, the winner of tonight's Jello wrestling match… Miss Arabella Mason."

Colt whistled through his teeth and the crowd erupted in applause. I cringed. *I hated being center of attention.*

Avery kept his eyes on me and lifted the back of my hand to his lips in a gentlemanly manner.

"There is hope for you yet," I said, failing to hide the tantalizing quivers that ran up my body as his lips made contact. His mischievous eyes took in my reaction to him. I narrowed my eyes at him. He did that on purpose. *Bastard.*

He was smiling like he held all the secrets to the world. My eyes flashed to the bright pink and brilliant white wild orchid blossom he just slipped in my hand. I sucked in a breath as he leaned in towards my ear.

"Tomorrow, 7 o'clock. I'll pick you up at your cabin." I nodded. "Oh, and Aria, wear jeans."

When I came to my senses, I closed my hand around the soft velvet petals. I tried to reign in my excitement, but I was caught up in Avery, again. I couldn't help it. A fire took hold of my heart and I knew in that moment that I would do just about anything to be with him. *I was so screwed.*

◆<u>Week Three:</u>

⌘

DAY FOURTEEN:
SUNDAY AFTERNOON
BUNGEE JUMPING

I had stared at the clock for the last twenty minutes. I had been ready and nervously filing my fingernails so that I would have something to do. It was ten minutes until he arrived and my stomach had that funny feeling you get when you drink too much caffeine; only I hadn't had any caffeine today. It was nerves. I don't know why I was looking forward to this so badly. It was not a date. Just the prize from last night's Jello wrestling.

I pulled my hair into a ponytail and grabbed my sweatshirt off the kitchen chair then sighed deeply. This was the most clothes I had on since my arrival at camp and the most comfortable I could be besides my running clothes.

I paced the floor feeling very uncertain about this whole thing. I didn't know if I wanted to be in the same room with him after he pushed me away the night of the Ball. I reminded myself that he had been hurt before. And I realized it was my softer side that kept giving him second chances. My only hope was that I wouldn't regret this. My compassion for him could not be allowed to rule me. I needed to be smart about this. Keep my head on straight.

The only problem was, when I got around Avery, my wit escaped me. My heart wanted to lead my body. *How do I fight someone that makes me feel so good and yet is so bad for me?*

I was setting my self up for heartbreak and I knew it, but I kept hoping there was a chance. Even a million to one shot is still a chance. *But I might have a better chance at being struck by lightning,* my subconscious sneered.

I was pulled from my contemplation when the quad pulled up outside. It was Sunday, laundry day, and my bra-and-panty-sets were hanging all over the cabin to air dry, so I scurried to the front door before he turned off the engine.

I slowed my steps trying, to read his mood. He wore a smile that said he had a secret that he wasn't sharing. He switched off the four-wheeler and handed me a helmet. He was still straddling the quad but I took in his tight black AC/DC t-shirt and dark denim jeans. My mouth wanted to fall open. I wanted to crawl across his lap and let him bury himself in me.

"Hi," my voice cracked. He winked and I stepped to take the helmet.

"Sorry about the helmet," he said pulling his helmet over his head. "You'll need it for where we are going."

I nodded, too afraid that my voice would betray me again. I weaved the braided strap through the silver ring and tightened it with my shaky hands. He waited patiently until my hands were through, and then checked the strap to make sure it was tight. I looked at his hands and longed for him to touch me.

He slid forward and I straddled behind him. He started the engine and I let the vibrations pulse through me. I felt liberated. I didn't know if it was because Avery was in control, or if I was just getting swept up in his world, but I smiled and felt myself relax against him. He revved the engine and I could see that we had several onlookers.

I waved to Sienna as she stepped out of her cabin in the distance and she gave me a 'go get em' look. I busted out laughing. *Oh, if she only knew how I really wanted to.*

I tightened my sweatshirt around my waist then wrapped my hands around his tight abs. He followed my gaze to Sienna. I couldn't help but notice the bewildered look she gave him as we pulled away.

When we got clear of all the people, Avery's body relaxed, then he shot through the woods past all the cabins.

Along the way, I could see his place in the distance through the trees and my heart raced. I had already forgiven him. He had shown me so much of himself and I knew that scared him. That was his true game. I told myself he wanted to get close to me but he held onto his fear. I realized Avery thought too much, just like me.

We started to climb the ridge up the mountain and I leaned into him more. The non-sensible side of me wanted to find the hem of his shirt and slide my hands over his warm skin. I pushed the thought from my mind and scolded myself. *That was not why we were here. This was not a date. I won a contest. He'd just hurt me again.*

We rode up the mountain for about thirty minutes over old dusty trails past half buried cabins from a bygone era. The thick canopy of forest thinned as we rode higher and the tires of the quad dug deep into the rutted trail.

Finally, we arrived at the top of a lightly wooded lot. He turned to the left and headed toward a cliff. We reached a large wooden bridge with planks missing every few feet as it swayed in the stern breeze that flowed up from the valley.

He pulled off to the side and turned the motor off. I climbed off, wishing I didn't have to let go and tried to loosen the strap on my helmet. He had already taken his off and stepped to help me with mine. He loosened the strap for me and I tugged the helmet from my head. I smoothed down my bangs and untied my sweatshirt then draped it over my arm.

"Are you ready for this?" he said. *Did you really have to ask?* I said to myself. Instead, I took it upon myself to be a smartass and yawned in fake boredom. Avery chuckled.

"Bold and beautiful," he breathed. His eyes danced with excitement. He stepped to the back of the quad, pulled out a backpack, secured the strap over his shoulder, and we walked toward the bridge. He led me past the bench next to the bridge and onto the rickety, swaying structure. I stopped to wonder where he was headed, and then I shrugged when I realized I would probably follow him anywhere.

Bits of wood flaked off under my running shoes as we made our way to the center of the bridge. He stopped mid-center, finding several secure planks that hadn't as yet fallen to the river below, lowered his backpack to the deck, and then knelt to the ground. You could feel the wind swaying us to and fro. *This was insane to sit out here.*

He spread the throw blanket open wide and lowered it to the creaking planks. I took in a deep breath, steadied my nerves, and realized there was no place I would rather be. I swallowed nervously as I watched him bring out plastic cups, cheese, crackers, and grapes. *This bridge could snap at any second.*

I pushed my hands into my front pockets and waited for him to arrange everything as a strong gust picked up, causing me to lose my balance temporarily. He glanced up in concern then gestured for me to sit. I dropped my sweatshirt beside me and wearily sat cross-legged on the blanket. I couldn't believe I was here, alone with Avery, drifting side to side, over a valley at least fifteen hundred feet below. I tried to reign in my thoughts as he sat next to me.

He opened the wine with grace and poured a glass then handed it to me. I sipped on it, grateful I had something to do with my hands, and watched as he poured himself a glass. I saw him study my KSU t-shirt.

"Do you like your nursing classes?"

"I guess. Nursing is all I've ever wanted to do since my best friend broke her arm when I was ten years old and I didn't know how to help her."

"You didn't want to become a doctor?"

"Nah. The nurse at the Emergency Room was so caring and gentle to my friend during a really scary moment of her life. The doctor just barked out orders. It was the nurse who really helped her."

He blinked then studied me. "You have a soft spot for the less fortunate don't you?"

"I guess I always have," I nervously played with the silver chain around my neck and let my hand fall around the rectangular metal. It was a habit of mine that I seemed to resort to when I was lost in thought – which was pretty often; except that this was the first time I'd had a chance to wear it since I got here.

"Are those Military tags?" he asked. I unclasped my hand around them and held them out for Avery to read. "Lieutenant Terry Joseph Mason, Air Force."

"They were my father's. He was a pilot. He used to take me flying every time he came home on leave. I loved how it was just him and me surrounded by nothing but blue sky. I always felt safe with him. He was killed in Iraq. It's just me and my mom now."

"I'm sorry." He paused for a moment. "What does your mom do?"

"She's an executive for a large business firm in Cleveland. I don't see her much. She works long hours. I usually only see her on holidays when the business world is closed."

I downed the remaining wine in my cup and Avery quickly filled it. We sat in silence looking out at the forest below, just taking in the scenery, munching on cheese and grapes.

"I started running because of my dad." Avery looked at me curiously. "He told me if you ever wanted to work something out in your head there was no better way to do it then by running outdoors. He was right. Nature seemed to consume me and make all my problems feel small."

I looked to see Avery staring at me. His emerald eyes seemed to shine amongst the sky in the distance. We were so high you could barely hear the waterfall in the distance but the mist layered itself above the river below us.

"My father gave me two other pieces of advice, want to know what they were?" I rambled nervously. Avery nodded and popped a piece of cheese in his mouth.

"Always read a newspaper and stay current in what is going on in the world today. Second, listen more and talk less. I've done all the talking. Now it's your turn."

"Your arms are very solid. Tell me about being a gymnast back in high school?"

I narrowed my eyes at him. *He was not opening up to me.*

"My best friend in middle school talked me into joining with her. I found it was a great way to let out frustration. I liked the independent part of the sport. You are only as good as you want to be. I suppose tumbling made me feel closer to flying. It was a way that I could feel closer to my dad when he was always gone." Avery's face softened. "Why all the questions? When do I get some answers from you, Mr. Jameson?"

Avery chuckled. "Alright, you can ask me all the questions you want until the sun touches those trees. Then we'll have some real fun."

I looked to see the sun just above the tree line. I playfully glared at him. *He thought he was so clever.*

I chewed on a red grape while I filed through my long list of questions in my head and tried to ask the most important one. I knew he wasn't going to talk about the woman that crushed him so I went to my second choice.

"The only one that is pressing is why did you start Camp Jameson? Don't you worry about what people might think?"

Avery looked toward the setting sun and shifted nervously, bringing his arms out behind him, and leaned backwards.

"That's two questions," he smirked gloriously to me. I wanted to melt right there.

"You can't stall waiting for the sun to go down. It doesn't work that way," I said.

"I'm afraid we don't have enough time for me to tell the story properly. But I will start by saying this," he said leaning into me. "If I never opened this camp, I never would have met you."

I chuckled. "That has got to be the worst pickup line I ever heard."

"Maybe so," he grinned. I blushed as he gave me a heated look.

"I will tell you this, it all started right here in this very spot. My brother and I hiked this ridge with the intent of rock climbing but we found this old bridge. On our way back down the mountain to our truck and hitch-trailer we missed our trail to the parking lot and veered off course. It took us around the far ridge across from the parking lot. At the edge of a clearing beneath an overgrown bush was a 'for-sale by owner' sign. Before I knew it, I had the owner on the phone asking for a price and how many acres they had to sell. Because I had graduated a year early from high school and I only had one more year left of architecture school, I decided to use some of my trust fund from my grandfather to buy the land."

The base of the sun touched the trees, bathing the horizon in a shimmering orange glow. Avery stood, wiping his hands down the front of his jeans, as he steadied his feet on the ever-swaying bridge.

"Time to have some real fun."

I turned to see a Club Car utility 4x4 pull up across the bridge. Pierce jumped out and rounded to the back of the cart. He pulled out a bag of gear and strode casually but carefully toward us. He'd obviously been on this bridge before. Neither one of them had any fear of it. I glanced toward Avery and I could see his excited smile on his face and then I studied Pierce. This was week three of camp and I still hadn't really talked to him. His shoulders were wide and he wore a deep tan like Avery.

"Aria, you know my brother, Pierce." Pierce whistled loudly through his teeth. I could feel my face heat up under his stare.

"Hi," was all that I could say.

"Yummy." He looked me over from head to toe. I took a step behind Avery as the breeze stiffened a bit, causing me to reach my hand out to Avery's shirt to steady myself. Pierce studied me. "Shy one, aren't you?"

"Let's get the gear ready. We're losing daylight," Avery interceded. I was thankful he did. Avery leaned over and lowered his mouth to my ear.

"Look who else doesn't trust easily," he breathed. He was smirking at me when he pulled away and I blinked at him, not sure how to reply. I realized then that he was quoting my words from the morning I had breakfast with him.

I watched as Avery and Pierce went to work with unpacking the gear. They both took out several lengths of rope, clamps, and harnesses, and I watched, intrigued by their knowledge. They had the same build. Pierce was younger and his eyes were blue. I still had no idea what I was in store for. It seemed very dangerous to try and bungee off this rickety old thing. I waited patiently until I saw Pierce begin to mount the support device to the side of the bridge. Avery laughed at my nervous stance.

"Nothing will make you feel more alive than bungee jumping off Jameson Bridge. I knew you'd like this."

"You named the bridge after yourself? Of course you did. But what if I'm afraid of heights?"

Avery laughed. "You're here aren't you? Now, step in."

I put my hands on Avery's shoulders to steady myself as he secured the harness around me. His time near me was too short and all I wanted him to do was close the space between us and kiss me. His hands, even though they were touching me through clothes were in all the right places and I was just about to explode with desire. I guess this was pretty exciting, being up here on a bridge that could snap at any moment and sharing that moment with Avery. It was amazing.

When I thought he was all through, he stepped closer and put his hands around the back of my neck. I tried hard not to overreact by his warm hands on my skin. I was glad when he lifted my father's military tags from my neck and gathered them in his hand.

"We wouldn't want to lose these." He stepped to the backpack, set them in, and zipped it up.

I was so blown away by the gesture that I just stood in awe as I watched him secure his own harness as Pierce double-checked his straps.

The mountainside glistened even more with the glow of the setting sun as Avery helped me climb under the rope to the ledge of the old bridge. I didn't want to look down but I couldn't help myself. I just stared at the rushing water flowing over the rocks kicking up a fine mist and the waterfall in the distance. The supreme foliage of the thick forest covering the mountains that led down to the valley was stunning. We were at least fifteen hundred feet in the air as he pulled me near and clipped his harness to mine.

"You didn't think I was going to let you do this without me, did you?" I smiled up at him. "I want to be the one to catch you when you fall," he said in a low voice. Those words did more to me than I wanted to admit.

"Put your arms around my chest." I was nervous and excited.

"Ready?" I nodded.

"On my count of three." He let his fingers trail under my chin and tilted my face to look at him. "Don't you dare look away. Keep your eyes on the ground and take it all in. Fly with me, Aria." He studied my face as if he was trying to memorize me then wrapped his arms around my waist. It was the most intimate gesture I could have ever hoped for. Avery looked at Pierce and nodded then looked back to me.

"One, two, three."

I could feel Avery lean over the ledge and I let myself fall with him.

The rush was exhilarating. The wind pushed my cheeks back away from my mouth and I could feel them rippling in the wind. I screamed in delight and louder than I ever have before. I felt Avery's chest rumble with laughter.

I knew I was secured to Avery, so I let my hands fall out to the side and leaned my head back. I was flying.

"That a girl," Avery breathed in my ear and wrapped his arms around me tighter.

I took it all in. I took in the smell of Avery's cologne as the tears streamed down my cheeks from the air rushing past my face. The mixture of the forest made of pine and oak, nature was all around us. The river gushed below us as the summer heat drifted by in waves off the mountain. The sun had a warm glow in the distance and the river below us was fast approaching. I was plummeting at a fast rate and I didn't once think of how dangerous this really could be or if the bridge would hold when our bands reached full tension. I was in Avery's arms, and I felt safe.

We dropped down within feet from the water. I stretched out my hands farther and let the water brush my fingertips. I laughed aloud as the adrenaline coursed through me. The cords recoiled and pulled us up about six feet, and then we dropped downward again. The ropes swayed us back and forth like a pendulum on a grandfather clock. I looked up at Avery as he wiped the tears from my eyes. My eyes met his and I could see wonder and exhilaration in his.

"What a rush," he said closing his eyes. His brown hair was tousled now and all I wanted to do was run my hands through it.

"That was incredible," I shouted.

We both hung upside down just taking in each other as the rope stopped swaying. His eyes sparkled in awe. All the blood was rushing to my head. My heart thumped loudly in my ears. Adrenaline pushed through my veins. He readjusted his body and angled it closer to mine. His arms tightened around my waist. I could feel every inch of Avery. His hot breath on my lips. I was caught up in the moment. I couldn't take it anymore. I leaned in and pressed my lips to his. I brushed my tongue over his lips and Avery groaned then deepened the kiss.

I tightened my arms around him and pulled him closer. I tilted my head back as he broke away and trailed kisses down my neck. He sucked in a breath but then I felt him stiffen and pull away. I could see the panic that shot through his eyes.

"I can't," he said. Anger spread through me like a wildfire.

"What do you mean? You can't kiss me but you can fuck me then leave me? You're just like Nate," I seethed. I could feel Pierce beginning to pull us back up. I took advantage of the time we had. It was a long way back up. *I know that I was the one to kiss him but had I really read his body language wrong?*

"Avery, why do you pull away every time we get close?"

"I can't be with you, Aria. I'm sorry if you thought that this was something more than the contest prize."

"Bullshit. So you would have done this with anyone? Even, say, Caitlyn?"

"It was just a prize. You won the prize."

"You know Avery, that's the thing. You're not being honest with yourself. You remember what you said to me the first day I arrived?" I didn't wait for his answer. "You said don't think, just feel. You should really follow your own advice."

The rope jarred and came to a sudden halt. Pierce cursed. "It's jammed guys. Give me a minute," Pierce called out. I heaved a sigh and tried to diffuse the situation. *What more could I do.* I was being held in his arms and held against him by straps with no place to go.

I looked at Avery. Here we were, hanging upside down, and between the adrenaline and my frustration, I could feel my brain falter.

"Don't you think you're being too hard on yourself? You push people away in your life that are good for you and you don't even see it. And you say *I* think too much. Everyone has been hurt one way or another in the past. You learn from your mistakes. That's life. You can't run away from your past forever. I have heard the stories about how badly you got hurt in the past, but that's no reason to treat every woman you've met after that like a piece of shit. Get over it already!"

Avery's eyes widened then traced back and forth from my eyes to my mouth as he took in my words. "You really care about me don't you?"

"Hah. Don't you dare turn this around on me, Jameson. This is about you. I've made a fool out of myself twice now. It's your turn."

"I got it," Pierce called out over the edge of the bridge. The rope began to pull us back up again.

Avery studied me. "Just tell me one thing. What do you see in me that has you so intrigued?" he asked in a rough voice.

"Oh, no you don't. No more. I'm done opening my heart to you. All you do is rip it apart. I don't want to be a part of your stupid games anymore."

"Fair enough." He lowered his voice. "Just so you know, I didn't know I was playing a game. I'm just…"

"Sorry about that guys. Almost there," Pierce called to us. I didn't really register what Pierce had said. I was too busy seething.

"You're just what Avery? Scared?" My voice rose up an octave. "News flash, we're all scared to show people who we really are. It's about who you want to take a chance on and who you don't!" My voice echoed off the ridge of the mountain but I didn't care. He looked so lost in that moment. I regretted my words instantly. *Once again, I had no filter.*

"Avery, give me your hand," Pierce said.

I didn't realize we had stopped at the underside of the bridge. The wind was starting to pick up drastically. Avery and I looked to each other, letting my harsh words sink in.

He unbound his hands from around my waist and stretched towards Pierce. The wind pushed us away from Pierce then back towards him. His hand was just out of reach as Avery stretched further.

Finally, Avery's hand clasped Pierce's and he pulled us up so that my hands could reach the rope rail. I pulled myself to the edge and held onto the side on the decaying planks. Pierce had two Coleman lanterns lit on high beside him. The sun had sunk down behind the mountain as we were mostly bathed in darkness. I couldn't help but feel how close it reflected my sinking mood.

"Hold on tight. I'm going to undo my clip. Don't let go."

I nodded as Avery undid his clamp and climbed under the rope rail. He lifted me with ease over the ledge and set me on my feet. We both could see his brother studying us. I'm sure Pierce could sense the tension between us.

Avery ran his hand through his hair and closed his eyes. He looked back at Pierce and I could see Avery's guard go up.

"That was awesome. I had never done this at twilight before. It really is amazing. You should try it," Avery said to Pierce.

"No, I need to get back. Help me pack up, would ya?" Pierce said shifting his gaze to me.

Avery dexterously untied my ropes and harness. I wish I could have done it, but I had no clue how it was hooked. I was at his mercy.

I stepped out of the harness, pulled my hands away from his shoulders, and turned toward the blanket. I reached into the backpack, retrieved my father's military tags, grabbed my sweatshirt, and threw them both on. I walked to the edge of the bridge and stared down at the dark ridge below as I waited for Avery and Pierce to get the gear packed.

I looked up when I heard the sound of the gear thrown in the truck.

"See you later, Aria," Pierce called out.

I waved and looked to see Avery packing up our half-eaten picnic food. He didn't take as much care when packing it away as he had unpacking it. He seemed frustrated and pissed.

I sighed, knowing that the next thirty minutes back down the mountain were going to be the longest minutes of my life. I'll admit Avery was more stubborn than I was. I could only do what he wanted. I had to keep my distance.

The silence between us was deafening. The only thing shining in the darkness was the headlight of the four-wheeler illuminating our way down the dirt trail heading back towards camp.

I didn't hold on as tightly to his abs as before and wished that I could touch him like I did on the way to the bridge. It was the most excruciating awkward silence, broken only by the sound of the engine and rubber tires grinding through the dried mud.

He stopped in front of my cabin and I got to my feet and tried to find the right words. I had wanted to say so many things in that moment but because my mouth had already said too much, only regret hung in the air between us. I had planned to soothe things over, but when we arrived, I saw that Caitlyn was sitting on the front porch of the cabin next to mine watching our exchange. *God, she was exhausting.*

"Avery, there's something wrong with my shower. Can you please come and take a look?" she said in a whiny voice as she stood and leaned over her rail in the bright porch light, exposing her double D's.

"You can call maintenance for that, Caitlyn. The number's in your manual," he said barely looking at her. He mostly kept his eyes to his quad beneath him. His jaw was clenched and I couldn't help but feel angry with myself for shooting off at the mouth tonight. I ruined a perfectly romantic evening all because I couldn't keep my damn mouth shut. All because I pushed him too far too fast. I was honest to a fault. And I knew that most people didn't want to hear the truth and Avery was no exception.

His eyes landed on me and he nodded toward me like I was some stranger he was passing by on the street then lowered his helmet and pulled away.

Caitlyn smirked, knowing she interrupted us. *I really didn't like that woman.*

I clenched my fists and turned on my heel toward my cabin. I had enough of the cold, distant Avery. I was done chasing him. I was done opening my heart up to him and laying it out for him to walk all over. I didn't want to be with a man that didn't want to be with me. *What was the point?* It was definitely time to move on.

⌘

DAY SIXTEEN:
TUESDAY NIGHT
SIENNA'S CABIN

"Aria, wait up," Sienna called out. I pushed the backpack over my shoulder and turned toward her. I smiled, feeling elated that I was able to completely relax and let go in my toys class today.

"Hey, I was wondering if you and Sara wanted to come over to my cabin tonight. We'll drink some wine and hang out."

"What time?"

"I need to clean up here, then I want to take a shower so, how about nine o'clock?"

"Sounds great," I said. As I turned to leave she put her hand on my forearm.

"Oh, and Aria. Way to let go today. You really are breathtaking to watch while you pleasure yourself."

I genuinely smiled back to her as I filled with confidence. "Thanks," I replied.

I left my hour and a half Tantric Breathing/Sex Toys class at Kit Kat cabin and headed back to Jasmine.

I showered and slipped on my jeans and a tight fitting t-shirt over my bra and panties and laced up my running shoes. It was quarter til nine. The night had gotten cooler as the sun set and I was hoping we could sit out by the fire. I reached for my Air Force hoodie instead of my father's military tags.

I had realized after talking with Avery about my father's death that it had been three years since he died and something in me had changed. I loved my father more than anything in the world but it wasn't healthy to cling to the necklace anymore. I was a different person now and there would always be a special place in my heart for him. I smiled at the memory of him as I glanced at his tags resting properly on my bedside table then I snapped off the light and exited my bedroom. I met Sara in the living room. She was grinning at me and bouncing with joy.

"Girls night. I can't wait. I am so happy that you hit it off with everyone."

"Me too. I really like everyone here," I said, putting on my hoodie.

Sara giggled. "I know. I can tell." She studied me. "You're different." She searched over my face again. "What's different about you?"

I shrugged. "I guess I'm just finally letting go of everything. I had a great class today. I'm sure Sienna will tell you all about it." I still hadn't told her what happened between Avery and me.

She squealed in delight, picked me up, and spun me around. "Yay! I'm so excited. The rest of the camp is going to be a blast. I know it."

I giggled. "Let's go. I need wine. And lot's of it."

I pulled the door shut to our cabin and glanced up to the sound of a four-wheeler driving towards us. I cringed, then relaxed some when I could see it was only Pierce. He whistled through his teeth at us arm in arm.

"Now that's what I'm talking about. Girl on girl is what this camp is all about." He whistled. "Where ya headed, Kittens?"

"Sienna's. Wanna come?" I asked.

"Always," Pierce winked and headed down the road toward the Cub section. Sara giggled and leaned into me.

"I *so* want to do him," she purred.

"So do him," I replied.

Sara hummed. "I'm saving the best for last," she said, wrapping her arms tighter around my left arm.

Pierce's statement made me realize then that I hadn't really enjoyed everything this camp had to offer yet. It got me to start seriously considering having a threesome experience. But other than Sara, was there a girl I wanted to be with? *Could I even go through with it?*

I pushed the thought from my head and walked with Sara toward the instructor's section of the camp. It was only a short walk from ours. We reached Sienna's cabin after a few minutes. The night air was cool for mid-summer, the sky was clear and the stars shown brightly down on us like the rhinestones on Liberace's cape. Sara knocked on the door and we let ourselves in.

"Sienna, we're here," Sara called out.

The décor was similar to our cabin but it was bathed in earth tones.

"Okay, I'll be just a minute. Make yourselves at home. There's wine already open for us. Help yourselves," she called out from her bedroom. I stopped cold and stared towards the corner of the room. My eyes landed on Caitlyn sitting on a dark brown leather couch.

"What are you doing here?" I quipped.

"I was invited," Caitlyn shrugged, looking bored as she sipped her wine and thumbed through the latest GQ magazine.

"No, Caitlyn. You invited yourself," Sienna chuckled as she stepped into the room.

"What evs," Caitlyn said as she rolled her eyes as if she really didn't pick up on Sienna's hint that we didn't want her there. Yet, we didn't want to start anything by getting rid of her. Sometimes, it just isn't worth it, but I haven't forgotten about her turning the lights on while I was peeing. I just didn't have the right idea yet as to what I should do to get her back. But I promised myself I'd think of something and soon.

Sienna mouthed the words 'I'm sorry' on her way to the kitchen to pour a glass of wine.

I casually strode around her living room taking in all the photos. One was of Sienna and an older couple I could only take as her parents. She looked just like her mother. It was taken on a beach in front of a pier. I saw photos of her and Sean on the same beach. He had her swept up in his arms and he was kissing her. I looked to the next photo to see Sienna with Sean and Avery. On Avery's arm was a tall brunette. She was kissing him on the cheek and he had his head pulled back in laughter. My heart dropped.

"That's Emily. She's the best," Sienna spoke those heart-wrenching words over my shoulder. I turned stiffly and took the glass of wine she held out for me. *Was this a girlfriend?*

Sienna eyed me curiously. "Emily is his sister," she added.

Oh. Okay, I'll admit it. I was a little jealous for like two seconds when I thought it was an ex-girlfriend. Okay, maybe a lot jealous. Then anger surged through me. *Avery was a player. He made it clear he didn't want me.*

"Let's sit out back. I started a fire," Sienna said. I nodded, afraid my voice would betray me, then followed her and Sara outside. Caitlyn was already sitting in one of the chairs waiting for us. I narrowed my eyes at her. *She was up to something. Why did she want to hang out with us now? She hated me.*

We sat in the low chairs next to the fire and I forced myself to block any and all thoughts of Avery for the night.

"When did you start working here?" I asked Sienna before I could stop myself. *Why did I just do that? I didn't want to talk about Avery,* I scolded myself.

Caitlyn just gruffed at my question like talking about anyone but herself bored her to death. *Yes, that's how I can get my revenge on her. I can keep talking and bore her until she dies…wait that came out wrong, that just implies that I'm boring… damn…you screwed me again bunny fucker.*

"I had known Avery a short while before he started the camp. I had just graduated with my Bachelor's in fashion design and I was currently working on a new lingerie line when he had told me his plans and asked if I wanted to help. I hadn't met Sean yet. I was single so I said, why the hell not. I've been working here since it opened. I love it. I can't imagine doing anything else."

"You know Avery pretty well then?" I asked. She studied me for a minute and I shifted nervously under her stare. *Ugh, I hated when she did that.*

I looked to Sara to see her eyes on me. I winked trying to deflect their attention. Sara giggled and I relaxed some. Caitlyn just rolled her eyes again like every question about Avery was just so boring. Yet she wanted him, too.

"Yes, I would say so. He's a good guy. He's always been there for me. I owe him a lot."

I took a sip of my wine and stared at the fire.

"Aria, I have to ask. The night of the Leather and Lace theme party, it really looked like you were dancing just for Avery. So were you?"

"Isn't it obvious," Caitlyn sneered. I spurted forcibly into my glass and choked on the wine as I inhaled. Sienna patted my back until my coughing fit slowed. She tenaciously waited for my reply.

"No," I said, answering Caitlyn, then I looked to Sienna and backpedaled quickly. "I don't know. I was doing what you taught me to do." I coughed again as my mind tried to rationalize my behavior. "Find someone in the audience to focus on. The audience was in total darkness. He was in the middle of the lighted table. It's as simple as that."

"Too bad. I was hoping for some good gossip," Sienna chirped. I laughed at her honesty. I sipped my wine, hoping for a subject change. I was glad neither one could see through my lies.

"Speaking of which, you didn't say much about going bungee jumping with him," Sienna said.

"Did you have fun? Did you guys have sex out there?" Sara teased.

274

I chuckled both sarcastically and horrified at the same time. "There's nothing to tell. We just went bungee jumping that's all. Well...that bridge we jumped from sucked. It was very old and swaying. I thought for sure it was going to fall. The bridge was scarier than the jump itself. I will admit it was a little weird when he brought out the picnic basket and wanted to have a picnic in the middle of the bridge. We could have died just sitting there having wine and cheese."

Sienna stopped with her glass in the air and studied my face. "Seriously?"

"Yes, why?" I asked.

She lowered her glass to her lap and sat silent for a moment.

"Because Aria, that's his move when he wants to fuck someone. He says it breaks down a girl's barriers and creates an emotional connection and that it makes for better sex. Did he make a move on you? If he did, I'm going to kill him," Sienna said glaring at me.

"What happened up there?" Sara added.

I stiffened at their words, trying to hide my true feelings from the two most perceptive people I knew. I ignored Caitlyn glaring at me over the fire.

"It doesn't matter. He didn't make a move on me," I said heavily. Caitlyn snickered.

"He better not have," Sienna said.

I let her words sink in, knowing that Sienna and Sara both were protective of me. I smiled softly, realizing that I learned so much more about Avery in one afternoon than I had known. I was plagued with insecure thoughts until I finally settled on the most pressing. *Why did I have such feelings for him?* But then my twisted mind shouted at me...

being strapped in a harness with Avery while bungee jumping off a bridge – was nothing. He really didn't want me.

I took a sip of wine and tried to shut out my wicked thoughts. Then Sara did me a favor by changing the subject.

"Sienna, tell me about Aria's class today. What happened? I want all the juicy details," Sara said.

Again, I choked on my wine. *Why did they keep making me the center of attention? Ugh. I didn't want to talk about me.*

Caitlyn was rolling her eyes so much that they looked like twin propellers on an airplane. I thought she was going to take off for a second.

Sienna embellished her story of how I finally let go. I had to admit the way she told it kinda turned me on. Sara sat with her mouth open through most of it. Her eyebrows rose in surprise as Sienna spoke of how Colt ravished me with Avery's new product, a dual rotating vibrator with a G-spot wand, and how I crumbled down around them and mewed like a kitten when I was finished.

"You suck, you know that Sienna," I said, shifting in my seat, trying to hold back my nervousness. *But, that thing was exquisite.*

"I want one," Sara gushed. Our laughter, even Caitlyn's, carried out into the backyard when I saw four figures step out into the light of our fire. Caitlyn lit up with excitement when she saw them. Then it hit me, Caitlyn was here because of whom we hung out with. I, on the other hand, was relieved when it was just Sean, Colt, Pierce, and Ethan. No Avery.

"I've got one inside. But you only get it if I get to use it on you first," Sienna said.

"That's my girl," Sean's face was lit up like a child at Christmas. We broke out in laughter again as I watched Sean take a seat next to Sienna. Ethan sat down beside me. I smiled crookedly at him.

"You wouldn't be talking about Aria, would you?" Colt asked.

"You just missed it," I said. I was glad the guys weren't here to hear Sienna's tall tale of my orgasms.

"Damn, you women go right to the good stuff, don't you?" Colt said.

"Yep," I radiated. "How are you doing after class today, Colt?"

"I've had a hard on for two straight hours now. How do you think I'm doing? Speaking of which," he said as he pulled Sara to her feet and kissed her passionately on the lips, then pulled her through the patio doorway into Sienna's cabin. "We'll be back in a bit," Colt said, grabbing Sara's ass and growling. "Or maybe not," he added. Sara giggled and followed behind him.

I rolled my eyes, in a very Caitlyn-like manner, and glanced at Pierce. He was standing with his arms crossed, leaning against the redwood privacy fence grinning at me.

"What?" I chirped.

"I'm sorry, but I have to hear this. Sienna, do tell."

Pierce moved to an empty chair and propped his feet up on a nearby stool.

Sean lifted Sienna and sat her on his lap then looked to me.

"When are you going to share that fine piece of ass, Aria?" Sean asked.

I raised my eyebrows at him and downed the rest of my wine.

Sean's, Ethan's, and Pierce's heated looks all rested on me while Sienna replayed the story for them. I had to admit, I felt sexier than ever before.

"Ok, I just have to ask. Why does everyone care so much?" I said.

"I don't," Caitlyn snipped.

I ignored her and looked to Sean for his reply, but it was Pierce that answered.

"Your innocence is very sweet. It's like honey to a bear. You indulge in it until you are submerged head to toe and left quivering from exhaustion. That's the only way you can tame the monster."

I blinked in shock at his words. *Oh my!* My arousal quickly fell as his words sunk in. *Left quivering from exhaustion.* The memory of my unmentionable night with Avery at the Ball flooded to the forefront of my mind. *It was too similar.*

My eyes searched Pierce's eyes for an answer to the question that rose to the front of my mind. *Did he know?*

He smirked and winked at me. *Fuck.* Of course he knew. He was Avery's brother and he was there to witness our argument during bungee jumping. The feelings of that evening only brought back my anger about how naive I'd been. *Pierce probably wanted his turn.*

I shifted in my chair as my hand tilted my glass back and I took a big gulp of wine and emptied my glass. That was my only escape.

"Need a refill?" Ethan said to me, holding out his hand for my glass.

"Yes, thank you," I replied. Our hands brushed and I glanced up to his eyes. They were kind. I smiled softly and gave him my glass. Ethan was so nice. He hadn't pushed me away yet, so there was hope. Maybe he could help keep my mind off Avery. I was so tired of being played. If I knew what to expect in a relationship it would be much easier. Just sex. I could do that. I smiled to myself. Ethan interrupted my internal monologue with a full glass of wine. He held up his beer to me in our own private moment. His eyes were soft brown and he had dark hair. He could pass for Avery's brother but I bet he could make me forget all about Mr. Jameson. I quickly decided I wouldn't let Avery hurt me anymore.

"Penny for your thoughts," Ethan said, leaning in toward me.

"I'll give you a thousand pennies if I don't have to answer that," I quipped. I glanced over the fire to see Pierce's eyes boring down on me. Caitlyn giggled and flirted with him but he wasn't looking at her. He was listening intently to my conversation.

"Pierce, you and Avery could be twins. I love the highlights. They make you look sexy," Caitlyn's prickly voice rang out amongst us. Pierce grimaced.

I closed my eyes, trying to get the image of Avery's face from my mind, then looked to the flames in front of me.

"Don't feel like talking?" Ethan asked.

I shook my head and tightened my hand around my glass.

"So, let's get drunk," Ethan said.

WENDY LEA THOMAS

"Sounds wonderful," I replied, not looking up at him. I felt myself loosen up immediately. There was no pressure with Ethan. He was so laid back.

I took another sip of my wine, hoping that the alcohol would make me forget Avery. Deep down in my heart I knew that I never would. He was already a part of my being. I had given myself to him from the very first day of camp. He just didn't know it. So, I took another sip of my wine and told myself that I needed to let him go. He was never mine for the taking. I inwardly chastised myself for being a fool and for thinking that I could fall in love in a place like this.

"How do you like your classes?" I asked. I had to think about something else before my anger got the best of me.

"This place is awesome. I never could have imagined anything like it." Ethan cleared his throat. "I'd like to take you into a room sometime. The offer is always open."

"I'd like that," I said, before I could stop myself. I saw Ethan visually relax next to me. He was just as nervous about asking me as I was in accepting.

"Maybe Wednesday?" he asked.

"We'll see...I'd say there's a good chance," I replied.

Caitlyn scoffed and rose to her feet and stomped in front of Ethan.

"You'd go in a room with her but not me?" she barked to him. Ethan nervously ran his hand through his hair.

"Mind your own business, Caitlyn," Pierce answered, witnessing the entire exchange.

Caitlyn looked back at Ethan. "I don't believe this. I've been asking you for two weeks and you said you weren't ready."

280

"I said I wasn't interested. You heard what you wanted to hear, Caitlyn," he sighed. Caitlyn turned on her heels and stormed away.

"What is it with that girl? Can everybody just get over her already? She's not even that pretty. She's lanky like a hotdog, I mean really, who wants to fuck a hotdog?" Ethan asked.

We all snickered as we watched Caitlyn leave. She just kept yelling to herself as she disappeared into the darkness. *Just great,* I thought. I didn't need another reason for Caitlyn to be mad at me.

"What the hell was that about?" Colt asked, stepping out of Sienna's back patio door and putting his shirt on. Sara was in front of him looking at me with curious eyes, but her body screamed sex and satisfaction.

"Caitlyn," we all managed to say in unison. Laughter rang out amongst the back patio and we quickly fell into comfortable chitchat.

A few hours later, and countless bottles of wine and beers between us, we finally said our goodbyes and dispersed for the night.

Back at the cabin, I crawled into bed and slipped under the covers. I drank more than I intended, but I was so relaxed and my mind was at ease, so it didn't take long for me to fall deep asleep.

∞∞∞∞

The piercing sound of an air horn beside my bed jolted me from my sleep. I screamed out in surprise. My eyes snapped open to a large costumed bunny head that was staring at me only inches from my face.

"Aaahhh!" I screamed again. I jerked about like a freshly caught flounder slipping through a fat kids' greasy hands. A blood-curdling scream erupted from my lungs again as I convulsed and rolled to the other side of the bed onto fiery pinching and snapping on my body. *Snap! Snap! Snap! Pinch.*

"Owww!" I screamed, then rolled off the bed and hit the floor with a loud BWWUUMP! And suddenly the room burst alive with great thunderous noise that burned against my skin as it sounded. The pain pinched my bare legs, through my panties and tiny white t-shirt at a rapid firing pace. It took the breath right out of me. *Snap! Pinch. Snap! Snap! Snap! Pinch, pinch, pinch. Snap!*

"Owwwwww!" *Pain, pain, and more pain!* I struggled to turn over but everything happened so fast. *Pinch. Pinch. Snap! Snap! Snap! Snap!* "Owwwww!"

"Sara!" I screamed out. "Owwww!"

The bunny person ran into the living room and out of the back patio door. *Snap! Snap! Snap!*

"Owww!" I reached my hand out and gripped something small and rectangular from underneath my right hip. I brought it up to see what it was. *Snap, Snap, Snap!*

"Mousetraps! Mother fucking mousetraps!" I yelled. *Snap. Snap.* "Owww! Jesus!" The more I moved the more they snapped. *Snap. Snap.*

"Oww! Fuck!" There were hundreds, maybe a thousand of them. *Snap. Snap.*

"Owwww! Where do you get this many fucking mousetraps?" *Snap. Snap. Snap. Snap.*

"Owwwwww!"

Sara came storming into my room with wild bed head and broad eyes of a deer in headlights, trying to figure out what all the noise was. Her mouth dropped open.

"What is going on in here? Who filled your fucking room with mousetraps?" Sara asked in a fevered pitch.

"I'll give you one good goddamn guess who!" I seethed at the very top of my lungs. *Snap! Snap! Pinch. Snap!*

"Owwww!" I squealed.

The traps went mostly silent and I was finally able to sit forward. Red blotchy marks filled my entire body. Every so often, you'd hear a singular *Snap!*

Sara reached out, and helped me to my feet. We both turned and looked at the widespread layer of mousetraps beside my bed.

"That bitch is going down!" we said in unison.

⌘

DAY SEVENTEEN:
WEDNESDAY NIGHT
NAUGHTY SECRETARY THEME PARTY

"**I** just finished my third year of Law School at Berkeley. That's all my life has been for three years. Being here is a nice change," Ethan said.

I was getting comfortable with Ethan over the last few days. It was the Wednesday night Naughty Secretary Theme Party. We were the last ones sitting at the table. The music was pumping through me and I had to admit the atmosphere was intoxicating. Everyone was getting very drunk. I filled Ethan in on last night's prank and explained why I had so many red welts and bruises. Makeup just couldn't cover them all. I looked like a red felt pen.

I really liked naughty secretary night. I wore a short black lycra skirt and tight white blouse unbuttoned enough to show a very generous amount of cleavage. My stockings were thigh highs but I opted not to go with a garter belt as the stockings stayed up nicely without any help. As always, my black platform heels and thin librarian glasses rounded out my look. I took a sip of my Jameson and Diet Coke then licked my lips. Ethan's eyes darkened and I noticed he was staring at my lips.

"What?" I inquired. He chuckled.

"What's it going to take for you to put that beautiful mouth on me?"

I giggled as he stood from his chair and pulled me up towards him. He leaned in and planted a soft kiss on my lips. I returned his kiss gratefully.

"Let's go," he urged. Before I knew it, he was leading me down the hall toward our own room.

He brought me in and slammed the door shut with his foot, locked the door, and tossed me onto the bed. He slipped off his shirt and laid over me.

"You are the most beautiful woman I have ever laid eyes on. Let me fuck you, Aria," he said, waiting for my approval. I grinned and nodded.

His lips rushed to mine and we both let out an urgent breath. He stripped me from my blouse, bra, and panties and trailed his rough hands over my skin. I closed my eyes and let him devour me with his lips. My heart pounded in heavy rhythm beneath my chest. My hands found the button of his dress pants and I quickly undid them. He slid them away and urgently returned to heavy kisses against my neck and down my body. His stubble grazed across my navel as he made his way downward.

He trailed kisses down my thigh and up as his knee forced my legs apart. My hips moved upward in anticipation. My body hummed with desire as his tongue found my red velvet canyon. He let out a guttural groan and his tongue went to work tasting me. Apparently, he loved how I tasted and I loved how our bodies craved one another. Lusting after each other but nothing more, this wasn't emotional. This was lust and I loved it.

I was so close to climax when he flipped me over, smacked my ass and took me from behind. I let out a loud moan as he buried deep inside me. He was inexorable in his quest to feel every inch of my insides.

I came quickly the first time but he didn't stop and let me fall limp around him; he pushed me further, and harder.

He brought me back up onto his lap and slowed his pace. I was sitting back against his legs when he reached around and began circling my clit. I threw my head against his muscular chest and let him take me.

We pulsed into each other. He was deep inside me and very intimate. He planted soft kisses against my temple as my legs stiffened. His hot breath beat against my neck. His body wrapped itself around me from behind. All I could feel was him sliding in then out, but that was all I wanted.

Our bodies were glistening in sweat. He pressed one hand against my lower stomach and pulled me tighter against him. I was lost in him, but he was found in me, as he ground slowly in and out of me for what seemed like an exquisite eternity.

His fingers refused to yield against my clit. My body exploded around him and he thrust into me three more times and let himself go. We crumbled to the sheets in coital bliss. He pulled me against his chest as we both desperately tried to catch our breaths. He kissed my forehead.

"That was well worth the wait," he panted. "I'm in awe of your body, sweet girl." He ran his hands over my breast and down over my buttocks.

I smiled at his compliment and let my eyes close for a few minutes, until I felt him hardening against me. I smirked up at him. *Round two.*

∞∞∞∞

A few hours afterwards, exhausted and barely able to stand we dressed inside our bedroom of inclination. Ethan then went to the bar to get a drink and I stayed in the bedroom a few extra minutes to freshen up and reapply some much-needed makeup and fix my hair. I was looking a bit haggard with my hair mussed and makeup smeared.

After I finished my transformation from the beast back into beauty, I stepped out of the bedroom to make my way down the hall to go find Sara. I never got the chance to tell her where Ethan and I headed off to and I didn't want her to worry.

"There's little Miss Popular. Have fun with Ethan?" Nate stepped in front of me blocking my exit. I stepped back against the wall to distance myself.

"You were in there a long time, Aria. Did he satisfy you? Did he finally make you forget about me?"

"You are such an asshole, Nate!" I said as my voice starting edging higher.

"I bet you like it rough don't you. Ethan's known for tossing girls around in bed. If I'd had known you liked that sort of thing maybe I would have kept you around longer," he said, rubbing his hard shaft against my pelvis. I pushed him away with my hands.

"Fuck off, Nate," Sara's voice called out from down the hall as she headed my way helping me distance myself from him even further.

I glanced to movement in the doorway behind him. Caitlyn was there, leaning in the doorjamb, watching the whole thing. I scowled at her, thinking of those fucking mousetraps she left for me in my bed this morning. I clenched my fists at my side and took a step forward toward her to knock that smirk she was wearing off her dumpy horse face. But Nate quickly stepped in front of me and then stepped back to take hold of Caitlyn's hand and both of them snickered with their snakelike grins. I swear they were both pure evil. *God, I hated them both. Why would you even come to a camp like this just to be assholes to people?*

"See you later, Aria." His eyes were cold and my body trembled. There was something off about him. Caitlyn followed behind Nate, holding his hand. They both deserved each other.

"Fuck you, Nate!" I said. "Maybe I'll come slap those grins off both your faces." When I finally snapped out of my fury, Sara was holding me back by the arms and trying to calm me down.

"Let it go. She'll get hers. That's a promise," Sara said through clenched teeth. She was fighting this as much as I was.

We walked back toward the main ballroom when laughter broke out all around the hall. Everyone gathered around the multiple TV screens that lined the entire room, watching something attentively.

"Nice bed head, Aria," Kennedy snickered.

My mouth dropped open as I noticed I was in my bed as someone filmed me from my bedroom window.

I watched as the bunny, who was clearly female, leaned forward and put her face right next to mine and blew the air horn point blank in my face causing me to startle awake and roll off the bed onto those fucking mousetraps. I could see them snapping away and me screaming for Sara.

Laughter filled the great hall as the bunny scurried away but not before someone else grabbed the camera.

I couldn't look away. It was like a bad car accident, only I was the intended victim, and I knew the outcome. My face reddened as the laughter grew with the finger pointing. Now I was the mousetrap girl. *Great, another nickname,* I thought.

The recording was looped because it began all over again. The laughter rose louder each time it started over, but then suddenly the monitor went dead as I turned to see Avery with the remote in his hand.

"Aria," he said with deep concern in his voice. "Tell me who did this."

I shook my head at him and barreled my way through the hall. I pushed past Ethan, who was heading back with a drink for me, as tears of anger were falling from my eyes before I could stop them.

Avery was the last person in this world I wanted to deal with right now. I could feel both Ethan's and Avery's eyes follow me out of the ballroom and into the warm night.

⌘

DAY NINETEEN:
FRIDAY AFTERNOON
LAP DANCE CLASS

Sara and I hurried through breakfast ignoring the people still pointing and snickering at me out in the open. Lunch was the same way. They didn't even have the decency to hide it. These people may be rich, but some of them weren't very classy.

After we finished lunch we headed toward Prentice cabin. Sara stopped me.

"Don't worry about it, Aria," Sara said. "We have to wait until her guard is down. She'll expect it if we retaliate right away. Let's make her think that she's won. Let her gloat." I smiled weakly and nodded.

"I'll see you later," I said, then turned and walked into Prentice cabin.

When I arrived at Prentice, I hadn't even realized that Colt hadn't been to lunch with us until I saw him talking on the cell phone in his office. He looked surprised to see me. I was earlier than usual but today was my solo lesson so I wanted to get as much in as possible.

"Sienna's covering another class today, it's just you and me," Colt said.

I pulled off my pink baby doll t-shirt and shimmied out of my shorts then set them on the bench beside me.

Colt switched on the sound system of the pole-dancing classroom and moved his chair closer toward the center of the room. I looked to him curiously as slow sexy jazz filled the room. I had no idea what he was planning. He wore a wide grin on his face as he blacked out the one-way mirror that led to the hall and locked the door. *I didn't know that was an option.*

"What are you up to?" I asked pouring myself a glass of whiskey. I took a big gulp and felt it relax my body almost immediately.

He dimmed the lights with the remote and looked up to me with a heated look.

"For what I have in mind, I don't want any interruptions," he said sitting in the chair in front of me. "Come here and sit on my lap facing me, you gorgeous girl."

I stared back at him, enjoying his compliment. I straddled him and lowered myself to his lap. He instantly reached up and gently released my hair tie. He let it drop and ran his hands through my hair then down my shoulders.

"You are all mine today, so we're gonna have some fun, Aria."

I opened my mouth to ask him what he was planning but he stopped me by placing his fingers over my lips.

"You're going to give me a lap dance. No blindfold, it's just you and me." *Oh.*

"We'll start slow, but here are the rules. Most of your lessons have been about you learning about your body and feelings. But in today's scenario, it's all about your partner. In this case, it's me. As much as you have to know about yourself, you have to know how to please someone else. That is if you want to be a good lover. You have to make me want you. I want you to block out all your insecurities. This is almost the end of week three now and I know you want me, Aria, so show me. Seduce me. Pretend I'm whomever you want me to be. Don't be afraid to touch yourself for me. I want your breathing heavy and your pupils dilated by the time this session is over or I will have to admit I'll be disappointed."

I chuckled nervously. "No pressure."

"You have all the sex appeal you will ever need inside of you. I've seen it. Here we are in a dark room with no one watching. What will you do with me? Better yet, what do you want to do to me?" I swallowed nervously. "Don't think about it. Just feel the music and dance for me. I won't touch you unless you ask me to."

My heart was pounding in my chest. *Was he really trying to seduce me?*

I closed my eyes and tried to clear my head. *Who was I kidding; I've fantasized about turning Colt on so many times in the last two years. I could still imagine him in my mouth from oral class two weeks ago.*

A slow grin spread across my face and I stepped off his lap. I tried to remember all that I had watched Sienna do for Sean and let my desire guide me.

I rocked my hips in front of him and let my hands trail over my breasts, down my sides to my hips and back up again. I bit my lip and turned my back to him. I bent over so that my ass was in the air in direct line of his eyesight and rounded the curves of my behind. My fingers skimmed over my light purple panties over my honey pot and I stood and lifted my hair in my hands then turned toward him.

Colt shifted in his chair and his eyes traced the length of my body. "Tease," his voice was deep and raspy. His eyes began to glaze.

I stepped closer and pushed my breasts closer. I ran my hands over them and circled twice. I could see him swallow hard as I ran my tongue over my lips leaving them wet. I could see his fingers itching to touch me as I pressed harder against his cargo shorts. I felt the urge to go further and before I could change my mind, I reached up and unlatched the clasp of my bra. The straps skimmed my bare arms and I quickly tossed it toward him.

His eyes widened three times their normal size. A slow, sexy smile played across his lips and he drew my bra up and breathed in my scent. This took me back, and deep down inside me, I felt my body tremble in need for him.

He was gripping my bra in anticipation and when his eyes darkened, I knew I had him. I rolled my nipples between my fingers and felt them grow harder while I moved to the bass of the music. I don't know what possessed me but the words were out of my mouth before I could stop myself.

"You like what you see, Colt? Do you want me?"

He threw his head back and looked up at me as I towered over him. He groaned and took in a slow tantalizing breath.

"You know I do, sweet girl. I'm kicking myself right now for not having Sara bring you into our bed earlier," he grumbled.

I swayed my hips and let them brush his knees. "Why's that?" my voice was low and breathy.

"I want to run my hands over that delectable body."

I shook my head seductively at him. "That won't do," I said, straddling him and pressing my nipples against his shirt. "If you can restrain yourself then I'm not doing a good enough job. I'm gonna have to try harder."

I lowered my hips over his hard cum-gun and ground my moist lips over him. The friction of his shorts and his stiff shaft sent quivers through me. I reached up and ran my fingers through my hair and ground my pelvis harder against him. I threw my head back and brushed my fingertips over my neck then I moaned as I tweaked my nipples again. My breathing was hard, uneven and I was certain lust filled my eyes.

"You want to touch me, don't you," I asked.

His eyes looked almost pained and I could see him fighting the urge. I ground against him again and teased him further. I let his lap-rocket rub against my clit over and over. It wasn't long before I was crying out and cuming powerfully.

My chest heaved as my eyes met his. He licked his lips and blinked to me, waiting for my command.

"Touch me Colt, please," I said softly.

His hands fell to my ass as he pulled my hips closer. His lips urgently found mine and I dug my fingertips into his hair to bring him closer to me. He cupped my breasts.

"God, Aria. You are so beautiful," he breathed.

My hands found my way to the hem of his shirt and I pulled it from his chest. Colt pushed my panties to the side and sunk two fingers deep within me. I moaned loudly and pushed my hips further against him, wanting him to ease this ache deep inside me.

He pressed his lips harder against mine and his tongue forced open my mouth. I unbuttoned his shorts and reached my greedy fingers in and freed his cock from his boxers. I moved to straddle him and started to lower myself over him, finding I wouldn't be satisfied until he was buried deep within me, but then he stopped me and pulled away. I opened my eyes to see a mixture of lust and something else I didn't comprehend.

"Aria," he whispered.

"Yes," I breathed against his mouth.

He leaned back further away from me and I looked to him questionably. I didn't understand why he stopped. He shook his head, telling me no. It's against the rules. I could see he was guarded now. Then my brain caught up to what we were really doing and I felt myself stiffen. He wrapped his arms around me and kissed the top of my head. I leaned into him, feeling a mixture of exhaustion and guilt. Both of our breathing was hard and fast.

"That was close," I gushed.

"Yes. I'm glad we stopped or I would be out of a job right now." We both chuckled nervously, expelling our pent up sexual frustration. He helped me to stand up and handed me my bra. I took in a deep breath but smiled up at him.

"Why are you smiling?" he asked.

"I guess fantasies really do come true."

He beamed back at me. "That's why we're here, Aria. But to be honest, now I can't wait until we get back home."

"Why's that?"

"So you, me, and Sara can finally fuck," he grinned like a Cheshire cat. And I blushed like a damn virgin.

⌘

DAY TWENTY:
SATURDAY NIGHT
CHRISTMAS IN JULY THEME PARTY

As Sara and I got ready for the Christmas in July party, we chatted about what had happened the day before with Colt. I had learned my lesson about keeping Sara in the dark so I came clean as soon as I got back into our cabin. She assured me that I would get to experience Colt soon. She wanted to see me with him as much as I wanted to be with him. She was truly the best friend in the world to want to share her man like that.

Sara had bought us matching little Sexy Santa outfits. They were red velvet with white fur trim. The tops sat right below our shoulders and the skirts barely covered our asses. We wore our black go-go boots which Sara had glued white fur trim to the tops of this morning.

As we got to the Main Lodge, Avery had every pine tree trimmed in Christmas lights with a Candy Cane walkway as we approached. Christmas music blasted through the PA outside the building. I recognized it as the Chasing Seven Christmas CD – which was my favorite. He really out did himself this time. He even had snow machines brought in which dusted the area in beautiful snow across the lodge's front lawn.

We settled in and started doing whiskey shots right away. The night became a little blurry before long. I socialized among my friends not caring about the pointing fingers and little snickers as I was getting as 'mousetrap girl'. Then I spotted Ethan and Wren as they rounded the table in my direction. In this dim lighting it was like looking at two Averys. I swear they looked more like Avery than Pierce did.

"Aria, go in a room with me again tonight," Ethan begged wrapping his arms around my hips and bringing me closer. Before I could reply, Wren scooped me up and twirled me to the dance floor. I mouthed the word 'sorry' and let him sweep me away toward the music. Wren had already asked me to dance earlier. I saw a somewhat dejected look in Ethan's eyes but Wren quickly distracted me from worrying about it. Wren growled into my neck and I giggled and threw my head back, letting him devour me.

This was just what I needed, to lose myself tonight. I liked Ethan. I really did, but maybe what I needed was just to let go and play the field a bit. Besides, this twin thing had my chicken tongue buzzing with the tingles.

The music pulsed around us as Wren brought me closer to him on the dance floor. His hands found my hips and he cupped my buttocks.

"I want that sweet ass straddling me tonight. Say you'll let me ravish you."

"What about your brother?" I asked. I glanced over at Ethan and our eyes locked. He shook his head and just turned away and headed to the bar.

"Don't worry about him. He'll be okay."

Somehow Wren's words, or maybe it was the whiskey, made it all right to let go and not feel obligated to Ethan. He was sweet and handsome and certainly, a great lover, but tonight I just wanted to explore and see what else I've been missing. Besides, it was better to blow Ethan off before he did it to me, just like Avery and Nate did. There was no doubt in my mind I was doing the right thing.

I turned my back to Wren and ground my behind against his hard cock. We were in a sea of red and white lingerie. It was the Christmas in July theme party and Wren wore a Santa hat, a black dress shirt, and slacks but his dress shoes were red with white trim and matched his hat nicely.

I lifted my arms back behind me and let them drape around his neck. I leaned into his ear, giving in to my desire. "I want you," I purred in his ear. I felt his body tremble against mine.

He lowered his lips to mine and I could feel his need for me in each urgent kiss. His eyes met mine and he intertwined his fingers with mine and pulled me down the hall towards the bedrooms.

He passed several of the immediate rooms and led me to the furthest hallway. He locked the door behind us and turned toward me. He wrapped his hands around my hair and made a make shift ponytail and forced me to look up at him. He searched my face for a moment then trailed soft kisses on my lips.

"I want you in the swing," he growled in my ear.

I nodded as he released my hair and let his hands skim over my breasts. He freed my nipples from my bra and lowered down to suck on them. His warm tongue licked and bit each one, causing my insides to tighten. He slipped the straps over my shoulder and took his time undressing me.

"I've never done it in a sex swing before," I said, eyeing the complex device with straps and loops and buckles to change the lengths of the straps. I could feel him smiling as he trailed kisses down my neck and shoulders.

"Oh, sweet Aria, this is going to be so much fun. Don't worry, I'll be gentle until you tell me not to," he quickly turned me toward him and devoured me, undressing me as he went.

He backed me up toward the swing and lowered my panties. I stood naked before him and he briefly pulled away to take me in. His calm facade didn't last long as his mouth closed around mine and he quickly deepened the kiss.

He helped me into the swing all the while planting kisses all over my body. I tried not to show how nervous I was. He didn't falter as he gently showed me where to place my feet and how to lie back into it.

"Close your eyes," he said, as he kissed my lips one last time. I heard him pull his pants off. "I just want to touch you, Aria."

"Okay," was all I could muster.

He stepped between my legs and kissed my forehead. His hands cradled my face then he led a trail of kisses from my mouth to my chest. His hands stroked my body in the midst of passionate kisses.

I closed my eyes and let my head fall back, enjoying how he absorbed me. He took each nipple in his mouth and teased me until I was clutching my nails into his back and crying out in pleasure. *I didn't know I could orgasm from someone sucking on my nipples like that. Jesus, he was good.*

He moved lower and my hips squirmed for their own attention. He smirked up at me knowing what I wanted most. He ran his hands down over my navel and across my hip. *He was teasing me.*

"Wren, I want you," I begged.

"Not yet, sweet girl. I'm gonna push your body to the extreme before I sink my soldier into you," he said, moving back up and whispering into my ear.

My body quivered in excitement. I watched him pull out a package and open a new small oval vibrator from the bedside drawer. Then he moved between my legs and switched it on. He trailed it up my inner thigh, up and over my mound, then back down the other side.

Repeatedly, he stroked it over every part of my body except where I really wanted it until I was wriggling and panting. When he pressed it to my clit my back bowed off the swing and I whimpered. His slender fingers ran up over the instep of my foot and my insides convulsed without warning.

It wasn't long before my entire body was building with anticipation as his hands and vibrator worked magic over almost every part of my body.

He paused only once to raise the swing to his hip height then he dropped to his knees between my legs and set to work on my pooty tat. My body was wound tight and it begged for release. The second he stroked the wall of my pink heaven I cried out loudly.

When he finally stood and I heard the crinkle of the condom wrapper I was panting in need. He positioned himself between my legs and slowly sank into me. My body bowed instinctively, wanting him to go deeper.

"You are so wet," he hissed. He paused for a moment and I could tell he was fighting back the urge to lose control.

"Fuck me," I begged.

Wren smirked and set out on a course that lasted well into the morning hours. We paused once for me to lie on my front. The he raised the swing so my ass was in the air and as he sank deep within me, I knew in that moment what Colt was referring to that day in class that he first showed me the swing. He was hitting the ache deep in my belly square on.

My body trembled from fatigue but my want and need for another orgasm didn't want him to stop. I was reaching my fifth orgasm. *Yes fifth.*

My body burned with desire and I soared one last time as he gyrated his hips and pushed on the front wall of my vagina. I screamed out Wren's name as he pounded into me three more times then found his release. He helped me to the floor as he embraced me against his chest. We both panted hard and fast, trying desperately to catch our breaths.

"Tired?"

I chuckled. "Yes, and I think I need a shower."

"A shower it is then," Wren said, kissing the top of my head. He helped me to stand and I could feel the soreness everywhere in my body. I couldn't wait to let the hot water soothe some of this.

We made quick use of the shower then I found my clothes and got dressed. I didn't slip on my top. I was too warm. I just left it off, opting to walk around in my bra, Santa skirt and boots.

Wren lowered his head and kissed me tenderly. "Let's get something to eat. I'm starving," he said.

My stomach growled loudly in response. I nodded and he led me out of the door and down the hall that led to the buffet table. *Christ. It was morning already.*

◆Week Four:

⌘

DAY TWENTY-FOUR:
WEDNESDAY NIGHT
NAUGHTY SCHOOL GIRL PARTY

I couldn't believe it was the next theme party already. I was still sore from Saturday night with Wren. I hadn't seen Ethan or Wren since Saturday and I hoped they weren't fighting over me.

Ethan seemed a little dismayed over my going into a room with Wren but that's what these parties were for, to experiment. I didn't want to hurt Ethan, but I was numb emotionally after my supposed connection with Avery turned out to be a milk dud. If Ethan truly liked me, then he would let me ride this out so I could figure out what I wanted. I needed to get myself together before I could free myself the way Sienna and Colt were teaching me.

But when it came to Ethan and Wren, I kept wondering what it would be like to have a threesome with both of them. They had different styles of lovemaking that seemed like they would compliment each other. Since I met them, I wondered what having both of them at the same time would be like. This was week four and I still hadn't had a threesome yet, and I was starting to think about it more and more. I bet it would feel wonderful having two guys shower me with attention at the same time, having a set of twins taking turns using me for their own pleasure. God, it seemed hot.

The time seemed to fly in between the parties. Classes were going fine and I was learning a lot about myself. I finally felt like an empowered woman not afraid to admit what I liked as far as my own desires were concerned.

Tonight was the Naughty School Girl theme party and the women were dressed in different styles of plaid skirts, tight fitting button up collared dress shirts, knee-highs, and Mary Jane's. The night got started in the usual way by Colt getting us shots of Jameson and beers from the bar. Both Ethan and Wren joined us at our table and each took turns flirting with me and casually touching me as they spoke. I guess Ethan came to terms with sharing me because he didn't seem too put out when Wren touched me as we talked. This really got me thinking that maybe tonight was my night to try out the twins together.

I must have had five or six shots by the time Avery approached the table to talk to the rest of the group. He didn't even acknowledge me. I was pissed. *What was his problem?*

It had been at least a week since I'd seen him. *Where does he always disappear to?*

But even though I was surrounded by my friends: Wren, Ethan Travis, Maya, Colt, Sean, Sienna, and Sara, I found that deep down, I still missed talking to Avery. It was Avery's fault, though I'm sure the whiskey helped, that I was feeling emotionally numb since he ripped my heart out at the Masquerade Ball. I wasn't wasted though, just tipsy. *Maybe I was building up a tolerance like Sara kept saying.*

But at least Ethan and Wren paid attention to me and after an hour or so of drinking, they begged me to let them do body shots off my navel and my breasts. I finally agreed after some coaxing. They hoisted me up onto the bar and had me lay flat.

Wren unbuttoned my shirt and let it fall open. I reached down and lifted my bra as a round of applause broke out from all the guys standing nearby. The bartender poured a shot between my breasts as Wren licked it off me. It tickled and made me squirm all over the bar. I couldn't keep still as they took several shots off different parts of my body and convinced a couple of the guys standing nearby to do the same. But while they were sucking whiskey off me, my thoughts circled back to why Avery wouldn't talk to me. It really started bothering me and I couldn't get it out of my head. However, my confusion about Avery got put on hold when a guy named Ben licked a shot off me and then started getting rough. His hands groped my breasts and started to slide down into my panties.

I sat up abruptly, batted his hands away, and ended the shot fest. I had to get some air, so I jumped off the bar, pulled my bra down, and said goodnight to Ethan and Wren as I watched their faces fill with disappointment. Several of the guys standing close complained about not getting their turns. I promised them some other time.

I stepped out of the Main Lodge and turned toward the lake. I hadn't sat down here since my first night at camp. The moon had a beautiful crescent shape and color to it tonight. It was crimson and rather large for this time in the month. I sat on one of the benches down by the water to watch the moonlight skip across the slight waves kicked up by the breeze. After awhile, I heard footsteps approaching from behind and a voice called out to me.

"Hey, Aria. You make a very sexy shot table," Sean said, walking toward me with Sienna beside him.

"Anytime," I smiled back at them. Unfortunately, the way I was treated tonight, made me feel more like a doormat than a table, but I appreciated him making the effort to cheer me up. I loved Sean and Sienna. She was becoming my new best friend.

Sean stepped closer to me and lowered his mouth next to my ear. "I want to be part of your threesome, when you're ready," he whispered in his low sexy voice. Sean pulled away to search my face and without warning, he kissed me hard on the lips.

"Soon," I responded, glancing over to Sienna to make sure it was okay. She winked at me in approval. Then as quickly as they came, Sean scooped Sienna up and threw her over his shoulder. She squealed as he carried her away.

I walked toward the Cub cabins to a secluded spot near the boathouse. It was one half mile farther away from Avery.

The night was still, except for the crickets chirping beside me. The breathtaking crescent moon created a soft, warm glow around me. I found myself walking the width of the lake, throwing stones as hard as I could until my shoulder hurt. I didn't know what made me angrier, the fact that Avery wouldn't talk to me or that he didn't want me. I was haunted by the memory of the night with Avery. Ethan and Wren had made me smile. They made me forget about him for a short time but deep down, I knew that Avery was for me. There could be no other. If only he thought about me in the same way.

I was lost in deep thought when a blindfold gently slipped over my eyes and the world went completely dark. No crescent moon or glow off the amiable lake. I didn't hear the footsteps coming up behind me and for a moment I started to panic when a somewhat familiar voice calmed my fears. I just couldn't quite place who it was. I just knew it wasn't Avery, Colt, Ethan, Wren, or Nate. But I knew I'd heard it before.

"Hot night, and a hot girl, how could I be so lucky?" his voice purred in my ear. Then he placed a gentle kiss on my temple.

"Okay, you've got my attention. Who are you?"

His warm hands wrapped around my waist from behind me as he replied, "Where's the fun in that?"

I moved my hands to my blindfold.

"Ahh, Ahh, Ahh," he trilled. "Ever have hardcore sex with a stranger and never ask his name?"

"I'm not really a one night stand kind of girl," I pouted playfully. He ran his rough fingers over my lips.

"Hmmm. I would have said that when you first arrived. But from what I've been hearing, you've been a naughty girl lately," he said, with his warm breath on my lips. It sent shivers up my spine.

"Seduction is the key element to any good sexual encounter. I heard you don't like foreplay?" he said, teasing me with kisses beside my ear.

I smiled, rising to his challenge. "Who said that? I like it when it's exceptional. Words to me are boring. A person's actions prove everything." I felt his smile, then his hands trailed up my white knee-highs past my thighs and over my buttocks.

"God, you're exquisite," he said turning me toward him. "I bet you taste divine," his voice was hoarse.

"If you play nice, maybe you can find out," I said, raising my chin in defiance. I could play his game. I still didn't recognize the voice but I was intrigued enough and needed the distraction. Besides he was turning me on and I didn't want to think about Avery anymore. Maybe this mystery man could help me forget about him. Even if was just for a short while. He let his hands fall to my waist as he leaned me back against the outside of the boathouse.

"Talking is a mere distraction. You still don't recognize my voice?" I shook my head. His hands trailed beneath my red and black plaid schoolgirl outfit and he cupped my sex.

"No more talking," he pushed my red lace panties to the side and slipped his fingers into me. "This won't do," his deep voice said next to my ear. "You're way too tense. You need to cum, Kitten." He pulled his fingers out slightly then pushed them back in deeper. I leaned my head back and moaned in delight. *A good cum was just what I needed.*

"Tell me, in your fantasies, are you standing or lying down?" He moved in and out, slowly stroking my g-spot while he spoke seductively in my ear.

"Standing." My body involuntarily leaned into him.

"Are you pressed against something hard? Is he giving it to you hard and fast?" he asked, but continued rubbing me.

"Yes, oh god…yes."

His smile was wicked against my ear. "Perfect." He bent in front of me and planted kisses up my inner thigh. Wanting more, my legs widened.

"You're so deliciously wet already," he breathed, and then his tongue licked my wet velvet lips as his fingers pressed on my front wall. He let his tongue circle around my now sensitive clitoris. I breathed in his musky cologne and my body begged for release. I didn't care who he was, I just wanted his perpetual repetitive motion against my snake cave.

"Let go, Kitten. You won't regret it."

My body wound tight in anticipation but soon I convulsed over him and his fingers spilled out of me to be replaced by his tongue as my insides quivered.

"That a girl." He stood, then pinned me up against the boathouse with his body. Then slowly, he slid his fingers back into my sensitive entrance and he stopped. I frowned. *Was he stopping now? Just when it was getting good.*

He chuckled and I felt his other fingers slide under my mask and take off my blindfold. I opened my eyes.

"Pierce." My brows raised in surprise.

"Aria, you really are scrumptious. I don't think I've tasted better." His fingers teased in and out of me and I could feel my body craving more.

I stiffened. "What are you doing here?" *Damn it. This was the last man in camp to help me forget about Avery.*

"Now don't go and get all tense again, sweetie, or I'll have to start all over," he playfully scolded.

"What do you want from me, Pierce?" I said in a short tone.

"Isn't it obvious?"

I scowled at him. Maybe it was the night air, or maybe even the six shots, but my head was feeling fuzzy. And I had no idea what he wanted.

"Is that any way to treat a man who just gave you pleasure? And from the feel of it, I still am." I tried to step away, but his fingers held me in their grasp, still teasing out of me and filling me.

"No fair. You're using my body against me," I sputtered.

"I'd have to disagree. I think you don't listen to your body enough." He let two fingers sink in and I will admit, I was distracted. His eyes glistened in the now ivory moonlight. My heart clenched because all I could see was how similar he looked to Avery. How more than anything I wished that it was Avery standing here pleasuring me, wanting me. I pushed all my thoughts of Avery away and narrowed my eyes at Pierce.

"Do you know how you tame a man, Aria?" I shook my head, not trusting my own voice. His fingers felt good. *Too good.* His lips brushed my cheek. "The same way you tame a woman."

I wrinkled my brow trying to figure out where he was going with this.

"You let them fall in love," he whispered.

"Stop finger fucking me, Pierce."

He let his fingers slide out of me and he stood with a smirk on his face.

"I'm sick of the games your family plays. Leave me alone."

"You've excelled in all your classes. Actually, you've gone above and beyond. You and he are more alike than you know."

"What are you talking about?"

"Getting you to orgasm was the only way I knew you'd listen," he said.

"Go away," I said.

"Not until you tell me what I want to hear," he said wrapping his hands around my waist. His blue eyes bore into me as if he was looking into my soul.

"I am nothing like that douchebag," I scolded.

"He was hurt very badly once, a long time ago. He drowned his heartache in sex too, just like you're doing." He studied me as my chest rose and fell fast with anger. "Just because you push your feelings way down deep inside you doesn't mean they will go away. They will resurface eventually."

My eyes widened at his revelation. He knew he had my attention now.

"Don't worry. I won't tell him you're in love with him."

"I don't know what you are talking about," I said calmer than I felt.

He looked at me with disapproval. "You know...I have never seen him so intrigued by a woman before. He's into you."

"He doesn't want me," I scolded. "He made that blatantly obvious the night of the Ball."

He laughed. "Oh, trust me. He's into you in a way I haven't seen in years." He stepped away and led me to the wooden bench beside the lake. He peered out at the lake, then looked to me. "You've changed him."

"I haven't done anything. Besides, I can't forgive him for the way he treated me that night. It was like he was Dr. Jekyll and Mr. Hyde. I don't like head games." I stood and walked to the water's edge, taking in the serenity of the night. I could hear the waves lapping against the shore with a calming rhythm.

"You're just as stubborn as he is. I won't tell you Avery's whole story because it's not mine to tell. But he was shattered. I had to pull him from the depths of despair and help him pick up the pieces. He's been running from his past for six *fucking* years. That's what he does, Aria. He creates fantasies and lets the people around him fulfill them. That was the only way that he could recover. That's all he knows. He needs you to show him what is real. That you're the real thing."

I sat down beside him gaping. Avery acted like he hated me. I was so confused.

"I've never seen him like this. He's never taken a woman to our private spot up on the bridge. He's never gone to anyone's classes to watch them. He's never offered a trip to Maui. He just doesn't do that." He sighed, reigning in his emotions. "I know you don't understand because you haven't known him very long, but I can see it. I see how you've changed him. He told me about the night you had together," he stopped for a minute then chuckled sarcastically. "And that song at your birthday party. All I can say is… wow!" His eyes fell serious. "He was drawn to you. I've seen the way he smiles when you walk in the room. There's a light in his eyes now that he's met you. He tries to hide it. But I can see it." Pierce turned my face to look at him. "I am here confessing *his* undying love for you because… because he can't break through the wall he's built so high around his heart. But you can, don't you see… you're the one that can."

Tears filled my eyes and I quickly brushed them away. I stood and stepped closer to the water's edge.

"He crushed my heart that night. I don't know if I can come back from that. You saw how we fought when we went bungee jumping."

"I saw more passion in him that day then I've ever seen. If you don't fight for him now, then you'll lose him forever. Think about that, Aria. Can you really leave this place knowing that you didn't try your hardest to be with him? That you didn't do all you could. To say to him that you're the girl he's been waiting for. That the past is the past and that it should die with the memories of his lost love and that it's time to be reborn…in love."

I turned my back toward him and drew my arms around my waist. He stepped in front of me.

"You love him, Aria. I can see it when you look at him. Go to him. Tell him how you feel."

I shook my head. "I can't." *I'm not good enough for him.*

Pierce sighed, exasperated. "You can't give up on him."

I crossed my arms.

"You are so stubborn. Christ, Aria, he threw you a birthday party the instant Sara told him it was your birthday. He worked his ass off to put together that barbeque for you. That wasn't a normal activity. That was special. If that's not love then I don't know what is."

"Wait. What?" I said, placing my hand on his wrist searching for more clarification.

I thought of Sara and Colt and how I envied the relationship they shared. How they were so open and honest with each other and here was Pierce telling me that I could have the same thing. Then I realized what I had to do.

"Let's go," I said. I was going to do it. Go all the way and admit it to the world that I was in love.

"Not until you tell me what I want to hear. Say those magic words out loud." Pierce always had a catch.

"Fine," I sighed heavily. "I'm in love with him, okay," I whispered.

He smirked and clapped his hands together. He grabbed my hand and pulled me down the hill toward his Swamp Thing styled club car. It was green and black with a roll bar and mini-mag tires.

"Are you going to tell him what we did earlier?" he asked when I opened the passenger door.

"Yes," I said, climbing into the passenger seat. I wanted to be completely honest with him.

"Oh shit. Then I'm dead," he said.

I smirked, waiting for him to start the engine. "Why did you do it then?"

"I wanted to see what you tasted like. Besides, it was the only way to relax you enough to listen. It worked didn't it?"

I giggled. *He was right. It was strange to think how much I had changed this past month.*

The dust carried behind us as the cart barreled down the all too familiar road. My stomach twisted in knots the closer we got to Avery's cabin. All the lights were on as we pulled into the drive. I stepped out of the passenger door and walked toward Pierce who was waiting in the headlights for me to follow. I wobbled on the loose ground in my black Mary Jane's and wished I had changed beforehand.

"Careful," he said, reaching for my hand to help steady me. I took it, and heard a woman's giggle as I stepped toward the front porch.

I heard Avery's laugh before I saw him. My eyes focused in the porch light. He was in his boxers with a semi hard cock poking out of the top, had his arms wrapped around a blonde and was whispering in her ear. She didn't have any bottoms on and her ass stuck out from the bottom of her shirt as it rode up while they kissed. I couldn't make out who it was because her face was still covered in shadows. The woman giggled again and I thought my heart was going to shatter.

As they kissed, I stepped back and my foot crunched on a branch as it split in half. His eyes locked with mine, then his gaze fell to me clutching Pierce's hand. His eyes fell cold.

"Well, well, well. What do we have here, my brother and my Kitten wandering around together so late at night? How sweet. Are you two fucking now?" His voice was condescending. There was no way I was letting him get away with that.

My Kitten? "You're a dick, you know that." I sounded more confident than I actually was.

"You didn't complain about my dick the night of the ball. In fact, if I remember correctly, you were begging for it." My mouth fell open. *His comment was so mean.*

My hands fell into fists at my sides. I was going to slap him, then Caitlyn stepped out from the shadows of the

317

porch wearing nothing but that dress shirt and it was barely buttoned. My heart sank into the pit of my darkest hour.

"Hi, Aria," Caitlyn's nail-ridden voice trilled. "Avery honey, where did you leave my panties after you pulled them off with your teeth?"

My lower lip trembled and my skin prickled. I unknowingly took another step back, twisted my ankle slightly on a loose rock, and fell backwards into the mud. I sat stunned as I stared at them. Then Pierce lifted me up by my arms. Caitlyn just snickered.

"I'm sorry. I didn't know you had company," I said sarcastically to Avery. "Pierce, get me out of here," I gritted between my teeth.

With Pierce's help, I hopped to the passenger door as my traitorous heart sought out the little trail that led to the waterfall behind his house. Tears filled my eyes as Pierce turned around in the front yard and peeled out of the drive. I let my head fall into my hands and sobbed quietly. I was too late. I was such a fool to think we had a chance. I know it wasn't fair to expect Avery not to be with another woman but he chose Caitlyn. *Of all people, Caitlyn!*

I let my guard down and let Pierce get my hopes up, and my hopes just crashed to the ground, in one massive thunderous fireball. The thought of Avery fucking Caitlyn made me sick. She had just fucked Nate, now she got Avery. It was as if she was following me. It was so gross.

"Aria, we're at your cabin."

His words barely penetrated my mental meltdown. He shook my shoulder gently. I couldn't move. I felt lifeless, depleted, and defeated. He must have realized I didn't have the strength to stand. He lifted me from the car and carried me inside.

I barely remember him knocking on the door. I vaguely remember Sara's confusion. I scantly remember him carrying me to my bed and taking off my muddy clothes as my tears and gasps of breath erupted from my chest.

"I'm so sorry, Aria," Pierce mumbled. "I really fucked up. I didn't mean to expose you to that."

I buried my head into my pillow and shut out the world. Avery had broken my heart again. And Caitlyn was winning.

⌘

DAY TWENTY-SIX:
FRIDAY MORNING
PIERCE

Friday morning came and I still didn't want to move. I had stayed in bed all day yesterday and there was still no way I was going to class today. I didn't want to rise out of bed, or eat, or see anyone I knew. I still felt sick to my stomach about what had happened Wednesday night. But somehow, I knew I had to find the strength to get up. I thought that maybe if I went for a run it would help me feel better. I was really struggling to understand how I could have let Pierce talk me into going over there. *I'm so stupid…so stupid.*

I dragged myself out of bed and I put on my lacy bra and panties and covered it over with my long sleeved t-shirt and running shorts. It had rained most of the night and morning and it was significantly cooler now. A chill ran up my back as I jogged quietly reflecting on my argument with Sara yesterday. I wouldn't tell her what happened Wednesday night, and I think that was the first time in our relationship that I didn't confide in her. I could see the hurt in her eyes but I couldn't tell her the truth, not after she warned me to stay away from him. *God, I was pathetic.* The man crushed me twice and I was still being loyal to him.

Sara would kill him if she found out what Avery had done. Then she'd kill me for falling for it. I wanted to crumble.

"Aria, wait!" I cringed at the sound of his voice and kept jogging. I had hoped it was all a nightmare. But reality bites.

"Aria," he said again, breathless, running up to my side.

"Leave me alone, Pierce. What else do you want to do to me? I don't want anything more to do with either Jameson."

"Ouch. Are we going to need a safe word here?" he joked. I stopped, crossed my arms, and glared at him.

"One word. Whiskey," he said.

"I hate to break it to ya, I will never need a safe word with you because I'm done with both of you. Now leave me alone," I snapped.

He ran his hands through his hair and sighed. "I can understand why you're bristly over this. Let me try this again. Whiskey brings out his jackass side and Avery was drinking whiskey Wednesday night. A lot of it."

"What makes you think that I care? He's stomped on my heart for the last time," I said.

"Don't you see…?" he started.

I took a step forward. "No, *don't* you see? I can't take anymore. I'm done!" I said.

"You wouldn't have any way to know this, but I am telling you, you stubborn woman, that he drinks whiskey when he's hurting – *really* hurting."

"Let me guess, it's been six years right?" I said bitterly.

He blinked in surprise. "Well, yes, actually. How did you know?"

"Because that's what you always fucking say!" I spat.

He shook off my insult and continued. "He probably only allowed Caitlyn to tag along because he got hammered at the theme party. Which he rarely does, by the way," he added.

"I don't care. I'm done with him. Please just leave me alone."

He frowned and stepped away from me, putting his hands in his pockets. I could see his guilt for what happened Wednesday night. How was he supposed to know that his brother brought another woman to fuck? *Because that's what a man like Avery does. He preys on innocent girls, well in Caitlyn's case, slutty girls, but he was a player and was never going to change,* my subconscious sneered.

I shook my head at that thought then lowered my voice. "Thanks for getting me home safely. But please, just leave me alone. I can't do this anymore."

He nodded politely. "I am so sorry, Aria. I screwed up everything," he said, rubbing his hand over my arm.

I glared at him and he dropped his hand. He turned toward the Main Lodge and I watched him walk away. I felt eyes on me and turned to see Avery a short distance away. His eyes reflected what I knew too well, sadness and hurting. I could see he thought Pierce and I were together. I just didn't care anymore.

I closed my eyes, turned my back on him, and started running again. I didn't get very far when my mind started processing everything Pierce had told me. Thanks to Pierce, I knew the reasons why Avery did some of the things he did.

For once in my life, I didn't want to feel with my heart

anymore, but it was a sad lie I told myself to ebb the pain. I didn't want to admit the truth that deep down, my heart only wanted to find a way back to Avery.

◆Week Five:

⌘

DAY THIRTY-FOUR:
SATURDAY NIGHT
NAUGHTY NURSE THEME PARTY

Week 5 had come and gone and I pretty much just went through the motions the whole week. My period came this week so it was an easy excuse to keep a low profile and hide, which I preferred over telling anyone I was depressed about Avery.

Last Saturday I left after dinner at the Topless Men and Ladies Naughty Nighty Party. I told Sara and Colt I had really bad cramps and just wanted to go to bed. She knew it was a lie but didn't call me out on it. I wasn't on my period then and I never had severe cramps before in my life. But then, my visitor came Monday and didn't leave until late Thursday, so I stayed in bed most of the week anyway.

Sara kept bringing me food so I didn't really have to leave the cabin. We still weren't really talking but she didn't press the issue. We still hadn't spoken about what had me so upset that night Pierce had to carry me in the house and put me to bed. And I never brought it up. She'd been watching me closer, making sure I was all right but she never asked. She knew I would tell her eventually. I had to work through it on my own. *I just had to.*

Wednesday's Theme party was a Wet & Wild. I made the effort to go but I didn't stay very long. I didn't even make it to dinner. *Why did this have to be so hard?*

Ethan and Wren were my saving grace in more ways than one. They were always there if I needed them. One would stop by to visit me, then the other would come by later. Sometimes they both dropped in at the same time. They could tell I was upset but they never asked me to talk about it. Instead, they did what they could to induce laughter and cheer me up. Sometimes it worked but never for very long.

It was Thursday afternoon when a thick mist settled over the camp and drowned the day in grey dreariness. It was a day made for staying in bed when their familiar knock hammered against the bedroom threshold as they had begun letting themselves in.

"What's up suggie-pop?" Wren said, plopping down on the bed beside me.

Ethan sat towards my feet. My hair was pulled back into a loose bun and I couldn't help but feel self-conscious with two hot guys sitting next to me. Both were wide-eyed and bushy-tailed and I couldn't help share in the excitement and energy that was pooling off of them in waves. I smiled warmly up at them as they broke into their cheer me up routine.

"Did I ever tell you about my first day at camp?" Wren asked. I shook my head.

"I was wandering lost through the woods for days…"

"You just said it was the first day of camp, idiot," Ethan reminded him.

326

I couldn't hold back my laughter at their exchange. Ethan and Wren were sharing this sexual experience together and I couldn't help but be envious of their closeness. I felt alone at times and wondered how I was going to make it through to the end of camp.

"Okay, so it was more like a few hours. Let me start over." Wren cleared his throat and began again. I giggled.

"You really suck at story telling," Ethan chided. I laughed aloud. *I was just thinking the same thing.*

"So, I was wandering through the woods for what seemed like hours on a hot and humid summer day…"

"Yea. Lost was more like it. This guy here couldn't find his way around this place with a compass," Ethan interrupted him again.

"Shut the fuck up. This is my story, dude," Wren spouted.

Ethan and I snickered. "Did you just say dude?" Ethan teased. Wren ignored his brother and went back to the story.

"When I came across this tall wooden booth. Probably about eight feet tall and wider than a car, and inside this booth was a wall separating it from another booth…"

Ethan sighed heavily. "Just get to the point. It was a glory hole booth. Aria, you know what that is right?"

I nodded. There were several located like small cabins on the trails throughout the camp.

Ethan continued, "There, that should cover anymore confusion. You don't need the blueprints or how many damn nails each board had in it. Unless you got a damn splinter from sticking your penis in the hole then we don't care what it looked like. Just tell us what happened."

"Fuck off, dude," Wren said. "It's my goddamn story. And besides, women like the details." Ethan and I both chuckled.

Wren ran his hand over the back of his neck and shifted next to me on the bed. He reached over and grabbed my hand in a melodramatic fashion.

"Oh, Aria. It was the most awful thing ever," he said with a southern drawl.

"She knows we're from California, not West Virginia, dumbass," Ethan said. "You can't just pluck a twang accent from the air like you're Mark Twain. And it couldn't have been that awful; you've been talking about it almost every day since then," Ethan added.

"But it wasn't at first, and it wasn't Aria's sweet mouth on me so for the sake of my story, it *was* awful," Wren winked at me and continued on. "So, I stuck my wrinkle-beast through this padded hole and I felt her warm tongue run down over my shaft. I was in heaven until she glazed it with her teeth and as I tried to pull back to escape her my crank was too big to slip out. Aria, you've seen it. You know!" Wren said raising his voice but his eyes held a wicked gleam. "There I was, trying with all my might to get my hedgehog out of the hole and she's chomping down on me like I'm a fucking hotdog." Ethan sighed loudly.

"You mean wiener, and we all know how big you wish it was," Ethan teased.

I was wiping away the tears that were running down my cheeks from laughing so hard. All I could think of was, it was probably Caitlyn. She liked to bite.

"Yea. Yea. She bit you, and then you moved along and found a goddess that sucked you almost blind. You came gloriously. The end," Ethan said. Wren pouted playfully.

"Yea. I suck at story telling," Wren laughed at himself.

"My turn," Ethan said. "Move over, Romeo," he said nudging his twin brother out of the way. Wren scooted down and two sets of mischievous eyes looked back at me.

"The day that Wren and I first met you we finished playing our basketball game and I wanted to ease my sore muscles. The workouts were getting tougher and I wanted to hit the hot tubs. I made my way into the Main Lodge and stepped into the hot tub room and stripped naked when I was met with this beautiful dark haired starlet. Her breasts were spilling over the bubbling water. My mouth was watering. I couldn't wait to get a taste of her. I sat next to her and began stroking my cock, giving her the invite to come sit on my lap. She pushed her breasts in my face and I began sucking each one. She let out this moan of pleasure that made my dick hard and ready. I told her to climb on so I could sink my missile into her silo and give her what she wanted. I let my hands trail down her body as she moved toward me. I skimmed over her stomach, making my way toward her wet heat when I felt her hardness. I'm sure she saw my confusion when she leaned over and in a sexy voice she said to me, 'Honey, I'm a hermaphrodite. Are you bi?' I don't remember anything else except her complimenting my ass as I pushed her off me, jumped out of the water, grabbed my clothes and got the fuck out of there," Ethan said.

I laughed aloud. Ethan continued on with another story about his outdoor adventure involving him lying naked on an anthill. It turned out they bite too. And he had the welts on his ass for four days to prove it. And just like that, I was lost in Ethan and Wren and my gloomy world didn't seem so grey.

When Saturday came, I decided to try to pull myself together. I had enough of feeling sorry for myself. It was week six, and since my visitor was gone, I had no real reason to stay in bed. It had been ten days since the night I found Caitlyn in Avery's arms on his front porch. Ten days before I finally said "fuck it."

It was the Naughty Nurse theme party tonight and I found that I kept thinking of having a threesome with Ethan and Wren. Even as bad as I felt this week, something about that kept pinging inside my head. So I figured why not live it up my last week here.

Sara and I started getting ready around 5pm. The party started at 8pm. She took great care to act as if nothing was wrong between us and I went along with that. As I showered and got ready I started feeling much better. I looked really good in this dress and felt extremely fuckable. I wore a red mini dress in a stretch knit fabric with short sleeves, and an extra short hemline that fell right below my ass. The front of the dress came adorned with white buttons running down the center. Framing these buttons are white stripes on either side as well as white crosses. The ruffled white sleeves matched perfectly with the white ruffle used at the dress's hemline. The nurse's cap in red with a large white cross on the front made the complete uniform. I was going to get somebody's heart racing tonight.

Sara was going to fix some broken hearts tonight herself. She was smoldering in a hot bad nurse's costume. It came with a black pleated skirt, zipper front black corset with white crosses, white trim, and black nurse's hat. In fact, she got my temperature rising looking as hot as she did. I wouldn't mind ending up on her ward tonight. She rounded out her look with black patent lace-up boots and black fishnet stockings.

As Sara looked me up and down she said, "Damn, Aria, I might want to get a taste of whatever medicine you might prescribe tonight."

"Well, then I hope you've got your insurance paid up!" I said. We both burst out laughing then hugged. Sara offered me a couple shots of Jameson whiskey as we prepared to head out to the party.

We met Colt just inside the door and quickly found the bar. Colt got me a beer and the three of us did two more shots of whiskey in unison. We headed over to our table where Sienna and Sean were already sitting, drinking and chatting with Ethan and Wren. Maya and Travis stopped by with Jello shots as we raised a toast to our last week at camp.

Avery entered the room but moved along the side surrounded by a small crowd as he talked and chatted with them. He never once looked over. But by now, I wasn't feeling any pain. In fact, I started to feel more daring and reached over and put my arm around Sara and declared to the table how happy I was to have found them and how much Sara meant to me for bringing me here. Of course, Ethan and Wren were getting rowdy and started yelling for us to kiss.

I'm sure it was the whiskey taking hold of me, but I

leaned in and kissed Sara hard on the lips. Then I saw her eyes light up as my tongue pushed deep into her mouth and lashed her tongue. All of the guys at the table cheered as Sara returned my kiss. I felt her tongue slip back into my mouth to return the favor. It was a very hot scene as even the table next to us cheered. The kiss might have continued even longer but was broken when Colt grabbed more Jello shots off the tray of a passing waitress and offered them in celebration of me finding my sexuality.

After a couple more beers, I was spinning slightly, when Sienna and Sara both pulled me out on the dance floor. We dirty danced and grinded on each other while we strutted in our little outfits. We danced for quite awhile, and at some point, both Ethan and Wren moved over to the bar and began chatting up a couple girls, but I was lost in a sea of whiskey and beer and just kept grooving on the dance floor with my two best girlfriends. Sara saw my eyes follow Ethan and Wren over to the other girls and even though my disappointment was only momentary, she danced over and hugged me and then reached up, caressed my cheek with her hand, and tucked the stray hairs behind my ear.

She stared into my dazed eyes, "Would you have a threesome with me tonight?" she asked. I simply nodded at my kind and loving friend. I was hers. Then she took my hand and led me to the hallway of bedrooms. I just followed along dutifully.

I walked with Sara down the hall toward the bedrooms, both of us turning heads as she led me around. We walked by the various couples making out and preparing to hook up. We passed Tara and her husband Jim in the hall. For the first time since I've known them his face wasn't wrinkled in frustration. He was smiling. Tara was dressed in a Zombie Nurse Costume that featured a white nurse's dress that was spattered with zombie dirtiness. The dress had a syringe loop and a beverage dispensing shot syringe to squeeze cherry Jello shots in people's mouths. She also wore a matching cap. *She was so weird.*

Jim stopped midstride and pushed her against the wall. He growled and started kissing her neck. Tara giggled. Then he dropped his head and started sucking on her nipples. Tara's shyness was practically non-existent when her husband lifted her legs around him and plunged deep into her in the middle of the hallway. Tara raked her newly French manicured nails down his back and I saw him quiver and thrust deeper into her. They were both gloriously into it and best of all; they were both glowing in happiness. Jim even looked like he'd been working out. His belly was a flatter hump now. Sara wriggled her eyebrows at me and we both bit back our laughter. *Guess they worked through their sexual frustration.*

Our eyes rested upon a group of women gathered in the hallway. Travis held Maya by his side in a loving embrace and they were both grinning ear to ear. Maya held out her left hand to Meredith, showing her the five-carat princess cut diamond glistening on it. Meredith squealed in delight and the other women gasped and moved closer. *Wow. Travis proposed here at camp?*

Sara and I said our congratulations and then Sara pulled me down the hall to our destination.

We entered the side bedroom where Colt was waiting for us. I smiled and stood near the bed, nervous but wanting. Sara unzipped my naughty nurse's outfit as I stepped out of it. I stepped to the edge of the bed in my panties and bra to see Colt hold out the blindfold for me to take. I shook my head. "I don't want it anymore," I said to Colt.

"Even with other people watching? Because I'm going to leave the door open," Colt teased.

I'm sure if I wouldn't have been drunk, I might have objected. It meant that other people could gather around and watch it all happen. I swallowed my nervousness down. It was the end of week five, no sense being shy about it now.

Colt dimmed the lights and I smiled – genuinely smiled for the first time in a week. *The one thing I could count on was Sara and Colt,* I thought as I looked at them with erotic desire.

I pulled the elastic rubber band from my hair and let it fall to the middle of my back.

"Are you ready, sweetie?" Sara said. "Because I have a surprise for you."

"I think so. Wait, are we having a fivesome?" I said, as Sienna and Sean walked in.

"I just came in to switch you Sean for Colt," Sienna said. My eyes heightened.

"Come on, handsome, let's go get some drinks and let the kiddies play," she said. Then she grabbed Colt's hand as he gave Sara one last kiss and they headed out of the door, which they left wide open.

"I can't believe we're really doing this," Sara said, stripping off her nurse corset and pleated black skirt.

"You brought me here. Opened me up to all these sexual experiences, I'm glad my first three-way will be with you." I smiled again. "And Sean definitely seems happy," I said, looking over at the widest grin I've seen so far at camp.

"I'm gonna rock both of your worlds, trust me," Sean said.

"That's the plan," Sara and I said together. We both giggled. And I was glad that we had gotten over the hard feelings that I caused when I couldn't tell her about why I was so upset the other night. I looked at Sean as he stepped up to the bed and took his shirt off. He was all solid muscle and tanned. I let my eyes roam over his body as sexual ripples spiked in my tummy. Sara and I beamed to one another. *God, I wanted him.*

Just then, Britney Spears "3" began to echo from the dance floor. Sara looked to me and smiled.

"How appropriate," she giggled. And I knew she meant the song.

Sean guided me to the bed and Sara followed. Sean grabbed me by the waist and drew me near. He opened my mouth with the pressure of his on mine. He pulled Sara along side of him and did the same to her, then pushed both of us down to the bed. He turned us toward each other. We were in an upright kneeling position. Sara smirked and reached for my bra and pulled it off. She rushed forward and brought her lips to mine.

I'd always been attracted to Sara. She was beautiful. I trailed my hands up her hips and brought her near to me, closing the space between us. As our bodies touched, my hands enveloped her breasts. My bra lay next to us on the bed where it fell. Sara rolled my nipples under her fingers, teasing as they hardened under her touch.

Our kisses deepened as I felt a warm hand run down over my back to my backside. Soft kisses pressed against my hip. His hands threaded under my panties bringing them down in one swift motion. I shifted my legs up one at a time until they were off. His lips found my buttocks as Sara pulled harder on my nipples.

Sean trailed kisses up my back to my neck behind my ear. Sara trailed her hands down my stomach and then cupped my lovebox. She spread my legs with her hands as I knelt there, and placed her fingers at the lips of my honey pot and began rubbing her hand against me, feeling how turned on I was, then she began stimulating my clit. I threw my head back and moaned into them. Sean slipped his fingers from behind, deep into me, stealing the breath from my lungs. Between my nipples being devoured by Sara, his fingers inside me, and her rubbing my powerhouse, I felt magnetic.

Sean continued to press kisses across my shoulders. I ran my hands between us, down his abdomen to find his engorged penis. I stroked it and he hissed under his breath. He turned my head toward him and kissed me. Sara painted light kisses across my breasts as I focused on Sean. She kept stimulating me. Sean's fingers eased in and out faster and faster as I stroked his shaft. I grew wetter with each passing minute. I felt his hands lower me over Sara and I found her soft lips. I skimmed my hand up her body and reached for her breasts. I heard the rip of a wrapper and Sean slowly sunk into me. I cried out into Sara's mouth.

After savoring a moment with Sean burying himself deep into me, I trailed kisses down Sara's neck and breasts. I let my tongue glide lower down her navel. She threw her head back as I reached her kitty cage. Sean rammed into me from behind again. My mouth kissed her bare skin and I let my tongue explore her wetness. She tasted like sweet honey. I loved it and craved more.

I licked her outer lips and then pushed as deep as my tongue would go. Sara squirmed with delight beneath me. I swirled my tongue into her and then alternated flicking against her clit. Sean's warm hands pressed into my hips harder. I could tell he was enjoying every inch of me completely hypnotized by every detail of the girl-on-girl display below him. I reached up and pinched Sara's nipples harder, and rolled them between my fingers. A grin spread across my face. I knew what she really wanted.

I traced her slim hips down to her wet vagina beneath my tongue. I inserted two fingers into her and let her acclimate to me inside her. I felt her hips rise up for more. I moved them in and out as my tongue stroked her clit. I could feel her inside walls tighten.

Sean swiveled his hips and pushed deeper inside of me. I lost all concentration for a moment. Sara did too. I pressed my tongue harder and Sara moaned softly. Her eyes looked down at me then up at Sean behind me taking in the view of all of us moving together. I smirked and rubbed the front wall of her vagina with my curved fingers as if I was beckoning her to come here. Her head fell back and soon her legs were stiffening.

I clenched my walls around Sean's hot length. *Jesus, watching Sara turned on was steamy as hell.*

Sean reached around me to rub my slick clit, driving me close to explosion. "That's it, feel it baby," he said.

Sean rammed into me over and over, then he stopped deep inside of me. I could tell he was trying to control his orgasm, but I involuntarily kept moving my hips, thrusting back into him. I needed more of his camshaft.

Sara's breathing was hard and fast. I watched her letting go beneath me and I smiled to myself knowing I was giving her this pleasure. My tongue circled around, and as I traced into her vagina, her body quivered and I slipped deeper into her again and stroked her front wall faster. I could feel her insides spasm and she convulsed beneath me. I smiled victoriously and raised my head. Her expression was of awe.

Sean took the moment to pound harder behind me. I cried out as my orgasm erupted. Sara's lips moved down to mine to absorb it. I let my body take over and let go. A moan escaped into Sara's mouth as she kissed me harder. Sean thrust into me three more times then groaned as his orgasm overtook him. He shook violently, stabbing into my vagina with desperate long strokes until he finished and calmed down. He then lay across my back and I could feel his warm breath against my neck. Sean rolled to the side. I lay down next to him. Sara was beside me. We were each gasping for breath.

My eyes caught movement by the door and I looked to see those emerald gems sparkling amongst a small crowd, wedged in around the doorway, staring back at me. Everyone around him applauded. I was totally exposed. Totally naked and the man I wanted more than anything stood in a doorway watching me have a threesome for the first time.

I lay spent and couldn't move but all my heart wanted to do was to go to him. I smiled softly to him. His eyes broadened in surprise. Then his features softened and his lips turned up into a smile. I looked to see who else was watching. Ethan and Wren stood beside Avery and Colt. Colt was radiating a smile at both Sara and me with lust and pride as he clapped. Beside him was Pierce, who winked to me as I looked back to Avery. My face reddened, but I didn't care. It was so good.

"I'm feeling a tad bit obsolete," Colt said, as he moved to the bed and kneeled beside us, looking to Sara and me.

"You taught me well," I replied.

"That was all you, Kitten. You've surpassed your fears. I would say you've overcome all your shyness." His eyes danced around the room at the guys as the clapping trailed off. "And you're becoming a favorite to watch." Then he turned to Sara and kissed her hard on the lips then once on the forehead. She turned to me and smiled. Colt cleared his throat and now they were both looking to me.

"Our Kitten is now a beautiful butterfly. Fly girl. Fly," Colt said.

My eyes locked on Avery's as Colt's words sank in. I was brought back to the secluded bridge and Avery saying those exact words. I smiled softly.

I swallowed nervously. "I suppose I just did."

Avery's eyes turned sad. My chest tightened. *Why was he upset?*

Sean's hand smacked me hard across my buttocks. My eyes darted to him as he moved to my ear.

"Round two, my beauties."

My face split wide with a grin. I looked toward Avery to see him storm away through the exit. I tried to hide my discouragement as the door closed behind him. I closed my eyes as Sean kissed me passionately and I drowned myself in sex again. Maybe Pierce was right about me.

I was distracted by Sara's tongue skimming my body and quickly moving south. Something didn't feel right in that moment. My heart seemed to be elsewhere. It was where I never wanted it to go tonight. It was with Avery.

When we finished, I was still in my post-coital state from my threesome when Sara mentioned getting a seat at the bar to celebrate. We quickly dressed.

"You guys go ahead. I need a minute. I'll be right there," I said, as I headed into the private bathroom that each bedroom contained to finish cleaning myself up.

As I was pulling my hair back and reapplying my makeup, I heard the outer door open and quickly close. After I finished, I stepped into the bedroom figuring Sara had come back to yell at me for taking so long but as soon as I entered, I froze. The blood ran out of my face and a cold chill ran up my spine, but quickly my fear turned to anger.

"What are you doing in here, Nate?" I glared at him as he locked the door behind him. He purposely waited for me to come out to witness his locking the door. He didn't say a word as he stepped over to me rapidly, and as he did, I stepped backward. He pressed me back against the wall and pinned both my arms on each side of me. He rubbed his hard shaft against my pelvis as my eyes narrowed up at his. He must have been stalking me. He never seemed to be too far away whenever I walked out of a bedroom. It was beyond creepy.

"Get off me, you creep!" I yelled.

"That's not going to happen until I get to fuck you again, Aria. I want to see what you've learned since you've been here. I hope you've gotten better since the first time. The last time you just lied there stiff as a board staring up at the ceiling. You never even opened your mouth to accept my kisses, but now I bet you're much better. I've heard you've grown into quite a little whore. Well, now it's my turn to see what kind of whore you've become. Come on you know you want me, I've seen how you always look my way. I can't enter a room without your eyes following me. You've been wanting to fuck me ever since we ran into each other at breakfast… wanting to show me what you've learned." I struggled to free myself but he had me pinned. He quickly made use of his free hand unbuttoning his pants. I heard his zipper come down as his knees forced mine wider.

"When I saw you up on the dance floor shaking that ass tonight, I could only think how I couldn't wait to have you again." He took in a slow savory breath and I felt him push his hard shaft into the palm of my hand. "You like this don't you, Aria?" I turned my head away. "There are so many things I want to do to you, my little slut. That's what you've turned into isn't it? Doing twin brothers in the same week and having threesomes with your best friend." He forced my hand around his shaft and let himself glide in and out so that I was jerking him off.

"Nate. Don't do this," I warned. A slight panic started to envelop me as I considered what would happen if he succeeded in getting inside me.

"Come on baby, I'll make you scream like all the others did." He leaned into my neck and took a slow deep breath in. "I heard you calling out their names during sex. You liked fucking all of them didn't you? Do you know what I would have done different?" He didn't wait for me to answer. He grinned widely and turned my head so that I was looking at him. "I wouldn't have been so gentle and you wouldn't have been able to walk when we were done. You would have to crawl."

"No!" I let him slide his penis closer into my hand and then I dug my nail into his penis. "You fucker that's never going to happen," I said through clenched teeth. He didn't have time to react when someone kicked the outer door open and two tall figures stormed into the room and grabbed him by the shoulders, spun him around and threw him against the wall.

"Get away from her you stupid fuck!" Avery bellowed. Colt stood beside Avery then two security guards ran up behind him.

"Avery, I…" I started but trailed off.

"Give me a second, Aria," Avery said, moving closer toward Nate and towering over him. He wrapped his hand around his shirt and yanked him upward so that Nate was lifted up on his toes and slammed into the wall as he spoke through clenched teeth.

"You have fifteen minutes to get your stuff packed and get the fuck out of my camp. Do you hear me you piece of shit? Get the fuck out of here and never come back or I will shove my hand down your throat and pull your dick out of your body from the inside!" Avery glanced over to see if I was all right then turned his attention back to Nate. Nate's shirt was covering him but his hard cock pushed through

342

his shirt and poked into Avery's cold belt buckle. Nate pushed Avery back by thrusting both his hands forward.

"I didn't do anything she didn't ask for," he said sounding unrattled. *He was such an asshole.*

Avery stepped toward him again and backed him up against the wall. "You're a piece of shit liar," Avery huffed in anger. His veins were sticking out in his neck as Avery raised his fist and thrust it toward Nate into his stomach causing Nate to lose his breath. Then he grabbed him and tossed him like an old shirt across the bed and into the adjacent nightstand smashing a small lamp against the floor.

"Get him the fuck away from me before I kill him," he said, still glaring at Nate. The guards strolled forward while Nate tucked himself back into his pants. The two large men began pulling him away as Nate turned to Avery.

"I'm not the only one that's broke your rules, Avery," Nate smirked.

"I don't have time for this. Get him out of here," Avery seethed. I could see his chest rising rapidly but he was trying to calm himself.

The guards started to drag him away. "You sure? You might want to know that your precious little Aria and Colt aren't as innocent as you'd might think." My eyes widened as I looked to Colt. Then Nate got out one last comment. "Aria, should I tell him how you have been fucking Colt during your lessons?" he laughed dryly.

"Jay, Danny, get him out of my sight," Avery said to the guards. I stared at an angry Avery as he walked towards Colt, as I tried to figure out how in the hell Nate knew that Colt and I almost had sex. Avery ran his hand through his beautiful hair then looked to Colt. "What's he talking about Colt?"

"Avery, I…" Avery held his hand up to me, cutting me off. I stepped back shocked by his look of anger.

"We've been best friends for over five years don't fucking lie to me. Did you fuck your student?"

I drew my arms around myself and looked to Colt. Colt drew his lips into a straight line.

"No. I got caught up in a lap dance and we fooled around a bit but we both stopped it before it went too far." I could see Avery visually relax. But it wasn't because of me. It was because he didn't have to fire his best friend. Avery gave me a mixed look as he stormed out of the room towards the bar. One of relief that I was in fact okay and Nate didn't get his way with me, and one of anger. We followed behind him but kept our distance.

"Kim!" Avery shouted. The bartender stepped out from behind the counter with a wide-eyed gaze. He lowered his voice as he walked to the bar. "Get me some ice for my hand, please."

"Aria, are you okay?" Sara asked coming up to me.

"Stop being so nice to me. How can you not be mad at me for almost fucking Colt behind your back?" *God, who was I turning into? I didn't even recognize myself right now.*

She chuckled and I looked at her dumbfounded. "Because you already told me sweetie and thanks to you, he took out his sexual frustration on me," she grinned at me like a giddy schoolgirl. "You know the important thing was you stopped yourself. That's why I wanted Colt to be your teacher because, I figured, if he slipped up and lost control it would at least be with you. I love both of you."

344

I tried to wrap my head around that. "That's messed up," I said trying to fight a smile that was spreading across my face.

"Besides, I enjoy how you torture him. He has a hard on all the time," she said smiling as Colt planted a chaste kiss on her lips.

"Oh, and Aria," Colt added. "We spent most of last night talking about what we want to do to you when we get you home." I gulped then smiled crookedly at both of them.

"You only talked about me one night?" I pouted playfully. Their laughter filled the bar as we started pounding shots. I thought about how Avery rescued me from Nate. How at any moment Nate could have forced himself inside me. Thankfully, my friends were there looking out for me. Avery was always there for me when I needed him. Because of him, I was safe.

I looked across the bar to Avery holding an ice pack on his right hand as he sipped a glass of whiskey. He scanned the rest of the room before he leaned against the inside of the bar and let his eyes fall on me. I smiled appreciatively to him and waved him over to us. Avery stared through me and shook his head. There was something in his expression that I couldn't recognize. I picked up my whiskey and raised my shot glass to him. He followed suit and downed his glass then turned away.

"Aria, that was the sexiest thing I've ever seen," Ethan said with a heated look. "I want you to know that I'm going to fantasize about your threesome probably until the day I die," he chuckled. "You are so damn hot, woman."

"I'll second that," Wren said, stepping closer. "I just wish you would have chosen us," he groaned. I looked at them regrettably.

"No worries, Kitten. We get it. This place is all about new experiences. It's all good." Ethan smiled at me warmly. I grinned back, relaxing a bit, knowing that they understood why I didn't wait for them.

Ethan and Wren were amazing but Sean was incredible. My body trembled thinking of all the wonderful things he did to me tonight. I sat on the bar stool in my red lace bra and panties and let Colt suck me into a new joke he was telling. He nodded to Kim and she quickly got Sara and me another round.

We were on our seventh round and the Main Lodge was loud and hectic. It was toward the end of the night and it was filling with couples and singles coming out from their private rooms and glowing in sexual bliss.

I got up from my bar stool and felt my world sway just a bit. *Okay, it was a lot. How much have I had to drink? Shit. I forgot to eat dinner. I was too nervous about tonight. What was I so worried about?* My thoughts slurred.

I giggled to myself and made my way toward the main hallway toward the bathrooms. I couldn't get my eyes to focus well but I knew the way by heart. I reached my hand out to steady myself on the wall beside me and that's when it happened – It wasn't a wall I tried to grab hold of, but one of the giant displays that Avery brought in to resemble a hospital sign. The entire ballroom was decorated with huge monitors flashing EKG vital signs, heart rates, and pulse readers. It was huge and expensive. Probably cost thousands.

As soon as I leaned against it, it was like the dominos I used to set up when I was a child. One by one they fell, crashing into the other, smashing into themselves as they toppled around the entire ballroom. Louder and louder it sounded. It was like the heartbeat of a giant, BOOM, BOOM, BOOM, BOOM, BOOM, as they fell until at last, the heart gave out and there was silence. Thousands of dollars lay on the floor sizzling and excreting electric pops, until the monitors went dead.

Everyone in the room stopped and just stared. It was the kind of silence you only hear at a funeral parlor. I felt warm hands around my shoulders spinning me around. I blinked my eyes, trying to get him to come in focus.

"Aria, you alright?" Avery asked. His lips pulled into a straight line.

I blinked, then, blinked again. "Yep. Couldn't be better," I slurred.

He narrowed his eyes at me. *Or at least I think he did.* I swayed in his grasp. Then I hiccupped. *Damn. Hiccups were a dead giveaway.* Then I heard the most annoying sound in the world.

"Colt's been feeding her drinks all night since she got back from her little threesome. Looks like someone likes to break the rules," Caitlyn said, in her sickening-sweet irritating voice.

I hiccupped again. *Damn it.* I needed water.

Avery disregarded Caitlyn and dragged me back toward the bar where Colt and Sara were gathered with all our friends.

"Colt, Sara, come with me." He pulled me toward the buffet and piled on French toast and bacon. I couldn't help but recognize the similarities from the first breakfast we shared at his lagoon.

"All of you need to eat," he barked.

Sara giggled at his serious tone. I snickered with her. She and I both erupted in a fit of giggles. Alcohol made everything funny. Even the buzzkill of Mr. Serious, Avery Jameson.

He set the plate down hard on the table in front of me and sat me in the seat. I felt stunned by his need to take care of me. I guess it was a good thing. At least now, my hiccups were gone.

Avery left, then came back with three tall glasses of ice water. He stood for a moment and took in a deep breath, then looked down at me.

"Aria, please eat something. You skipped dinner and you've had at least seven whiskey and Diet Cokes on an empty stomach."

I nodded stiffly. *How the hell did he know that?* I took a big bite of French toast and I moaned, enjoying the taste of the warm syrup in my mouth.

Avery blinked at me and I could see his eyes darken as he shifted from one foot to another.

"God, Aria. You're killing me when you moan like that," his raspy voice said. His heated look disappeared and it was replaced with determination.

I took another bite as he waited for Sara and Colt to join me at the table. They were both ignorant to the fact that Avery had just had a moment of weakness. Avery leaned over so only the three of us could hear.

"Colt, I don't want to hear about you breaking any more of my rules. More than one person saw your group getting her wasted. Look around at this mess. This is what happens when rules are disregarded. I'm stuck having to clean up the mess. I'm afraid your punishment will be kitchen duty tomorrow. You can help unload the supply truck." Colt's eyes narrowed at him.

"It's the Olympics shipment," Avery added, "And the temperature is going to be ninety five degrees with seventy percent humidity. Eat something then get to bed."

"Shit," Colt grumbled.

My eyes flashed to Colt as he fidgeted in his seat. His eyes filled with defeat as he looked to Avery and nodded.

"See all three of you at noon," he smirked.

My eyes fell to the clock. It was nearly 4a.m. *Oh hell. I was going to be hurting tomorrow.*

"What?" I asked, as both Sara and Colt stared at me.

"The supply truck that's coming tomorrow is for the three day Camp Olympics. It's the biggest shipment we receive during a session. It's a very big truck and it'll take us hours to unload."

My eyes followed Avery as he walked across the Main Lodge toward Kim. He whispered something in her ear and she nodded. She glanced at us and winked. I guess that answers that. Kim wasn't in trouble. Just us.

◆Week Six:

⌘

DAY THIRTY-FIVE:
SUNDAY
KITCHEN DUTY

It was Sunday and the weather was sweltering. It was barely noon and it was so hot and humid that it was oppressive. I was so hungover that I barely remember arriving at the party last night, let alone smashing all of the displays in the ballroom. I felt terrible, about not only my head pounding, and the bouts of nausea, but about destroying $20,000 worth of electronics. Avery was so pissed last night. He seemed to get angrier the more he thought about it. Colt wasn't ever supposed to be supplying his students alcohol, that and the fact that I was only twenty years old was bad enough. Avery did look the other way most of the time. That is, until something happened like someone getting out of control and destroying private property.

I finished my energy drink and stepped up into the back of the supply truck to help unload it. My heart clenched when I saw him. Avery had his back to me and was bending over grabbing the next case of food. He stood and pivoted then faltered as he registered that I was standing there.

"You're late. Where are the other two?" Avery sneered then handed off a case of canned peaches to me.

"I know. I'm sorry. I'm a little under the weather. Sara and Colt are on their way." I rambled nervously. This was the first time I'd been this close to Avery and alone with him in a long time. He pushed the case into my hands and his fingers brushed mine. An electrifying touch coursed through my body and he gasped audibly. *He felt it too.* I ignored it and asked, "You didn't punish Kim?"

"No, I didn't. It wasn't her fault. She was giving the drinks to Colt. What he did after he got them was the problem."

"Then why after all these weeks of camp did you let us get away with it?" I asked, confused and angry.

He took a step closer. I could see his breathing had spiked. He was angry. I studied him.

"Are you taking all this out on me because you weren't part of my threesome? You didn't have to watch," I said.

His nose flared and he stepped closer. "Let's see, shall we. Let's check the score of Aria the Tornado so far. You destroyed private property. You broke most of my camp rules, broke the underage drinking law and you continue to be mean to Caitlyn."

"What?" I asked, hastily.

"She told me how you forced her to turn the lights on while you peed on my back lawn because it was your fantasy to be watched, and about how you two planned that mousetrap video for a YouTube prank video, and how you made her play it for the entire ballroom. She told me how she tried to talk you out of it but how you needed the attention so she went along with it. She was so distraught that she said she had to come apologize to me over and over again."

"Oh, really? And you believed her?" I pulled my mouth closed and I recomposed myself. Then Avery continued.

"And yes, it would have been nice if I would have been invited into your little threesome with Sara. I am the owner of this goddamn camp and can bring a little something to the table. Besides, is it so wrong that I wanted to spend time with you? It seems I have to schedule the fucking time just to see you because you've become little miss popular," he concluded.

I took a second to gather my swirling thoughts. "You're the only one I want to be with. You're the only one that makes any of this matter and you've made it clear you've wanted nothing to do with me! I've done what you've wanted and it's still not good enough. Tell me what I have to do because quite frankly, you're giving me whiplash," I said, raising my chin.

His eyes narrowed as Pierce stepped out of the cold section of the truck carrying ice cream.

"Am I interrupting?" Pierce asked.

Avery rolled his eyes. "As always, brother, your timing is impeccable."

"Hey, hot stuff," he said, looking guilty toward Avery. Before I knew it, Avery was growling and pushing Pierce against the wall. The ice cream that pressed between them was Pierce's only form of protection.

"Did you sleep with her?"

"You were with the blonde boxhead," I called out to him. I couldn't bring myself to say Caitlyn's name. His eyes filled with regret as he looked to me. Then he loosened his grip on Pierce as he turned to me.

"KIM!" he called out.

"Yes, Avery?" she asked, as she appeared in the doorway.

"Find Ethan and Wren Cartwright. They just got put on barn duty tomorrow." I narrowed my eyes at him. But he just narrowed his eyes right back at me.

"And find Sean Seeley, too. He's on barn duty with them." A fleeting satisfaction crept over his face.

"How could I ever think you were different?" he asked. His words struck me deeper than I ever wanted to admit to myself.

"I am different than all those other girls. You just chose not to see something that's good and standing right in front of you," I yelled back at him. My blood boiled. My hands were shaking and I almost dropped the case of peaches. I purposely tightened my hands around the cardboard box to steady myself. "And just so you know, Pierce and I talked about you most of the time that night, so fuck off, Avery!" He blinked in disbelief.

I turned and stepped off the truck and carried the case into the cabin, slamming it down on the counter beside Sara, who finally made it and went to work unpacking boxes. I huffed loudly. Sara glanced at me sideways. She knew that when I was in this kind of mood it was best to wait until I calmed down before she started her inquisition.

I didn't speak but I stayed to help Sara unload the boxes onto the large metal shelves. I let Colt and Sara bring the remaining boxes in, preferring to stay in the kitchen unpacking them.

"I don't want to get stuck with kitchen duty ever again. My head feels like a cannonball after it's been shot out of a cannon," Sara said, bringing in the last of the boxes.

I quickly went to work on breaking down the boxes and leaned them up against the wall for recycling.

"Go see what's taking Colt and Pierce so long," Sara said.

I heard the shouting before I emerged through the doorway.

"How could you? You know how I feel about her."

Colt was trying to push his way between them. Avery's fist met Pierce's jaw. He stumbled backwards and righted himself. He rubbed his jaw as Colt held Avery back.

"I had to pin her down somehow," Pierce said, rubbing his jaw.

"You son of a bitch," he struggled out from under Colt's grasp and lunged for his brother.

"Stop this, you idiots!" I shouted. "Avery, don't you dare try to play the angel here. You crushed me and Pierce was only trying to help you. We didn't fuck. I told you we talked about you. Are you happy? Is that what you wanted to hear? Is that what you wanted to know?" My voice rose up an octave. "How about I tell you how he convinced me to tell you how I felt about you and when we drove to your house you were with, Cait...you know what...never mind. I'm not doing this. Not in front of everyone."

His eyes scanned those around us, and let his hands fall to the side. Pierce cursed and mumbled something about getting some ice, then turned toward the quad, hopped on and peeled out towards his cabin. Avery was left breathing hard and fast, looking at me with a confused expression on his face. Sara stepped beside Colt. Avery's eyes flashed toward them then back to me. He ran his fingers through his hair and cursed under his breath as he jumped down out of the truck.

Avery had always been in control, strong, confident. In this moment he looked rattled. I could feel Sara and Colt's eyes on me. I looked to see a questioning look in their eyes.

Avery slammed the back door of the truck and stormed through the cabin's side door. I kept my eyes on him until he was out of view. I just stared at the door, wishing he would come back. But he was just like me, he knew how to run from heartache. Pierce was right. We were alike in so many ways.

"You have something you need to tell me?" Sara inquired loudly.

"No, there's nothing to tell," I said, surprisingly calm, while looking to the ground.

"How could you not tell me about you and Avery?" She waited for my response but when I didn't give one, she continued. "All I have to say is I'm really disappointed in you. I warned you to stay away from him," Sara said heatedly. I shifted my eyes to see my best friend's disappointment reflecting in her eyes.

"I know!" I said. But before I could storm away, Kim reappeared in the doorway.

"Aria. Avery has put you and Sara on barn duty. Report Tuesday to the stables," she said.

"Mother fucker!" we both cried in unison.

⌘

DAY THIRTY-EIGHT:
WEDNESDAY AFTERNOON
BARN DUTY

For two days, I had spent all my extra time with Sara grooming the horses in the nearby stalls. Avery was on a rampage, punishing everyone that slept with me, including Sara.

It was awkward running into Ethan, Sean, and Wren since it was easy to figure out they were being punished because of me. But I found an instant calm each time I was near one of the horses. I purposely only groomed the white one and kept away from the brown one. It was childish to think a horse had the same color hair as Avery but I kept that to myself. I had done well so far, avoiding any explanation of my situation to Sara. But the Camp Olympics were starting tomorrow. Three days of more competition. *Yippee!*

I knew I needed Sara to get through this week. I had never seen her so mad at me before.

I brushed the white Arabian, thinking how Sara and I hadn't spoken since unloading the truck outside the Main Lodge and I was overwhelmed emotionally. I hadn't slept since then, thus the bags under my eyes, as I looked in the mirror above the bench trying to figure out how it all went wrong.

I moved to the doorway of the stall and looked out to the extravagant barn that Avery had built. I could hear Sara filling water buckets at the outside spigot. The fragrant wild orchids nearby made me think of Avery's Lagoon. I breathed in the fragrance of the horses and tried not to let my thoughts go down that path. I walked over and sat on one of the benches in the barn along the row of horse stalls. Avery kept returning to my thoughts. He thought I slept with Pierce. He knew about Ethan. He knew about Wren. He saw me with Sean and Sara. *God, who was I turning into?*

I finally let the floodgate release as I laid my head over on the bench and cried. I felt Sara sit beside me and lift my head onto her lap. She gently ran her fingers through my hair.

"Aria, you're scaring me. I know you don't want to, but please tell me what happened," Sara begged.

I sucked in a deep breath and turned toward her. I studied her. She was my best friend. I let out the breath I'd been holding and started from the beginning.

Through my tears, I poured out my soul to Sara. I had so much built up inside me that I had to get it all out. How Avery seduced me emotionally the first day of camp. How we had breakfast by the waterfall, and how we had sex during the Masquerade Ball. I told her how fantastic the sex was and how caring, passionate, and kind he was. How he fulfilled one of my fantasies and he took me up against the wall. The way he took me in the shower, and the delicious time in the bedroom. I told her how we made love to the most perfect song. How I saw so much caring and compassion in one man's eyes that it took my breath away.

Just like the song was speaking to my soul, I knew then I could never let him go.

It hurt too much to relive all of my emotions that night. Then I told her what happened during bungee jumping. And later how Pierce took me to confess my love to Avery and how it devastated me to find him with Caitlyn. Then to find out how Caitlyn blamed me for all the pranks she pulled on me and said it was all my doing. I told Sara everything that led up to this point. She sat with her mouth opened, stunned as I spoke. It felt good to get it all off my chest, not to hide it from her anymore.

"Oh, Aria. I didn't realize. If he doesn't want you then he's a fool," Sara bellowed. I loved that Sara supported me. She always had my back. I frowned, knowing she was right. "Look, we go back to Ohio next week. You'll be back in school and you'll soon forget everything."

"I don't think I can," I said. "How can I forget all of this? I love it here," I said, as the tears fell again. Sara's eyes bored into me. It was what she always did when she was trying to read me.

"You love him don't you?" Sara inquired. I didn't respond. She sighed heavily. "Look, Colt has been coming here since the camp opened. He said he's never seen Avery like this. He's never taken interest in anyone. Work was all he knew. All he's ever done."

I let her words sink in then looked at her. More tears fell from my eyes and I quickly wiped them away. She studied me.

"What am I going to do with you?"

I shrugged, "Want to know something else?" I asked.

She looked at me curiously. "I got my belly button pierced."

She gasped. "When?"

"After the fight," I frowned.

"Let me see," she said pulling up my shirt. Her fingers traced the shimmery sapphire blue butterfly bead and she smiled at me. "Whore," she teased. We both giggled. It was what I had said to her when she got hers pierced right after she met Colt.

"I know," I chided.

"Aria," Caitlyn said. I bristled at the sound of her voice as she walked up to us.

"What do you want, Caitlyn?" I replied, stagnantly not bothering to look up from the bench.

"You to back off from Avery, that's what," she said.

"What are you talking about?"

I saw Sara get up and walk a few feet to her horse and start grooming the same side I just finished. I knew it was only to be within striking distance if this got ugly between us.

"I see the way you look at him. He would never give you the time of day. So, just stop embarrassing yourself," Caitlyn snapped.

I finally looked at her. She was wearing tan breeches; black riding boots, a navy blue short sleeved riding jersey, and her hair was pulled back into a tight ponytail, everything about her wardrobe screamed money.

"Funny. I was just thinking the same thing about you." I'm pretty sure I heard her growl as she took a step closer. I didn't know what really happened between her and Avery and truthfully, I didn't want to know, but a part of me knew that if he still wanted her then she wouldn't be here now.

"You better watch it," she hissed then went on. "Look, Bambi, I hate to break it to you but a man like Avery would easily get bored with a girl like you. Look at you," she said, scouring me with her eyes from head to toe. "Fantasies don't come true for people like you. You could never be the woman Avery wants." She stalked around the barn like a tiger about to eat its prey. But I didn't care.

"Get over yourself. Gold digging dried up a long time ago. Maybe you should try a paint-by-numbers class or something that wouldn't interfere with all that silicone."

She stomped her foot. "Little girl, I'm warning you. Back the fuck off of Avery."

I laughed at her absurdity. She stepped closer. She was taller than me, but I was pretty sure I could take her if we fought, and my stubbornness overrode my common sense as I stepped closer to her. I had a lot of fuel in the fire.

"What makes you think he'd want you anyway? I mean look at you. Let's see, fake hair. Fake teeth. Fake boobs. Fake tan. What more could a guy ask for?"

"Why, you little bitch," she said, pulling back her fist.

"Is there a problem here, ladies?" his magnetic voice rang out through the barn walkway.

I cringed when I heard his voice. Caitlyn could have spun on a dime the way she dropped her hand and smiled pleasantly to him. *Oh, she was good.*

"Hi, baby. Aria and I were just having a difference of opinion on riding saddles is all. Weren't we?" She widened that bleach white smile of hers and I suddenly imagined her teeth all knocked out and I laughed at her. *She was ridiculous.*

I motioned for the horse to follow me into its stall and I closed the door. I slammed the brush into the wooden crate for cleaning and turned toward the exit.

"Avery, did you come here to go riding? I'm free right now, I could go with you," her voice was like nails on a chalkboard.

All I could think about was getting away before I lost my temper on her. I was halfway down toward the exit when I heard Avery blow her off and run after me. I picked up the pace and ducked out the side door.

"Aria, wait!" Avery bellowed.

I didn't stop. I just wanted to get away from him. My body was shaking with anger. Avery put his hand on my arm and I recoiled it. "What?"

"I heard what Caitlyn said. I could never want a woman like that," he said.

"That's not what it looked like on your front porch that night," I seethed.

"I got very drunk on whiskey that night and yes, I fucked her," he huffed. "Look, I'm sorry. That wasn't one of my proudest moments. I got back from the party that night hammered. I was trying to drown out the thoughts of those guys all over you at the party when Caitlyn was waiting for me there on my front porch. She offered herself to me and I just went with it. I needed a good cum to clear my head."

I blinked up at him as the harsh reality of it all set in. *That sounded really familiar.*

"Like I care about your sex life. Why are you here anyway?" I said, crossing my arms.

362

He raised his brow at me. "My Kitten has claws. You seem to have a lot of pent up anger."

"I am not your Kitten!" I stuttered. "And I only act this way around you!" I dropped my arms to my sides with my fist clenched. I shook my head and took a slow deep breath, trying to calm down. "Don't do that. Don't act like you care about me when you don't," I seethed, stepping closer.

He grabbed both my arms and closed the gap between us. "I care about you. Christ, Aria, why can't you see that?" he said in a husky low voice. I ignored the way his voice vibrated through me and struck me down deep.

"Because you have a really lousy way of showing it. Why can't you open up to me? Tell me what you're thinking. Tell me *now*, Avery, because I'm losing my mind over all of this!" My voice echoed off the barn beside us.

His eyes fell away and he brought his hand up and rubbed the back of his neck. "I can't..."

I held up my hand cutting him off. "You're exhausting. Here I'll save you the trouble and this time *I'll* walk away."

I jogged up the path farthest away from him. I knew this was his camp. I knew I couldn't leave here for five more days, but damn if I had to be within ten feet of him. He crushed me and I let myself get crushed. I was such a fool. I ran up the beaten path toward my cabin. I fell hard into my bed and threw the pillow up over my face. I screamed into it. *God, Avery's head games made me so mad.*

363

⌘

DAY THIRTY-EIGHT:
WEDNESDAY NIGHT
LADIES' CHOICE KEY PARTY

It was the night before the camp Olympics, and only four more days until I could get away from Avery Jameson for good. *And once I've gone from here, I am never coming back.*

I stepped through the doorway of the Main Lodge to the Ladies' Choice Key Party. Every girl got a key when she entered the ballroom tonight. When she saw a guy she wanted to sleep with, she was to give him her key and then they would meet up later in the room that the key unlocked.

Each of the bedrooms had a theme but you wouldn't know the theme until you unlocked the door. It might be Western, Moroccan, Hawaiian, Chican or a Doctor's Office. Avery kept it unpredictable. The idea was that you didn't know until you unlocked the door and got in there.

I stood taking in the gold and silver key decorations. Giant golden and silver keys hung from the ceiling and lined the walls. Combined with those keys, were giant gears and cogs representing the locks that turned and moved showing whatever secrets were being unlocked.

With each party, Avery seemed to outdo himself each time with grander and larger themes. But as I stood in the ballroom looking around taking in the massive display, the words of my psychology professor echoed in my head. He used to say that keys are important entities in our lives, and most of us never give them a second thought. Keys are powerful commodities that symbolize the opening of one part of our life's journey and the closing of another. They represent the knowledge, mystery, and curiosity of that journey. Always, there is a door to be unlocked.

When you think about it, unlocking a door can bring you knowledge. But it also can expose your secrets and this place was full of them. The knowledge of what lies inside can lead you to new experiences and a completely new way of life, or it can awaken your fears and force you to retreat from that life. The mystery of it comes from unlocking those closed doors and seeing what's inside. You might be unlocking something inside your heart or unlocking desires that can breathe new life into your journey. Who knows what adventures wait for you when you unlock something that is hidden. Those new adventures might be more than you could have ever imagined.

But there is a certain empowerment that comes from being curious enough to turn the key in the first place. When the door opens, when you're strong enough, and brave enough, to step through not knowing what you'll find waiting for you on the other side. Without the curiosity to turn the key in the first place, we wouldn't be able to step into that new way of life. Or find our way to happiness, or whatever lives beyond those locked doors. But it all starts by the turning of a key. I bet all those people wandering around this ballroom never gave any of that much thought and I bet most of them didn't care. But I cared.

Camp Jameson was the key that unlocked my sexuality and for that I was forever grateful. I was a much different person now than when I arrived a few short weeks ago and, good or bad, this new person was here to stay. Of course, Avery unlocked my heart, and even though I am suffering on the inside, I know that someday I will be a better person for it. At least I learned to quit falling for every guy I sleep with. I was pretty sure that revelation had cost me a relationship with Ethan, because I was sure he wanted to be my boyfriend until I slept with his brother Wren. So now, I was in the friend zone with both of them. It was just another chance at love ruined. *Maybe someday, I'll get it right but until then, I might as well find someone to fuck.*

As I continued my search for that special someone, I made my way around the ballroom looking for Sara, who was supposed to be meeting me at any moment. As I pushed my way through the crowd, that sad echo of a once beautiful child interrupted my daydreaming with her sour puss.

"Looks like you didn't get the guy after all," Caitlyn sneered. Her voice was like stepping on a rusty nail in your bare feet.

"Your point, Catface?" I said harshly, not making eye contact with the annoying troll. I still hadn't spotted Sara yet.

"Rumor has it, Avery has a girlfriend. Like I told you he would when he got bored and moved on," Caitlyn smirked.

I figured Caitlyn started that rumor herself, but she was wrong. The whole camp knew Avery was a player, except for me, and that he would never have a girlfriend. He didn't need one. This camp was his personal procurement center. The women came here to him.

"Caitlyn, Travis needs you," Sara trilled. "There's a leaky window in Kit Kat cabin that needs silicone to seal it. Why don't you run along and help him out with that," Sara said, molding her hands around each breast and giving them a little wiggle. "I would help him, but mine are real," she said, in mock disappointment.

Caitlyn huffed, then spun on her heel and headed toward the bar. I was thankful for Sara rescuing me. I wasn't sure how much more I could take.

My eyes scanned the room. Avery was nowhere to be found tonight. He must be getting ready for the Olympics tomorrow. There were decorations and bleachers going up all over the camp. I actually passed a medal ceremony stand on my way here tonight. The whole place was transforming, into what... I don't know.

Sara and I were in tight fitting sequined mini dresses. Hers was gold. Mine was a silver, short, sparkling mini with a sweetheart neckline and glimmering teardrop-shaped sequins. It favored my rhinestone silver strappy heels that Sara had bought me. Gold and silver seemed to be the color scheme tonight. Most of the women passing by had on something similar and the guys, as always, wore black. I walked with Sara across the hall toward Pierce. He was leaning against a support beam near the bar with his arms crossed, watching us from across the room with interest.

"Taking care of the trash, Sara?" Pierce asked.

"Always," Sara answered.

He grinned mischievously. "I have to be dreaming. The two hottest ladies in the ballroom, are standing in front of me. What do I owe the pleasure?"

"I'm saving the best for last." Sara slipped her key in Pierce's hand and winked. I was shocked at Sara's forthrightness and Pierce smiled wide as he looked to me with hope in his eyes. I shook my head lightly and looked away. I was saving mine for now.

"How are you, Aria?" he asked.

I shrugged, not wanting to answer. I kept my eyes on the high priced flooring, trying to distract myself with something other than looking at him. Except for his eyes and blonde highlights, Pierce was a younger version of Avery and it was difficult for me to be so close to him like this.

"That bad, huh?" he inquired.

I put on my best smile and looked at him. "Have fun you two," I said, taking a few steps toward the bar but making sure that it was the opposite side that Caitlyn occupied.

"She's miserable," Sara muttered. I tried to ignore the fact that they were talking about me like I wasn't three feet away.

"You can see me standing right over here can't you?" I asked sarcastically as they ignored me.

"So is Avery. I tried everything I could." I heard Pierce say as they walked away toward a room. *Was Avery really suffering like I was? If so, why the hell wouldn't he tell me how he feels? Ugh. All I wanted to do tonight was get drunk.*

A while later, I'm not sure exactly how long, but I was on my fifth or maybe sixth…oh god who knows…*wheeee…*

my head was spinning…. Jameson and Diet Coke. I looked up to see a smiling Sara bouncing on the balls of her feet.

"Done already?" I said, surprised and trying not to slur.

"Yep, and guess what?"

I quirked my eyebrow at her, *Well at least I think I did, I wasn't sure it came across the way I wanted it to; the alcohol was limiting my muscle movement.*

She snickered at me. "You're wasted. Happy you've succeeded?"

"Yep. I fought hard and won this round," I chirped.

Kim handed me an energy drink and a tall ice water. I frowned at Sara.

"You're such a buzzkill," I whined.

"Down them, and hurry," she urged. "We have something to do."

"What evs," I said.

Sara and I snuck out of the Main Lodge in our mini dresses and stilettos and we made our way toward the Pinky Princess Spa Cabin. Sara reached down behind a bush and pulled out her camp backpack and slung it over her shoulder. I followed her to the back of the salon to a single glass door and she knelt down and started to pick the lock. My eyes scanned the perimeter sluggishly. *Too much alcohol tends to slow your reflexes.*

"Did you know that Caitlyn goes spray tanning every Thursday morning?" she said casually like we were leisurely getting a manicure or just hanging out in a coffee shop gossiping like two old ladies would. *I knew that bitch spray tanned. She always passed it off as natural outside tanning. She was so phony.*

Sara stopped what she was doing to wait for my reply.

"No," I said, shrugging my shoulders at her. Sara went back to picking the lock.

"Did you know she has the first appointment of the day? Yep, every Thursday at 9am," she added concentrating on the lock. "And she always uses bed number three because that's the only spray tanner. The other two are regular UV beds.

"Okay," I said, crossing my arms and looking around to make sure no one was able to see what we were doing. "How do you know this and what's your point?"

"You'll see," she said. She strolled up to the computer and the screen popped awake. She scrolled through and tilted the screen for me to see that she was right. Caitlyn was the first appointment of the day tomorrow. I nodded. "Booth 3," Sara added.

Sara stepped down the small maintenance hall to the back of booth three and lowered her backpack to the floor. She rummaged through it and pulled out a large wrench that looked like something a plumber would use and set it beside her feet on the floor. Then she pulled out a Phillips screwdriver and started unscrewing the screws to some kind of access panel.

"Did I ever tell you that my cousin Ronnie was a plumber?" she asked in that casual tone again.

"No, but that doesn't surprise me. I'm thinking that you picked up a few tricks from him over the years," I whispered.

"Why are you whispering?" she said loudly, startling me and causing me to jump as she kept moving to undo the second screw.

I fanned my hand out to the empty and dimly lit salon, showing her that I thought we should be quiet and not chatting as if we were browsing through a shopping mall.

"No one's here. Stop worrying," she pressed. "Anyways, my cousin used to take me on some of his house calls when he babysat me and I used to help him. That's how I got pretty handy with tools," Sara said, moving to the bottom of the panel. I watched as Sara unscrewed the bottom two screws and stood.

"Help me with this panel," she said.

I went to the other side and helped her lift it away and set it down against the nearby wall. She reached over for the large wrench.

"Pipe wrench, the best tool a plumber can have," she said with humor in her eyes. She was having fun with this and I was freaking out inside. I saw a shadow dance on the wall beside us and I jumped. My eyes focused on it a little more and I realized it was just the wind blowing a nearby tree.

"So," she said placing the wrench on one of the fittings and went back to her work. *I still didn't know what she was planning to do. And I was sad to say I had lost my buzz.*

"When you need to unfasten any fixture you use this tool," she added.

I stayed silent watching her turn a valve to the off position. Then she made quick work of untightening a long metallic flex hose with brass fittings.

"Hand me that container from my backpack, would you?"

I reached inside the backpack, brought out a large cylindrical tube, and handed it over to her. She poured the entire contents into a copper reservoir at the back of a large tank and put the pipe back together.

My eyes widened in curiosity of what Sara was planning. *Holy shit.* I ducked when I heard the sound of a key being turned in the front door and a flirty giggle echo across the cabin's hardwood floors. I grabbed Sara and we knelt behind the booth. Our dresses might as well have been a flashing gold and silver neon sign the way we were sparkling from the sliver of white light that danced through a small window on the side of the cabin.

Two voices, one male and one female, delicately danced across the cabin to our hiding ears. All I could think about was Sara and I peeling potatoes and shoveling more horse dung when we got busted in here. I decided I'd give myself up, hopefully causing a distraction enough for Sara to get out. When I went to stand up, I felt Sara's hand on my skirt yanking me down hard on my ass.

"Oww," I whispered. "What did you do that for?"

"I'm keeping you from getting both of us busted you dumb ass. Now don't move," Sara said, leaning over to get a glimpse of who came in.

"I've wanted to fuck in here since I've got to camp," the female said. "I fantasize about it all the time while I'm here at work," she purred in the male's ear.

"All right, baby," he shrugged. "Just tell me, when are you going to put that beautiful mouth on me?"

"Wait a minute," I whispered to Sara. "That fucking asshole used the same line on me?"

"Who?" Sara whispered back.

"I'll show you who." But as I went to stand up, I felt Sara's hand grab me and yank me hard on my ass again.

"Oww," I barked. "Quit doing that. You're gonna bruise me."

"Then quit acting like a dumbass," she repeated. "Who is it?" she whispered again.

"Ethan," I whispered through clenched teeth.

"Oh my," she said, with concern in her eyes.

We knelt there while the couple made out for what seemed like an eternity. Every time they went to move to a booth they started back up again and didn't make any forward progress. Sara would go to stand up then have to fall back down.

"Shit. I wished they'd hurry up already," I whispered.

"Let's go get into Booth 3," the female voice said.

Fuck. Damn. We were about to get caught.

The female's back was to us as they kissed and tongued their way toward the booth, knocking over bottles of tanning lotion and smacking into the counter. At one point, he was dry humping her on one side of the counter, jarring it into Sara and me, dropping flowery smelling lotions and bronzers on our heads. They would press harder on one side of the counter and as it would start to tip, Sara would brace it and push it back up, and then they did it again...and then again, *holy baby Jesus*.

Finally, they stood back up as Sara and I nearly lost our grip on the counter a couple of times. The couple slowly sidestepped backwards while they kissed, heading back to their rendezvous.

As they passed the counter we were crouching behind, my eyes locked on to Ethan's even as his tongue was tickling her tonsils. He froze, trying to take in what the hell we were doing there. Sara and I both just shrugged cutely. *I mean, what are you gonna do?*

My consternation was evident on my face as I visually scolded him with my eyes for using the same pick up line on me. He stood there shocked as her tongue took its turn invading his mouth. I held my finger to my mouth to shush him and he nodded, moving her head in unison with his. He tightened his arms around the woman to keep her from turning toward us and he kissed her hard on the mouth.

"First, I want you to suck me off then I will take you anyway you want me to," he said, lowering her to her knees. *Oh really,* I thought.

She giggled in excitement and unzipped him. His breath caught when her lips made contact and his head tilted back. He seemed caught up in the moment for a minute then he motioned with his chin for us to hurry up and go. He kept his hands on the sides of her face so she couldn't see us. Ethan groaned loud as we set the metal back up against the back of the booth. *Nice way to cover Ethan, you asshole,* I thought, as Sara made quick work on tightening the screws.

I felt like I was watching a tennis match. I kept looking back and forth between the woman and Sara. But then I stopped for a moment, to watch the woman pleasuring Ethan. And then my eyes fell on his. His eyes locked onto me and I could see what he really wanted even in the dim hallway. He still wanted me. *What a player.*

He was seducing me with his eyes while getting a blowjob. *I admit, it was kinda hot.*

I clenched my legs together, remembering that delicious night we shared together. He just shrugged his shoulders as if this was all perfectly natural. I gulped as Sara gripped my hand and dragged me up, tiptoeing down the hallway. I looked back to Ethan and mouthed politely 'Thank you'. Sara turned back toward him and mouthed, 'Lock this' and he nodded and waved us to get going.

As we stepped out of the spa, I heard Ethan's command, "Come on Bridgett. Let's fuck, baby."

I didn't hear her answer but she was always too polite to talk with her mouth full.

We barely made it three steps before we erupted in giggles. We both managed to run to our cabin. Even in our stilettos we could still haul ass when we needed to. Sara and I landed on my bed and broke out in another fit of giggles. Sara wouldn't tell me what she put in the machine. She said I had to wait and find out with everyone else. I laughed even harder. It was like Christmas for the underappreciated.

⌘

DAY THIRTY-NINE:
THURSDAY AFTERNOON
CAMP OLYMPICS DAY 1
POLE DANCING COMPETITION

The entire camp was buzzing about the Camp Olympics today. I slept well for the first time since getting to camp. Maybe because, as far as I was concerned, this was like Christmas morning and I would get Sara's present sometime today when I finally got to see Caitlyn.

Everyone at breakfast was chatting about the games and predictably, most of the guys were complaining that they weren't eligible for the trip to Hawaii. It was only for the Kittens. It was always about the Kittens but the Cubs were eligible to win some very nice cash prizes for their events. The men's competition had events like basketball, beach volleyball, canoe races, kayak races, logrolling, and a 10k trail run. The games were held in all different areas of the camp. Banners were strung throughout the camp showing that the winning Kitten would win a trip to Hawaii and sidebars were set up everywhere as the drinking rules were relaxed, since these were the last days of camp. Avery definitely wanted everyone to have a great time during the games. You could tell he was planning a truly fantastic finale to our time at camp.

The first event of the afternoon was the pole-dancing contest. Sara and I made our way around the back of the Main Lodge to the big stage where a tall brass dancing pole stood about mid-center and a judge's table was out in front surrounded by a large horseshoe of bleachers that spanned either side. It looked like a small football stadium.

I suppose by this time in camp we weren't supposed to get nervous performing in front of so many voyeurs but then just like everything else, voyeurism had its own place here at camp as so many people loved to watch the fun live. There were six of us entered in this event. We were all finalists from the previous rounds. The crowd filed in for a small opening ceremony to wet everyone's appetite for what they came here for, to see the women dance. Almost everyone at camp was here except for one person who was noticeably absent. *Damn, I wished she'd get here so I could see my present.*

The air was dry today and overcast with the temperature coming in around eighty-two degrees. It was very comfortable.

Avery took the stage and walked up to a podium that was set up on the far side from where they seated us contestants. "Attention, is this thing on?" he said tapping on the microphone. "Testing…. testing…1…2…3…4… ssss…syphilliss… ssssyphillis," he chuckled. "Check… check." His voice crackled but then the soundman quickly dialed him in. Like everything he did, Avery brought in a massive stage set up with expensive lights and a large aluminum truss that outlined the stage in a giant rectangle.

"Hello everyone and welcome to the Camp Jameson Olympic games." The crowd cheered. "Today we begin the greatest of all parties. For the next three days, we will cheer for those who strive for excellence in victory, and praise those who fall to the agony of defeat. Some will distinguish themselves as they rise to the challenge and ascend to the victor's podium and others will fail to obscurity. But to all who enter these brave contests, let me just say, you can't win if you don't play. So let's get this fucking party started!"

The crowd went ballistic, standing and cheering loudly as Avery jumped down off the stage and was handed a drink by Pierce. The place was going bat-shit crazy at his speech and it left me wondering who was this Avery, who finally decided to live a little himself. *I bet real money that he had whiskey in that cup.*

Tara was called to the stage as the judges took their places at the center table. Everyone was toasting and drinking shots that they picked up at one of the two bars that were set up on the opposite sides of the event. Tara put her request in for music and headed toward the pole. I could see her husband Jim beaming up at her. She gave him a sultry look and took hold of the pole. Tara's hair was longer and silky. Her makeup and manicure were nicely done. She wore a rainbow rhumba bikini top with the Camp Jameson logo embroidered in dark green over the left chest and a colorful techno skirt to match. She was beautiful and glowing. This place had really changed her. She was a swan. And most importantly, she looked happy.

Chasing Seven began to play the song 'If I Didn't Have Eyes' as Tara shook her ass on the pole. A part of me wondered if my routine was good enough. She twisted and churned in a seductive dance on the pole. She finished her routine by kicking her legs out and climbing the pole, showing her arm strength. The large crowd cheered and whistled as Tara dismounted, held her arms up high and waved at the crowd. She then jumped off the stage and ran into her husband's arms and he twirled her around and kissed her deeply.

Ivy strutted her stuff in black side tie shorts and a red lace wrap top, with the Jameson logo, exposing her well-defined breasts. Kennedy took to the stage, after her, in a gold shimmery halter-top and matching boy shorts.

Amber followed next on the stage in pink tie front top and matching string bikini. Each girl danced her heart out and rocked the place. Each outfit had the Camp Jameson logo to reveal who were participants of the games.

I was getting nervous about going last. Then Becca blew everyone away with her badass black leather front closed corset and fantastic routine. These women were serious about winning and showed they'd been practicing.

Then my name was called, and the crowd seemed to have enlarged – if that was even possible. I made my way to the DJ booth and requested 'Pony' by Far then stepped center stage. *Why was I so nervous?*

Sienna had been privately coaching me, and until a second ago, I was confident I had a good routine. I looked down at Avery. His hair was tousled in just that way that made me want to run my fingers through it. His nose was perfect and his square jaw had a day old shadow. I forced myself to look away because thoughts of Avery wouldn't help my concentration.

I nodded to Sienna and she whispered to Rodriguez. He lowered a lever beside the stage and the floor rotated so that a second pole rose from the floor. The crowd mumbled their confusion. I felt the bass of the music pulse beneath my feet and I began swaying my hips. I had to do something extreme here. I couldn't do just the same old basic moves that we learned in class. I had to take it one step further in order to win this so Sienna and I came up with the two pole mcgillicutty.

I started with a barbed wire move Sienna taught me. I placed my hands on each end of the pole facing outward then lifted myself up and bent my body sideways around the pole. I held it there for a moment, and then dropped down to curve my feet around the pole and used gravity to spin myself around. I could honestly say that I liked the rush it gave me when I was floating around the pole. I dipped down, turned around and shot my ass in the air at everyone watching. I caressed my behind, arched my back, and then resumed into a standing position. I shimmied a little then skimmed my hands down my body.

My hair was pulled back into a long ponytail today. I chose to wear a black and white checkered halter-top with the dark green Camp Jameson logo, black mini skirt, black thigh highs, and black platform shoes today. I put extra grips on the bottoms of my shoes because I would need them for some of the moves I was planning.

I twisted around and anchored myself to the pole by bending my knee and flexing my foot around the pole. I pushed my leg up as high as I could and reached up high above my head to grab the pole with both hands. With my elbows bent, I pushed up with my legs and pulled myself up onto the pole, then gripped with my legs and extended my lower leg out. I released one of my hands and slid down the pole until my feet were planted firmly on the pole midway down then I kicked off the pole and I quickly turned into a back hook spin and twisted around. I spun around like a fireman then stepped to the floor. I did a few more spins around it, trying to build up the confidence to pull off my next move. I crawled up the pole and hung from one arm as I spun around building momentum, then when I was going fast enough I positioned my legs until my feet met the pole and I pushed off and leaped to the other pole. I flew through the air until my hands met brass then and I clung to it like a monkey and pushed the air that I had been holding from my lungs.

The crowd roared as I looped my left arm around to hold myself then twisted downward in a somersault and held myself mid-air. I locked my leg around it and held myself with my leg and only one hand. The music was blasting through the speakers. The lights were mesmerizing and a part of me got swept away in my performance. I slid down the pole and let my feet touch the ground. I did another lift onto the pole then with all my upper body strength I flexed my arms and pulled myself up to the top. I pushed my right leg out to the side and pointed my toes. Holding myself up with both hands, I twisted so that I could kick my legs out into a scissor kick then tightened my legs around the top of the pole. When I felt secure, I let my hands go and leaned backwards on the pole and squeezed my legs to hold me upside down. I could feel the brass pole behind me as I let my hands fall over my head, arched my back, and reached back to the pole. I thought of it as the balance beam – *it wasn't much different.*

As my hands made contact with the brass, I let my legs go and did a back flip. I felt exhilarated as my feet landed firmly on the floor. I righted myself then snaked my ribcage and breasts against the pole. I jumped upward and latched on to the pole while I spun around, found my footing, and pushed off. I soared through the air then I reached out for the other pole and tightened my grip as my hands came in contact with it. I dangled from my right arm and pulled my body in against the pole. I crawled up the pole like I was walking up it. I held the pole tightly and pulled my legs above my head then wrapped my legs around it and let my hands go. I trailed my fingers and palms down the sides of my body, gyrated my pelvis and dipped into the pole as the artist 'Far' urged me to ride his pony. I let my hands trail down both my breasts, my navel, then I dipped my fingers into the sides of my barely there skirt. I pulled it away from my skin to tease him. I shimmied and rolled my body while I still hung upside down and my legs held me tightly. I reached upward, gripped the pole, and kicked off and somersaulted back to the other pole. I let my hands loosen so that I could spin around softly and descend in a gentle spin to the floor.

As the song neared the end, I leaned back to find the pole, and bucked downward, spreading my knees in the process. As I slid down the pole to my knees with the bar pressed against my back, I looked up at Avery while licking my lips and trailing my hands up my legs. Then I shimmied back up the pole one last time, and scissored my legs in the air, anchored myself, and pushed off to the other pole, then braced myself upward with my arms, and then back flipped to the floor.

The song ended and I could hear the crowd erupt all around me. I rose slowly as I heard Sara cheering for me.

But the heated look in Avery's eyes was the only thing holding my attention. Sara jumped up to the stage and broke our gaze.

"That was amazing, I am so turned on right now. You just killed it on two poles. You have to teach me that back flip," Sara gushed, pulling me from the stage. The crowd erupted in catcalls and cheers for us to kiss as I waved them off generously and tried to get my breathing under control.

"All right, let's hear it for all the contestants," Avery's warm velvet voice filled the courtyard as he took center stage. My ears filled with applause. It only took a few minutes then the crowd quieted, waiting for Avery to announce the winners. Travis brought him the envelope and Avery quickly opened it.

"Third place goes to Amber Benson." The crowd cheered.

"Second place goes to Tara Evans." The crowd roared louder and whistles zipped through. When the crowd settled down Avery continued.

"And first place goes to…" His eyes darkened as they found me amongst the crowd. I squirmed under his heated stare. "Miss Arabella Mason!" A massive set of applause thundered through the bleachers.

My smile was weighted. It suddenly occurred to me. I had just won. If I won three events, I would be going to Hawaii with Avery. *Fuck. Did I really want that?*

⌘

DAY THIRTY-NINE:
THURSDAY LATE AFTERNOON
MEET SMURFETTE

"Will the contestants for the oral competition please come to the stage. We will begin in fifteen minutes," Avery announced through the PA system.

It was later in the afternoon around 5pm and the stage had received a makeover as Rodriguez and his crew removed the dancing poles and replaced them with six chairs to make way for the oral competition. Sara and I had walked down by the beach to watch the kayak races until the stage transformation was complete.

The loudspeakers sounded sharply as they announced the events and where they took place. It was nearing the start time when Sara and I made our way back to the back lawn and took our seats in eager anticipation of the contest, mainly because this was Caitlyn's first event and she had been mysteriously absent from public today. No one had seen her, not even her cabin mate, Kennedy.

It was a very large crowd that spilled back into the mini stadium. The bleachers were full, and getting hot in the afternoon sun, and that left only standing room on both sides of the stage. Six male instructors, including Colt, stepped up to their plush chairs and disrobed. The contestants made their way up to stand next to their chairs waiting for the signal to start. It was getting very close to starting time but only five girls made it to the stage so far. The loudspeaker rang loudly again.

"Are all the contestants on the stage? Can we get a count of the participants?" Avery said, while Sienna and Maya shuffled the contest sheets, seeing whom they were missing. "Can the last contestant, please step to the stage?"

"She's not going to show," I said to Sara.

"Don't be too sure. She desperately wants that trip with Avery. He's her golden goose. Plus, I'm sure she doesn't want you to win equally as much as you want her to lose."

"Too true, " I smiled. This suspense was killing me.

Maya handed a piece of paper down to Avery and as he read it, he nodded. "Caitlyn Camden, please come to the stage or you will be disqualified," Avery said.

Standing awkwardly on stage dressed only in their matching black bras and lacy boy short panties with the words 'Camp Jameson' in white across their backsides were Tara, Kennedy, Amber, Nora, and Lucy and all were awaiting the arrival of the last girl. As they fidgeted and waited to show the large crowd their oral gifts, a tall female body pushed her way through the crowd in a black trench coat and wide brim hat with dark sunglasses. She kept her head down so it was hard to get a good look at her. Then she stood next to the stage, undid her coat, and tossed away her hat. The crowd gasped audibly.

"Told ya she wouldn't miss this," Sara said, squeezing my leg and shaking it from side to side in her excitement.

At first, shock and awe spun through the crowd like a black widow spins her mystical web. Caitlyn walked proudly up the stairs next to the stage and stood before the entire crowd in very sheer canary yellow bra, panties, and matching high heels. She was the only girl not in black but from the look of defiance on her face everyone could plainly see that she just didn't care. She had coordinated her outfit nicely with her hair. But she was really…really blue. From her head to her toes, she was blue, not a light matching the sky in the Simpson's kind of blue, but that kind of blue you'd see on a Smurf. Sara had put blue dye in the spray tan reservoir and it dyed every part of her body and it worked stunningly well.

At first, the snickers started here and over there, one person, then another and another, then, like a deadly virus it spread across the crowd until the entire mini stadium was roaring with laughter and pointing their fingers, and every single one of them, wondering what the fuck was going on. Some thought she did it to psych out her competitors, while others just thought she was out of her mind. Damn she was blue. *Really blue!* I smiled proudly, *revenge was prettiest when it comes in the color blue.*

The entire time everyone was laughing, Caitlyn just stood there stoically, not looking at the crowd. She was ready to begin her quest of getting that trip with Avery. Sara and I high-fived each other, and it was at that moment when I decided there was no way I was going to let her win that trip with Avery. It was Hawaii after all. *Caitlyn could go fuck herself.*

I was going to do everything in my power to deny her that one thing that she wanted in the entire world, and why not? She was prepared to do the very same thing to me. Sara looked over at me and nudged me then she cupped her hands around her mouth and started chanting Smurfette…

Smurfette...Smurfette, and soon others joined in until three-fourths of the Stadium was hollering Smurfette.

The other girls on stage stood dumbfounded. I could see Kennedy was torn. She looked like she wanted to go hug Caitlyn but she hesitated and stayed in her spot. Avery just turned his head toward the crowd, scanning the sea of people until his eyes found me. Behind the fatherly look of disapproval, his eyes were laced with humor. I shrugged my shoulders as innocently as I could. He then turned and sounded the bell for the competition to begin.

Colt shook his head fiercely at her as Caitlyn approached him. I snickered, remembering the brutal mouth lashing she gave him that first day in oral class.

Tara then stepped up to Colt as Caitlyn made her way over to Travis. I knew from what Sienna said that it was difficult to make Colt cum. I smiled to myself remembering how turned on he was for me that day.

Avery leaned in and spoke into his microphone. "Rules are... first one to make her guy cum, wins. These men can go for a while, Kittens, so make yourselves comfortable. Each Kitten can set a pillow under her knees."

Each girl lowered to her knees on a large pillow and exposed the white imprint of Camp Jameson on their behinds.

"Let's go, Smurfette," Sara called out as most of the steady jeers lightened up.

Caitlyn narrowed her eyes and glared at Sara. Sara leaned close and threw her arm around me and wriggled her eyebrows at me playfully. Our prank turned out way better than we had planned. Caitlyn was blue from head to toe except for her blonde hair. Even her eyelids had that wonder shade about them.

The buzzer went off then suddenly everyone started cheering again, "Smurfette…Smurfette…Smurfette," repeatedly.

I could see Caitlyn trying to maintain her composure and do her best but it was getting to her. I looked to see Tara pleasing Colt. Her jaw was swallowing him up and her tongue was dancing around in her favorite technique. The sun danced off their blonde hair as I looked to Jared sitting next to him.

Nora was taking her time with Jared, licking every inch of him like a melting popsicle while her long lashes batted playfully up at him. Except for playing with her on the powder-puff football game, I didn't know Nora that well. She was tall, 5'7" with sandy colored hair and long loose curls. The one thing I would always remember about her was that she had a great laugh. Jared was the beefy bodybuilding type with broad shoulders. His brown hair and dark eyes made any woman want to melt.

Next to them was Lucy with her golden brown straight hair and larger curved frame and she was going all out with Pierce. Deep throat was her specialty. And it seemed to make Pierce happy as he leaned back and thread his hands behind his blonde highlighted hair to enjoy the pleasure.

Kennedy was her elegant self. She wore her poker straight blonde hair back in an immaculate tidy ponytail and she didn't look a bit out of place as she sheathed her teeth with her lips over Jessie's large caramel lollipop while she twisting her hand up and down at the same time.

Amber's pouty lips couldn't stop smiling around Danny's cock. Her eyes were closed and her ebony hair fell all around her. Danny seemed to be in heaven. Danny was a redhead and his cheeks were covered in freckles. When he smiled, his dimples would stop any girl in her tracks.

Travis moaned and I looked back to him. Travis still had his short buzz haircut and his hazel eyes seemed to sparkle in the sun. I could see the large tattoo with Maya's name across his left chest.

I bit back a smile as I looked to see blue Caitlyn still going strong. I watched as she lowered her finger down his sack and massaged the smooth skin of his testicles. His buttocks were out past the edge of the cushion and he was resting against the back of the chair with his head tilted back in pleasure. Slowly, she worked her way down further and I could see Travis fidget in his plush chair. He was enjoying this way too much. *Damn.*

She worked her way towards his tight hole and spread some lube over it without taking her mouth from his cock. Travis pushed closer, wanting more. Caitlyn dipped her finger inside and he hissed through his teeth. His hips bucked upward and Caitlyn smiled around his shaft. She moved in and out slowly and Travis couldn't contain his moan.

Her mouth continued to work erotically over him as her finger went in deeper up to the knuckle. Travis gripped the sides of his chair and Caitlyn continued to work her magic with her finger. She started pulsing relentlessly on both areas and before I knew what was happening she did some crazy trick with her tongue in concert with her jackrabbit grip and Travis was shooting cum all over her face. His

389

moan of pleasure rang out through the back courtyard over the music and Caitlyn stood, smirking valiantly. *What the hell?*

I gave Sara a 'how the hell did she do that' look and she grimaced.

"Damn her. The prostate massage will make a man cum every time." Looks like Caitlyn and I were tied for first in the Kitten race for Hawaii. *Well, fuck me!*

After the oral competition, Sara and I headed back down to the beach for some beers and to watch some of the men's events. As we neared the lake, I could see Ethan playing volleyball with a team of guys. I made my way over to them as Sara went to get us some drinks from the tiki hut on the beachfront. The game broke up as I neared.

Ethan grinned his sexy grin at me and scooped me up in a big hug.

"Hey beautiful. Come to watch me kick some ass?"

"Always," I joked. Ethan kissed me on the top of the head and set me down.

"Thank you for your help last night."

Ethan closed his eyes and grinned. "I had the best orgasm thinking about your delectable body. So thank you for that." He leaned into my ear and threw his arm around my shoulders. "Shhh, don't tell Bridgett," he whispered. I threw my head back and laughed.

"Your secret is safe with me," I grinned. I felt Ethan stiffen for a moment and I looked up into Avery's emerald eyes.

"Aria, can I speak with you for a moment," he said. His nostrils flared but his words were even. I nodded and stepped away from Ethan. I waved to Ethan and walked with Avery to an empty spot by a lounge chair. I stepped beside it and waited for him to speak.

"Are you responsible for Caitlyn's new look?"

"What? Well...I...uh," I sputtered. "Why would you think that?"

"Because, this is starting to get out of hand, so I'm telling both of you to cool it," he said sharply.

I studied him, trying to see how mad he actually was.

"I see you've entered in the Sybian Rodeo tomorrow. That's the toughest event and I won't play favorites during the judging," he said, stepping away. His eyes scanned the area to make sure no one was listening.

"And Aria," he said, turning back toward me. "You'd better get your rest tonight. You're going to need it."

I swallowed nervously as I watched Avery walk away. Sara stepped up next to me. She glanced over her shoulder at Avery storming away. She raised her eyebrow at me. I shook my head at her.

"I brought your bathing suit and a towel for you. Everyone's swimming at the lake tonight at the Beach Party," Sara said breaking me from my uncertain thoughts of Avery.

"Thanks," I said, heading toward the Main Lodge to change. I made my way toward the bathroom trying to figure out why Avery was so mad at me. Caitlyn started it. She kept getting the upper hand, even with Avery. I was just another notch in his bedpost. I pushed open the door too hard and it bounced off the wall behind it. *Crap!*

I held the door back and let it rest against the wall then stepped into the bathroom. I made quick work of changing into my red bikini then I picked up my backpack with my change of clothes and threw it over my left shoulder. As soon as I stepped out of the bathroom to head back to the party I ran right into Pierce leaning against the wall waiting for me to come out. He was in a white polo shirt with the dark green Camp Jameson logo over the left breast and tan cargo shorts with sandals. He looked scrumptious. I mentally shook myself.

"Great performance on the pole today. I've never seen anything like it," he said. I just stared at the ground. Then I lifted my head towards him.

"Thanks," I replied. *Great, couldn't I say more than one word answers?*

"I want you to know he's acting like this because he's afraid of what he's feeling for you," he continued.

"I've put my heart out there for him more than once and he's afraid?" I balked.

"He cares for you deeply, Aria," Pierce said. I heard his words but I just couldn't let myself believe in him again.

"He has a funny way of showing it," I huffed. "Look, Pierce," I said, exhaling a deep breath. "Where I come from, if you really want to be with someone then you'll risk it all, sometimes more than once, to get it." I ran my hand over the back of my neck. "I've risked it all for him and both times, I've got burned. If he really wanted to be with me then he wouldn't be running in the opposite direction. It's as simple as that."

"Fair enough," he said, glancing at the doorway of the men's room. "But my life has taught me that if you stop fighting for what you really want, then you aren't risking anything at all." He stepped away from me out into the main hallway.

I glanced up to see Avery standing just a few feet away from us. I frowned. *How much of that did Avery hear?* By the look on his face, I would guess the whole thing.

I walked away, rubbing my hands over my face, and then shook my head not believing that really happened. *Ugh, I didn't want to think about Avery tonight.* I would worry about all this tomorrow. After all, tomorrow holds more promises and more events. *But tonight I'm gonna party like it's nineteen ninety…something or other…oh fuck it.*

"Sara! Where's my beer?" I hollered.

⌘

DAY FORTY:
FRIDAY NIGHT
CAMP OLYMPICS DAY 2
THE SYBIAN RODEO

I smiled through my hangover and nausea. Caitlyn was the most talked about subject during breakfast today. Every table was buzzing about the bright blue blonde, and finally it was her, and not me, that got the fancy nickname. Smurfette had such a nice ring to my ears. I loved it.

After breakfast, everyone filed out into the back courtyard. Techno-dance music rang out as the early events got started. This was not good for my splitting headache. We must have been out drinking until 4am.

The sensual couples massage event started off slowly. From the looks on most of the six couples' faces, maybe everyone was still hungover from the night before.

As we walked by the tables, some of the men were breaking out the toys to help get their Kittens going. I recognized Oliver and Anne. Next to them were Brooke and Alan. They were in their early forties and still looked decadent.

From what Sara had told me, Oliver and Brooke worked together in a big law firm in Seattle. They both are happily married but one night over dinner with their spouses they found that they had more in common than they thought. After a few bottles of expensive wine, the night turned kinky and ever since they have declared themselves swingers and have shared in the pleasure of each other's company for the last five years. They even came together to Camp Jameson to fulfill a few more fantasies.

The instructors Jessie and Danny were monitoring the event. Each one was wearing their white polo shirt with the standard camp logo and khaki cargo shorts. Jessie announced that he was deducting points from their total score since they were using toys. Danny announced that the only way to win this event was to make the woman squirt so everyone could see her climax. And the more hand techniques you used the higher the score. The only couple seemingly to get each other off cleanly was Tara and Jim.

Jim trailed his tongue down the center of Tara's navel and began teasing her clit. He worked his fingers inside of her and soon she was aching in need for release. He slipped his finger into her back entrance and continued with his ministrations. Tara bucked upward, exploded around his fingers and squirted. I had never seen a girl do that, though Sara told me Colt made her squirt before.

Jim crawled over Tara and pressed his mouth to hers as she mewed like a Kitten and cried out. It was loving but kinda gross, though I was still happy for them finding their passion again. He swallowed her cries and they were awarded first place. They didn't seem to care when the instructor announced it. They were too wrapped up in each other to notice.

Sara and I left in case they started fucking because I just did not want to see that, so we made our way to the canoe races to visit Colt.

The loudspeaker soared with the results of the 10k trail run. I guess they had a really good turnout for that.

"What do the Cubs get if they win?" I asked Colt. The Cubs didn't win the same prizes as the Kittens. Their games were more athletic in nature, probably just to give them something to do while the Kittens sexed it up.

"The winner gets five thousand dollars and moved up to the top of the list to become an instructor." I lifted my brow at him.

"What guy wouldn't jump at the chance to do that plus get a nice chunk of change? This place is heaven," he said, giving Sara a chastely kiss.

I frowned when I thought of Avery and how he'd created this world just to fuck women. According to Pierce, he submerged himself in women. His only rule was that he never got emotionally involved. No matter what the closest person in his life said, Avery couldn't love me. I was just another woman he seduced. I was part of his never-ending fantasy. Not love.

What scared me the most, was if I won the trip to Hawaii and went with Avery, could my heart withstand the time I spent with him? Because for me, our night together was more than just a one-night stand and no matter how much I tried to deny it, I was in love with him.

Even though Sara warned me from the beginning not to fall for him, I couldn't classify my heart as weak or strong in this situation, it was a little bit of both. And in two days time, I would take what was left of it and go back to

Ohio. I would do what I did best. Pretend that I lived out the last six weeks of my life in a fantasy. *Now, tricking my brain into believing it was the hard part.*

As we walked past the canoe races, I stopped momentarily. I could see that Ethan and Wren were in the lead. Each one had his shirt off and sweat dripped down their chests. I licked my lips as my eyes wandered over the grounds of this beautiful, surreal place and I felt my heart grow heavy. I would miss the friendships that I had made. I would miss the erotic foreplay and the way I'd grown comfortable in showing my naked body.

"Aria, you coming?" Sara said, interrupting my sentimental rambling. I nodded and followed beside her. I smirked knowing that each time I heard that word, I would think of this place. I would remember how the classes combined with all my sexual experiences brought me into my prime. And now I was captivated by it all. I felt confident and sexy.

Sara snickered as we walked back in to the main stage for the masturbation event. I looked to see Caitlyn's Smurf blue body lying on the table and she was exposed in all her glory. *Wow that dye really went everywhere.* Even her choo-choo lips were blue, and she wasn't shy about it.

She easily slid her fingers down inside her love cave all the way in one motion. She slowly and steadily rotated her fingers in and out as if it were the first time until they hit her cervix and you could see the juices flowing down her blue ass cheeks. *Oh my, I can feel it starting again*, I thought as I felt the wetness once again begin between my legs. *I must be sick or I need to get laid*, I thought.

When her orgasm started, she came as if she were cuming for everyone watching. Sienna and Maya looked to the heart monitor beside her as it spiked while she orgasmed. I could see the three leads stuck to each one of the contestant's chests to monitor their heart rates. I guess Avery thought of everything. Had to make sure they weren't faking it. It was like the crowd felt every little tremor as it passed through her body right into the core of the audience. I heard Caitlyn cry out and the instructors announce her as the winner of that event. She was determined to win the trip to Hawaii. She'd just won two events.

Within in a few seconds the heart rate began to fall back to normal. Amber quickly followed beside her, and then Jen. Jen was a petite Asian American. She was beautiful. Her father owned one of the worlds largest oil industries in America and she'd never worked a day in her life. My eyes shifted towards Ivy, Nora, and Lucy, they were still going strong. Each one spread eagle and trying to tip over the edge.

I shook my head, trying to get the mental image of blue Caitlyn out of my head, and made my way to the outside bar for a cold beer. *Hair of the dog, ya know.*

The sun was starting to sink down below the trees when they finished setting up the main stage for the Sybian Rodeo. Rodriguez and his crew had moved out all of the masturbation tables and set up one lonely apparatus in the middle of the stage. This was Avery's big secret project. It was very large and sat in the center of the staged area under a large white sheet ready for its unveiling as dusk peaked and the campfires were being lit around the fire pits. The lawn lights were slowly coming to life.

I looked over at the main scoreboard. There were ten women in this event. Caitlyn had just won two events. Tara was a close second. I was third. I was behind but I only entered three events so it was pretty much win or go home. And I didn't have a fancy backflip to help me win this one.

The Sybian Rodeo was run just like a real rodeo. Each contestant would have three minutes to reach the highest level they could withstand from one to ten. Country music blasted through the PA and all the girls wore plaid shirts tied up baring their tight midriffs.

My outfit was about as simple as you can get, but it was still super adorable. My tie-front plaid shirt, with the camp logo over my left breast, was sexy without being old-fashioned, and my short daisy dukes with the dark green Camp Jameson initials on the right back pocket completed the sultry country girl-next-door look. Sara went all out buying this outfit for me. It even came with cool brown leather harness cowboy boots. It was perfect for driving a pickup to the hardware store, or riding a mechanical bull, or in this case a Sybian.

My eyes fell on Avery as he sat at the judge's table. He nodded to Travis and then he announced the beginning of the Rodeo. There were three rounds. I was in the second round. Five women were in the first round then five in the second. The winner of each round would then compete against each other.

I was feeling shaky from being hungover this morning. Avery warned me to get a good night's sleep like he knew we were going to stay out late ahead of time. If I had any hope of winning at all, I would have to ride the Sybian twice. I had no idea if I could win this because I'd never been higher than a level two.

"Wait, why didn't you enter this? You've been talking about this from the beginning of camp," I said.

Sara gave me a small smile. "You need to win this. Not me," she said.

"What if I don't win?" I asked Sara, who was standing next to me.

"You keep going until you do. You only entered three events," Sara winked. "This is a must win. No one's ever scored higher than an eight in this rodeo and whatever is under that sheet looks like a monster, it's huge. Remember just relax, don't clench your muscles together. You'll cum faster that way. Keep everything loose and ride it until you can't stand it anymore."

The loudspeaker crackled to life as Avery addressed the crowd.

"Ladies and gentlemen, welcome to the 5th annual Camp Jameson Sybian Rodeo!" The crowd applauded and cheered vigorously. "I would now like to present to you this years Sybian wonder horse...the Arabian Fabian...the Black Beauty...the Country Clogger..."

"What's he doing?" I asked.

"Shh, he's on a roll," Sara quipped.

Was he drunk? I've never seen this carefree side of Avery and I couldn't fight back the smile that spread across my face as he continued on.

"The Canter of Canterbury...the Italian of Stallions... friends and neighbors...I give you....Teeaaa cup!"

Was he serious? With a name like Tea Cup how bad could it be? The sheet lifted high in the air as one thousand pounds of mighty hydraulic dynamite sat center stage.

"Can you believe that thing cost $75,000 for Avery to make? It's his own design," Sara said, grinning.

My eyes scanned the very ornate piece of machinery. It was a large black rocking horse with a vibrator sticking up from the authentic leather saddle. It had glowing blue eyes and spitfire out of its nostrils. Its legs displayed in mid gallop and actually moved in animated motion. Its bridle was handcrafted leather with real golden inlays, and it was bigger than a Clydesdale. It was pulsing and you could feel it hum and vibrate from ten feet away. Saying it was intimidating was a total understatement. I only had one experience with the Sybian and it was nothing like that mustang. Most Sybians are about the size of a large suitcase, but this thing was mammoth.

"Holy fuck," I sputtered.

The first woman, Clarissa, approached the Sybian with fear in her eyes as she shimmied out of her shorts and underwear, leaving her in just her tied plaid shirt with the Jameson logo. Colt helped her step up over and mount it sliding the phallus slowly into her hoo-ha. Colt had lubed the shaft up nicely. The bell sounded and before she knew it the Sybian...I...er...mean Tea Cup bucked to life. Travis clicked the timer and the scoreboard that stood high above the stadium-like stage sprung to life.

Everyone alternated their eyes from her to the scoreboard above. Some of her friends cheered for her. She started off at level 1. Then Colt, who was running the control switch, progressed it up one level at a time slowly.

Clarissa bucked and writhed as the vibrating shaft pulsed, spun and moved inside of her. Then Colt increased the intensity up to level 6 and everyone could see the strain it took on her. Her face clearly showed pain and she stood up. The mechanical monstrosity came to an abrupt stop.

The crowd cheered for her and Colt helped her step down. She winced. Her score remained on the board as the next contestant Lucy, stepped up and waited for Colt to replace the latex phallus with one fresh from a new package. He then quickly lubed it up then helped her into the stirrups and up over the horse.

Lucy only made it to level 5 before she could no longer take the beating it was giving her and rose up off it with her legs trembling in the stirrups.

Then Tara stepped up to it. She let Colt lower on another latex rod and she mounted it with a smile without waiting for him to lube it up. She was already very wet. Determination reflected in her eyes.

The saddle started rocking and tilting side to side as Tara relaxed her body around it. She had the right idea. *Just let yourself move with it. Don't try to fight it. Go with it.*

Tara closed her eyes and threw her head back. The relentless vibrator pushed further into her as it spun and vibrated. She had just passed level six and she didn't seem to be tiring. She lowered her hand and her fingers found her clit and began rubbing. *Wow, this girl could take a fucking.*

She cried out in pleasure and after her release she couldn't take much more. She made it to level 8.25. It was intriguing to watch. Ivy and Katie followed but neither one could hold out past level 6. Tara was the winner of the first round.

The second round began with Becca. The crowd hissed as she barely made it to level 6 and she clutched her abdomen in pain as the mighty machine tilted and twisted. Just when I thought Colt had shown everything it could do, he'd press a sequence into the controls and the horse would give something new.

"Uh-oh. Looks like contestant six has a cramp," Travis announced into the microphone.

"Too bad, Becca. Nice try," he added. The crowd applauded lightly for her.

Caitlyn, dressed as a bright blue cowgirl, made it to level 7 as cheers for Smurfette rocketed from one end of the stadium to the other.

After that, I couldn't watch anymore. *Holy hell that looked painful for her.* I didn't remember it being painful. I remembered really enjoying myself. I don't suppose it was on the level of intensity that these women were experiencing. A shiver ran up my spine. *How was I going to win this?*

I could hear the hard slapping of the saddle smacking against their asses and the force that the Sybian was pushing into them as it spun and pulsed. It wasn't gentle by any means; it was terrifying. I swallowed nervously, trying to find the courage to approach this beast. I had never been fucked that hard by any man and certainly not by a piece of machinery that could hospitalize me.

I let my gaze wander back to see that Kennedy was dismounting the mechanical device after a very brief try at level 5. Amber held her own and tied with Caitlyn at level 7. *This was it.*

My name was called and I shook myself and redirected my focus to Colt standing beside the powerful mustang. He smiled his wide smile of encouragement and I slipped out of my daisy dukes and black panties and let Colt help guide me into the stirrups and up on the massive stallion. I slipped down on the fresh vibrator and felt it fill me. It was larger than any cock I had yet experienced in my life. That alone was challenging.

"You have to beat level 7, Aria, to win this."

"No pressure," I said nervously.

"I'll start low then I will increase it one level at a time up until level 7. After 7, I will increase it in quarter increments. After 9.5 I'll increase it by tenths. Keep your thighs relaxed no matter how hard it pushes into you. That's the only way to win this. Stay limber, and don't forget to breathe. You've got this," he encouraged. I nodded.

"Ready?"

"Ready as I'll ever be."

Colt switched on the mean machine and the loud hum pulsed into my body like a vibrator normally would. Not too bad so far, I thought. I took in a slow deep breath and once I got acclimated to the speed, he sped up.

I kept my thighs relaxed no matter how hard I wanted to fight against it. The mechanical cock seemed to thrust deeper and twirled inside of me with every increase in level.

The giant beast swayed side to side as I passed level 5 and I tried to keep my breathing steady when Colt announced I was at level 6. I had never experienced anything like this before. Then the horse itself began to spin in the opposite way that the vibrator was moving. Fire belched from its nostrils as I rode it for dear life. Sweat glistened my brow. *Two more. I could do this. Jesus, this thing was beating the hell out of me.*

Colt called out, "Level 7." I gasped and my head was spinning as it jolted me in pleasure and sank deeper into me as it rocked from side to side. It was hitting my G spot and I wanted to cum right then and there. I could hear the cheers for 'mousetrap girl' racing through the crowd.

"Come on, Aria. Not much farther, hold on. Focus on my words and use them to distract you from the beast," he coached.

"Aaahhh," I felt the sounds slip out of me as I twisted jolted and turned, all the while, the machine pumped faster and harder than I ever thought was possible. My eyes rolled back in my head. I thought I might pass out at any second.

"You're at level 7.25, Aria." Colt said.

"Keep going, you can do it," Sara cheered. I could feel my legs start to stiffen.

"7.5, Aria," Colt encouraged. I looked down to him out of the corner of my eye to see him advance the controls. I could no longer fight it. It felt like it was ripping me in two and felt wonderful at the same time. There was a fine line between pleasure and pain and I was experiencing it first hand.

"I'm raising it to level 8."

"Please, no higher…no higher," I sang.

"You just passed 2 minutes and 25 seconds, you're almost there," Colt said.

I squeezed my eyes shut, trying to block out the stadium and the cheering around me. I felt the increase in the speed and it was bittersweet. I was moving in all directions now as the vibrator slammed into me, twisting with every thrust. I focused on Avery for a minute but the thought of him being the one who thrust into me was about to make me cum so I quickly thought of chemistry. I hated that class. Elements, what were the elements again on the periodic chart? *Seriously, was I really going to think of chemistry at a time like this?* My breathing paced rapidly in short tiny bursts as I held on.

"Keep going," Colt urged.

Okay, I could do this. Fuck chemistry. *What was the song that Sheldon always sang on The Big Bang Theory? It was something about a goddamn kitty.* I swear my insides were vibrating out. I rose up. I couldn't take anymore.

"8.5, Aria. You've won," Colt cheered. The machine stopped suddenly and I broke through my internal chant. My insides clutched and I had to take a deep breath before I climbed off the thing. *Jesus that was freaking hot as hell.*

That thing beat the shit out of me but I loved every minute of it. *Did that make me a sadist?*

The crowd roared and I could hear catcalls from Ethan and Wren. I smiled up at Colt as he helped me down from the machine. I wrapped a towel around my waist and fell to my knees as Travis announced me as the winner of the round and that there would be a short break before the third round commenced.

I didn't know if I could do it again. Once was beyond the extreme already. I looked around to see that the other events had concluded. Most of the camp had gathered to the stadium seating and watched every moment of my ride.

Night had spilled out over the camp and the lights were at full glow on the back courtyard, illuminating the Sybian on the main stage so that nothing would be missed. The fires around were burning high and a small crowd of people moved to the one nearby. People were drinking and enjoying themselves in the last days of camp. The mood was electric and the chatter and laughter seemed to ring out over the grounds. Everyone was enjoying the festivities.

Sara and Colt shoved two doubles of whiskey at me and I downed the first.

"This will help keep you relaxed and numb any soreness for a little while, anyway. Tara goes first, then by the time it's your turn, you'll be nice and loose," Sara said.

"My easy bake oven feels three miles wide," I panted up at her.

"It's between you and Tara now and there's a good chance that she won't make it up that high again. The second time can be more brutal. You'll both be sore, so we'll just take it as it comes."

I sat in a chair, leaning my head on Sara's shoulder, still feeling the raging behemoth between my legs like a phantom.

"Round two," the PA rattled.

Tara climbed up to the Sybian and dowsed it in lubricant this time. She lowered herself onto it and tilted her head back.

I could see she was stiff and trying to adjust to it. Colt switched on the controls and started a little higher at level 3. The crowd cheered her on and I couldn't help but wonder if they wanted her to win. The wild ride escalated and Colt continued to increase the power.

At level 8, Sara leaned over to me and whispered, "She must really want to win that Hawaii trip."

My eyes found Avery. He was watching me as I shifted nervously, trying hard not to freak out. He glanced at the scoreboard and my eyes followed his.

"She's at level 9 everybody. I don't believe it. No one in the history of this camp has broken their own record. I must say, this is a first," Travis announced.

Tara grunted and groaned loudly.

"9.25," Colt called out and Tara collapsed forward. The crowd whistled and hollered. *How the hell was I going to beat that?*

The crowd started chanting Tara's name and I could feel my confidence wavering. Sara placed both hands on my cheeks to turn my attention towards her. I could see confidence and determination in her eyes. I downed my second shot and handed the glass to Sara. I tried to squash the fear as she gave me her pep talk. I felt his warm touch on my forearm and looked up to Avery.

"Can I have a minute alone with her, Sara?" Sara nodded and winked to me, then walked to the edge of the crowd.

"Avery what are you doing? Do you know how this looks right now? You can't favor a contestant…" He placed two fingers over my mouth to quiet me, and then moved to cradle his hands around my face.

"I don't give a damn what they think. I want you to win this and I'm not going to stand by and watch you internally doubt yourself." I blinked in disbelief.

"You are the strongest person I know, Aria. You've shown more courage and grace than anyone here combined. I realize what I did to you squashed a big part of your soul and I regret being the one that put the pain in your eyes that's there every time you look at me."

I swallowed nervously. Avery held me by both arms and his eyes bored into my soul.

"I saw the most beautiful and seductive woman from the moment we met. Take the drive that I saw on the first day of camp, the one that peaked as I backed you up against that tree, and use it." His eyes danced over me. "You took my breath away," he said, tucking a loose strand of hair behind my ear. "You were so new to this world and instead of running, you kicked its ass until you had it right where you wanted it. Now do the same here. Win this for me. For us. I want you to be the one to go to Hawaii with me," his voice wavered as I looked at him with wide eyes. "But most importantly, don't do this because I ask you to. Do this because you want to," his eyes softened, there were so many things I wanted to say in that moment, but not with a full stadium audience. Avery had just bared a part of his soul to me and I was bursting inside.

"Okay, I got this," I breathed. As I made my way toward Colt, my eyes scanned the quiet crowd and I was met with curious stares from my friends as well as Caitlyn. I glanced toward Colt.

"Did everyone see that?"

"See what?" he winked, trying to help ease my anxiety. I smiled up at him as he helped me to the Sybian. Sara crossed her fingers at me as I lubed up the shaft in front of me. I eased myself down onto it. I glanced up at Colt and nodded.

He started at level 3, then 4, and then moved to level 5. My insides wanted to blast off into space. I shuddered, quaking into my first orgasm. The latex shaft was pounding me mercilessly once again.

He quickly moved to level 6, then 7. I looked down at him and gave him the encouragement that said 'keep going'.

At level 8, my orgasm was begging to be released again. I convulsed terribly into my second then third orgasms in rapid succession. I screamed. I was swaying to and fro with the horse, as everything intensified.

"More," I belted louder. Now anger replaced hesitation, as I wanted this giant Mustang to fuck me harder than anyone before me. Colt nodded and kept clicking higher.

"More," I screamed. "Fuck me you beautiful beast!" I squealed as my fourth orgasm claimed me. My head was spinning as it pounded into me. I reached down and grabbed the neck of the machine as I hung on for dear life as it spun one way, then back again. Sometimes, I felt as if I was moving in several directions at once.

"Level 8…8.5," Colt said. "Hang on, Aria," he urged. I tried to keep my breathing at a steady pace but the machine was bucking and causing me to tremble. My legs burned and I felt the numbness all the way to my toes. My insides started to quiver and my orgasm began rippling through me yet again. I threw my head back and cried out.

"More," I demanded, as orgasm number five took its hold on me.

"9…" Colt said in a strained voice.

My sixth orgasm pushed through my body and I was still convulsing. "More," I bellowed.

"9.25," Colt shouted.

My body felt like it was exploding in all different directions. As if I was tossed from a raft during a white water rafting trip, flung under water, not able to figure out which way was up as the water swirls all around me. And no matter how hard I try to reorient myself, the current holds me tight in its icy grip. The only way out is to swim with the current until at last, my head breaks the surface of the water and I can gasp for breath again.

I rocked side to side with the machine as I hung on with one arm and dipped my finger down over my wet clit and began rubbing it. *I was taking control and kicking its ass.*

"Aaahh," I said. I felt Colt increase it again.

"9.5," he said, with excitement in his voice. I screamed and my whole world thundered around me. " 9.6…9.7," he said.

I was lost in darkness and stars in my periphery flashed in my eyes. I cried out in a strangled raspy voice as I came again intensely. It was the seventh time. My legs were like jello.

"No more," I gasped, trying to find my breath as the machine suddenly slammed to a halt underneath me.

The cheers were so loud it was deafening. I blinked, trying to reign in my focus. The crowd stood in awe as my eyes flashed toward the large LED monitor displaying level 9.7. It was a new record.

The celebratory alarm was ringing as fireworks' exploded overhead declaring an end to this day's events and the crowd was chanting my name. I felt myself sliding to the side then Colt's arms around me as he lifted me off. I couldn't stand. I fell to my knees once again. I was spent.

Sara wrapped another towel around me and held my upper body upright as I shook in her arms. Avery knelt to the ground and held up a shot of Jameson whiskey. I smiled and downed it. Then he followed it with a beer.

A scouring bright blue Caitlyn was standing nearby with her arms crossed. She really did look good in blue. We were tied, two events each.

I chuckled. Her blonde hair was glistening in the light. She was just standing there glaring at Avery and me. *God, she looked like a pissed off Smurfette.*

The partiers fell out of their seats and spread across the whole lawn. Then the PA whistled on and Travis announced me as the winner.

The crowd filed out of the stadium and I just sat there on the ground next to Sara and Colt, trying to catch my breath. I watched Avery as he walked back to the judges table pointing and giving out orders like a general as they began to tear down from this event and set up for tomorrow's Jello wrestling.

Avery glanced over at me and even from the distance his eyes were blazing and for the first time since the night of the masquerade he was truly smiling at me. My mind kept repeating... *do this for me. For us.*

⌘

DAY FORTY-ONE:
SATURDAY AFTERNOON
CAMP OLYMPICS DAY 3
JELLO WRESTLING

Saturday morning came and I couldn't move. Most of the camp stayed up until 5am partying and carrying on. I came home around 2am, but Sara said that people were having drunken sex all over the lawn and in the bleachers and by the campfires. I guess it was a good party.

It was almost noon by the time I climbed out of bed, feeling the soreness that Sybian monster released on me last night. I stiffly made my way to the shower, hoping the hot water would soothe my achy muscles. I still had one more event today with Tara, Amber, and Caitlyn. We were the four remaining girls with the most points. I had no room for error. Jello wrestling was the last event and I couldn't let Caitlyn win this.

I finally shut off the hot water and stepped out of the shower. I toweled off and put on my red bathing suit. I waited for Sara to finish primping and we made our way to the Main Lodge for lunch. I was glad that I stopped drinking when I did last night. I had been too sore to stay out as late as most. And by the sluggish movements of Sara and everyone else, they looked very haggard and hungover.

Sara was in the middle of telling me about the massive orgy that broke out on the back lawn after I left when Caitlyn shouldered me.

"Hey thanks there, sweetpea!" I said. *Geez, would her childishness ever end?*

I grimaced and rubbed my shoulder, then kept walking. *She was so not worth my time.* But still, I snickered at her blue skin and knowing how Sara and I had everything to do with that made me feel better.

We ate lunch then headed toward the beach by the lake. I wanted to get there early and try to get my head in the game.

As soon as we arrived, Sara left me to go get us a couple Hurricanes at the bar. Three large pools of Jello came into view. They were again sunken into the center of boxing rings with the one in the center being the largest. The bleachers had been moved over on either side of the tournament area. Flags lined the rear of the beach area flowing briskly in the strong breeze today.

Caitlyn was already there in her canary yellow bikini with her golden hair flowing over her shoulders. The lake water reflected a bright bluish hue that didn't quite match Caitlyn's but yet they didn't clash either. Sometimes when you paint a room you might have two different shades of a color, like royal blue walls and country blue kitchen cabinets, and it just doesn't fit right. That wasn't the case between Caitlyn and the water. The blue hues were complimentary.

I looked to the tally boards to see Caitlyn and I tied for first. Tara was in second place and Amber was in third.

Because of the lottery round, they had every bit a chance to win this as much as I did.

We stepped to the podium where Pierce drew the names of who would compete against each other first. Caitlyn and Amber's names were drawn first. Tara and I would go second.

Tara and I stepped over to the edge of the crowd that was growing more and more by the minute and I felt a warm hand on the small of my back. I knew his touch. It was electric. There was no mistaking it. I tilted my head up to look at him and Avery smiled his panty-melting smile.

"How are you feeling?" he asked as he handed me the Hurricane Sara was supposed to bring me.

"Sore. But okay," I said as I took a really huge sip.

"Ready to kick some ass for me?" he whispered in my ear. I could feel his hot breath below my ear and my body shivered involuntarily. My eyes lit up and suddenly I had the urge to tackle him right then and there. I didn't care who was watching. Avery stepped away, reluctantly letting go of my waist, and headed back to the judges table. I hadn't taken my eyes off him when I heard Tara speak.

"You've really got it bad for him, don't you?"

"Yea," I gushed. I stiffened when I realized I said that a loud. I started to panic.

"After the way he was fawning over you yesterday before the final Sybian round, I would think its safe to say that he's crazy about you, too," she smiled. I studied her swanlike face. Her hair was groomed and perfectly colored. It was cut in wavy layers with wispy strands covering her accentuated features. She now wore contacts and had on a perfect amount of makeup. She glowed like an angel. *Tara was kind. I wished that there could be more genuine people like her in the world.*

I smiled softly back at her and then looked over at Avery. I could feel Tara's eyes on me but all I could think about was that after this competition, Avery and I needed to talk.

My attention was drawn back to the match when Pierce blew the whistle. Caitlyn and Amber stepped into the pool of lime green Jello and began wrestling.

Caitlyn was a blue ball of blind fury. She was determined to win that trip. Amber looked like she was trying to defend herself but Caitlyn was too quick and too fast. She attacked her like a hyena attacking its lunch. I snickered to myself. *Caitlyn laughed like a hyena, too.*

After one very hotly contested match, Travis announced Caitlyn as the winner. She simply destroyed Amber. *Just fucking peachy.*

The women stepped out of the pool and Colt and Pierce lined up to hose them off. Tara and I stepped over to the edge of our pool of cherry Jello.

Most of the camp had arrived by now. The beer lines over at the two tiki bars were humming. The crowd spread wide across the beachside as Pierce blew his whistle and Tara and I stepped into the gushy crimson Jello. It squished between my toes as I steadied myself. I sidestepped Tara as she lunged for me. She moved toward me again and I stepped away but Tara gripped my wrist and pulled me down so my ear was close to her mouth. She mumbled something too quick for me to be sure I heard her correctly.

"Come again?" I said, pulling away to lock my arms with her as we tossed each other about. She leaned into my ear again.

"I want you to kick Caitlyn's ass for me," she reiterated. I stared at her, trying to understand what it was that she was saying. Then Tara did the most absurd and yet noble thing; she grabbed hold of her calf and cried out… "Cramp!"

Then she toppled over and faked slipping in the Jello. She reached up and pulled me down on top of her, and as I fell she held me in place pinning her.

"Why are you doing this?" I asked.

"You deserve to have your happy ending, too," she winked.

I was stunned. Tara just let me win and as I looked down at her I whispered, "I will kick her ass all the way back to Nantucket."

I fought back the tears that were threatening to spill from my eyes and looked up at Avery. He stood off to the side with his arms crossed over his chest watching the whole thing. He grinned and I found myself smiling in return. My eyes looked at Tara. *One opponent down, one crazy bitch to go.*

I wiped my face with the towel Pierce handed me and stepped up to the pool's edge. Pierce chuckled.

"Aria, there's a thirty minute break then we'll meet back here."

The crowd cheered as the two bartenders brought out several trays of shots and handed them out. Catcalls filled the air while Colt hosed off Tara and I.

People were still teasing Caitlyn and calling her Smurfette as they walked by. Sara took the towel from me and helped to dry me off. Before I knew what was happening Sara was kissing me on the lips. The guys whistled and whooped and I fed into the hype and deepened the kiss. The crowd went nuts. I pulled away, giggling. Sara licked my lips and looked at me like she couldn't wait to have more.

"That's my girl," Colt said, wrapping his arms around Sara and kissing her deeply.

"See what you're missing, Avery," Sara purred.

I looked up to those green emerald eyes gazing down at me and felt my heart clench in my throat. Ignoring Sara's comment, he stepped up to me and quirked his eyebrow.

"She let you win, didn't she?" he said. I nodded. "Why?" he asked.

"I'm looking right at him," I said honestly.

Avery's eyes went wide for a moment then he looked like he was at a loss for words.

"Wow," he finally said ineloquently.

"Oh, that and she wants me to kick Caitlyn's ass," I laughed, trying to lighten the conversation. He chuckled.

Thirty minutes later, Pierce called me over to start the final round and butterflies danced in my belly. I giggled at myself for my inward silly butterfly monologue.

Caitlyn and I both climbed into the center ring with the blue Jello that matched Caitlyn.

"It's a death match, Kittens. The gloves come off. Rules are simple. No choking, scratching, or knees to the stomach. Everything else is fair game."

I glanced across the pool at Caitlyn's narrowed glare. Pierce blew the whistle and I swear I heard Caitlyn growl. Caitlyn leaned in and tried to uppercut me openhanded. I dodged it, smacking her hand to the side, then I felt my feet slip. I stumbled to regain my footing.

Caitlyn lunged forward, grabbed me around the waist and reached up and pulled my bikini top off exposing my breasts. The crowd cheered wildly. *Now I see why Jello wrestling is such a big deal, the guys just want to see tits.* So I thought I'd give them some more. I reigned in my surprise and then tackled her, ripping off her top. *There if they want tits let them eat fake.*

I squinted through the slime to see Caitlyn's blue bulbous fake globes exposed. I regretted my decision instantly. I struggled to stay on top of her. She wriggled like a fire horse. *Where did she get her energy?*

She struggled out of my grasp like an oiled pig at the farmer's market. We went around each other like steamrollers coating ourselves in the blue Jello and choking on it in the process.

Caitlyn squirmed out from under me and jumped onto my back. Before I had anytime to respond she was pushing my face into the Jello. *I swear this bitch was trying to kill me and she kept screaming obscenities the whole time.*

I shoved my head back and head-butted her. She paused for a moment looking dizzy, and I rolled out from underneath her. The crowd hissed and I looked to see she was clenching her nose. Blood dripped from her blue nose.

The crowd then cheered for me. That seemed to only fuel Caitlyn's rage. She kicked my feet out from under me with a leg swipe as her manicured fingers dug into my thigh.

Damn, that hurt!

"Kick her ass, Aria," Tara called out. Sara and Colt joined in. I pinned Caitlyn for a second then looked to see Sara not far from the ring jumping up and down cheering for me. Colt was next to her holding up his beer and cheering me on.

Caitlyn took advantage of my distraction and pushed me over onto my back. I kicked back and Caitlyn grabbed her stomach in a protective maneuver. I was spitting out Jello trying to catch my breath. My heart was pounding. Caitlyn rose to her feet, still clutching her side. I took a moment to breathe.

I found Avery in the crowd and he mouthed 'do it for me'. I somehow pushed myself to a standing position and without hesitation I slid down and kicked her feet out from under her and then hopped on her and straddled her. I leaned all my weight into her then gasped when she pulled my ponytail backwards, causing my head to look upward. I rolled sideways off her and climbed to my knees and fell back down as Caitlyn dragged me backwards into a chokehold. I was kicking my feet as she was closing off my airway, so I reared my elbow up then back into her gut, causing her to quickly release me as she lost her wind. I glanced at Pierce. *Wasn't that one of the rules, no choking.*

He frowned and I could see he wasn't going to call it. She got away with that one I guess because it wasn't technically choking.

I pummeled her, forcing her to the bottom of the pool, and grabbed her arm and leg, pressing my weight into her. She screamed from the pain I was causing. She dug her nails into my side and I let go instinctively. We both backed up and rose to our feet. Caitlyn stepped forward and landed a square blow right into my belly. Then I returned the favor with an uppercut.

We stood facing each other trading blows like prize fighters. The crowd cheered uncontrollably, she'd slug me, then I would return the blow, then again her fist into my belly, and my fist into her face, again and yet again we reigned blows down on each other until she finally lunged at me and dragged me down into the slime.

I rebounded quickly as Caitlyn and I backed up and circled each other like jaguars waiting for the other to show weakness. I squinted through the Jello to see her evil smirk. Then she charged me and at the same time I charged her, but at the last second I slid just like I was sliding into third base back in softball. I took her feet out from under her as she fell over me into the Jello. But before she could react I made it back up and grabbed onto those canary yellow bikini bottoms of hers and atomic wedgied the fuck out of her. I pulled up with all my might. It took every last bit of strength I had, but I hoisted her into the air, driving those panties up, and deep into her crack of nastiness. *Desperate times call for desperate measures.*

Then I rolled over on my back, using my feet to brace into her sides, and using my momentum, I pushed her up and over me, out of the pool, and into the hot sand. Pierce blew the whistle.

"Caitlyn's out of bounds. Aria wins it," he called out.

A slow grin moved over my face as I watched her face fall as Pierce's words sank in. Her mouth fell open and she narrowed her eyes at me. I finally sucked in a deep breath and rose to my feet.

The crowd went berserk. Everyone was closing in on me, congratulating me and cheering my name over and over. Sara scooped me up and spun me around. She pulled away giggling. Now we were both covered in Jello.

Sara grinned devilishly, leaned down, and sucked one of my exposed nipples into her mouth. Then she switched to the other one, licked her lips, and drew back to look at me.

"Yum," she said, then led me over to the edge of the water.

We both jumped in to wash off. I could see Avery standing by the shore watching Sara and me splash around. I suddenly felt shy and I put my bikini top back in place and climbed back out. Caitlyn had already rinsed off and stood off to the side looking defeated. I walked past Avery towards her and waited for her to look at me. When she finally did I spoke.

"Dip a washcloth in white vinegar and scrub, scrub, scrub." She raised her eyebrows in confusion.

"That's how you get rid of the blue dye from your skin," I added.

Her eyes widened then she nodded and went back to pouting. I jogged back to Avery, feeling my heartbeat pick up the closer I got toward him. I knew we needed to talk. But with all these people around, I knew that was next to impossible. Once again, it would have to wait.

⌘

DAY FORTY-ONE:
SATURDAY EVENING
ALL HAIL THE KITTEN QUEEN

It was Saturday evening and the Island Beach/Farewell theme party was rocketing full blast. The torches were lit and glowing brightly around the beach, waiting for dusk to come. Fires blazed in the multiple fire pits and more lined the shoreline. Tonight was our last night here. The camp was winding down and Avery, as usual, was busy with final preparations so I still hadn't had a chance to talk with him.

I had showered and changed into a sundress and wedge sandals. My hair was pulled to a low side ponytail that lay over my left shoulder. I stood amongst my friends sipping on a frozen Hurricane as I watched Avery take the stage for the final time.

The crowd was chattering low and everyone seemed to be savoring the last moments of camp. Colt and Sara stepped up to join us and everyone seemed to talk amongst themselves while I plotted a way to get Avery alone.

Avery stepped to the center stage microphone and cleared his throat. The crowd quieted and all eyes were on him.

"I wanted to thank you all for coming to Camp Jameson this summer. It has been fascinating to see each and every one of you grow sexually. It is with my dearest

435

hope that each of you found what you were looking for. Tonight is the conclusion ceremony and our last hoorah so please enjoy yourselves. Oh, and tonight, there are no rules except the obvious one; no means no."

Everyone cheered as Avery nodded to Pierce, standing on the side of the stage, to come forward.

"Our final ceremony includes one last award, the crowning of our Kitten Queen." His eyes landed on me. "Ladies and Gentlemen, may I introduce to you our Kitten Queen, winner of Camp Olympics, and the trip to Hawaii, Miss Arabella Mason," Avery's velvet voice echoed out into the camp.

I smiled nervously while I climbed the stairs to the stage. Pierce handed the four-inch rhinestone crown to Avery and he lowered it onto my head. As I stepped beside him, cheers of 'Aria' broke out from the crowd. It was deafening. I realized then how much I missed him. I took a deep breath of Avery's cologne into my lungs. I fought against my heart pounding in my chest. He pulled away just enough for me to see his wolfish grin appear and I wanted to melt right there. Avery stepped up to me and cupped the back of my neck with his hand. I scanned his face.

"Avery, what are you doing?"

He smirked. "I'm risking it all," he said with a glow in his eyes.

I sucked in a breath just before his lips crushed to mine. I felt us both shudder as the crowd cheered bombastically. He growled possessively, pulled me closer, as I threaded my hands into his hair and pressed harder against him. We were breathless, but neither one of us wanted to pull away. I felt Avery grip my hips and pick me up and I instinctively wrapped my legs around him. His desire pressed between my thighs. I leaned my head back and held my crown as he moved to my neck. My surroundings dropped away. *God, I could get lost in him so easily.*

The applause filled every part of the beach. Everyone was cheering, whistling, and catcalling. We pulled away from each other to see the onlookers. I can honestly say it was the first time I ever saw Avery blush.

Sara, Colt, Sienna, Sean, and Pierce stood near the stage with big smiles plastered on their faces. Sean whistled loudly. The crowd joined us in the celebration.

I turned my head into Avery's shoulder and hid my face. Avery chuckled and kissed my forehead.

"About fucking time," Pierce called out to us. Avery touched his forehead to mine and I felt my heart flutter. *God, he was beautiful when he smiled.*

I didn't realize how much I missed his touch. His eyes held hope and something that I wasn't sure that I'd ever see. Love.

Avery cradled my face in his hands and met my eyes. "Come home with me, Aria," he breathed. "We have a lot of time to make up for," he added.

I nodded to him and grinned like a Cheshire cat. Avery released my hips and my feet barely touched the ground when he tucked me in to his side and guided me towards the courtyard.

When we got to the edge of the beach, Ethan and Wren stopped us.

"Did you hear the good news? Wren and I are coming back next session. We're his new instructors," Ethan said.

"You are? That's great." I stepped out from under Avery's arm and pulled them into a big hug. A part of me was sad to leave. The other part of me, the grown up part of me, told me I had to go back to Ohio and start class in a couple weeks.

"We always knew you two would hit it off," they both said in unison. *They knew?*

"What about the bar exam?" I asked Ethan.

He chuckled. "I'll study. I promise. It's not scheduled until December." Ethan extended his hand to Avery and Avery reached out and shook it. "Take care of our girl for us," he added.

"Always," Avery said.

"Bye, gorgeous. Come back and see us soon," Wren said, kissing my forehead. I remembered I still wore the crown Avery had just given me and lifted it off my head.

"Can you do me a favor and give this to Sara and tell her I left with Avery," I asked Wren. He smiled widely and nodded, then I waved goodbye as I made my way to the four-wheeler with Avery.

My heart raced the closer we got to his house. The sun was setting and the glorious sunset urged Avery to go faster. I didn't want to waste anymore time.

We raced into his drive, parked in front of his house, and then he turned off the engine. I jumped from the seat in time to see two grey and white husky wolf mixed breeds bound off the front porch.

"Hey guys," he said to the excited dogs.

I smiled to them and ran my hands through their soft coats. He smiled in awe like he was truly seeing me for the first time.

"Meet Bo and Luke."

I walked toward him. I quickly remembered his biography in the manual and how it said he had two dogs but I had never seen them until now.

"How have I never met them before now?"

He shrugged. "Because I only let them meet those I'm closest to."

His eyes searched mine and then looked to my lips. He closed the gap between us. His hard muscles pressed against my chest. His lips hovered in front of mine.

"No, not like this."

He pulled me across the wraparound porch and we stepped down the path. My heart quickened as I realized where we were going. My smile widened.

We barely made it to the waterfall and his lips were melted to mine. My body fell into his, knocking him backwards. We both stumbled to the outdoor mattress, laughing. His eyes danced over me as he climbed on top of me.

"God, I missed that sound," he said brushing a strand of hair away from my face and tucking it behind my ear. "There are so many things I want to tell you, but when I look at you…" Avery struggled to get his words out. His eyes were ablaze as he ran his hand through his hair. "Christ, Aria, you steal my breath away."

I knew in that moment that he needed to hear the words I had been longing to say for so long.

"Avery I…" I stumbled over my words. I had to do this. This is why I came here with him. I had to say what was in my heart. His eyes looked to me with hope, with love, with yearning. I closed my eyes and steadied my breathing.

"I don't want to be without you anymore. Somewhere in the middle of this fantasy world you created, I fell in love with you."

He sucked in a breath. His gaze fell to my lips then back to my eyes. His lips kissed me gently and he groaned into my mouth. His lips sought out every inch of my body as he ravished me with kisses. I let my hands trace the muscular curves of his body then I took his face in my hands and drew him in front of me.

"Avery, don't be afraid. Please tell me what you're thinking." He smiled a crooked smile.

"I can't seem to form a sentence when you're near me," he said. I placed my hands over his eyelids and left them there like a blindfold.

"Slow your breathing and clear your head," I said.

He smiled nervously but he didn't move. I watched as he took slow, deep breaths and relaxed his body. He let his fingers find my hands.

"That really does help," he said pulling my hands away from his eyes. "No wonder you did it for so long."

"Keeping tabs on me, were you?"

"You know I was." He cleared his throat. I could see him gathering his confidence. "I want to look at you when I say this." We were nose to nose with only a small distance between us.

"You, beautiful Aria, exploded into my heart from the very moment I saw you." He kissed my lips tenderly. "Maybe even before that when I heard you call out, 'spill it

Cox,' that first night in the ballroom. That was the sexiest thing I'd ever heard."

I giggled. He chuckled with me. I could feel his chest rumble with laughter. That was the most beautiful sound in the world. I smiled widely. *God, I loved this man.*

"It stirred something in me. I know, I'm not explaining this right," his voice shook. He closed his eyes a moment then looked back to me. "The night of the ball, I got lost in you and for most of the night, for the first time in a very long time, it was beyond any of my fantasies. You were my paradise. You were what I have been searching for…for so long," he swallowed roughly. "You weren't the only one that night to let go. I saw the look in your eyes and how happy I made you. How the real part of you actually worshipped the real part of me without you even knowing who I was. And then we made love to that song and I realized that I haven't felt anything like that in so long." He exhaled deeply. "I was falling for you and suddenly I had no control of how I felt and my whole world crumbled like a giant stone wall enveloped by a torrent of flood water. I couldn't get my bearings. I freaked out." He swallowed hard.

"The more time I spent with you the more I ached to be near you and it really scared me. But Jesus, Aria, I want you to know, I wanted you so badly. But I couldn't be that selfish. It was the hardest thing for me not to tell everyone to back the fuck off and that you were mine. I wanted to crush my lips to yours no matter who was watching. I wanted to bust down your door and crawl into bed with you so many times that I had to bury myself in work. But each time that I did, something or someone would remind me of you. And I'd end up daydreaming about how you tasted. The feel of your warm breath on my cheek. The feel of me buried deep inside of you. The way your body quivered underneath mine when you came." He brushed his hand down my cheek as his eyes danced over me. "It was worth the risk."

"What risk?" I asked.

"My heart," he swallowed dryly.

"You'll always have my heart," I said.

"Somehow deep down inside, beyond anything I can ever understand, I just know."

"Will you please tell me what happened to you? I can't help you heal if you don't share with me what you're feeling," I said.

"Are those the wise words of a nurse?" he asked.

"You're avoiding the question," I replied.

"Yes. Yes, I am." He lowered his head to my chest and wrapped his arms around me tighter. "I promise I will tell you when I'm ready. But right now, I need to be close to you. I need to feel you. I need to be buried deep inside you." I nodded as he trailed his hand up my sundress and lifted away my panties.

"You're strong in so many ways. You have held me together more than you realize," he said, unzipping his pants and freeing himself. "God, you have no idea how badly I need you. Not just your body, but this," he said pressing his hand over my heart. "It's your heart that made me realize there are people in this world that still care. I see so much passion and love in you it took my breath away," he rocked his pelvis against mine. "I feel so drawn to you when you're near. It still scares me," he whispered.

"Make love to me, please," I begged. He softly pressed his lips to mine. I kissed him harder and a deep moan escaped the back of his throat as he sank into me.

"I want to see you all of you." With him still inside me, he stripped me from my sundress and bra then tugged off his shirt and pushed his pants off with his feet. He ran his hand down the middle of my chest as he memorized every inch of me. His eyes widened, then a slow smile spread over his face.

"I love this," he said, running his hand next to my belly button piercing. "You have the most beautiful body."

The sun had set now and it was only us in the soft light of a solar lamp nearby. I smiled as his warm skin connected with mine. He was mine. All mine. And I would forever cherish him.

He smiled triumphantly to me and eased out slowly then delectably back in. We kept that pace for a while, a long while, as our hands glided over each other as if at any moment one of us would disappear. He threaded his hands through mine and drew them over my head. We were lost in each other. Hand to hand, skin to skin, heart to heart, soul to soul, surrounded by beautiful wild orchids. I had never felt so close to anyone before and I knew just by his touch how much he loved me. Words would never be able to describe what we felt. Only our bodies as one could ever come close.

"I love you, sweet Aria," Avery breathed.

When he whispered those words to me, I knew I would be his forever. I would never forget the six weeks I spent in Paradise Lake, Pennsylvania. Camp Jameson would always be a part of me. And Avery, I knew, would forever be in my heart.

∞∞∞∞

5 days later...

I rode in the black limo to the Pittsburgh airport to meet Avery. The driver came around and opened my door where a private jet awaited to take Avery and me to Hawaii.

The driver helped me out of the car then grabbed my bags. I walked the short steps to the jet and my mouth fell open when Avery stepped to the stairway. He was drop-dead gorgeous. He was dressed in cargo shorts and a dark green polo shirt with a white Camp Jameson logo on it.

It had been five days since I'd seen him in person. The things we did over the webcam still made me blush, but nothing compared to when he put his arms around me and kissed me all consuming.

"Hi," I breathed. His face broke into a wide smile and he kissed my forehead.

"I have a surprise for you," he said in his delicious voice. He stepped to the side and I was met with Sara and Colt beaming back at me.

"Like my new dress I bought for Hawaii?" she bounced on the balls of her feet in a short coral dress.

"How?" I sputtered. "I just left you at the apartment," I said glancing back and forth between them. Colt shrugged.

"The limo brought you. Avery sent a helicopter to pick us up." I looked up at Avery. He smiled his wolfish smile back at me.

"They're coming with us?" I bleated.

"Of course," he said, tenderly kissing my temple.

"Tonight, sweet girl, we'll have our first foursome," Colt said seductively in my ear.

My eyes shifted to Avery and he smirked knowingly. I shivered as Avery led me through the cabin of the jet. *Holy hell, this was luxurious.*

I sat next to Avery as we buckled up and the flight attendant skittered up and offered us a drink.

"So is it true, Avery?" Sara asked. He quirked his eyebrow at her questionably, "Do we really get to see your new yacht?"

He nodded and grinned widely. *Boys and their toys.*

Sara winked at me with a mischievous look in her eye. I knew what she meant. The first night at the meet and greet Avery had ignored Caitlyn's inquiry regarding his yacht and now I was going to share it with Avery.

In the beginning, I had wanted to flee when I heard that Sara had tricked me into coming to a sex camp, but looking back now, all I wanted to do was run back to it and I wished that it never ended.

I leaned over and pressed a kiss to Avery's lips. He could sense my urgency and he deepened our kiss. He threaded his fingers through my hair and drew me closer. I wanted to unstrap my belt and straddle him right then and there. We were lost in each other when a familiar voice cleared his throat.

"Sorry to interrupt this snuggle fest, but I miss this beautiful woman, and I feel with all my hard work to get you two together I deserve at least one kiss as a thank you," he boasted.

Avery pulled away but didn't look at him. His eyes were still on me. "As always, brother, your timing is impeccable."

I giggled and turned toward Pierce. His eyes lit up when I moved in to give him a kiss. At the last minute, I moved to the side and kissed his cheek. He playfully frowned then I moved back into Avery's arms. Pierce grumbled something about me being a tease but I could only concentrate on Avery's kisses. Avery pulled away when the engines switched on and threaded his hand into mine. Pierce was looking between Avery and me then Sara and Colt. He fastened his belt, then cursed and mumbled something about being the fifth wheel and everyone busted out laughing.

"You're adorable when you pout," I teased.

His eyes lit up when he saw the flight attendant and undressed her with his eyes. She gave him a seductive look telling him 'soon' with her eyes and I knew then that Pierce was going to be just fine as soon as we got in the air and he got her alone.

The jet began taxiing down the runway and when we lifted off, I couldn't help but wonder what the next week would hold. If Avery had anything to do with it, it would be heaven.

I smiled as Avery pressed a soft kiss to the palm of my hand. His eyes were gleaming back at me. The butterflies were doing somersaults in my belly. But I liked them. *Butterflies were a beautiful thing.*

End of Book 1

OTHER BOOKS BY WENDY LEA THOMAS

THE CAMP JAMESON SERIES:
Sara & Colt Novella
Camp Paramore

About the Author

Wendy Lea Thomas, R.N. lives in Northeast Ohio
with her hubby and twin tuxedo cats. When she's not
writing you can find her at various Comic Cons.
She is an avid cosplayer.

Feel free to visit her at:

www.wendyleathomas.com
or
Follow her on Facebook, Goodreads, & Twitter:

Wendy Lea Thomas